PRAISE FOR THE VA'

I absolutely adored this novel. It's a b
meets-girl that manages to never fall into the dreaded classification of
"cliché and predictable." The narrative is wonderfully written, with
exquisite attention to detail. I've never been one to "fall" for a religious
man, but William Brook is likely to get fans fluttering and cheeks
flushing.
Alexia Bullard for eBook Review Gal

I am completely, unabashedly in love with this book. Many books claim
"fans of Jane Austen will love this" - this one lives up to the claim. It's an
enchanting read that pulls you into it and carries you happily along. It
was so refreshing to read a high-quality book that was clean all the way
through.
Heather from Word Menagerie

I thoroughly enjoyed this delightful read. Highly recommend it. The
characters were perfect together. Well drawn and realistic.
Barbara Silkstone, a reader at Amazon.com

I enjoyed this fast-paced, charming, historical romance. The narrative is
so well done with a lot of attention to detail. I loved the description of the
countryside – green fields, tiny hamlets and Tudor buildings. The author
is obviously familiar with the country and the era. This debut novel is a
delightful, clean read that will capture the hearts of readers who enjoy
historical romances.
Sandra at Library of Clean Reads

As an avid admirer of Jane Austen's work, this sweet Regency romance
was right up my alley. As a young good-looking vicar of marriageable age
and a forward-thinker, William reminded me a bit of Sidney Chambers
(of Grantchester). The romance was nicely woven together with the
happenings of the village, which gave it a nice village chronicle feel,
similar to Cranford. Great story with interesting characters.
Midnight Attic Reader

One of my favorite things about The Vagabond Vicar was Brentwood's original story filled with interesting plot twists that kept me turning page after page. The suspense, action, and development of characters rose as the novel neared its close, bringing the ending to a touching conclusion. This is a Regency novel worth adding to your to-read list.
Katie Patchell at Austenprose

I loved this book. I find it extremely frustrating that there are so many historical romances which are merely fronts for endless, anachronistic sex scenes and so few genuinely affecting love stories like The Vagabond Vicar. A truly moral hero who holds true to what is right even though it threatens to cost him his livelihood and the woman he loves, a heroine who isn't just after a husband and who grows throughout the book into a strong, independent character, a wonderful setting and an interesting cast of supporting characters made this the best book I have read in a long time. I couldn't put it down.
Carolyn Cooke, a reader at Amazon.co.uk

The Vagabond Vicar is a sweet and charming regency set historical romance with many swoon-worthy moments. Though I don't usually read regency romances, I was intrigued by the plot and as I read, I fell in love with the characters. For a classic romance, the characters felt fresh and complex and I would definitely pick up the next two books in the series.
Stephanie's Book Reviews

Ms Brentwood weaves a pleasing tale. Her characters are vivid and she brings them to life on the page, capturing the small-mindedness of a remote community with care. An unashamedly romantic novel, The Vagabond Vicar moves along at a great pace and is never boring. There is enough love and sentiment but rarely too much, and there are plenty of sub-plots to keep everything interesting. A lover of Georgian romance will enjoy this, particularly as it is not solely concerned with earls and dukes, but takes a wider view of the world. An indulgent read.
Nicky Galliers for the Historical Novel Society

The Vagabond Vicar

THE **HEARTS OF AMBERLEY** SERIES

The Vagabond Vicar
Gloved Heart
Heart of a Gentleman (coming soon)

Go to www.charlottebrentwood.com and sign up
to my email newsletter for book news!

HEARTS OF AMBERLEY
BOOK ONE

The Vagabond Vicar

CHARLOTTE BRENTWOOD

*For my parents, who are the definition of
unconditional love and support.*

I love you and appreciate you more than words can say.

Chapter One

London, June 1805

Maybe it would be India. William pictured himself building schools, feeding the hungry, and translating prayers. Perhaps a longer journey to the Far East would be required, or overland to the dark heart of Africa. Wherever his calling might be, he was ready. He'd committed himself absolutely to do God's calling, and he'd always sensed he would be used in a strange land. He yearned for adventure, for a strong purpose in his life. There would be physical hardships, to be sure, but the knowledge that he would be making a real difference would see him through.

William strode through the streets of London towards the rectory at St Mary's and the meeting which could change his life. The journey from The Foundling Hospital would normally take twenty minutes, but today his quick steps ate up the distance in half that time. As he left for the hospital earlier that morning, he'd received a note requesting he speak with his rector Jacob Roberts, also the influential Dean of the City of London, regarding an assignment. Surely his friends within the Clapham Evangelicals had put in a good word for him within the missionary society just as he'd requested. What else could it be?

He took a deep breath of the damp morning air, trying to calm his racing pulse. He'd barely been able to concentrate during the lesson with the orphans, and it was with shaking hands that he distributed the bread and cheese to each hungry child. His imaginings of possible quests grew wilder with every step. Would there be warriors, voodoo or disease? Cannibals? He could handle it. He'd been a deacon at St Mary's for eighteen months now. He was ready to take orders and fulfil his destiny. He marched across a cobbled courtyard and gained admittance to the rectory, steadying his hand before the dean's office door. He managed a gentle rap.

"Yes, who is it?" a deep voice called.

"William Brook, sir."

"Ah yes, come in."

William was inside the office in an instant, taking the chair the dean gestured toward.

Dean Roberts had appeared to take an instant liking to William right from the young graduate's ordination as a deacon, apparently recognising a special sort of potential in his protégé. The heavy-set man stroked his greying beard and smiled at William, then took a breath.

William leaned forward, unable to hide his anticipation. Five minutes later, he sat back aghast. He felt the blood drain from his face, and it was a full minute before he mustered the voice to utter, "Shropshire?"

"Yes."

"Shropshire, England?"

The dean smiled broadly. "The vicar has just passed on, and in lieu of other candidates I was asked to recommend a gentleman for the benefice. Usually I would be wary of entrusting a whole parish to one so young. However, you have proven yourself to be an exceptional servant of the Lord, with a depth of compassion and strength of judgement unmatched by your peers." He sat back in his chair and folded his hands across his stomach.

"Uh... thank you, Mr Dean." William ran a hand through his dark brown hair, becoming sensible of the immense compliment being paid to him. Livings were generally bought or bestowed upon relatives, and he had not counted on being granted one by distant recommendation. "However, I must confess I had thought I would be assigned to a foreign land. The missionary society..."

"No, no." The dean chuckled a little. "I would not risk yellow fever or malaria on you. You shall be safe in the English countryside."

"Yes... safe." *And bored out of my wits.*

"It is the village of Amberley," Dean Roberts said, leaning forward over some papers on his desk, and popping his monocle in. "Your patrons are the Barringtons, Lord and Lady Ashworth. I have known Ashworth since my Oxford days. They are attending services here at St Mary's during the season, and your teachings have met with their approval. You will meet with them formally this week. You should find them to be kind and generous benefactors."

William began to sweat. He'd had no idea prospective patrons had been evaluating him for months. "And of what size is the parish?" he asked, grappling with an unexpected future. "Are there many needy people within the vicinity?"

The dean ran a finger over the paper in front of him. "The population of Amberley numbers two hundred. I am led to believe the surrounding lands are fertile, and the people quite self-sufficient. You needn't worry about too much pressure concerning funds for the poor."

William's eyes roved about the office restlessly as he racked his brain for an escape. "And there is no-one residing locally who would benefit from taking up the living?"

The dean frowned. "There is no-one... suitable. The Barringtons prefer that a gentleman take up the post, and I am led to believe any local genteel younger sons are otherwise engaged."

"Do the Barringtons have sons?"

"Aye, there are two sons of age, but I believe the younger is not desirous to take up the living, as he is likely to be given a property elsewhere."

William nodded. Would there be anything meaningful for him to do, besides reading from the prayer book once a week? "And the parsonage?"

"A cottage with a glebe totalling some fifty acres. Your income will be around a hundred and fifty pounds per annum. Not enough to hire a curate all the year I'm afraid, but there is already a maid-of-all-work in residence."

Roberts looked up and fixed his protégé with an authoritative stare.

William could sense this interview was nearing its end. His head spun.

"Mr Dean, are you certain this is the appropriate time for me to be assigned a living? Surely while I am young and agile I could be better utilised in physical service abroad?"

The dean held up a palm. "Now young Brook, do not be hasty. I believe you have great potential, and perhaps a mission is in your future. You still have much to learn about managing a congregation. This is a golden opportunity. Starting a church in a foreign land is a lot harder work than you think. Even stepping into an established parish is not without its challenges. You shall see." He lifted his eyebrows in a dismissive gesture.

William stood, knowing further arguments would be fruitless. "When am I required to leave?"

"Within a fortnight. The Barringtons will return to their seat directly upon the closure of Parliament, and you need a week or so to settle in before your first Sunday service. Prepare to take orders later this week." His eyes softened. "Take heart, my boy. You will no longer be a deacon."

William left the rectory with his head hanging low. Surely *this* could not be his calling. How could his dynamic, inspirational dreams be reduced to a life sentence in a small village? Even as he walked into open spaces, he felt as if the sky was bearing down on him. How could he live in only one place, forever?

Despite spending his entire childhood at a country estate in Cambridgeshire, since leaving for university he'd travelled frequently to preach, assist the poor and counsel the morally bankrupt. At Cambridge he'd gone beyond the limited syllabus, consuming all the knowledge he could not only in theology, but also arts, science and literature. Being in London had afforded all the more opportunity for enrichment. What possible enlightenment was to be had in a minor village in a far-flung county? Surely he was needed more elsewhere. He would be trapped for the rest of his days, with only a few weeks respite a year. William collapsed on a park bench and dropped his head into his hands.

He dare not defy the dean. It would be career suicide. The man was infinitely well connected, and a slight to him would mean being slighted by others.

William lifted his eyes to the heavens and prayed desperately for some kind of guidance. At once he felt an urge to go down and visit the evangelical group in Clapham. Surely they would understand his frustration, sharing as they did his passion for spreading the good news far and wide.

As he crossed the river then passed through the city blocks, he resolved to call upon his dearest friend, Thomas. They'd met at Cambridge and graduated together. Leading a somewhat nocturnal existence in London, he and Thomas frequently ministered to the inner city folk. Seeking out the needy and the depraved, they would assist with both physical and spiritual wants.

When he arrived at the small house Thomas shared, he was informed his friend was out. He waited half an hour in the tiny vestibule, growing more agitated by the minute.

At last Thomas returned and pulled William into the parlour, a grin plastered over his face.

"Will, you'll never believe it." He gestured for William to sit on the battered couch, then pulled a chair over and sat on it backwards, drumming his fingers on the top.

William had never seen him so excited. "Well go on, man, do not keep me in suspense."

"I am bound for India," Thomas announced. "Simeon has arranged for me to join him on a voyage from Portsmouth this coming Saturday. I have not a moment to lose!"

"Simeon?" William whispered. He stared at Thomas dumbfounded, a lead weight dropping in his stomach. This was the opportunity he was longing for. Charles Simeon, a passionate rector in Cambridge with strong connections to both the Clapham group and the British East India Company, was the very man he had been depending on to send him abroad. Surely it wasn't God's will for Thomas to go and leave him behind. They were brothers in arms, destined to fight together against bigotry, small-mindedness and cruelty.

"You will come with me, will you not?" Thomas clapped a hand on William's shoulder. "Our time has come."

William sucked in a breath. Was this the sign he craved? Should he go back to the dean and beg to be released from the Shropshire benefice? "Thomas," he began, "I have been offered a living."

Thomas let go of his shoulder, and his eyes clouded. "A living?"

William nodded. "Lord and Lady Ashworth of er, Shropshire, have been so generous as to bestow their parish upon me."

Thomas released a slow breath and his eyes strayed to the floor. "When do you leave?"

Will you not convince me to stay? "Next week." William got up and began pacing the floor. "But I know not if I can accept this assignment. It is so unlike the calling I have long desired."

"Will, don't be a fool."

William stopped pacing immediately and his eyes flashed to his friend. "What?"

"We are younger sons. We have no guarantee of income or security. This appointment is a godsend. You have a chance to become invested in a community and make a real contribution to their lives. A house and land at your disposal. Of course I want you to come with me to the new world, but even I would not throw away such an opportunity."

William sat before Thomas again. "I only... I never thought I would have to commit to such a staid existence so soon."

Thomas stood. "I shall miss you terribly, old chap, but one does not look a gift horse in the mouth, does one?" He stuck out his hand.

William hesitated for a moment, unable to find peace. At last he shook Thomas' hand. "No, I suppose one does not."

"Now I must not remain idle; I must take account of my possessions and prepare for my departure. As must you."

William rose to his feet, his mind slowly adjusting to his fate. "Indeed. Thank you, my friend. I pray we will serve together again before too long."

☙❧

William did not go back immediately to his quarters near St Mary's. Instead he found himself at his family's London apartments in Grosvenor Square. Presided over by his eldest brother since the death of their father, William had never felt completely at home in these fashionable rooms.

The baronet Sir Charles Brook kept him waiting in the drawing room for a quarter of an hour before condescending to acknowledge his presence. William was nearly ready to stalk through the house in search of him.

Charles drifted into the room languidly. "Ah, if it isn't my baby brother," he said, affecting a smile. The brothers shared the same strong physique, dark hair and eyes. Where they differed was in that William had inherited Lady Brook's straight nose, while his two elder brothers shared their father's Roman proboscis. Even though Charles Brook shared the same given name as William's evangelical mentor, the two men could not be more different. The rector was the sort of man he wished his brother could have been.

William rose and took his brother's outstretched hand for a moment.

"And to what do I owe the honour?" Charles asked as he indicated they should both sit.

William swallowed his ire, ignoring his brother's supercilious countenance. He wasted no time with pleasantries, explaining what had transpired at the deanery that morning.

Charles had the grace to cover his mouth even as he failed to swallow his audible amusement. Recovering, a smile remained on his haughty lips. "Well, my dear brother, I must proffer my congratulations... if being sworn in as a priest is indeed good news. I believe I shall now call you our Vagabond Vicar."

"Very clever, Charles, but sadly the 'vagabond' description will no longer be appropriate. The living is in Amberley, Shropshire, and I shall not have the means to travel."

Charles did not bother to hide a chuckle this time. "Cast off to the far reaches of the kingdom, eh? Well I daresay we will still see you from time to time. I will keep your old room as it is, for now."

"How kind of you."

William only remained at the residence long enough to clear his wardrobe of the fine evening clothes he had left behind. He had not needed them since taking up his post as a deacon, shunning the few social invitations within the *ton* he'd received.

∽⸙

As he boarded a stagecoach ten days later, William was resigned to accept his task, but no more eager. It must be God's will for him, but why? Since he'd taken orders he'd tried to face up to the challenge that lay ahead. He only wished it was *more* of a challenge. He avowed to himself that he would accept the post as a temporary commitment, to appease the dean, but he would try to persuade the man of his unsuitability for the task. Perhaps even the Barringtons would understand his need for a quest elsewhere. Mayhap he need only stay for a few months.

His final farewell to Thomas had further disturbed his heart. As they'd both assembled their worldly possessions, the difference in their final destinations loomed large as a deafening unspoken subject. Thomas promised to write as soon as he was able, but it could be over a year before any letters would find their way back. William's heartbeat thudded heavily in his chest with the pain of losing his best friend of nearly five years, perhaps forever. He could only pray they would one day be reunited.

As the coach rumbled out of London's stretching suburbs and into the countryside, William turned to the window. The sharp green of the pastures shocked his senses. It had been some months since he had left London, and he'd grown accustomed to the muted greys and browns. He supposed he'd have to get used to thatched cottages and half-timbered shops instead of the soaring Georgian townhouses and grand public buildings he'd so admired in the city. He'd even miss the dowdy slums and dark alleyways, perhaps even more so.

After a full day of travel and a fitful sleep at an inn, William found himself elbow to elbow between two other travellers in another coach. His mind wandered to his final interview with the dean, in which the senior man had attempted to give William advice which would help him adjust to life as the leader of a flock. There were certain rituals that would need to be carried out, and he was given a list of key townspeople who volunteered their services to the church. The dean's last words rung in his ears like the shrieks of a crow.

"And Brook, seek to make a wife in a timely fashion. Single vicars are looked down on. Granted, you will not have a large choice within the village, but marrying a local girl will ensure you are accepted more readily into the community. Make it a priority."

William shifted in his seat, grinding his teeth. Marriage? A wife? He'd sooner have a noose around his neck. There was no time in his life for romancing maidens. His emotional energy was spent in his work, and besides, he doubted a woman could provide him any intellectual stimulation. From growing up as the youngest of three sons, to college life in Cambridge, to his existence at St. Mary's, he'd become used to mainly male company. With the maid-of-all-work, he'd have no need of a wife to provide domestic comfort. And he'd seen enough unwanted children come into the world to last a lifetime. This directive only served to further fuel his resentment towards the post. An overseas mission would have negated the need to marry for the foreseeable future.

After they stopped for lunch and to change horses, William glimpsed a large hill on the skyline as he headed back to the coach. A fellow passenger followed his gaze.

"That's the Wrekin, sir," the man remarked. "Famous throughout Shropshire."

William regarded the round mound with disdain and stepped into the coach with heavy feet.

His journey finally came to an end near sunset that evening, in a hackney coach he'd hired from Shrewsbury. In the dull light the farming land gave way to some large houses and then a series of cottages, before they turned into what must be the main street of Amberley. The Tudor buildings and bay-windowed shops were not a surprise; the thirty seconds it took to drive through them was however shocking.

"Is that it?" he murmured involuntarily, barely noticing the few villagers who had stopped in their tracks as the carriage drew past.

The church tower at the end of the village was silhouetted against a sky of pink and purple streaks, and the carriage pulled up outside a house next to it. It was a two storied white-washed structure, with a row of three windows on the top floor, and one either side of the main door below. A candle's light flickered from within the bottom left window. William got out as his bags and trunk were deposited on the ground, and tipped the driver. He took in the low rock wall around the property, containing an overgrown flower garden. A row of stone slabs led the way to a small wooden door. *The path to my dull destiny.*

He picked up one of his bags and started up the path on tired legs. Perhaps if he slept soundly enough, he'd wake to find it was all a horrible nightmare.

A breeze picked up, rustling the leaves in the weeping willows and causing the oaks to groan. Cecilia Grant turned her face to the wind as she strolled through the woods near the river. She thrilled at the delicious feeling of a shiver up her spine as one of her long curly blond tendrils tickled the back of her neck. The summer breeze was a welcome foil to the hot July afternoon.

She stopped and surveyed the bend in the river, observing the way the slanting light hit the water as it tumbled over the rocks. She nodded a little to herself, and headed for the bank, discarding her shoes along the way. At the river's edge, she put her satchel down and glanced around furtively with a mischievous glint in her eye. *All clear.*

A moment later she dropped down to the bank and slipped off her stockings. Hitching her buttercup-coloured muslin up to her knees, she slid her toes into the cool rushing water. A sigh escaped her lips as her head dropped backwards and her eyes fluttered shut. She swished her feet around and pulled her head back up, leaning over to empty the contents of her bag. A large notepad, a palette of watercolours, several brushes and an empty jam pot were spread across the grass. She dipped the pot into the stream, opened her palette and picked up a large brush. First dropping it in the pot and then into a bright green pigment on her palette, she began broad, bold strokes across the paper.

Two hours later, Cecilia awoke when a beetle crawled across her forehead. She sat up with a cry, batting at the insect. At once she sensed the sun was lower in the sky, and the realisation of her slumber in the sun hit home. *Oh no! I shall miss Mama's visitors!* She had promised her mother she'd attend tea with one of the families from the neighbouring village. She gathered up her things, hurriedly closing her notepad and spilling the remaining liquid paints over the meadow. Pulling grass from her hair, she smoothed her dress and reached for her stockings.

When she entered her family residence a quarter hour later, she was met by their maid Lucy in the hall.

"Miss!" Lucy cried. "Your mother fair turned the house and garden upside down looking for you! The Wallaces have been here this half an hour."

Cecilia went to the grandfather clock and took in the hour. Three-thirty.

"Miss, your dress is green!"

Cecilia turned around and tried to inspect the back of her dress in the hall mirror. It was indeed tainted with large grass stains.

Lucy's eyes widened. "And your face is blue!"

Cecilia whirled around to confront her reflection, and instantly licked her fingers, rubbing paint from her forehead, nose and cheeks, which were almost as blue as her eyes. "Thank you, Lucy," she said. "I shall have to keep my back to the wall."

"Cecilia, is that you?" Her mother's voice drifted through from the drawing room.

"Yes Mama, I am coming!" Lucy fussed with her hair, which was really past saving, until she opened the door to the room and crept inside. Sitting with her mother was another woman of middle age, and what were to be assumed to be her children: two young girls and a boy about Cecilia's age.

Mrs Grant cleared her throat pointedly. "This is my daughter, Miss Cecilia Grant," she said, directing a hand towards her. "Cecilia, this is Lady Wallace, Miss Wallace, Miss Anne and young Mr Wallace."

Their guests stood, and Cecilia returned their bow and curtsies with a quick bob before edging her way around sideways to the vacant chair. "I am delighted to meet you," she said with an uneasy smile.

Mr Wallace did not try to hide his examination of her, and she returned his stare. His cheeks turned red, and he smiled at her. He was tall, with a scattering of freckles across his fair nose and cheeks, and a fine blue jacket tailored to his slight frame. While he was dressed as an adult, Cecilia couldn't help thinking he still belonged in the schoolroom.

"Miss Grant, are... are you well?" he enquired a little breathlessly.

Pitying his attempt at conversation, and not at all mutually affected by his person, she replied, "Quite well, I assure you. I apologise for my late appearance."

"Indeed," said Lady Wallace, "I fear we must depart else we will be late for dinner." She stood at once.

Mrs Grant's face fell. "I do understand. Thank you for visiting with us."

Lady Wallace ushered her children from the room and the house, and her son had no further opportunity to seek Cecilia's favour. When they had disappeared from sight, Mrs Grant turned a pale countenance to Cecilia and pulled a strand of grass from her hair with agonising deliberation.

Cecilia bit her lip and averted her sheepish eyes from Mrs Grant's glare.

Her mother harrumphed, then turned on her heel and marched into the house. She led her daughter back into the drawing room, and waited until Lucy had left with the tea tray.

"Cecilia," she began through clenched teeth. "How am I going to get you a husband if you behave in this manner?"

"I am sorry Mama," Cecilia said sincerely. "I lost track of time. But really, even if Mr Wallace will inherit a title, he was no more than a boy. He is yet to go to university and finding a wife must be far from his thoughts."

Mrs Grant sniffed, gracefully perching on the edge of a chair. "It is no harm to make connections. In the little time you afforded us, he seemed to be taken with you. It may yet lead somewhere."

Cecilia dropped onto the sofa and folded her arms, a pout threatening to possess her lips. Even if Mr Wallace returned to claim her in a few years, would she want to claim him?

"Now Cecilia, don't sulk. You know full well our options are restricted. We have not the means to give you another season, or travel throughout the county seeking you a husband. You should be grateful that I am thoughtful to engineer such meetings."

While Cecilia had been acknowledged as pretty during her season in town the previous year, her lack of sophisticated manners and more importantly, her modest dowry, had caused her to be slighted by most men. She had danced with many gentlemen, but seriously courted by none, with certainly no hope of a proposal.

With an heir and a spare, there was not a desperate need to get her married, but Mrs Grant still aspired to settle her soon so that she wouldn't be a burden to her brothers. Besides, she had little else to do except plot how to get rid of her daughter.

Cecilia sighed. "Thank you, Mama."

Lucy returned to clear away the cups and plates. Mrs Grant was reminded of another grievance.

"I desired you to practise serving the tea. How are you to learn ladylike manners if you do not practise the arts?"

Cecilia squirmed. How did she always manage to disappoint, despite always having the best intentions to please? "Let me make it up to you, Mama. Shall we practise tomorrow?"

Mrs Grant pursed her lips, but her daughter's eager expression made a smile tug at the edges of her mouth. "We shall see," she said.

Lucy reappeared and picked up the cake stand. "If you please ma'am, Cook wishes me to tell you she baked a Madeira cake we didn't end up using for the tea."

"Thank you Lucy. You may tell her to serve it with the dried fruit course at dinner."

The maid curtseyed and left with her load.

"Oh Cecilia," Mrs Grant said archly, "I heard some news this morning from Mrs Croxley."

"Oh, did you?" Cecilia responded drily. She would be more surprised if their neighbour had *not* imparted some sort of news.

Mrs Grant nodded. "The new vicar arrived yesterday. She saw his hackney coach going past yesterday evening, so she spoke to Miss Hicks this morning, and found out it was he." Miss Hicks' cottage was directly opposite the vicarage. "She did not get a good look at him, but she said he seemed younger. We have it on good authority from Mrs Fortescue that his name is Brook."

Cecilia nodded and stifled a yawn. It wouldn't be a hard achievement to be younger than their previous beloved vicar, Mr Johnson. He had enjoyed an extraordinary length of life, aged well over seventy when he passed. She imagined the new vicar must be closer to fifty or sixty. Any age over forty was old in Cecilia's eyes, as she was newly nineteen. "I suppose we will all meet him when he conducts his first service. Was that all the news?"

"Yes, but any new arrival is always a source of discourse." Mrs Grant brightened suddenly. "I say, would it not be a friendly gesture to send him that cake? He is probably living on bread and water until he has his accounts in order. And rather than have a servant take it, would you be a dear and drop it over?"

Cecilia frowned. She wondered if sending her on an errand was a punishment. She'd have to tidy herself up properly, but she shared her mother's generous streak. "Of course, Mama. We should welcome him." It would be like going to meet an elderly relative for the first time. Her conversations with Mr Johnson had always been cordial, but rather boring. "Should I need to take Lucy with me?"

This unusual deference to propriety was purely to please her mother, and it earned a small smile and a shake of the head. "A short unchaperoned visit through the village will be fine."

Cecilia chose not to go through the village, preferring to ramble along the dry farmyard paths behind the buildings instead. The day was still warm, and the sun cast a sheen over the pastures. Cecilia inhaled the heady scent of meadowsweet and chamomile. She entered the vicarage from behind via the glebe, which was occupied by grazing sheep. She held her package up above their noses, but couldn't resist giving one a scratch behind the ears.

Coming around to the front of the house, she rapped on the door, and prepared to encounter an amiable, benevolent, older gentleman.

Chapter Two

Cecilia waited, and while there was some movement inside the house, no one came to the door. She knocked again, and glanced at a ground-floor window. Perhaps old Mr Brook was indulging in an afternoon nap. After all, the summer warmth had induced her to do the same thing earlier that day.

"I have it, Emma!" a deep voice bellowed.

Suddenly the door was thrown open, and a tall young gentleman stood before her, wrestling with his cravat. His brows were knitted together into a scowl above coffee-coloured eyes, and he braced himself into the doorway with one arm. As he focussed on her, his demeanour changed slightly. His eyes grew larger, and he stepped back a little, but seemed no less irritated. "Yes, may I help you?" he said, though his manner seemed to imply he wished he could slam the door shut again.

Cecilia was confused. Could this really be the vicar? He seemed to be neither amiable, nor benevolent, nor old. In fact, he seemed to be impatient, young and grumpy. He couldn't be more than five and twenty. She looked from him, to the cake, then tried to peer in behind him to see if this was merely a curate, and the real vicar was hiding somewhere within.

"Well?" he demanded. He ran a hand through his hair, which was the dark stain of peat.

"Are... are you the vicar?" Cecilia stammered. "I came to give this to

15

the vicar." She jiggled the cloth-wrapped cake, but did not hand it to him.

"Oh. That is, yes, I am he. William Brook, at your service." He affected a small bow.

"And you are?"

His stern look disabled Cecilia at first, but then she curtseyed and looked him in the eye. "I am Cecilia Grant. I live with my parents at Harcourt Lodge, nearly a mile that way." She pointed towards the village.

He nodded. "And you have no brothers to accompany you?"

Her features darkened. He must think it inappropriate for her to have visited alone. With each moment she was also becoming convinced it had indeed been inadvisable. "I have two elder brothers... Gerald is still in town and Duncan is a lieutenant in the navy."

"Ah." He shifted and his gaze drifted down her form to the cake in her hands.

"Here you are," she said, finally handing it to him. "I do hope you are settling in well."

"Thank you... tolerably. As well as one might expect considering the circumstances."

What circumstances? Cecilia was again perplexed, but she nodded. This vicar was unlike any she'd ever encountered before. "Well, if I am unable to assist you in any way, I will be off."

He nodded. "Forgive me, Miss Grant. I am still tired and somewhat bruised from the week's journey."

Cecilia blinked. Was it proper for a vicar to be discussing bodily harm in such a way?

"Do give my regards to your parents. I look forward to seeing you all on Sunday." He attempted a lopsided smile.

His effort at civility, and something about his countenance, prompted a spark of empathy within her. Of course he was tired, and he was without any of his friends or family in a strange new place. "Do not be shy to ask if you need anything," she said with a smile. "From anyone. Amberley is a friendly place and there will always be someone to help you or give you any information you seek."

His expression had softened, but at the end of her speech his brows plunged down again. He straightened and put a hand on the door. "Yes, I am sure everyone is well acquainted with everyone else's business. Good afternoon, Miss Grant."

৵৽৽

"Thank you, Emma." William nodded to his maid as she curtseyed and left the parlour. He turned to his breakfast, but the kippers and toasted bread held no interest for him. He took a sip of tea and turned to the weekly newspaper produced in the nearest large town, Milton. The stories were basically society gossip, such as the society was. He was hungry to learn of hardships or vice... something he could find to get his teeth into.

It seemed as if Emma would be a satisfactory maid. She had served the late vicar for ten years, and he guessed her age must be nearing forty. She appeared fit and well able to do all the housework, and of a good temper. Thus far he had hardly needed to give her any instruction, as she carried out her duties and routines just as she had always done. While she'd welcomed him in on his arrival two days before, she hadn't tried to make conversation except for asking after his journey. He appreciated her regard for his solitude – or perhaps it was merely shyness – he would not question it either way.

He made himself take a bite of toast. Today he would be meeting with the parish vestry, before which the rural dean was coming over from Milton town to perform the rituals. He could then officially start to find out about the community.

The previous day he hadn't managed to speak to all the business owners in town as he'd meant to. He had hardly slept at all during his first night. At first the quiet was maddening, and then a dastardly cricket took up residence right outside his window and chirped as if its life depended on it for hours on end. Just as he was drifting in and out of sleep, the chickens in his yard began to stir, before a rooster's crow heralded the start of a full country dawn chorus.

When daylight arrived he waited for the sounds of Emma starting the fires, and then had risen to fully inspect the parsonage, as both the darkness and his exhaustion the previous evening had prevented him taking in his surroundings. The stone house was in relatively good repair, with a parlour and library, the kitchen, pantry, Emma's quarters and the mudroom downstairs. Upstairs he had a small suite and there were two further bedrooms. It was obvious from the decor Mr Johnson's wife had occupied the room next to his, and he guessed that at one point in time their children had resided in the last. Outside, there was the front flower garden, and an overgrown pottage garden between the house and the churchyard. Then the glebe stretched out before him past the church, being grazed by sheep, and further out, cattle.

He'd dressed and forced down some breakfast, before going out to explore the lands for a few hours. The dewy grass had squeaked beneath his boots as he strode out across the meadows. He breathed in the scent of it, along with the smell of animals and some sort of floral fragrance. The sun had lifted above the crest of the far hill, throwing long shadows over the village. He climbed to the top of the rise behind the vicarage and looked back over his new home.

The stone of the church shone in the light of dawn. He had to admit its position overlooking the village was picturesque. The township lay in the valley, the rows of shops and houses nestling together snugly. He could make out a small river winding to the south of the built up area. The fields within his benefice were peppered with large oak trees, beneath which the animals grazed. It was all just so perfect, and so *English*.

And therein lay the problem. He despised the perfect hedgerows and the perfect thatched cottages. He gazed at the lazy cattle with contempt, and regarded the wildflowers with revulsion. He wanted to be in an unfamiliar land, where the air was filled with strange spices and the sounds of an exotic language foreign to his ears. He yearned for the heat of the tropics, the challenge of converting pagans, the comradeship of his fellow brothers in Christ. Yet here he was in this sodding idyll, charged with only reading weekly lessons from the prayer book, keeping widows company, and distributing funds to the poor if he was lucky.

Once back in the vicarage, he had settled in a comfortable chair in the library overlooking the glebe. He'd slipped into slumber, and it was only his stiffening neck which made him stir later in the morning. He was then aware of Emma hovering, wanting to know if he'd like some bread and cheese, as he'd had such an early breakfast. After partaking of a brief meal, he returned to his room and knelt by the bed in the quiet, quiet room. He thought of Thomas striking through the seas, wondering how far from England the ship had sailed. He immediately began to pray for his friend, asking for fine weather for the journey, no illness, and a speedy passage to their destination. Then, sucking in a huge breath, he asked the Lord to guide him during his tenure in Amberley, pointing him toward where he could be of use. Then he despaired, crying out in prayer even as tears spilled over onto his cheeks. *Why, why did you not send me to a land where I could bring your word to fresh ears, to those who desperately need to hear it? How long must I remain here? When will I commence my true calling?*

He'd been sitting on the bed engrossed in the book of James, which always gave him solace, when he thought he heard a gentle knocking. He rose and took up a cravat, going down the stairs with some trepidation. In the hall he almost collided with Emma, who was scurrying in from the kitchen, covered in flour.

There was a second, louder knock. "I have it, Emma!" he said, dismissing her in a fluster. Perhaps a town elder had come to welcome him, or one of the farmers who leased his fields wanted to discuss terms.

He had not expected to find a young girl on his doorstep. His stomach tightened at the memory, and what it meant.

It had already started. No doubt every family with a daughter to spare would have them knocking on his door. He wouldn't be able to escape after Sunday services without the farmers' wives recommending their offspring, and if he dared to attend a social gathering he'd be preyed upon by every available miss and the gathered dowagers would spend the evening plotting his matrimonial fate. Well, he'd have none of it. He was only here to humour the dean, and he'd have to make it clear he was not on the marriage market... while trying not to offend the villagers. A delicate operation, to be sure.

The Madeira cake had been an excellent treat at suppertime. He'd given Emma some funds to restock the cupboards, but the first few meals had certainly been basic. The only trouble was he thought of the cake's delivery girl with every moist bite. Her eyes, an extraordinary shade of topaz blue, had become as wide as saucers at the sight of him. She almost seemed a little scared, especially once he'd opened his mouth. His words reflected his frustration and exhausted mental state, and once he'd realised she was a single girl, his suspicions of premature matchmaking were aroused. It was obvious she was a lady, and he did think it odd she would be sent to him without a chaperone. Still, he told himself, he was in the country now – deep within it – and the rigid manners of London and his own upbringing were probably more stringent than those of Amberley village.

Her hinting of the way all the villagers lived in each other's laps did nothing to lift his mood. He had been intending to walk about his immediate surroundings, and introducing himself. But the idea of forming a bad impression when he was in such a foul mood put him off. He didn't want the villagers to be gossiping about him so early in his tenure. He'd leave the introductions for one more day. Justifying his procrastination brought him more satisfaction than it probably should have.

Perhaps he had been too hard on Miss Grant, not gracious enough, maybe even a little rude. He should make more of an effort towards civility with the villagers. He'd been dog tired when she arrived. She didn't attempt to flirt with him, only showing polite sympathy. The thought of her standing there in all her youthful beauty stuck in his mind. She was a little taller than average, with a well-proportioned slight figure. Her smile had transformed her countenance from wary to winsome, and he remembered golden curls peeping out from under her bonnet.

William pushed his plate away and rose from the table. He'd better not be unprepared to meet with the dean. Despite his intention to escape from Amberley as soon as possible, it was in his nature to do his best with whatever tasks lay immediately before him.

かゝ

Having passed the tea-serving test later that same morning, Cecilia took up some mending, and did not notice when a family manservant took up residence next to her elbow.

Joseph cleared his throat.

Cecilia barely glanced at the mail tray he held, saying nothing. She hardly received any mail so it must be for her mother.

"Miss Grant, a letter," Joseph said.

"Truly?" Cecilia's head swung towards him, her eyes bright with excitement. She snatched the letter up from the salver, instantly recognising the small, neat handwriting on the parchment. "Amy," she murmured, and then, looking up at her mother, she said, "A letter from Amy! You know what this means."

Mrs Grant lit up as she watched her daughter open the missive with a flourish. "This late in the season it must mean they are returning to Amberley." She couldn't help rising, moving around to stand behind Cecilia as she read the note.

Amy Miller was the only child of a tenant farmer and his wife, and Cecilia's closest friend. Their friendship was tolerated by Cecilia's parents rather than endorsed, as Amy was not of the gentle classes. However they learned early on that the bond between the girls was not to be broken.

Amy's father had passed on a few years earlier, and on the death of Mrs Miller, Lady Ashworth had offered Amy the position of lady's maid to her second daughter Catherine. This year had seen Amy's first season in town with the Barringtons.

The letter confirmed Mrs Grant's assumption of the family's return within the next week. She paced around the room in excitement. "We must prepare, Cecilia."

Cecilia looked up from her second reading of the letter. "Prepare, Mama?"

Mrs Grant stopped pacing long enough to toss an impatient look in her daughter's direction. "I told you, did I not, of the letter from my sister? Only a week ago she was quite certain that while Lord Marsham has formed an attachment with someone, his younger brother remains unattached. Oh, it is a most eligible match, my dear. He surely cannot be so puffed up as to refuse you because of your small dowry. You are a beauty, and he will have more than enough to live on when he takes up residence in Mulberry Manor."

Mrs Grant referred to another property the Barringtons were in possession of, a cottage ornée. While the lands were not as great as Ashworth Hall, the manor would indeed provide a generous income and it was widely known that the second son was to be granted possession of it.

Mrs Grant drew near to Cecilia and took up her hand. "Now is our chance. That is – your chance – dear daughter."

Cecilia was overcome by the rare display of motherly affection, and already excited with the prospect of Amy's return, any sensible thoughts flew from her head. "Yes, Mama," she whispered.

She was not to know her words were interpreted as a solemn promise: a verification of her desire to become Mr Barrington's bride.

Chapter Three

William was sure to study the Book of Common Prayer from end to end before his meeting with the dean from Milton. He was relatively familiar with the morning and evening prayers, but the weekly service had never been his major focus. He assumed in Amberley it would be the most important duty, next to the obligatory weddings, funerals and christenings.

As the dean laid William's hands upon the church door and spoke prayers of commitment and servanthood, a surprising bevy of emotions overtook the new young vicar. Despite his intention to quit the village as soon as possible, he could not perform the swearing-in ceremonies with anything less than sincerity. The dean was the Lord's representative, and William must give him, and the rituals, due respect. It was a sacred undertaking, and he was unexpectedly overcome as he was given responsibility for the souls of the parish.

Even so, as they went inside and the dean directed William to ring the bells, he was uncomfortable. In his heart he wasn't making the lifetime commitment required. He felt false, even as he reached for the bell pull. The striking of the bells then penetrated his heart, his soul perhaps. With each note, he felt God was telling him he must be of use, no matter where his situation, no matter what the tenure. They rang again and again, convicting him.

He fell to his knees. *Yes Lord, I will serve you here... for as long as I must remain.*

࿇

William had only recently recovered his composure after the dean's departure when the members of the parish vestry began to arrive. The group consisted of the highest ranking local people: Mr Fortescue the solicitor, Mr Stockton, a gentleman farmer, Mr Morton of the counting house, Mr Lindsay the physician, Mr Jones the shopkeeper, and Mr Grant, of the landed gentry. Although Lord Ashworth officially presided over the group, William was informed it was not unusual for his Lordship to be absent from meetings even when in residence.

"Welcome, Mr Brook," said Mr Stockton, shaking his hand enthusiastically. "It is wonderful to have a fresh face in the village."

This sentiment was more appreciated than the farmer could have realised. William smiled at the new faces as he shook hands with all, and the group took their positions around a well-worn table within the vestry.

Mr Fortescue presented William with the keys to the parish chest, where all the town's records were kept.

Mr Morton seated himself next to William, and he said quietly, "Doubtless there will be some… adjustments, and you may find that some of the village people are not used to change." His brow had furrowed, but then his expression softened. "However, we will all do what we can to ease the transition."

"Thank you, Mr Morton," William said. "I confess I know not quite what sort of reception to expect."

Mr Fortescue's wife, the vestry secretary, handed out the notes from the last meeting, which had been three months before, when Mr Johnson was still in good health.

William took a quick breath, wanting to assume an air of authority right away, lest the group think him young and inhibited. "Shall I read the minutes aloud to acquaint myself with business?" he said, as more of a statement than a question.

He positioned his index finger underneath the first item, but the words on his tongue were silenced by a pointed feminine throat-clearing. He looked up. "Yes, Mrs Fortescue?"

"If it is all the same to you, Mr Brook, I shall read the minutes," she said. "Mr Johnson preferred to leave that to me."

"Oh, did he? I don't mind leading, so please do not trouble yourself in future. Now, item the first..."

"But, Mr Brook –"

William raised an eyebrow. How could he be doing something wrong in so simple a matter, when he was trying to save the woman effort?

"I would prefer to read through the business. That is, if the vestry members are happy to continue the way things have always been done." Mrs Fortescue eyeballed each member in turn, and they each murmured their agreement. She turned back to William with a triumphant smile.

He smiled back, impressed with her imperious command and not feeling the need to challenge her so soon, despite his enthusiasm to lead the group. "Please proceed, Mrs Fortescue. Thank you for your commitment." *It is more like domination*, he thought to himself, and as the meeting progressed, it became more and more obvious that she not only read the minutes, but controlled the flow and order of the entire meeting, including steering any decisions. He watched her from the corner of his eye, taking in her short yet solid frame, her immaculate dress and steely blue eyes. *The Mayoress of Amberley*, he thought. *If I am to succeed during my time here, you must be an ally.*

Mr Morton presented a review of the current financial status, and the group discussed how funds would be distributed to the needy. Mr Stockton gave a report on the state of the church roof, and there were calls for a new volunteer to keep the churchyard tidy.

A new hymn book was then placed in William's hands.

Mr Jones spoke up. "That's the updated edition, sir. Dated eighteen-oh-two. We have raised funds to purchase a set."

"Jolly good," William said. "But that is already three years old. What is the age of the current hymnal?"

The mutterings of the group belied their ignorance of the date, and one by one eyes settled on Mrs Fortescue.

"I believe it is over one hundred years old," she said.

"I say," William said, "it appears this purchase is well overdue. And you have ordered the books, Mr Jones?"

The shopkeeper nodded. "I got a good price for them, too."

William smiled, disarming the man's obvious defences. "I am sure you did, Mr Jones."

As the shopkeeper returned to his seat, Mr Morton whispered, "It was quite revolutionary, you know."

William turned to him. "What was?"

"Deciding to purchase new hymnals. It took a few years to convince Mr Johnson that it would be nice for the younger people to have new music."

"Indeed," William said, not altogether successful in hiding his smile.

The meeting went on for over an hour, and William concluded this group was more than capable of managing the clerical affairs with minimal guidance. The only notes he took were of who he would need to visit to deliver assistance. Mr Grant seemed to be the voice of reason, and Mr Lindsay wanted to appear as if he had all the good ideas, simply by repeating them the loudest.

William tried to visualise the moment when he would tender his resignation, which would hopefully be accompanied with the news of him heading a mission to an exotic destination. Would Mrs Fortescue be shocked? Would Mr Morton's spectacles fall from their precarious position on the end of his nose? He was sure with or without him their lives would go on as they always had.

As the group began to stand at the conclusion of the meeting, Mr Grant cleared his throat. "I have it on good authority," he said, "that the Barringtons will be in residence any day."

"Is that so?" William asked him quietly. He had hoped he would be the one to receive advance warning of their arrival. "May I ask whose authority?"

Mr Grant grinned. "Why, my wife's of course. The feminine information network is not to be rivalled." He clapped William on the back. "I have no doubt you will be made aware of their presence in due course."

"No doubt," William agreed. Privately he wondered how he could show the proper amount of deference to his patrons, whilst also indicating he would rather they look elsewhere for a permanent parson.

❧

"Only look at all the colours, Mama." Cecilia ran her hand over the dozen different shades of silk pinned to a page in Mr Jones' catalogue of new gowns from a Shrewsbury dressmaker. She drank in the bright shining hues hungrily, and they swam through her mind in a liquid frenzy.

Her mother beamed. "Mr Grant has been most generous. He understood the exceeding import of a new dress once I explained Mr Barrington has not seen you in your true bloom."

The gentleman in question had never returned to Amberley last year between seasons, and Mrs Grant was convinced Cecilia's beauty had developed since her time in London.

"You must look as if you follow the latest fashions," she continued. "I would not want those Barrington girls looking down their pretty little noses at you."

"No, Mama." Inwardly Cecilia shuddered. The Barrington ladies certainly did know they were better than the rest of Amberley society, although the younger sister seemed to rub their noses in it a little less.

With a dress design chosen, Cecilia pointed to the shade of green she desired, which shimmered like the colour of the river running deeply under the trees. "This one please, Mr Jones."

"Ah yes, I think that will do splendidly," said Mrs Grant. "And now we must find some shoes..."

Mr Jones had some shoes in stock, and Cecilia tried on three pairs obediently until her mother approved. Mrs Jones appeared from the back of the shop with a tape measure, and proceeded to discreetly take Cecilia's dimensions, noting down the numbers on a tiny notebook. When this was complete, Cecilia found her mother adding several lengths of ribbon to their purchases.

"I must re-trim my bonnets," she said in answer to Cecilia's questioning look. "Married ladies must be allowed some delights too."

When all the items were noted on their account, the Grant ladies slowly wound their way around the stands of merchandise – crockery, stationery, haberdashery – towards the door.

Mrs Grant grasped Cecilia's arm. "Only think, my love. You may be married by next spring, and then attending the Season as a bride! Oh!" She clasped her hands together. "Can you imagine?"

Cecilia could not. She preferred not to use her imagination for such hopes (or fears), rather utilising it for making her current surroundings come alive. In fact she'd rather not contemplate marriage at all. It was an unavoidable certainty which would surely change her life forever, but she'd never been one to speculate or dream about the future. She tried to please her parents, and she had made a genuine effort to be pleasant to the gentlemen in town, but her nature was such that she was consumed with the sensations of the present moment.

While the grace, manners and polished looks of the London men she'd met had been impressive, and while some of the local lads were entertaining, she had not yet experienced the first thrill of amorous intoxication. Her heart was still her own, and as of this moment it belonged to art, nature and any other object of beauty, tranquillity or worth in her eyes.

Even though in the secret places of her soul she nurtured a fantastical wish for a wild romantic attachment, she dared not hope for such. It was too fragile a dream to be dwelled on, and she devoted her energies instead to obtaining pleasure from surer avenues. In her experience, men – in fact, most people – didn't want to listen to her ideas or understand her for who she was. She must wring out as much enjoyment as she could from life now, for she knew her future husband may not allow her to indulge her fancies. She could see herself trapped in a drawing room all day long with visits and reams of correspondence. When the inevitable marriage finally transpired, she hoped happy memories would carry her through any disappointments.

"We are leaving now, Cecilia." Mrs Grant tugged on Cecilia's arm and dragged her toward the door, her tone indicating it was not her first attempt to break her daughter's reverie. As they rounded the last rack, they bumped into two elderly ladies entering the shop.

"Goodness me!" Miss Hicks exclaimed.

"Begging your pardon, ladies," Mrs Grant said. "It is a lovely day, is it not?"

"Indeed Mrs Grant," said Mrs Croxley with a bland smile. The ladies disappeared deeper into the shop. "In a world of her own," Mrs Croxley said in pointed exasperation, without any intention of hiding the sentiment.

"I did not see them, Mama," Cecilia said as they walked out onto the street, knowing full well she was the target of their malice, as usual. "It was not my fault."

Mrs Grant sighed. "I know, my dear."

❧

William was ravenous after the vestry meeting, and after some bread and cold meats he was fortified enough to face the rest of the Amberley populace. He set out from the vicarage at his normal brisk walk, but then reminded himself to slow down in order to appear approachable.

As soon as he began passing the huddled cottages, he could feel eyes on him. With his peripheral vision, he could see curtains fluttering aside, and figures moving. By the fifth house, he wanted to check that he wasn't just being paranoid. He stopped walking for a moment and turned his head slightly towards the second storey of the thatched cottage on his right. As expected, a female face in the window turned from curious to embarrassed, then disappeared.

The cottages gave way to Tudor buildings, housing businesses on the ground floor and, presumably, their owners above. He passed the blacksmith, glimpsing glowing embers and the sound of metal clanging on metal. Then his senses were aroused by the enticing aroma of freshly baked bread, and he made a mental note to return to the bakery on his way back to the vicarage.

The street itself was scattered with residents going about their business, most of whom were also pretending not to look at him. He saw Mr Lindsay, the physician from the vestry, and the man introduced his wife, who was also the church organist. No-one else approached him, and as they were mostly ladies he knew propriety did not allow him to introduce himself.

Passing by a milliners and the post office, he found the object of today's excursion, Mr Jones General Wares. He thought he saw the young lady who had delivered the cake leaving with a woman who must be her mother, but thankfully they began walking in the opposite direction and were so deep in conversation they didn't notice him. He didn't want to give that particular mother any sort of encouragement.

William entered the shop and exchanged a wave with Mr Jones, before withdrawing a list of requirements from his pocket. He sauntered along the first aisle, and when he turned at the end to go up the next, he saw two ladies at the end with their backs to him. They were examining embroidery patterns with their fingers, but engaged in fervent conversation with every other faculty. He could not avoid hearing their words as he moved about the shop collecting the items he wanted, but they appeared too preoccupied to notice his movements.

"And Miss Grant is yet unmarried, even after a season in London." The first woman's voice was frail, and her narrow frame was stooped over a cane.

"What will it take for her to charm a gentleman? She doesn't lack for beauty." The second woman was also of advanced years but stout, her grey dress covered in lace frills.

"It almost seems she is not interested in men, although she does not appear shy."

"Her demeanour to both sexes is sometimes lacking. One sometimes wonders what on earth is passing through that pretty head of hers."

"Perhaps she will end a spinster, pottering away at her drawings in her brother's house."

"I don't think young Mr Grant would like that!"

"And what a shame it would be, for such a lovely face to decline into dowdiness."

William did not wish to appear a tyrant, but as he concluded his business in the shop a righteous indignation burned within him and he could not condone the idle gossip any longer.

"Good afternoon, ladies," he said loudly, announcing his presence behind them.

They both whipped around, and faces of annoyance turned to surprise and perhaps embarrassment. "Good afternoon," the woman in the lace dress greeted him. "You must be the new vicar, Mr Brook."

He bowed. "That I am."

"I am Mrs Croxley, and this is Miss Hicks."

"I am your neighbour," Miss Hicks said with a smile which somehow sent a shiver up William's spine.

He cleared his throat. "I will call on you next week, if I may."

"Certainly," said Miss Hicks.

"It sounds as if you ladies know an awful lot about the, er, village. I should be glad to depend on you for any information." He wasn't sure, but he thought he detected some colour in Mrs Croxley's creased cheeks.

"Of course, we should be happy to assist you with anything you need," she said.

"However," William began carefully, "we must be wary of falling into hollow conjecture about others in their absence."

Mrs Croxley took up the challenge. "If you mean what we were saying just now about poor Miss Grant, I can assure you we spoke out of nothing but concern for her future."

"I am sure that is true," William said. "However if such a conversation *is* necessary" – here he raised his eyebrows to illustrate his belief it was not – "it is better conducted in a private place where it can do no harm to anyone who may be easily offended."

The two ladies stared at him. He grimaced, knowing he'd overstepped the bounds of dishing out advice to new acquaintances.

"May I help you with those, Mr Brook?" Mr Jones came to his rescue, eager to begin tallying up William's purchases.

"Indeed Mr Jones," William smiled at him in relief and handed over the items, before turning back to the ladies with a humble countenance. "So pleased to meet you both, and I thank you for enduring my sermonising."

Miss Hicks giggled, while Mrs Croxley smiled knowingly. "You'll see what we meant about Miss Grant, young man," she said. "You can make up your own mind about her."

Their words had certainly served to make the lady a little more intriguing, if only to observe if there was any truth in them at all. "Thank you," he said, "I intend to."

Chapter Four

After breakfast two mornings later, William found Emma polishing the mail salver industriously in the parlour.

"Good morning Emma," he greeted her. "I am sure you will be able to see your reflection in that tray by now."

The maid broke into an uncharacteristic smile. "I need to use this, sir. You have mail. Proper letters, like."

"Oh, really?" The possibility of news from the outside world was pathetically thrilling. "Where is it?"

Emma patted the right pocket of her apron.

"May I have it, then?"

She shook her head and looked wounded. "If you'll only sit down, sir, I'll bring it to you on the salver, properly."

William sighed and went over to the armchair, making a show of sinking into it and crossing his legs. "There now," he said. "At your leisure."

Emma held the salver at arm's length, examining it from every angle. At last she gave a satisfied nod, and laid it on the occasional table. She withdrew the anticipated items from her pocket, laid them on the tray, and carefully arranged them in an even pile with the edges all lined up. Then she lifted the salver as if it were balancing a dozen full glasses of wine, and grandiosely stalked across the room.

"Your mail, sir," she said.

William refrained from snatching it up and telling her to go away. "Thank you, Emma," he said, taking up the little pile of cards and notes. "Excellently done."

The maid beamed, and hugged the salver to her chest.

"I shall read the mail now," he said.

She nodded, anchored to the spot.

"I do not require, er, further assistance."

Comprehension finally dawned on Emma, and she bustled away.

William's correspondence consisted mainly of invitations to visit or dine. Three were from vestry households: the Fortescues, the Grants and the Stocktons. There was also a letter from another farming family, the Russells. The last item was a grand note card inviting him to take tea that very afternoon with the Barringtons. They must have arrived the previous afternoon while he was arranging his few possessions in the vicarage. Sadly, there were no letters from his acquaintances in London or Cambridge. He wanted badly to write to Thomas about his experiences thus far, but he knew not where to send the letter, and it would be months before his friend arrived in India.

He took up his pen, and began to reply to the invitations, being sure to allow days in between each engagement to recover.

∂◦↖

Cecilia half walked, half ran over to Ashworth Hall. Entering by the servants' door, she greeted the cook and scullery maid before taking a seat at the mess table. The last thing she wanted was a formal tête-à-tête with the Barrington ladies.

One of the newer footmen came strolling into the room, immediately stiffening on seeing her.

"Hello Miss, are you lost?"

"Why, no." She smiled. "I am Amy's friend, Cecilia Grant. Will you tell her I am here?"

He bowed slightly. "Very good."

Cecilia felt the self-conscious movements of the kitchen staff as she waited. She wanted to make some sort of conversation, but knew not what to discuss.

It was a good ten minutes before Amy burst in through the door. Her green eyes sparkled at the sight of Cecilia, and she brushed her twig-brown hair out of her eyes. Her attempts to form curls around her freckled complexion were in vain, for the strands were stubbornly straight. Her skin had paled considerably since their last meeting. Amy was no longer working in the outdoors, her work as a lady's maid transforming her appearance.

She rushed forward to meet Cecilia, who met her half way around the table.

"Oh," Cecilia cried as they embraced, "how I have missed you!"

As they pulled apart, Amy whispered, "Cici, I've got such good news!"

"Oh yes, what is it?"

Amy glanced furtively at the staff, and walked her friend towards the door. "Let us find a private spot to talk."

Once ensconced in the library, Cecilia was impatient to know her friend's subject.

"The Barringtons' governess is engaged," Amy said, fairly floating on her chair with excitement.

Cecilia motioned for her to go on, but Amy just smiled and nodded. "How wonderful for Miss Holt. But why are you so excited?"

"Because, silly, it means you can apply for the job. We could work in the same house, and be in London together every spring!"

Cecilia absorbed the idea with wide eyes. Being in gainful employment would lessen the pressure on her to wed, and she did like children. The Barringtons had two younger children, nine and seven years old. "But surely we will be apart for most of the day as the children will not be with the adults... and you."

Amy waved a dismissive hand. "'Tis true, Miss Holt did spend all day with the children, but in the evening she would socialise in the servants' hall. When Lady Catherine had no further need of me we would spend the nights chattering. And we could share a room!"

Cecilia let her mind conjure up fantasies of late night whispering, doing each other's hair, sharing their deepest secrets and always having a friend in such close company. She'd never had a confidant at home.

"And you wouldn't feel a burden to your family," Amy went on. "You'd have your own income until your prince comes to claim you."

Cecilia laughed at the very idea of a prince coming to call upon a lowly governess, but inside she had to admit self-sufficiency was very appealing. Apart from allaying the stress of having failed as a daughter in the marriage department, it would mean her mother would no longer have the worry of securing the hand of a wealthy gentleman. Surely Mama would be all too pleased to be relieved of that duty. Cecilia's main concern would be only having one afternoon off a week for drawing outside.

"I will think about it," she said, "and see what my parents will say."

Amy nodded, satisfied. She reached for Cecilia's hand. "Now, tell me how you are and all the news. I heard we have a new vicar and Henry Russell is positively apoplectic. He was foolhardy to think that Lord Ashworth would offer the post to a farmer who is not a gentleman, but I cannot but help feeling sorry for him."

"Indeed," Cecilia said. "It would perhaps have been easier for someone local to fit into the community as well."

Amy nodded. "Yes, I have heard the new vicar is a young upstart from London. Perhaps he will not have the patience for life in a small village."

Cecilia frowned. Her mother had indeed passed on various opinions from ladies who had met Mr Brook and were not impressed. However the young man's dark eyes remained in her memory, and she sensed a barrage of emotions lurked within. "Let us not pass judgement so soon," she said gently. "It is only that he is so different from our dear Mr Johnson. I do not think it would be easy to find anyone who we could love as dearly." Cecilia sighed, remembering the pleasant old gentleman who had been as a grandfather to most of the town. Not wanting to descend into melancholy, she changed the subject. "How are you enjoying your post? Were you able to enjoy much entertainment in London?"

Amy's face lit up in a grin. "Oh Cici, I have never been happier. Catherine is so kind to me, and I have to admit to being quite entranced by London."

"You were able to get out and about frequently, then?"

"Oh yes, Martha and I were always to accompany the ladies to the park or shopping, and I was even allowed out to the theatre once."

"Is that so?" Cecilia rested her chin on the back of her hands as Amy chatted, and thought that perhaps being in service might be exactly what she needed to avoid the question of marriage.

৵৵

William made his way to Ashworth Hall on foot. He was a little annoyed at the presumption that he would be free with a few hours' notice, but he supposed the family was used to their local vicar being at their beck and call.

Lord and Lady Ashworth had seemed innocuous enough during his brief meeting with them in London. He understood they had four adult offspring, all still at home, and two younger children.

As he sipped his tea half an hour into their meeting, it appeared the docile parents were entirely ruled by their headstrong children. Only the youngest of the four present, Catherine, turned a kindly eye upon him. Her sister and two brothers seemed impatient for him to be gone.

The conversation centred mainly around his background in Cambridgeshire, including veiled interrogations about the size of the family lands and income, and how his elder brothers had turned out. They might have heard of the Brooks in London, perhaps, but they could not be sure. Certainly William had not been present at any of the gatherings of the *ton*?

"Indeed," smiled William. "I attended to the aftermath instead."

This comment silenced his examiners, drawing a little of the haughtiness away from a few expressions.

Lord Ashworth cleared his throat. "We look forward to your first sermon, Brook," he said, ignoring the facetious glances exchanged by his sons. "I do hope we have given you enough time to get your bearings and prepare."

"Quite sufficient, thank you," William said.

There was another lull in the conversation, during which the sisters whispered and giggled. Finally, Lady Catherine leaned toward him archly. "You are not promised to a young lady, then?"

William's eyebrows flitted up briefly. "I am not."

Mr Barrington gave his sister a sardonic stare. "I am sure even vicars are reluctant to be tied down, Catherine," he said.

William eyed Mr Barrington, who seemed to be your typical child of privilege, with a strong proud brow and restless eyes, his expensively-clad body sprawled across the sofa. There was something lazy yet accusing in his voice whenever he spoke, which rubbed William up the wrong way.

"Well, I am sure we can find someone for you locally," spoke up Lady Ashworth. "No doubt a quietly spoken, but useful sort of girl will be just the ticket."

"I pray, do not exert yourself on my behalf, Lady Ashworth," William said, trying to hide mild panic. "I have more than enough on my plate at present."

"Of course. That is why the ball will be beneficial for you."

William stared at her blankly. "The ball?"

The elder son Viscount Marsham spoke up over his newspaper. "Mama and Papa always give a ball on our return to the country."

Lady Ashworth nodded. "The moon will favour us three weeks hence. It will be the perfect opportunity for you to socialise with suitable ladies." She smiled in a slightly patronising fashion, as if expecting his gratitude.

William was at a loss as to how to reply. At last he reached for his tea cup and decided on, "You are very generous."

It was, of course, generosity he could well do without.

As William walked away from the Hall, a flash of movement caught his eye. He checked to ensure no-one was watching, and then crept around the side of the hall a few steps toward its source. He saw a young woman negotiating the rose garden, meandering away from the house. He was certain it was not a lady of the house, but she was also not in servant's garb. Perhaps a lady-in-waiting?

Something about her movement compelled him to watch for a further few moments, and he held his breath when, just as she reached the end of the formal garden she turned to glance at the house. She didn't appear to see him; she only smiled a little before skipping off through the long grasses and wildflowers of a meadow.

He shook his head and resumed his own departure. It was his cake girl, he was sure of it: the infamous Miss Grant. And she hadn't been with the family or left the house through the proper entrance. Whatever could her business be?

William shrugged a little to himself and quickened his pace. He wondered if the rumours about her being bacon-brained could be true.

~∞~

"Absolutely not," Mr Grant said, setting his knife and fork down firmly on his plate of mutton. "No daughter of mine will be earning wages."

Cecilia was momentarily struck dumb. She had at least hoped the governess idea would be given due consideration. The image of a shared room with Amy shattered in her mind. "But Papa" she said, her voice shaking a little, "it will give me something useful to do."

"Cecilia," Mrs Grant said with a sigh. "You underestimate your own worth, or your *potential* worth. I would have you installed at Ashworth Hall, but not as the governess. We must have you married to Mr Barrington. Even as the younger son, his possession of Mulberry Manor will provide a considerable income, and you will move in the society of peers."

How quickly the conversation had turned away from what she wanted, toward her mother's aspirations on her behalf. That particular goal did not seem attainable in her eyes, and this time she intended to say so. "He has never given me a second glance, Mama, not even when I was in town last year."

"Then you must make him notice you here in Amberley, my dear," Mrs Grant said, and her gaze turned unyielding. "I will not rest until I see you married within a titled family. Your beauty will not be in vain."

Cecilia felt a rising dread, sure any efforts she could make would only end in disappointment. There was indeed a dearth of rich or titled gentlemen in the vicinity, so her mother was partly justified in grasping at such a convenient catch. The only other gentleman she would have considered eligible, heir to a neighbouring holding, had swiftly engaged himself to the daughter of a cotton-merchant with a dowry of ten thousand pounds.

"Cecilia," Mrs Grant prodded, "you will promise me you'll try to charm him."

"I shall try Mama of course, but I am not confident he will want me without much money."

"Some things are more desirable than money, dearest."

Cecilia chose to ignore the unsettling meaning in her mother's stare. She turned to her father. "Papa, would you have me throw myself on the gentleman?"

Mr Grant swallowed his mouthful and considered. "Perhaps," he said, dabbing at his mouth with his serviette, "it would be wise to see if you *like* Mr Barrington."

"I see." Cecilia's eyes dropped to her full plate, but she had no appetite.

"Now that's settled," Mrs Grant said swiftly, "tell me more about your visit. Were the Barrington ladies pleased to see you?"

Cecilia hesitated, trying to think how to best deliver the unsatisfactory news. "I did not see any of the family," she said, twisting her dress in her hands and not daring to meet her mother's gaze. "I sought out Amy and visited with no-one else."

Mrs Grant descended into an incredulous silence, although not for long. "But surely the butler must have announced you?"

"I – I did not trouble the butler. I approached via a, er, side entrance."

"You cannot mean... the *servants'* entrance?"

Miserable, Cecilia nodded, focussing on the mantel clock. "I did not know I was supposed to visit with the Barringtons. I only went to see Amy. They did not invite me... I had no reason to call."

"You could have requested to visit with Amy, as she is your particular friend, and someone in the family would have had to acknowledge you. Really my dear, do I have to explain everything to you?"

"I am sorry Mama; I do not mean to fail you."

"Yes. It is perhaps the accidental nature of your mishaps that is the most alarming."

Cecilia tried to hide the hurt she felt, only murmuring, "Yes, Mama."

Chapter Five

William chose his next movements within Amberley with care. In a purely political move, he decided to visit the Fortescues first. By intimating they were the next most important family after the Barringtons, he was hopeful his officious "mayoress" would be flattered into cooperation. For his part, he was eager to find out more about how this woman ticked, and how her husband coexisted with her.

He could see Mrs Fortescue was sensible of the compliment in the way she dismissed her maid and practically pulled him through to her drawing room, which was laden with tea and small cakes. She took control of the conversation, and seemed to think it a necessity to inform William she had not always been in the village. "I am originally from Milton," she said, "and I have some acquaintance in Shrewsbury."

"Indeed, Mrs Fortescue." William reached for a confection covered in pink icing. "Have you never been tempted to return to Milton? I daresay a woman of sophistication such as yourself would crave more diversions than Amberley can offer."

Mrs Fortescue coloured slightly in response to his flattery. "We visit every now and then," she said with an appreciative smile, "but a wife's place is with her husband's family, is it not?"

"I can see you take your duty very seriously, Mrs Fortescue." William thought that the lady also probably preferred a smaller community over which she could take dominion.

William was then obliged to talk about his family background and his education, which he did freely, but when Mr Fortescue asked him if he was contented with his new position, he faltered. He would not lie about his intentions.

"I am, er, that is I expect it would take some time for any new vicar to find their way." Before his hosts could draw breath again, he rushed to change the subject. "Mr Fortescue, did you meet Mrs Fortescue at a social event in Milton?"

"No indeed," Mr Fortescue began, but he was hushed when his wife placed a hand on his arm.

"No, it was in Amberley." Mrs Fortescue looked away for a moment. "I was staying with a family I am acquainted with nearby."

"How fortuitous," William said with a smile. "And have you children?"

William had thought he was on safe ground with the seemingly inoffensive question, but Mr Fortescue frowned deeply, and Mrs Fortescue took a deep breath before replying.

"Mr Fortescue and I have been unable to have a family," she said finally.

William was immediately remorseful. "Oh, I am sorry," he said. "I apologise for the intrusion."

❧◈❦

William sat in his small library late the following night, working on his first sermon for the next morning. When he was reasonably happy with it, based on the prescribed lesson from the calendar in the prayer book, he leaned back in his chair and stretched his arms above his head. He stared up at the low beams on the ceiling, and was suddenly aware of the stillness. As it had every night since his arrival, the huge silence seemed to swallow him up.

With a pang, he realised that the real feeling oppressing him was loneliness. This house with its many vacant rooms was devoid of company. Emma had long since gone to bed and didn't seem capable of more than two sentences together at the best of times. The emptiness was in stark contrast to a house full of deacons in London, coming and going at various times of the night. He missed the sound of activity outside in the street; he missed the very possibility that things might be happening, or that he could make things happen.

When a cricket began chirping loudly outside, he sprang up from the chair, sure the penetrating sound would drive him mad. "I must *do* something," he said to himself.

Stalking from the room, he picked up his jacket from where it was slung over a chair in the parlour, and marched out of the house, down the lane to the village. His steps led him towards the public house, where the lights still burned. Drunkenness? Debauchery? Why not. He would welcome any sin he could confront head on, with his talent for gently showing a lost soul there was a better way.

Some nights his whole ministry had centred on sobering up men so that their tempers cooled enough to prevent them beating their wives when they returned home. He assumed the level of desperate poverty and petty crime would be minimal in Amberley. But he was sure he could hunt out some kind of depravity, if he searched for it hard enough.

He didn't even reach the pub before he heard raised voices. The heavy wooden door to the tavern slammed shut, and from the light of the windows William could make out two men engaged in a shoving match, trading insults and expletives.

He stood back in the shadows for a few moments, hoping they would quickly exhaust themselves and collapse in drunken stupors. However, neither was apparently so far gone as to be rendered useless, and they began trading blows in an increasingly violent bout.

William quickly intervened, pushing between them with expert timing. He put a hand on each man's chest. "Leave off chaps; no one wants to cause an injury."

"Who are you?" one of the men demanded irately, still with his fists raised.

"I know who he is," the other one growled. "He's the new vicar, fresh from London. Come to spy on us, have ya?"

The first man eyed him up and down, his hands drifting to his hips. "Vicar? Ye don't much look like the kind of vicar we're used to."

William smiled ruefully. "So I have heard."

"Well clear out of here, vicar," the second man said. "We got a score to settle, and you've got no right getting in the way."

"I believe it is part of my job to keep the peace, and I have no wish to see someone injured because of a drunken argument, likely over something very trivial."

"Trivial?" the first man slurred.

"You're not wanted here, vicar," the second man said firmly, his thick ginger eyebrows knotting together. "Go home."

If only I could. Briefly William wondered whether the man meant he wasn't welcome at this particular spot, or in the village itself. He took a breath in order to begin the usual pacifying words he had spoken so often when diffusing such a situation. But when he looked into the man's eyes, he saw not just annoyance, but a seething hot hatred, as if William had personally done something to offend him. Instead he only said, "Advice you should take, I rather think."

He turned and walked back down the lane, but he stayed close-by to make sure the men had cooled down. He'd been in similar circumstances before, and hurt men were always glad to see him in the end, when they needed help getting their wounds attended to or a shoulder to lean on during the journey back home.

❧

William knew his first sermon, and indeed the entire service, was not the time to experiment or attempt to introduce the congregation to difficult or moving topics. He asked Mrs Lindsay to play the most well-known hymns, and he had rehearsed traditional prayers. He could not stop himself from walking over to the church half an hour early, and he nervously paced in the vestibule. Ten minutes to the hour, and his only company was the organist, Mr and Mrs Fortescue, and Mr Morton, currently serving as the churchwarden.

"Will anyone else be coming?" he whispered to Mrs Lindsay.

"Oh yes," she replied with a placating smile.

William pulled out his pocket watch. It was now only five minutes to the hour. "Er... when?" he pressed her.

"Why, at the hour of course." She busied herself with her music book, and William traded polite smiles with the Fortescues, who were occupying one of the front pews.

As the clock tower in the village stuck the hour of ten, William found himself dashing outside to see where on earth everyone was. At the doorway he collided with Lady Ashworth, who drew back with an imperious shock.

"Do have a care, Mr Brook," she murmured, before sailing past him.

William peeked into the churchyard, and to his surprise it was now full of milling parishioners. He shook hands with Lord Ashworth and his sons, then bowed to the ladies, and for an indeterminable length of time his sole occupation was thus as the pews filled from front to back, roughly in order of rank. He attempted to keep a mental register of all the names and faces.

He took his place at the pulpit, and was dismayed to find his palms sweaty. He surveyed the small sea of faces, and the many pairs of eyes made his stomach flutter. However, he took a deep breath, and told himself he'd preached to a far greater number in London on several occasions. *I don't need to worry about gaining their favour at any rate*, he told himself. *I will be here for a few months at the most before the missions board come to their senses.*

"Welcome," William said. "I must commend you all on your promptness." He laughed a little, but no-one in the congregation even broke a smile. "Well, then." He opened his prayer book and began the service.

Despite wanting not to care, William found himself looking for approval or judgement in the eyes of the villagers during the service. He sang quietly so as not to offend with his lacklustre voice. He began to grow concerned when as his sermon progressed, more and more people began to look away or just stare into space. *Are they even listening to me?*

He knew not all of the congregation would be devout; church was a custom or habit as much as worship. But he did hope that at least some of the attendees would be impacted by his words.

This was yet another reason prompting his desire to go abroad to preach to new Christians: they would be hungry to hear the Scriptures. As the third person yawned, William spoke more quickly. He rushed through the creed, thanksgivings and the Lord's Prayer. As the parishioners began to stand, he hurried to the back of the church to bid them all goodbye.

First he shook Mr Stockton's hand, glad to recognise the farmer.

"Wonderful service, Mr Brook."

William's relieved smile was genuine. "Thank you, I am glad you enjoyed it."

"You know, Mr Johnson would have done a longer reading and dwelled less on interpretation, but I am sure your way is fine."

William's smile disappeared. "I shall keep that in mind, Mr Stockton."

While some villagers were content to wish him a quiet goodbye, many others felt it necessary to offer similar comments.

"A very... thorough sermon, vicar," Mr Grant said, as his wife and daughter gave him polite smiles.

Mrs Croxley did not mince words. "A little long, Mr Brook."

Mrs Fortescue gave him her hand. "I have never heard the book of Matthew mused upon in quite such a way, vicar," she said.

"Thank you."

The look in Mrs Fortescues eyes flickered, betraying the notion that it was not a compliment.

William frowned, his already bruised spirits crashing through the floor.

Mr Lindsay escorted his wife from the chapel, and Mr Morton finished tidying up the prayer books. He patted William on the back. "Marvellous job," he said. "You have a gift for rhetoric."

William thanked him and shook his hand warmly. At least someone appreciated his efforts. But then he couldn't help but wonder if Mr Morton's compliments were more in a spirit of pity than appreciation.

His mind drifted back to the altercation he'd interrupted the previous evening. At breakfast that morning, he'd asked Emma about the irate man with red hair. She knew at once to whom he referred.

"That would be Mr Russell, son of a local tenant farmer. It's widely known he wanted the living, sir."

"Ah." It was jealousy which had caused the man's malice.

"Don't take it to heart," Emma went on. "He would hate any man in your position... and Mr Russell's a good sort. He's always quick to help out my Pa if ever he needs an extra hand about the place."

Now after the service, the farmer's words echoed in William's mind. *You're not wanted here, vicar.* They haunted him long after everyone had left, when he stood alone in the chapel.

Cecilia was not alone at last. She grinned broadly as she strolled down through the village after Sunday lunch, arm in arm with Amy. While her unfortunate news regarding the governess post had dampened the first moments of their meeting, they were now resolved to make the most of any time spent together.

"Do tell me more about London," she urged her friend. "I must know what all the latest fashionable colours are. I am sure Jones' catalogue is at least a year out of date."

"You do not care to know the cut of the gowns, only the colours?"

"Oh, well if you wish to tell me the hemlines as well I should be only too pleased to…"

Amy's eyes sought her own, and she realised she was being teased.

"You know me too well," she said fondly. "I am not a slave to fashion, but I do wish to know what hues are swaying through the ballroom." She closed her eyes. "I can almost imagine the scene now, with all the dark coats of the gentlemen and the whites and rubies of the ladies… do tell me all about it."

"Very well," Amy said with an affectionate smile, "I shall indulge you. It is my great pleasure to inform you that a sort of cerise seems to be the height of fashion this season, as well as a sort of leafy green."

Cecilia didn't open her eyes, only nodding. "Yes? What else… are there any particular jewels in fashion?"

Amy considered for a moment. "I did see many pearls and rubies… but you know I have only seen the ball thrown by the Barringtons – apart from that it was only what I saw on the street or in the park with the ladies, and at the entertainments I was permitted to attend."

Cecilia squeezed Amy's hand and looked into her friend's eyes keenly, knowing it was her dream to attend grown-up parties. "And were they lovely?" she asked.

Amy smiled and gave a little sigh. "Quite lovely."

"I am glad you have enjoyed yourself. The Barringtons are not too supercilious toward you, then?"

Amy giggled, which confused Cecilia, and she wondered why her friend had turned a shade of pink.

"No, they are quite tolerable. Almost amiable, one might say."

"Catherine does always appear to be very agreeable, on the few occasions I have had the leisure to converse with her."

"Catherine?" Amy seemed to shake herself out of a reverie. "Oh yes indeed, she is quite benevolent. She is very patient and does not behave in a condescending manner." She sighed again. "I am very fortunate indeed."

There was something in Amy's manner which baffled Cecilia, but she could not isolate what it was exactly. It was almost as if she looked more of a woman than a girl for the first time. It was something in the way she carried herself, and a new kind of assurance in her eyes. They were positively sparkling in fact, and this coupled with the blush on her cheeks made Cecilia wonder...

She looked away for a moment, choosing her words with care. "Did you make many new... acquaintances in town?"

Amy shrugged. "Only the London servants. I know of all the young people the ladies spent time with, but I cannot count them among my own acquaintance. Why do you ask?"

Cecilia shrank back under Amy's keen gaze. "Oh, no reason in particular. I only wondered if perhaps you had made any special friends, perhaps among the servants?"

Amy shook her head. "They were polite, but I think they saw us as a hindrance as much as a help. They have their routines and we have ours. But I was not lonely, if that is what you are meaning." She embraced Cecilia in an impulsive hug. "You have always been so kind to me. I do appreciate your concern for my wellbeing. You are the truest and best of friends."

Cecilia breathed an inner sign of relief. Nothing had materially changed. She supposed it was only that the season in London had caused Amy to mature. She hoped nothing would change between them. Except for those months when Amy travelled with the family, surely everything could remain exactly as it always had been.

Chapter Six

The baker's tithe consisted of each day's leftover bread, while the local farmers pledged milk and cheese. William chose to stockpile the spoils for a few days, and then set out towards the edge of the village with a food-laden hamper. He knew where the poorest citizens of Amberley resided, purely by the size and condition of their cottages. As he hurried down the lane, he caught himself whistling and chuckled. It was ridiculous how excited he was over being able to deliver relief to those who may want for basic sustenance.

At the first two houses, he encountered the families of farm workers, each welcoming and hospitable. They accepted his offerings gratefully but he was in turn plied with scones and numerous cups of tea as he listened to their stories. He marvelled at how often those with very little exhibited the most generosity.

When he arrived at the third house, the sound of feminine laughter made him halt at the door, poised to knock. He shrugged to himself and knocked thrice. The laughter immediately stopped and was replaced briefly with voices, and then to his great surprise the door was swung open by – "Miss Grant!" He was momentarily stunned by the sight of her at close range again, caught off guard by her beauty and an indefinable quality of pure radiance.

"Oh Mr Brook, hello." Her voice was soft and strangely comforting. She observed his bundle. "Mrs Kendrick will be pleased to see all that bread and cheese. I brought her some preserves but I fear she has not had the energy for kneading a dough."

She motioned for him to follow her inside. He had to bend down to go through the low doorway, and he remained slightly stooped under the low wooden beams of the main room.

He exchanged greetings with the old woman propped up on the corner of a sofa, recognising her face from the church service. Mrs Kendrick was frail, but with bright eyes shining from her crinkled face. She gestured towards a battered arm chair, and he dropped into it.

Cecilia placed an embroidered bookmark between the pages of a thick volume, putting it on a small shelf on the wall before sitting at the other end of the sofa.

"Miss Grant has been reading me Miss Redham's Revenge," said Mrs Kendrick.

The two women exchanged a smile.

"It is probably rather scandalous," Cecilia said, and turning to William, "I am sure you would disapprove." Even as she spoke a trill of laughter escaped her lips, and her hand flew to her mouth.

The effect of the joyous sound and her glowing countenance made her appear extraordinarily beautiful to him. He swallowed. He hated the notion that godly men were unable to enjoy themselves. The bible was peppered with stories of the apostles at feasts and parties.

"I do not fault reading novels on the whole," he said a little defensively, "as long as they do not break with the biblical moral code."

"Cecilia is a great reader," Mrs Kendrick enthused. "She speaks with a great deal of expression, although sometimes I am sure she varies from the text."

"Oh?" William regarded the young lady again.

A blush crossed her cheeks. "I confess I like to describe things in greater detail than perhaps the author has given us. I want to imagine the feeling of every object within the story."

Mrs Kendrick nodded. "She makes it come alive."

Cecilia rose to her feet. "Well, I must be going," she said.

William stood also. "Do not leave on my account."

"I will leave you to your visit." She kissed Mrs Kendrick and nodded to William on her way out.

William took a breath, regaining complete control over his faculties. He realised the basket of food still rested at his feet. "Now Mrs Kendrick, where can I put these things?"

She pointed at the rear wall. "In the store cupboard behind that door, if you please, dear."

When William had settled on his chair again, she motioned toward the shelf.

"The bible is just there, if you should wish to select a passage to read."

William smiled and shook his head. "Perhaps another day. If you will indulge me, I should like to find out more about you."

Mrs Kendrick's eyebrows rose slightly, but then her mouth was just as quick to curve at the corners. "Certainly, Mr Brook. Where shall I start?"

William's glance passed over the room as he gathered his thoughts, and a picture on the wall opposite caught his attention. "Who is that fellow?"

Mrs Kendrick looked up at the portrait of a little dog, a white terrier. It was an uncommonly fine painting. It was as if the animal was about to leap off the parchment, and there was an immense warmth in the creature's eyes. "That is – was – my little Tommy. He passed on during the winter. He was such a comfort when my dear Daniel died ten years ago. I haven't had the heart to seek another animal... and I doubt I would be able to care for one, in any case."

William reached out and took Mrs Kendrick's hand, looking squarely in her pooling eyes. "I am sorry," he said, and he didn't need to explain any further.

After a long shared moment, Mrs Kendrick gazed back up at the painting. "Miss Grant did a wonderful job of Tommy's likeness, don't you think? It almost feels like he's still here with me."

At the sound of the lady's name, William's head whipped back towards the picture, and he surveyed it with even more appreciation. The artist had crafted the animal in fine detail, and with great sensitivity. "Yes indeed," he murmured. Surely a lightweight could not be capable of producing such a work?

"She is a treasure," Mrs Kendrick went on. "She has her fancies, to be sure, but you won't find a more gentle soul anywhere. Amberley will be the poorer if she leaves to marry."

"I am glad you are not devoid of company," William said. He found himself gazing at the shelf, but not at the bible. He was tempted to ask Mrs Kendrick if he could borrow the volume Cecilia had marked, under the pretext of making sure it was suitable for a fine Christian woman.

He wanted to see what had made her laugh.

❧⚜

Cecilia swung her basket to a secret rhythm as she strolled back home from Mrs Kendrick's, alone with her musings. Why had she felt compelled to leave the widow's house when Mr Brook arrived? She had felt so self-conscious around him, in a way she never had with Mr Johnson. It was probably because she wanted him to believe her mortal soul was in good order. Miss Redham's romantic intrigues were likely far beyond anything of his imagination.

And yet, there was a feeling other than wanting to create a good impression. She'd been very aware of his presence and when he looked at her. The intensity of his gaze was unsettling – she remembered that from their first meeting – but there had been something different in his eyes this time.

She shrugged and turned down the lane to her house. It was likely nothing to do with the vicar at all, just an odd fancy of her own creation.

❧⚜

As the full moon neared, William's social calendar grew crowded. He'd accepted every dinner invitation, and at the end of them all loomed the Barringtons' ball. With the date set and invitations delivered, a general air of excitement pervaded the village. His second church service had passed without too many pointed comments, and he was glad to recognise many of the names and faces staring back at him.

He'd begun to establish a routine of sorts in his visits to all of the villagers. So far he'd managed to avoid the conundrum of being matched with any particular lady, but not without effort. During a visit with the Stocktons, for example, he felt as if he'd walked into a snare.

The farmer's wife greeted him in their parlour with almost maniacal glee, before Mr Stockton pointed out three clones of the lady.

"And these are my daughters, Mary, Anne and Jane."

"All are out," Mrs Stockton said meaningfully, directing a knowing stare at him that chilled him to the bone.

"Indeed, Mrs Stockton," William said, choosing a chair as far from the girls as he could. "I am sure they will all make some men very happy indeed." *But not me, please not me.* Oh, they looked like very nice girls, probably very capable and hard-working, but he did not mean to give even the slightest hint that he was in the marriage mart.

The last major hurdle before the ball was dinner with the Grant family. He did not suspect Miss Grant of having set her cap at him, as she'd made no attempt to flirt with him during their last meeting. And yet an odd sort of anticipation jumped in his stomach as he greeted the family. He met the mother, who seemed all formal politeness. He was then introduced to the eldest son, Gerald Brook, recently returned from town.

There was a noticeable absence from the drawing room. He could not help but ask, "And where is Miss Grant? Is she ill?"

"No..." Mr Grant said, looking to his wife.

She ran a hand back and forth along the arm of her chair uneasily. "She is not here, at present."

"Oh?"

"She is, er, very fond of exercise. I am sure she will arrive at any moment, and then we shall go in to dinner."

"I see."

Gerald Grant engaged him in conversation. He was a congenial chap and William took an instant liking to him. He was the first man in Amberley he felt a kinship with, although Gerald was shortly to head to a friend's estate in the north for the grouse hunting season.

After half an hour of idle chatter, William's stomach growled loudly. There was no hiding the extending whine of hunger, reminiscent of a dog moaning. As three sets of eyes turned to him, he bit his lip and stared at the clock on the wall. The sound of Gerald's muffled laughter reverberated around the white-panelled walls.

Mrs Grant suddenly bolted up off her seat. "Gentlemen, I think it is high time we went through for dinner." She rang the bell. "Cecilia will have to go without."

As they moved through to the dining room, she came alongside

William. "I do apologise for my daughter, Mr Brook. She has no sense of time. I quite despair as to what to do with her."

The irony of the situation was not lost on William. Ever since he'd arrived in Amberley Miss Grant had been popping up all over the place, and now that he was supposed to be meeting with her formally she was nowhere to be found. He was almost – *almost* – disappointed at her absence. He wanted to form his own opinion of her. He did not want to admit to himself how strong his curiosity had become.

He smiled at Mrs Grant. "I am sure all young people go through a phase of selfishness," he said.

She sniffed. "Oh that it were a phase," she said. "You do not know our Cecilia."

He didn't have a chance to respond to this interesting comment, as he was assigned his place at the table between the two Mr Grants, across from the empty chair.

Just as Mrs Grant gave the signal for the first course to be served, there was the sound of a door slamming and pounding footsteps. The dining room door burst open, and a slight blond sprite bounded in. Her hair was dishevelled, though she pushed her hands into it in a vain attempt to right it, which only made it worse. Her cheeks were flushed and her eyes a mix of embarrassment and zeal. She approached the empty place setting.

"Good *evening*, daughter," Mrs Grant said pointedly. "Take yourself away this minute and tidy up for dinner. Your appearance is quite shocking. Poor Mr Brook must think you a gypsy."

Cecilia noticed him properly. "Oh, I am sorry, sir, I completely forgot you were coming."

Mrs Grant emitted a kind of groan.

Cecilia cringed and whispered, "Sorry!" before dashing from the room.

William exchanged an amused glance with Gerald, clearing his throat to avoid letting laughter come to the surface.

A fairly normal dinner ensued, as William answered the typical questions about his background and his impressions of Amberley so far. Cecilia re-entered the room with more grace the second time, perhaps hoping that no-one would notice her tiptoeing to her chair. She'd changed into a lovely pale-blue dress trimmed in gold. It set off the shining curls on her head, which were restrained by a white ribbon. William did not realise he was gaping at her until her clear blue eyes came to rest upon him, and he looked away just as she sent him a shy smile.

"Tell me, Mr Brook," Mr Grant addressed him, "what is your opinion of these Methodists? Should they be separate from the Church of England?"

William's brain leapt into action. This was one of his favourite subjects. He had indeed embraced many of the Methodist ideals, such as concentrating on biblical study and ministering to the poor and the sick. His dedication to the cause was on shakier ground when it came to the dramatic style of preaching based on hellfire and damnation, and the expectation that one may attempt to lead a perfect life. He knew only too well that he could never be perfect, and he could never expect anyone else to be.

"Ah, Mr Grant," he said, "that is a most interesting question."

❧

Cecilia wished it was an interesting answer. As Mr Brook launched into what seemed like hours of dissertation, she retreated to her imagination.

She resolutely kept her focus on the vicar, but after some minutes the sound of his voice lost all meaning, and she found herself transfixed by the different shapes his mouth made as he spoke. She noticed the fullness of his lips as they repeatedly came together, then her gaze drifted to the other shapes on his face. His features were almost symmetrical, and she studied the shadow his straight nose cast across his cheek. His eyes were large and dark, and his brow line was punctured by a crease when he became particularly serious. Unruly curls occupied the lion-share of his forehead. It was a face unlike any other she'd seen, although as she mentally put all of the shapes together into a whole, she could not quite settle on why. She must ask him to sit for a silhouette drawing when she knew him better.

He gestured wildly with his hands, which she noticed were not the frail, effeminate hands she usually associated with clergymen. Instead their strength evoked a certain kind of power and grace, and though she had lost interest in the meaning of his words, his tone implied a deep conviction.

At length she could not even find interest in him as an artistic subject. He continued to expound, and her attention shifted to the fruit course laid out on the table.

☙❧

William feigned interest as Mrs Grant described the family's visit to London the previous year.

"We were quite delighted with the attendance of Cecilia's debutante ball, Mr Brook. A simply charming array of people."

William nodded politely. "How wonderful for Miss Grant. I take it you enjoyed your first grand social occasion?"

He turned to Cecilia, to find her completely absorbed in another realm. She reached for a grape and popped it into her mouth, and then she closed her eyes as she chewed on it, seemingly in ecstasy.

The sensuous look on her face held William captive, and when he remembered where he was he said, "Miss Grant, Miss Grant? Are you quite all right?"

"Cecilia!" Her mother snapped, forcing her to become sensible of her company.

Her eyes flashed open, and she gulped down the remains of her mouthful. "Oh sorry, Mama?"

"Mr Brook is attempting to converse with you. Do pay attention."

"My apologies, Mr Brook," she said with a disarming smile. "Do go on."

William shook his head a little, to make sensible thoughts re-enter his mind. "I only meant to enquire as to how you found your first ball in London."

"Oh!" Her smile faded and her eyes grew larger. "It was quite overwhelming, sir. I do not know if I remembered a single name. There were so many important people there, I was quite without the power of rational speech."

"Yes," Mrs Grant murmured, "Cecilia did seem to abandon any kind of rational behaviour in company of the *ton*."

Mr Grant cleared his throat. "I think we may pass the port now, what do you say gentlemen?"

His wife took her cue, escorting Cecilia from the room. Immediately the two Mr Grants seemed to relax, slouching in their chairs and helping themselves to liquor.

As he passed the bottle to William, Gerald said, "You will have to excuse my sister, Mr Brook. She does tend to get lost in her own world sometimes."

"Yes," William said as he filled his glass. "I noticed that."

"Poor dear, you can understand why she has a general reputation for eccentricity... even inanity."

"That's enough, Gerald," his father interjected.

William couldn't help exchanging a conspiratorial smile with Gerald, but he was moved towards something like pity for his sister. He could see the formidable task Mrs Grant had in trying to marry her off. She was beautiful, there was no denying it, but not any sort of company for a man who occasionally wanted to discuss more than the weather or the dinner menu. And with what was no doubt a modest dowry, being settled as a gentleman farmer's wife was probably the best thing for her. And he hoped to be long gone before he had the chance to officiate at the marriage ceremony.

"I am sure she has a good heart," he said, thinking of her visit to Mrs Kendrick.

"That she does," Mr Grant said. "She only wants a little understanding."

"And I am sure you will find her a patient man." Patience was not one of William's strong points. He decided it was time for a change of subject. "Had any good sport lately?" he asked.

Some quarter of an hour later, Mr Grant pronounced they had better join the ladies.

❧

Mrs Grant wasted no time in addressing her daughter as soon as they were seated in the drawing room. "Cecilia, you must promise me you will not be late to any more social engagements. I know this was only Mr Brook, but I cannot bear the thought of you disrespecting the Barringtons in this way."

Cecilia felt as if she spent her life apologising. There was no point in explaining the reason for her lateness (which was due to following a deer and her fawn deep into the forest). "If the Barringtons are due for a visit, I will keep to the house," she said.

Mrs Grant nodded, and after several minutes of silence her irritation seemed to extinguish. "What do you think of our new vicar?" she asked, idly toying with her brooch.

Cecilia decided not to tell her mother about her musings on Mr Brook's visage, considering instead his ponderous lecture at the dinner table. "He certainly is very... religious, is he not?"

Mrs Grant laughed. "I suppose one does rather expect that from a cleric, my dear."

"Yes but, I don't seem to remember Mr Johnson blathering on for quite so long."

"Hush dear, hold your tongue," Mrs Grant whispered. "Here come the gentlemen." She smiled broadly as the men filed in and seated themselves. "Would everyone like tea? My dear, perhaps you would like to pour?"

"Of course, Mama," Cecilia said, a little too brightly. This was her penance for missing tea with the Wallaces. She only hoped she would not spill anything on their guest. She inquired as to his preferences and made him a cup. Approaching him, she delivered it on a saucer with slightly shaking hands.

"Thank you," he said, his smile reassuring as if he had sensed her discomfort. "Do you know," he said quietly as he took up his spoon, "I have two elder brothers as well."

Cecilia found herself sitting on the sofa next to him before she knew what she was doing. "Oh, do you really? You must have had grand times with them growing up, being three boys." She hoped she hadn't betrayed any envy.

"That's a logical assumption," he said. His spoon jingled in his cup, and then he withdrew it and laid it back on the saucer. "However, they were much older than me, and spared me very little attention."

"It was the same with me!" Cecilia cried, much gratified to find someone who might understand her juvenile experiences. "That is, they are not so very much older, but I had to amuse myself most of the time. I was lucky to have a friend in Amy. We met in the churchyard as small girls, and were inseparable from then on. Who did you have to keep you company?"

The crease appeared between William's brows as he swallowed a mouthful then set his cup down with a clink. "No one," he said darkly, not meeting her eyes.

"Cecilia! We are waiting."

Only her mother's scold reminded Cecilia there were others in the room, and they needed tea, too. She jumped up and resumed her duties.

❧

William wasn't sure why he'd suddenly divulged personal information to the young lady. There were something unsettlingly appealing about her, which made her captivating and yet accessible at the same instant. It was time for him to leave before he revealed anything further. He politely indicated his intent.

"I insist you take our carriage, Mr Brook," said Mrs Grant.

"It is really not necessary," he said, wanting to hasten his exit. "The distance is a mile at most."

"But the roads are dark now, and we cannot have you getting lost or sick. We need you in good health for Sunday sermons, christenings and – marriages." At this she shot a significant glance at her daughter.

William's stomach hit the floor. He had thought this household was not setting that particular trap. Surely her brother would have recommended her to him if they were trying to marry her off to him.

He chanced a glance at the girl, expecting to see her batting her eyelashes at him coquettishly because of her mother's hint, or perhaps fanning herself.

Instead Cecilia looked positively gloomy, her head bowed and her eyes darting in every direction she could to avoid eye contact. If that was her idea of flirting, she was stranger than he had thought.

He was glad to be free of the place, conceding to their offer of the carriage. They were an odd bunch indeed and he was glad of the fact that it was only Mr Grant he would see frequently in the future.

Chapter Seven

As William prepared his next sermon in his library in the quiet of late evening, he stopped for a moment to take a sip of tea. Without warning, the image of Miss Grant's face from the dinner several nights before filled his mind.

He recalled the specific moment when she'd seemed enraptured by the simple pleasure of a grape bursting in her mouth. It was as if she'd been in another time or place, and even with her eyes closed her expression had been undeniably sensual. Something about the arch of her eyebrows, the curve of her cheek, the way her eyelids had fluttered and the undulations of her jaw had been slightly hypnotic.

He swallowed. At least, she seemed to be hypnotised. He pondered what could have caused such depth of feeling at the dinner table. Mrs Grant's food, while perfectly acceptable, was not such as to send one into congratulatory hysterics. Perhaps she was imagining her favourite place, a new dress... or a lover. He blinked. It was possible, though apparently no one suspected it. Was she nursing a secret *tendre*?

As far as he knew, no woman had ever been moved to regard him with such a spellbound expression, and briefly he wondered what it would feel like to be the sort of man who could entrance a woman so. But then he shook his head and sighed, impatient with himself. That would never happen, and besides, he didn't have time for such nonsense.

It was folly to sit there thinking such idle thoughts. He threw down his pen and reached for his jacket. He found his purse and checked for the presence of a few coins. Creeping carefully down the stairs so as not to disturb Emma, he took his hat from the coat stand by the door and went out into the night.

Still feeling irked by the confrontation with Mr Russell and his opponent during his first nocturnal outing, he headed straight for the public house. They'd see he couldn't be scared off. He'd *make* himself welcome if it was the last thing he did.

William stalked into the pub. As the doors closed behind him, he watched while every set of eyes turned towards him, and a hush settled over the bar. A man to his right paused with a tankard raised to his lips, and elsewhere around the room small groups assumed a similar rigidity.

William assumed a deliberately casual gait as he made his way over to the bar.

"Mr Granville, isn't it?" He extended his hand to the man behind the large mahogany surface, who was drying a glass with an ancient-looking tea towel.

The man did not take William's hand, instead merely pausing in his activity. He fixed the vicar with a hard stare. "This ain't a gentleman's club, sir," he said.

"Indeed," William said smoothly. "Amberley village is without such an establishment, I presume?"

"Aye. Any sensible gentleman stays at home or in other 'genteel' houses after dark."

"Perhaps I am insensible then. I will have a pint of your local ale, if you please."

A large man nursing a tankard further down the bar spoke up. "And now we'll all have to watch our P's and Q's, is that right, vicar? Would you deprive us of the only place we can relax?"

William smiled and shook his head, laying money down on the bar. "I would like to relax too, and I would not dream of stopping you from doing so." In the silence of the room, this conversation was well heard by all. The tension was palpable. William turned to address the patrons. "I come not to judge your words or actions, or to spy upon you. I assure you it would take a lot to shock me. I am part of your society, and as such I would like to partake in village life. Surely this establishment is at the core of village life."

"Get him a drink, Granville."

William whirled around to find the owner of the voice: Mr Stockton's son.

"It's over to him whether he chooses to be offended by our ways."

William nodded his thanks to Stockton, then turned back to lean on the bar, tapping his coins.

Granville said nothing, but slowly moved to put the glass and tea towel down before collecting William's money. He poured the ale wordlessly, all the time maintaining eye contact with William, and laid it before him with a lift of his eyebrows.

"Thank you, Granville," William said lightly, and then he took his ale to the nearest table. "Is this seat taken?" he asked, indicating the chair next the two Mr Russells and one of their farm workers.

Henry Russell, who William now knew envied his benefice, scowled and looked to his father.

William did the same, until the man shrugged helplessly.

"It's not taken," the older man mumbled, and William slid in. A hum of conversation began to fill the air of the pub around them.

The farm worker grinned at William. "I ain't never seen a holy man with a drink in his hand before."

Henry Russell agreed. "One of Mr Johnson's favourite subjects to preach on was the evils of alcohol. He'd no sooner set foot in here than dance a jig." William noticed the man was not speaking directly to him, but rather addressing the other two men. He had not actually spoken to William since the night of the fight.

William tried to read Henry's expression, but it was inscrutable. This conversation was at least an improvement on the stony silence he'd encountered with the young man at his family home. Of all the people in Amberley, William most wanted to build bridges with Henry, because a man who desired to work for the church should be an ally, not an enemy.

"The consumption of alcohol is not a sin in itself, of course," William said. "Christ did turn water into wine, after all. It is only when used excessively that spirits can lead men into sin. I look to set an example of moderation in all things."

"Well," Mr Russell said, raising his glass, "here's to your health, young vicar."

The farm worker immediately knocked their glasses together, but Russell had to eyeball his son to make him do the same.

"Don't go thinking you're one of us just because we're letting you drink with us, Mr Brook," Henry said. "You have to be here twenty years or more before they'll consider you a local."

Well then, a local I'll never be. But he liked the challenge in Henry Russell's countenance. "And if you marry into the village?" he countered.

"Then ten years ought to do it."

The men laughed together, though Henry's eyes remained narrowed.

❧

Mrs Grant hovered about Cecilia as Lucy pinned her hair, and then weaved a string of jewels around the curls.

"That's right; ensure you can see them from all angles... over here as well, Lucy."

"Mama," Cecilia said as she tried to remain as a statue, "please stop fussing. You are making me nervous."

"Nonsense, my dear, this is an important occasion. It is your chance to remind Mr Barrington of your beauty and... availability."

"I shall do my best, Mama, but I do not know what I shall say to him. How will I even get his attention?"

"Have no fear of that, my love. This is not London. Next to the Barrington girls, you will be the most resplendent lady at the ball."

"I only wonder why he did not choose someone in London."

"As the younger son, perhaps it is more that he was not chosen."

Lucy finished Cecilia's hair, and dropped a necklace over her head.

Mrs Grant assisted her daughter to her feet. "There, now. If you only carry yourself with confidence, you'll not want for admiration."

Her mother's predictions proved true. When she entered Ashworth Hall, Lady Ashworth remarked, "Don't you look lovely, my dear. A vision."

Lord Marsham smiled at her. "Good evening, Miss Grant," he said politely.

Mr Barrington took up his mother's cue however, taking Cecilia's gloved hand as she curtsied and pressing it to his lips. "A vision from heaven," he echoed, noting her blush with satisfaction. "May I claim you for the minuet?"

Cecilia recovered from his compliment sufficiently to look into his eyes. They were dark, yet glinting, carrying some sort of message she could not understand. His posture spoke of assurance and ease, and the sharp contours of his face matched the angles of his shoulders. "Of course, sir," she managed to say, curtseying again.

"I told you," her mother whispered in her ear. "Make the most of it."

They exchanged greetings with the Barrington girls. Catherine gave Cecilia a warm smile, but Louisa's welcome was delivered with a high chin and slanted eyes.

The family entered the grand hall and met their acquaintances. Mrs Grant immediately gravitated to Mrs Croxley and Miss Hicks, who were already deep in discussion with a bevy of matrons.

The Barringtons entered the room once all the guests had arrived. Cecilia felt the eyes of Mr Barrington on her, and when she dared to peek at him, he tipped his glass at her. Her insides fluttered, but she wasn't sure whether it was from nerves or excitement. She looked toward her mother, who was conversing with Mrs Croxley with a satisfied sparkle in her eye.

"Good evening, Miss Grant." The younger Mr Stockton stood before her, holding two glasses. "I brought you some elderflower cordial."

"Thank you, Mr Stockton. Are you well?" She was torn between her affection for her childhood friend, and not wanting to lead him on.

"Quite well, thank you. We are looking forward to a large harvest."

Cecilia smiled and nodded through a stilted conversation, feeling a familiar awkwardness which had only been magnified on the grand stage of London society.

The orchestra began to tune, and Mr Barrington was instantaneously at her side, presenting his arm. "Shall we, Miss Grant?"

"Certainly." She weaved her hand into the crook of his elbow, and her breath quickened as he pulled her arm closer.

He brought her into the line of dancers and deposited her opposite him. She smiled at Miss Jones, the merchant's young daughter, who was dancing with Mr Brook.

The dance began with several bars of silence on both sides, and Cecilia felt her cheeks burning as she stared straight ahead in embarrassed confusion. It was like her London season all over again. Would she ever think of anything to say? Out of the corner of her eye she could see Barrington looking at her, and her cheeks turned redder still.

When they began to dance together, she finally met his eyes to find him already smiling at her. It was enough to make her look away again.

"Are you quite well, Miss Grant?" he enquired gently.

"Oh! Yes, perfectly well, I assure you. It is only some months since I had… the pleasure of dancing in mixed company."

He chuckled. "And here am I, practically worn out with dancing in Town."

She made herself look at him again and returned his smile, slightly more at ease. "I hope it is not too much of an imposition," she said.

"On the contrary, I would have enjoyed the season much better if such a beauty as you had been present."

Cecilia giggled. "Really, Mr Barrington. I am sure I do not deserve such praise. I felt quite insignificant when I was in London."

"Then you were not in the correct company."

His compliments finally penetrated her reserve, and her confidence began to return. They were parted in the dance for a few moments, and when reunited Cecilia's thoughts sputtered out of her mouth before she had time to consider them. "I wonder that we did not meet in Town last year."

Barrington's eyes darted to the side. The smile dropped from his mouth. "Uh, yes, that is most…" He took her hand and moved through the next sequence. "I have been bound to seek other…"

Cecilia nodded to let him know she comprehended his meaning, an embarrassed glow spreading over her neck and chest. He had been seeking ladies of far greater fortune than her. At once she felt absolutely worthless, and she wished the floor would swallow her up. If they were in London, he would not spare her a passing thought. It was only now that he was starved for society that she became desirable company. When she turned away from him, she sighed deeply. Here she had been thinking her attempt at flirting was going so well, but he was merely bored, toying with her.

They danced in silence for some moments, and Cecilia caught her mother's eye. Mrs Grant was frowning, and she raised her eyebrows in a motion for Cecilia to keep trying.

It was Barrington who spoke first. "Miss Grant, I hope I did not offend. I only meant to say I wish we had met in London. Your company is very refreshing compared to the world-worn ladies with whom I have endured society these past months."

Cecilia was still confused, but she murmured, "Thank you, sir." She was very glad when the dance came to an end. The effort of trying to flirt with him was too much for her. She curtsied, and when he rose up from his bow he sent her a smile, and she could have sworn he winked. Whatever did that mean?

She stepped off to the side and was immediately approached by her mother. "Well?" Mrs Grant took her by the arm. "Have you made some progress?"

Cecilia shrugged. "I am sure I do not know. He kept comparing me to the ladies in London."

Mrs Grant considered this. "Was it a favourable comparison?"

"He said it was... but he implied I would normally be beneath his notice."

"Well, we must own that is true. But it was plain to see he was charmed by your presence. We must have him desire your company above all others before he returns to London."

A bolt of dread hit Cecilia's stomach. This was going to be hard work. She could not even force her mind to make the leap to matrimony. "Yes, Mama," she said.

☙❧

William detached himself from Miss Jones with some difficulty. He had not had a moment's peace throughout the entire dance, as she prattled on about the novels she was reading and the latest feathers for bonnets. He had only enough time to pick up a glass of claret, before he was approached by Mr Stockton and his daughter Anne. Mr Stockton talked about the weather and the state of his pastures, but as his eyes kept drifting to the couples moving through the quadrille in front of them, it was clear his intent was to have his daughter dance.

William waited until there was no chance of joining the current dance, politely fielding questions about the parsonage's glebe and his experience (or lack thereof) with livestock. Then, almost as a way of silencing the man, he suddenly said, "Mr Stockton, I wonder if Miss Anne intends to dance?"

Mr Stockton made a great show of gratification. "Why Mr Brook, I'm sure she does, don't you daughter?"

Anne blushed obligingly. "If Mr Brook will be my partner, I'd be delighted."

William nodded at her, but did not smile, hoping his politeness would not be misinterpreted for more than it was. Once the dance began, he wasn't sure whether this was more unbearable than the previous one. Instead of chattering, Miss Anne only stared at him adoringly, except when she stood on his toes, and began to apologise profusely. He tried to keep his eyes on the wall. This was torture. He renewed his gumption to beg Dean Roberts for a new assignment. He was not ready to be tied down to marriage, particularly to one of these simple country girls. Not that any of the city girls would likely be interested in him, if it came to that.

His eyes slid over the other dancers in the quadrille, and came to rest briefly on Miss Grant, who was partnered with Mr Morton of the counting house, and seemed a darned sight more relaxed than when Mr Barrington had taken her out on the floor. It was quite obvious the mother hoped to make a match there. Still, he was not entirely safe, on his guard since those strange hints at dinner, and recalling her errand with the cake. If Barrington turned into a dead end, he may well be in the firing line.

When her bright blue eyes found his, the bolt of energy which struck him made him look away with a start. His gaze settled on Miss Stockton by accident, and she smiled and blushed. At once he found a window frame to concentrate on and kept his sight there until they turned. Maddening.

Once his dance with Miss Anne was over, he deposited her with her family and made a hasty retreat to the table of refreshments. His respite was however short-lived, as Mrs Lindsay approached with a visiting female cousin. There was an unmistakable eagerness in her eyes, and William began to panic, unsure he could maintain his composure through two more dances. This was why he'd avoided society in London.

With the Lindsay women only a few feet away, William swiftly turned back to the table, only to come face to face with Miss Grant. He breathed a sigh of relief. Surely she was the lesser of two evils. "Miss Grant, would you do me the honour?" he asked quickly, extending his hand.

Chapter Eight

Cecilia hesitated, but then her face relaxed into a smile. "I would be delighted, Mr Brook."

William felt a ridiculous surge of pleasure when she placed her hand in his, and he tried to keep a straight face despite his satisfaction at having kept the more obvious ladies at bay. She curtsied elegantly, and he caught himself admiring her slim form as they began to move through the figures. The dearth of civilised company must be playing tricks on his mind. At least Miss Grant didn't attempt to engage him in puerile conversation such as he'd had to endure thus far. He cringed a little when, as their second dance began, she took a breath to speak, but the topic she raised hit straight to his core.

"I collect you are missing London, Mr Brook?"

He lost his composure for a moment, but regained it in time to keep up with the dance. This was not the undemanding conversation starter he might have expected. He met her eyes and saw only concern, rather than coquetry. "Yes Miss Grant, I'm afraid I am," he confessed. "What betrayed me?"

"Nothing, really. It only seems as though you are still adjusting to small village life."

She was right, of course, but he did not want to admit that she'd been perceptive, or to the fact that he would struggle to adapt to their simple society. When she was within earshot again he said, "I do hope I am not putting too much of a damper on proceedings."

She laughed, another surprise. "I would say to the contrary, Mr Brook, you seem to have inspired general appreciation and high spirits."

Could she be alluding to the range of females targeting his attention? Was she bold enough to address such a topic? A glance at her twinkling eyes told him she was. He couldn't help but feel lighter inside, and grinned at her.

When they were next in the range of conversation, she asked, "What do you miss most about London?"

He felt a pang. "Where do I start?" A tumble of images streamed through his mind... people, places, experiences. The hope for the future that he seemed to have left behind. After several moments he remembered his company, and looked back into her curious eyes. "The variety of society must be keenly felt," he began, hoping not to offend her. "Apart from my general acquaintance, the members of the congregation, and other clergy, I had a particular friend whom I am missing dreadfully. Thomas."

She nodded. "Perhaps Thomas could come and visit."

He shook his head sadly. "I am afraid not. He is on a ship this moment, bound for India."

Her eyes clouded. "Oh. Is that a dangerous journey?"

He gave a little shrug. "No more than most. The destination must make it worthwhile." The dance ended, and after thanking each other they continued to talk off to the side. "Thomas will be ministering to peoples who have not yet heard God's word," William told Cecilia, unable to hide the earnestness in his features. "He will be building churches and schools, and feeding the desperately hungry."

She nodded, warmth and understanding in her eyes. "One could be forgiven for thinking you would rather be in his place."

His eyes flashed to her serene countenance. How was it possible that this girl, who he'd practically written off as an eccentric oddity, had pinpointed his deepest issues within a few minutes of conversation? "You are very perceptive, Miss Grant," he said. "But I would not rather be in his place – I yearn to be beside him through the journey. We were a good team."

She nodded. "And Amberley is somewhat removed from the life of a missionary."

He looked away for a moment. "Yes."

Supper was announced, and William offered his arm to take Cecilia through to the dining hall. As they approached the long tables, William spotted Mrs Grant. She had saved a seat next to her, with Mr Barrington on the other side.

Cecilia paused as she also noticed the arrangement. "Look, there are two seats available over there," she said, pointing to a far table. "That is, if you can withstand my company."

William laughed and started in that direction, noticing Mrs Grant gesturing wildly towards them out of the corner of his eye. "It would be my pleasure."

Once they were seated and had filled their plates with salmon, vegetables and biscuits, Cecilia returned to their former topic. "I have been to London twice," she told him. "Once when I was a girl, and again last year for my debutante season."

He chewed and swallowed a mouthful. "I see. And how did you like it?"

She hesitated. "I did enjoy London itself, once I became used to the noise and bustle, but trying to hook a husband was a perplexing activity."

William smiled. She certainly did not shy away from the heart of matters. How refreshing. He wasn't sure if he should prompt her to go on. This was precisely the sort of conversation Dean Roberts would have preferred an unmarried vicar to steer well clear of. "Oh yes?" he said.

"I am a hopeless flirt," she said with a self-effacing smile. "That is – I am hopeless at it. I always just say what I think, or if I am nervous I don't say much at all. My mother despairs that I have not taken to the female arts."

William smiled again. "Does she now?"

"Indeed. She is determined to have me married well, but I fear I am not ladylike enough to impress the right gentlemen."

William was thinking she was the closest he'd come to a lady in the whole time since he'd been in Amberley. Even the Barrington girls, though they had assumed airs and elegant postures, did not have the natural grace of this creature. "Miss Grant," he said, "I am a gentleman, and yet you do not seem nervous."

"Oh, but you are a vicar!" she exclaimed. "You are not an ordinary gentleman."

William wasn't quite sure what to make of that. He was half perturbed by her assumption that he was somehow less male because of his calling, and apparently not in danger of seducing her, but he was grateful that it meant her trust was earned instantly. A wave of relaxation poured over him. He could be himself without worrying about her trying to make him into a husband. He weighed his words, considering the demands and expectations she carried. "Do not try to mould yourself to fit what aristocracy demands," he said quietly. "You cannot pretend forever, and a marriage based on false ideals is bound to be miserable."

Cecilia met his eyes, and her lips curved into a smile. "I can see why you are a vicar," she said. "You seem to have wisdom beyond your years."

William was surprised to feel a blush creeping into his cheeks and he looked away. "I thank you, but I think I have merely sharp observational skills." He hurriedly popped a biscuit into his mouth, and regrouped as he chewed and swallowed. "So you have been to London," he said eventually, "and I have been told you are an artist. One would assume you have visited the great art galleries?"

"Mmm!" Cecilia struggled to swallow her mouthful as she nodded and gestured wildly, her eyes sparkling. "Even in short visits, I learned so much from observing the old masters. I have never seen painting on such a scale, with every inch so meticulously rendered."

William was caught up in her enthusiasm. "I too find the masters inspiring. The insight into the human condition is remarkable. One finds depictions of people from all walks of life, as well as moving religious art."

"I was particularly excited by work I saw by a newer artist, Turner. His depictions of landscapes are unlike anything I have ever seen before."

He nodded. "Yes, I have seen his works too. In fact, I purchased a book about him. And I have many other books on painting, as well as sculpture and architecture."

"Do you really?" she breathed. "I have studied art as much as I could, but my governess only had a few books, and they were very old."

"Well, I would be happy to lend you any of my books whenever you wish."

"I would be indebted to you, to be sure," she said, and she smiled with such simple gratification that he was rendered speechless.

Tearing his eyes away, he said, "I was able to study art history at Cambridge, where I obtained many of my books, and though I did try my hand at the fine arts I regret I lack any kind of natural talent."

"Perhaps you could sit in on one of the classes I teach for the local children," she said, and then giggled.

He laughed too. "I would consider it, only your young charges will surely out-do me."

After supper, William was sure to circulate around the room. He was sensible of the many pairs of eyes on himself and Miss Grant during dinner, and he had no desire to provoke gossip. As he moved from a group of widows, to the publican, to the Barrington girls, he felt a lightness within his spirit. He did not dwell upon it, but he could not deny his opinion of Miss Grant was much altered, and his curiosity about her only intensified.

As he stood chatting with Lady Catherine Barrington, his eye was distracted by some movement. In the hallway, he caught a glimpse of Mr Barrington and Amy, the lady's maid, deep in conversation. While he assumed they were discussing something to do with the household management, the next time he looked at them, Barrington whispered something in Amy's ear. She giggled and batted playfully at his chest. William's eyes narrowed as he saw Barrington take the girl's hand for a moment before she pulled away and disappeared. Perhaps he would need to have a word with the gentleman regarding the appropriate treatment of servants.

❧

Mrs Grant entered Cecilia's bedchamber as Lucy took down her hair. "Well?"

"That was a pleasant evening," said Cecilia, "but my, how exhausting! I am well and truly ready for sleep." She regarded herself in the mirror while assisting Lucy in removing the string of jewels from her hair.

Her mother moved in front of the mirror, startling her.

"How did it end with Mr *Barrington*?" she asked, the words bursting forth in an unladylike rush.

Cecilia frowned, thinking back to their second dance of the evening after supper. "Well enough, I think, but I know nothing more about him now than I did this afternoon."

"But do you think he liked you? Did he flatter you?"

"I think so... his words were pretty, but I hardly understood his meaning."

Mrs Grant pursed her lips. "I hope you did not let on. We cannot have him thinking you are an imbecile."

Cecilia blinked to stop a sudden rush of tears. Even Lucy stopped moving for a moment. "Do you think that is what I am, Mama?" she asked, her voice wobbling as her chin quavered.

"It is not what I think that matters," snapped Mrs Grant.

It is what matters to me. Cecilia didn't reply.

"Come now, dear," Mrs Grant said, taking up her daughter's hand. "You are just tired. It will not do to start crying and end up with red eyes tomorrow. Your aunt is due for dinner, you know."

"My aunt?"

"Yes, Cecilia. Did I not mention it?"

She shook her head.

"I thought I did. Perhaps with the excitement of the ball I neglected to tell you. She will be with us for a fortnight while the Viscount concludes some business in London."

Cecilia smiled. "It will be nice to have her company," she said.

"Yes." Mrs Grant removed herself from her daughter's dressing table. "I say," she said, "it was rude of Mr Brook to monopolise you like that at supper."

Cecilia laughed. "Hardly, Mama. We merely happened to go in together after the dance. It could have been any other gentleman."

"Well, I wish it would have been."

Cecilia remembered her time with Mr Brook as the only interesting or comfortable moments of the evening. *I am glad it was not any other gentleman.*

⧉⧉

William was lost in his thoughts as he made his way to Ashworth Hall two days after the ball. The previous day had been Sunday, so he'd been fully absorbed in his duties for most of the day, and then on his best behaviour while hosting the Fortescues for dinner. This walk was the first opportunity he'd had when he could no longer avoid thinking about a rather dangerous subject: his rather reformed views on Miss Grant.

Cecilia was not dim-witted. On the contrary, she'd been surprisingly insightful, apparently able to sense his feelings as no-one else had. She was the only one who had dared suggest that he might have met the Amberley appointment with anything less than unbridled joy. If anyone else suspected it, they had kept it to themselves. In a society ruled by manners, her gentle frankness was refreshing, illuminating, rare.

Once engaged, her faculties seemed to be sharp, and she had a lively sense of humour. The way she had come alive when discussing her passions, and her obvious knowledge for the subject, had impressed him more than almost any young lady he'd known. And yet she was very humble. He suspected she was not obsessed with the superficial fripperies and rumour-mongering which seemed to occupy the minds of most genteel ladies.

Perhaps it was only that she was so absorbed in her senses and emotions that sometimes she appeared to be without her wits, careless, or haphazard. He had never known a female to be so wholly without airs, yet so elegant, and so honest and transparent, yet not insensitive. Her artistic temperament might explain her powers of observation, mingled with a carefree disregard for the mores of the world.

The exquisite sight of her smiling at him invaded his mind, in a most disquieting manner. He'd taken far too much pleasure from their conversations. His breathing quickened as he remembered her entirely too bewitching movements as they danced together. He hoped with all his heart that he had not revealed any admiration in his expression, for the very last thing he wanted was to be encouraging any sort of female attention – particularly from someone so irritatingly appealing. Could there have been something deeper in the warmth of her countenance? As soon as the thought occurred to him, he dismissed it: he was sure no-one like her would ever think on him as a romantic subject.

In a world of rich, dashing, polished beaus, he was an ordinary, serious, plain man, and he knew he could be something of a grouch. His countenance and demeanour were certainly not an advertisement for matrimony, nor did he ever intend for them to be.

Although he was now the target of many village families with daughters to marry off, his apparently certain position in life must be the only attraction. He knew any marriage of that kind would not be for love, and only an undeniable love would compel him to succumb to that particular life sentence. In the back of his mind he assumed it would happen one day, but he had no intention of actively pursuing it while he had so many other ambitions.

The prospect of a young lady not only turning his head, but hers being turned by him, was unfathomable. Surely he was too difficult, too righteous, too... *boring*, to ever be considered as a husband or even a beau on the strength of his romantic merits. He was sure his appearance was mediocre, and his lack of desire to appear in the latest fashions would render him more unattractive. What would Miss Grant possibly see in him? How could a female with such vitality and genuine warmth ever see something to admire in someone like him?

No, it was impossible. Any sign of affection was in his imagination. She might be flattered, she may be longing for attention from someone – anyone – but she could surely not have singled him out as worthy of a sincere attachment. And if she had – well, God help her. It could not end well.

On his arrival at the hall, he was shown to the drawing room, where Lord and Lady Ashworth awaited him. Lord Ashworth shook his hand and directed him to a seat. They exchanged pleasantries, before the elder man saw fit to engage in a critique of the previous day's church service.

"Your sermon was good, Brook," he boomed, "but I would tend to steer clear of any message that might lead to the village folk thinking they are equal with us."

William's eyes flashed. "In God's eyes," he said, "they are."

Ashworth smiled patronisingly. "Indeed, but we must not have them becoming uppity... demanding lower rents and such. There is an order to the world, and we must do our utmost to maintain it."

It was clear that the "we" in this statement meant William. "I see," he said.

"I only mention it because you alluded to some questionable passages yesterday... the rich man not entering the kingdom of heaven and such like. We cannot have the tenants and workers questioning our place as their superiors."

William's blood went from boiling to sparking, and something of his ire must have shown on his face, although it was misinterpreted.

"We understand you are still learning," put in Lady Ashworth. "Lord Ashworth's comments are to assist you, so please do not take them as criticisms or be offended in any way. We will continue to help you in any way we can."

William was tempted to give up the living there and then, but something held him back. "Thank you, my lady," he ground out. "I will do my very best to write the appropriate sermons for my audience."

A thick silence descended on the room. The tea tray arrived, and William chit-chatted his way through two cups before politely indicating his intention to leave.

As the front doors closed behind him, William caught sight of a gentleman across the courtyard dismounting a horse.

He approached with deliberate nonchalance, greeting Mr Barrington with a handshake as the man sent his horse off with a groom. "I wondered if I might have a word?"

Barrington's left eyebrow arched, but he smiled and said, "Of course, Mr Brook." He folded his arms across his broad chest.

William took a deep breath as he organised his thoughts. "I have heard you are to be settled with a very pretty estate. Is it far from here?"

"It is in Hampshire, a good three day's ride away. Mulberry Manor came into the family from my mother's side. But what interest could you have in my inheritance?"

"I take a keen interest in the future welfare of all my parishioners, Mr Barrington," said William mildly. "I suppose you will want to take a wife, before you begin your life there?"

Barrington fixed him with a steady stare. "It would probably be wise to do so," he said, "for there will certainly be a household to manage."

"Have you a young lady in mind? Perhaps you met someone in London this past season?"

Barrington put his hands on his hips. "I am not on the verge of issuing a proposal to anyone, Mr Brook. I fail to see why it is any of your business, unless perhaps you are looking to schedule the marriage into your pathetic diary. Now, if that is all..."

William realised his curiosity regarding Barrington's interest in Miss Grant was clouding his real intentions for this conversation. He didn't want the man to walk away until he'd come to the crux of the matter bothering him the most.

"I only enquire, my good man, because it is my observation that idle young men are wont to seek pleasures from, perhaps, the wrong realms. You would do well to settle soon, take a wife and direct your... desires to their proper place."

Barrington's mouth dropped open. "My – my desires?"

William was too impassioned to stop. "You are a man of the world, in a privileged position. You have nothing to lose with casual affairs. A young innocent lady is an easy target, and you should consider the consequences before taking advantage."

Barrington's lip curled, and his hands clenched into fists. "I don't take kindly to interference, Mr Brook," he said with quiet force. "If you are not careful, I will persuade my father you are not the right man for the job."

"Please do," William said easily. "You would in fact be doing me a favour."

"Is that so?" Barrington considered him for a moment. "Well, in that case I shall ensure you stay. For the moment."

William finally ran out of steam. "I only hope that you will consider what I have said. Good day, Mr Barrington." He turned and left the property with as much poise as he could muster, as an uneasy sense of foreboding sunk into the pit of his stomach. The idea that his fate may rest in Barrington's hands was exceedingly unsettling.

Chapter Nine

William had almost begun to look forward to his weekly visits with Mrs Croxley. She seemed to remember his chastising her gossip at their first meeting, and to his amusement, on each call she wavered between quiet courtesy, and sudden unstoppable bursts of "news".

On this particular visit, Mrs Croxley was poorly and in bed. He'd heard of her condition when calling on Miss Hicks, and after letting himself in he countered her protestations that she was in no condition to receive him.

"Mrs Croxley," he said, carefully advancing through the dark room, "it is my duty to attend to the sick. I have brought you some jelly."

There was a hesitation from the sickbed. "If you would just leave it on the table," Mrs Croxley said in a shuddering voice, "I will be well enough to attend you next week."

"Nonsense." His eyes now adjusted to the light, William found the bed and perched on the side next to his patient. He put a hand to Mrs Croxley's forehead, and she jerked back with a gasp.

"Now young man, there is no need to play the surgeon..." She dissolved into coughs.

"I do not think you have a serious fever," he said, "but I know you must be feeling quite dreadful."

Mrs Croxley gave a sort of whimper. "One bears it the best one can."

William smiled to himself. "You are very brave. Would you like some jelly now?"

"If you please."

He took the cloth wrapping from the bowl of jelly, and instinctively leaned forward to grasp Mrs Croxley behind the shoulders and ease her into a sitting position. Instantly she began batting at his arms and chest.

"Mr Brook! I say, Mr Brook! Unhand me at once. This is quite shocking."

"There, you will be better able to swallow now," he said, ignoring her protests.

The meal progressed in silence for some minutes, until Mrs Croxley began one of her characteristic outbursts.

"Do you know, one could be forgiven for thinking you and Miss Grant were forming an attachment."

William's hand paused for a moment with a spoonful of jelly in mid-flight. He forced a laugh, even as his pulse accelerated. "Now why would anyone speculate on such a theory?" he asked, jamming the spoon in her mouth.

Mrs Croxley gulped the mouthful down. "You spent an inordinate amount of time together at the ball. First dancing, and then during supper. I noticed private conversations and countless smiles."

Why did she not comment on all the other ladies who had commanded his attention that night? "Coincidence, I assure you," he said. "We are nothing to each other." Even as the words left his mouth, a betraying warmth rapidly engulfed him, and something in his spirit condemned his words. He was grateful for the dim light.

"Ah well, her family would never approve of it anyway," Mrs Croxley said, with a deal too much satisfaction.

William swallowed and took up more jelly. "Oh?"

"Oh yes, her mother in particular is puffed up, and seems determined to secure her a gentleman of noble birth with fine carriages and an estate of his own."

"It is just as well," William fairly snapped. "For I have no intention of courting Miss Grant or any other lady in Amberley. Ever."

To his horror, Mrs Croxley giggled, the infuriating sort of sound which proclaimed she knew better. "We shall see," she said.

"That is the end of the jelly," William said, placing the spoon firmly in the remains. "I shall leave you to convalesce, unless you wish me to light a candle and read some scriptures?"

He left the cottage rapidly, a new sort of indignation building in his veins. "Puffed up, eh?" he muttered as he stalked across the lane to his house. Then he shook his head vehemently as he entered the building. "It is of no consequence."

✄✁

Later that night, William tossed in his bed in sweat-soaked sheets. The events of the past few days trampled through his mind as he worked himself into a panic.

This was exactly why he did not want to be marooned in a small town like Amberley. He could not move without someone noticing or criticising. His future was being planned by strangers, and his dreams were consigned to dust.

As he gasped for breath, fear engulfed him. The worst of it was not that he would have to remain here, but that his heart could get tangled up. The risk of love meant the risk of pain. His life was a study of careful detachment, a myriad of lives he hoped to touch, without allowing himself to be touched in return. The only people in his life he'd ever fully let in were the rector, his first mentor, Thomas, and to some extent, Dean Roberts. Anyone else he'd sought to love was either gone or had rejected him. By and large the Church was safe, and even then he revealed precious little to most of his co-workers. Cecilia made him want to open up, and the way his words tumbled forth impulsively in her presence was frightening.

Suddenly, all of the criticisms he had endured these past weeks roared in his ears, and he convinced himself he was being ineffective in Amberley, of no use to anyone. His budding feelings for the people here were perilous. He wanted desperately to leave, but if he did so against the dean's wishes he'd be scorned by the wider church. On the edge of terror, he found a candle, rushed to his library and prepared a pen.

Dear Mr Dean,
I do hope you are well and the St Mary's congregation in fine

spirit. First allow me to assure you that I am in good health, in that I am physically well. The parsonage is a good size, with ample lands. If one looks hard enough, one can find all the material items one requires. The church is staffed with volunteers, and I am able to access funds for the poor. On the surface, a new vicar would find satisfaction with the general situation.

It is when one begins to act out spiritual stewardship that one encounters difficulties. The community resist any sort of change to the routine of decades past. Any effort at improvement, or injection of vitality, is met with strong obstinacy. It seems that Mr Johnson preached the same messages repeatedly, those which do not challenge his congregation to higher moral goals, or spur them into acting out their faith. Any change to the order of doing things, any change in expectations, or if I accidentally stumble into a different routine, I am met with a chorus of opposition. It seems I am unable to do anything right, and I wonder if someone with more experience would be better suited to the task. Though I grew up near a small town, the society of Cambridge and London are in sharp contrast to the environs in which I now find myself.

While Lord and Lady Ashworth appear to be generous benefactors, their spiritual outlook appears to differ from my own. I feel the post would be better suited to an older vicar, someone who is set in the traditional ways, and will be more pleasing to the conservative villagers.

I am still also longing for the opportunity to serve in the new world, to learn of other cultures and languages and bring the good news of God's word. I feel I would be of much more use, as a young and fit male, being of physical as well as spiritual service to the poor abroad.

By no means am I ungrateful for your generosity in recommending me for this post. But I must beg that you reconsider and send me elsewhere, preferably far from England's shores. Can my instincts for my calling be so wrong?

I remain,
Your faithful servant,
William L Brook

Cecilia welcomed the addition of her aunt, Honoria Holcombe, to their household. Her mother's younger sister, she supplied a wealth of diverse conversation during long afternoons of needlework, and also became a buffer from Mrs Grant's criticisms. Without Aunt Honoria, Cecilia's debut season would not have been possible, as she had hosted the family in her London townhouse.

Honoria had married well – almost too well for her sister to bear. Their father Mr Wright had persuaded Viscount Holcombe to stay with the family to break his journey on the way to a hunting party in Scotland, and while there the young heir Richard had fallen headlong for Honoria, who possessed an angelic singing voice. They maintained a steady, if long-distance courtship for several months, and at last on his father's passing, Richard presented himself to Mr Wright at once to claim his daughter.

Now settled at a large country seat in Derbyshire, and with the impressive city townhouse, Honoria became Lady Holcombe and this title was more keenly felt by her sister Susan than by herself. An heir was quickly produced and reared, and now Honoria was in the fortunate position of advisor to her friends and relatives on all matters matrimonial.

Susan met Mr Grant at a ball in Shrewsbury, and it was a love match. She nursed an unspoken envy of her sister, wishing that she had been the one to snag the title, the vast estate, and the seasons in town with all the clothes and jewellery one could ask for. Her only way of competing now was to see her sons distinguished somehow in the course of duty, or to see Cecilia settled with a title – perhaps even of superior rank to Honoria. It seemed unlikely now, but at least a marriage to the brother of an Earl would be advantageous. You never could tell what sort of accident might befall Lord Marsham.

Cecilia watched as the Wright sisters fell into their usual roles, her aunt attempting to assume the dominant position. As the ladies took tea a week after the ball, she tuned out the chatter from a window seat, observing the shapes of the clouds passing by. Her mind wandered back to the ball, and lingered on a certain Mr Brook.

Perhaps there was more to the gentleman than the serious, erudite cleric she'd encountered previously. She'd seen the longing in his eyes as he'd talked of his past and his friends. In the next moment, they'd sparked with interest and enthusiasm as he'd shared in her passions. Deprived of sympathetic company since Amy went to work at the big house, she longed to speak with him again.

She realised she was smiling. When her own name began to puncture the room's conversation, her attention returned with a start.

"Susan, I am sure I could find someone for Cecilia in Derbyshire, or in London next year."

Mrs Grant pursed her lips. "Now sister, I am quite capable of getting her a husband, and a good husband too. In fact, I hope she may make an impact on that score before the year's end."

Cecilia's teacup hit her saucer with such force that some of her tea splashed on her dress. "Mama," she cried, "it is mere months before the year's end."

Mrs Grant smiled. "In matters of the heart, my dear, that is an age."

A chill settled over Cecilia's heart as all words abandoned her. Any freedom she had known was surely about to come to a swift end.

§

William could not look at the tangle of weeds visible from his parlour any longer. He decided he would dig over and plant the land. Even if he wouldn't be around for long enough to actually eat the results of his labours, the next incumbent would benefit from having their own supply of vegetables and herbs. While he hadn't planted a garden before, he'd helped some poor labourers with their own gardens, so he knew how to wield a hoe. If nothing else, cultivating the land around the parsonage would give him something useful to do.

That Friday, he rose early to attend the market in the village green. He appeared to be the only gentleman among the throng of farming folk, servants and wives. As each set of surprised eyes met his he tipped his hat and smiled, but his presence caused a proliferation of unnecessary bowing and curtseying.

He surveyed the stalls of fruits, crafts, ciders, breads, and poultry. At length he found what he had come for. Next to a large vegetable stand, Farmer Russell was selling several rows of seedlings.

"Good day, Mr Russell," said William. He pointed to the small plants. "Are these ready to be sown now, for winter fruiting?"

"Indeed they are, Mr Brook."

"I will take all of them. I am sure my plot will allow enough room."

Mr Russell looked at him sideways. "Very good, sir. When shall I send them round to you?"

"I will take them now. Do you have a wheelbarrow or some such method of transportation?"

Mr Russell stood back from his counter and planted one large hand on his hip. "Sir, I think it best I keep them until your labourer is ready to plant them."

"I am going to plant them myself," William said, smiling. "I intend to start today. I found some tools in my shed. Is there any particular instruction I should bear in mind, regarding spacing the crops?"

The farmer nearly toppled over, and he steadied himself against the stand. "But sir, you're a gentleman. Do you really mean to dig over your own dirt? I've seen that parsonage plot. It's a right mess. You'll be there for days just pulling the weeds out."

"So be it. There is no reason why I should not do it."

"But surely I could arrange for my boy to do that for you, sir."

William imagined Henry Russell being conscripted to help in his garden. The man would probably think it a fate worse than death. "Nonsense," he said, "I am fit and able to do the work. I have seen the way a vegetable garden is laid out."

"Well, at least let me come and help you work out a plan."

William hesitated. He should not let his pride get in the way of progress. "If you are willing, I would be very grateful." He paid close attention while the farmer described the different crops, the size they'd take up and the conditions they liked. Mr Russell agreed to pay him a visit after the close of the market, and advised him to measure out the plot beforehand.

❧❧

Cecilia slipped out after breakfast on Saturday, intent on painting the late summer wildflowers. She worked near the river for several hours. On her way back home, she saw a distant view of the churchyard, and some movement caught her eye near the vicarage. There appeared to be someone working in the pottage garden next to the house, which she knew was well overgrown. She moved closer, with the intention of striking up a conversation with the worker, and asking about what he was planting. The Grants had an abundance of spinach seedlings, so she could offer a few.

She walked down around the base of a mound, and through a grove of trees. Upon emerging from behind a large oak, she gave a start. It was Mr Brook working in the garden, furiously tilling the hardened soil. *He always gives his all to whatever endeavour he sets his mind to.* He hadn't seen her, and though she felt she shouldn't disturb him, she found herself stealing closer, pressing herself behind another oak only about twenty feet from the plot. She couldn't help but examine him closely, as the sight of him was unlike she'd ever seen a gentleman before.

William had worked up a sweat. His dark hair was tousled across his forehead, and dirt was caked on his cheeks and neck. His torso and arms were only clad in a shirt, with no coat, cravat or waistcoat. Apart from her father and brothers, Cecilia had only ever seen gentlemen in jackets or coats. And she had never seen a shirt, or the man within it, in such a state as this. He had torn it open at the neck, and she could see a broad chest speckled with hair. The damp fabric clung to his shoulders and well-formed arms. Cecilia watched him drive his hoe into the soil again and again, breathing hard with the effort. She swallowed, realising she had been gaping with an open mouth, which had suddenly dried out. She knew there was no way she could talk to him, her agitated mind flitting from one thought to the next. She emerged from the tree, intending to creep past the vicarage and on her way home. Her heart beating wildly, she began to shuffle through the grass.

William chose that moment to pause in his work, stretching backwards and causing his shirt to pull out from his breeches. The glimpse of the muscles of his stomach made Cecilia gasp, and she clamped a hand to her mouth, too late. He bolted upright, and instantly his eyes were on her, freezing her steps. He held her stare for just a moment, before conflicting emotions washed across his face. First he smiled, then frowned, and then mumbled something as he looked down at himself. Even from her distance she could see colour creeping up his neck to his face, and she felt remorse for embarrassing him. He was working his own land, after all. She had no business spying on him.

"Oh Miss Grant, I do apologise..." William looked about the yard frantically, locating his coat hanging on a fencepost. He started towards it, but did not advance two steps before he landed on his rake. The instrument jumped up and smacked him squarely on the nose.

"Mr Brook!" Cecilia started towards him, coming to the low stone fence and hesitating for only a moment before sitting on it and swivelling into his plot. "Oh my goodness, you are bleeding!"

He touched a hand to his nose then observed the thick red liquid on his fingers. With dazed eyes he took in her advancing frame.

"I am so sorry, Mr Brook. I was on my way back home from the meadows and elected to cut through the glebe. I never thought... oh do let me help you." She hovered close to him as he produced a handkerchief and held it to his nose. She regarded his injury pitiably, her eyes widening at the sight of the blood in close quarters, before her gaze drifted irresistibly lower.

"Really Miss Grant, I am quite all right. You should be on your way immediately. I did not consider female passers-by when I reduced myself to this state."

"Well, I shall go then," Cecilia said reluctantly, her eyes clinging to the tail of his shirt. "But are you sure you will not let me attend to your wound? I feel terrible for causing you pain."

William stifled a laugh. "It will only bleed for a few moments more, I am sure. Then I will resume my work. Your concern is most kind, but I am afraid it is wasted. And I must be grateful to you for teaching me a lesson about leaving my rake lying on the ground."

Cecilia went back over to the wall, pausing as she sat.

William averted his eyes as she swung her legs over, and said, "Good day, Miss Grant."

She turned back just as his eyes met hers. He looked a little woozy, but magnificent. "Goodbye," she breathed.

Chapter Ten

As Cecilia looked up at the vicar in church the next morning, she tried to keep her mind on the words he was saying. But it was no good. All she could see was the dishevelled young man she had encountered the day before. Instead of the confident authority which masked his eyes at this moment, she remembered the shy sparkle she had glimpsed, and the dark curls which had strayed across them.

Mr Brook pressed his fists on to the lectern as he spoke passionately about Jesus being every person who needs help. The message impacted Cecilia for several minutes and she was moved by his kind spirit and conviction. Then she also remembered the toned arms that had worked the earth, and as she watched his fists she was sure his muscles must be flexing under his jacket. When his eyes connected with hers, heat washed over her body. As she felt the crimson rise over her chest and creep up her neck, she yanked her eyes away from him.

She blinked hard and looked down at her hands. *Cecilia!* she scolded herself. *This is the vicar! You cannot have impure thoughts about a man of God! This must be a sin.*

William invited the congregation to pray. Cecilia knelt down and fixed her clasped hands on the pew in front. At the end of the prayer, she quickly added, "And help me to concentrate on the sermon, not on the vicar's figure! Amen!"

She was still flustered as the family left the church, carefully avoiding the gaze of everyone lest her blush betray her thoughts. A few steps out of the door, she bumped into something, and was horrified to find herself faced with an elegant cravat. She screwed up her face for a moment, before slowly lifting her eyes to find Mr Barrington staring at her with laughing eyes.

His gloved hands caught her by the elbows. "Steady on, Miss Grant," he said with a chuckle. "What was on the ground that held you so entranced? It is advisable to find a clear path before charging ahead."

She stepped back, and he released her. "I am so sorry," she said. "I did not see you there, sir."

"Alas, I fear that is a common sentiment among the ladies."

She saw a twinkle in his eye. He must be daring her to flirt with him, to pass him some kind of compliment regarding how he could never be invisible. She took a breath but couldn't bring herself to do it. She just looked up at him with bashful eyes.

He laughed softly. "Come on, Miss Grant, let us get you away from the doorway." He took her elbow again and steered her off to the side of the exiting parishioners.

Cecilia allowed him to guide her, but she glanced back over her shoulder. Her mother looked on and gave her an approving smile, and just behind her, William left the church. His eyes swept over the crowd, before resting on her. She held her breath. His brows knitted together for just a moment, then he turned to shake the hand of Mr Morton.

"Did you enjoy the service, Miss Grant?"

Cecilia turned back to Barrington. "Yes," she replied. "The sermon was very... impactful." *In more ways than you could ever realise.*

"Indeed."

❧

William received compliments on his sermon with altogether less pleasure than he should have. It took all his strength not to keep watch over Miss Grant and the roguish Mr Barrington.

Before he could restrain himself, his eyes betrayed him, drifting over the churchyard to where the young couple talked. But he did not meet the gaze of Cecilia. Instead, it was Barrington who stared back at him. William could not help the narrowing of his eyes.

The gentleman first regarded the vicar, then looked back at Cecilia, then toward William again. A knowing smile played across his lips. He brought his hand to his face and surreptitiously tipped his hat at the vicar; a gesture so subtle Cecilia would not have noticed it.

William rushed back to the vicarage, nearly colliding with Emma on his way in.

"I'm off out to see my Ma, all right Mr Brook?"

"Yes yes, that's fine Emma, enjoy your afternoon."

He flew up the stairs to his bedroom and flung himself on the bed, but rose an instant later, beginning to pace about the room.

This was exactly the situation he had wanted to avoid. Not only was he stuck in a safe little town in the middle of nowhere. His stupid emotions were starting to interfere with even the simple job he'd taken up. How was he supposed to concentrate on preaching and teaching, when all he could see in his mind's eye were her dashed blue eyes and golden curls?

The entire service had been a nightmare. From the moment he'd taken the pulpit, he'd known exactly where she sat, even though he hadn't looked that way. He'd kept his eyes on the other side of the pews while they sang the hymns. Then when he'd begun his sermon, he'd made sure to look at each person in the congregation, as had become his custom.

As he read the passage from the book of Matthew, he surveyed the pew in front of the Grants, before moving his gaze over her father, then her mother. He contemplated skipping her altogether. He dropped his eyes to his bible again as he finished the verses, even though he knew the words by heart. Then he took a breath and looked up, right into her eyes.

The breath had been sucked right out of him as the warmth in her countenance made his pulse quicken. Dressed in her Sunday best, she looked like an angel, and in her eyes there was such an intense fondness, and her loveliness seemed to only but increase when her gaze fell.

He'd had to look down at the lectern to study his notes, whereas usually he spoke from the heart without the need for reminders. Today he'd needed prompting, at least for a few minutes while he recovered from... what? A moment's exchange of eye contact with a flighty young maiden?

He grasped one of the bed posts and leaned his forehead against his arm, forcing himself to take even breaths. This could not go on. He would only have to see her on Sundays, and he'd just have to avoid looking at her until this little inconvenience had passed.

He was still embarrassed from their little *tête-à-tête* in his garden. Not only had his unkempt appearance been ungentlemanly, unseemly, he then went and almost knocked himself out with a garden implement. The shame of it made his stomach turn, but he told himself out loud that there was no reason to be so mortified. She meant nothing to him.

He would not allow the distraction of a female to sway him from his purpose. Pretty she may be, but by all accounts there was not two sensible thoughts in her head to string together. And yet the night of the ball, she had been the only one he could get any sense out of. It was as if she had seen right into his soul. She was such an enigma: a confusing combination of fickleness and perception.

Stop thinking about her. Don't let her ruin everything.

He would not allow it. He must stem the tide of any trifling emotions before they got in the way. If a few innocent encounters could cause him so much upset, only think what a real entanglement might do. He'd run mad. His small ministry in this village would falter, and how would he then prove himself worthy of leading a mission abroad?

His mind jumped back to the churchyard, and seeing her with Barrington. His blood boiled at the memory. It could not be jealousy, but some sort of possessive ire surged through his veins. Surely it was just concern for her welfare.

He was certain he knew the meaning of Barrington's gesture, and it shamed him all the more that his regard for the girl was so transparent. Barrington meant to keep her from him, did he? Well, he was welcome to her. If he meant it as some kind of retribution for his meddling in Barrington's affairs, it would turn out to backfire on him. Attaching himself to an innocent such as Miss Grant could only raise Barrington's moral character, and she would benefit from the security of his position. He only hoped... he shuddered involuntarily. Surely Barrington would not sink so low as to abuse the trust of a young lady such as Cecilia.

If nothing else, he would try to protect her from any such harm, even as he stayed out of the way of any romance between them. As her spiritual leader, it was his duty to ensure her path to matrimony was innocent and honourable, was it not?

Satisfied, he sat back on the bed and opened his bible. He needed to work on the lesson for the village children which he was to deliver on Tuesday.

❧

If Amy had sensed there was anything different about her friend during their Sunday afternoon stroll, she hadn't let on. But though she wasn't yet ready to reveal it, Cecilia was irrevocably altered.

For the first time in her life, she felt a deep, hungry need. The building excitement of her attraction to Mr Brook consumed her every thought and emotion. When would she see him again? She craved just a glimpse of him, but also yearned to speak with him and discover what lay beyond his carefully cultured reserve. She yearned to know more of him, to discover his traits and desires, and find out if he would ever want her in the way she did him. And if he did...

Perhaps she would fight for her future after all; take control of her own destiny. Instead of merely wishing her life could continue with peaceful sameness until her future came to claim her, perhaps she could reach out and claim it... claim *him*.

Her mother may need to be worked on to adjust her expectations from younger son of an earl, to local vicar, but he was also of a respectable family, so she'd heard, and also a gentleman. Why should they be so particular in her choice? Perhaps she could live as comfortable a life at the vicarage as she could with Mr Barrington at his far-off estate. She would not have to leave the village she had known her whole life. And she was sure her feelings of warmth towards Mr Brook would only but grow. Quite sure, indeed.

Chapter Eleven

William made his way to the village schoolroom well before the intended time on Tuesday, grateful for the chance to occupy his mind and prove his use. Surely there could be no more important task than educating young minds and hearts in the gospel. He even found himself whistling as he walked through the village, waving cordially to passers-by.

He opened the door to the small classroom a little before barging in, as the silence surprised him. When he'd approached gatherings of children in London, it had always been to raucous chatter. He listened for a moment, and was stunned to hear a familiar voice. *Her* voice. Surely not. It couldn't be. Was there nowhere in the vicinity of Amberley safe from her presence?

He opened the door wide, and his suspicions were confirmed. There she stood, instructing the children in sketching a figurine of a cow. Even as she described its belly and horns, her face glowed with passion for her teaching, and he noticed the children were either intent at their scraps of paper, or gazing at her adoringly.

He caught himself employed likewise and cleared his throat. Her eyes swung to him, along with every other set in the room.

"Good afternoon, children," he said with a smile. "Miss Grant, I did not expect to see you here."

His tone must have been too severe, for her fine eyebrows knit together. "I take a class every week at this time, Mr Brook. They told me you were coming to teach the group, but I did not expect you as yet. Would you like me to stop now?"

At this a general moan rose up from the group of children, and a mix of scowls and pleading faces were directed at him.

He held up his hands in defeat. "No Miss Grant, I would not deprive these young artists. I am early. Will you mind if I sit at the back?"

She smiled. "No indeed, Mr Brook. Would you like a pencil and paper?"

William laughed in spite of himself. "No, no, I assure you my scratchings would be an insult to your instruction. Continue, and I shall watch in silence."

He found an empty seat at the back of the room, and made approving noises when some of the students approached to show him their drawings. He could not help smiling as Cecilia came nearer and praised a child's tragic artwork.

She'll make a fine mother. William started in shock. The thought had trespassed into his mind unbidden. *To someone else's children, obviously,* he qualified. There was nothing wrong with admiring such qualities, was there? It was perfectly innocent.

Rather than continuing in the errant luxury of observing Cecilia, he turned to his bible and began to think about the message he would give that Sunday. He became so engrossed in the book of James, that he jumped the next time Cecilia said his name, announcing it was his turn to address the students. They changed places, and she reposed elegantly in the hard wooden seat.

He began his lesson on Noah, managing to absorb himself fully in the effort of engaging the children for some time. However when he dared peek at the back of the class, he couldn't help noticing that Cecilia's eyes had slid shut. Was he that boring?

He talked on about Noah constructing the arc, but he couldn't stop his eyes from darting to her face, and he made out the faint trace of a smile on her lips. Daydreaming about Mr Barrington, perhaps? She might not be William's student, but she could at least show a little respect.

"Miss Grant," he said sharply. A little too sharply, for some of the children jumped.

Her eyes flew open. "Yes, Mr Brook?" she said.

"Would you be more comfortable outside?"

Her brow furrowed. "Oh, by no means, Mr Brook. I apologise if my demeanour was off-putting. I did not realise. I was simply imagining the story in my head. Drawing a picture. Do you ever do that, children?" She raised an expectant gaze to the room. Some of the children smiled, and she was rewarded with a couple of nods. Addressing William again, she said, "You tell the story with so much expression, I could not help but get carried away. Do continue, please."

She smiled at him so sweetly and with such gentle persuasion that for a moment he was dumbfounded. There was not a sign of insincerity or mockery in her stunning blue eyes. Recovering, he was struck by an idea.

"Miss Grant, would you care to illustrate the story?"

She flushed, obviously pleased. "Well, if you don't mind, Mr Brook, that would be great fun. What do you think, children?"

To a general cheer of encouragement, she rose, taking up her largest drawing pad and her pencils. William pulled a chair next to him, and she smiled at him as she dropped on to it. "Now Mr Brook, you mentioned a huge ship?"

He nodded, realising he was smiling back.

"Well then, let us see what it looks like. Do you think it might be like Lord Nelson's ship?"

The children agreed, and instead of drawing the bulbous arc of William's imagination, she drew a galleon with huge, billowing sails.

"And we need Noah and his wife, don't we?" She drew a huge man dressed in a toga, with a skinny and more modestly attired wife by his side.

"What is next, Mr Brook?" she said, turning to him with the pencil in her hand.

William froze for a moment, and then consulted his notes. "The animals," he stammered. "God instructed Noah to gather up two of every animal in the world. Then they could multiply and fill the earth once the flood was over."

"What's 'multiply'?" enquired a thin dark-haired girl at William's feet.

He turned a perplexed face to her. "Uh... it means they will have babies, and their babies will have children and then there will be many more animals."

"What sort of animals went on the arc, Mr Brook?" Cecilia prompted.

"Why, all the beasts known to man. He would need horses and cattle, to start with."

Cecilia got to work, drawing two horses prancing into the boat, followed by two cows grazing nearby. "What noises do these animals make, children?"

A chorus of neighing and mooing issued forth from their charges.

"Very good!" she said. Then, turning to William, "What else?"

"Pigs, I suppose."

The next minute, two porkers with huge snouts and long curly tails followed behind the other animals. Cecilia began oinking away with the rest of the class. She laughed gaily, delicate little snorts punctuating the trills.

He regarded her in wonder. He had never met a lady who would behave so in front of a gentleman. He was quite sure she had no regard for his opinion of her. Her only thought was teaching and entertaining the children. He wondered if she would be self-conscious in front of a man she wanted to impress. Indeed, she said as much at the ball. Poor Barrington would be missing out on seeing her natural charm in such a setting as this. It was unlikely he'd ever help with teaching children. It was obvious Cecilia had no interest in William whatsoever.

Once African animals of all sorts joined the farmyard creatures, William described the flood. Cecilia drew a raincloud, but thought it best to stop before trying to illustrate the elimination of all evil mankind.

When the class was over, William and Cecilia walked the children back to their homes, which were mainly farm cottages a small distance from the village. Once alone, they continued to walk together.

He turned to her. "You have a gift for teaching, Miss Grant."

"Oh, I thank you," she said, meeting his eyes with a blush, "but that is clearly your specialty."

"It is my profession, in a way, but I admire your enthusiasm to share your passion with the children."

"They are doing *me* a favour. I have never had anyone to share my artistic tendencies with, so it provides an excuse for me to talk about drawing and painting for an hour or two. That is, no-one before you arrived."

His heart pulsated with the meaning and sincerity of her words, and the look she gave him only seemed to emphasise the connection between them. Her colour deepened charmingly, and then she pulled her gaze straight ahead.

"Well," he said, "I can see that most of the children are greatly enriched by your gifts."

She smiled, but she did not look at him. "I only wish I knew more of the principles of art, and more opportunity to learn from the masters."

William's mind took a moment to catch up with her words, and he was reminded of their conversation at the ball. "Miss Grant, I have been remiss in not lending you the fine arts books I spoke of when we ate together. They are sitting on a shelf, of no good to anyone."

"It is no matter," she said. "I know you are too busy to be thinking of me."

He stared at her cheek, at the swirling blond curl drifting across the soft peach-coloured skin. Her focus on the road ahead only granted him leave to savour the sight. *Oh Miss Grant, if only you know how much time I spend busy trying* not *to think of you.*

They reached a fork in the road. She turned to him. "I can go on from here by myself if you like," she said. "I do not wish to keep you from your duties."

His heart ached to keep her with him. Before he knew what he would say, the words tumbled from his mouth. "The lesson for the children was my last duty for the day. I wonder, Miss Grant, if I could give you a lesson instead, by way of showing you my library."

She blinked a few times, staring at his chin, and then looked off in the direction of her house.

He'd over-stepped the mark. Of course it was inappropriate for her to come with him. She was probably thinking that even now, her maid should be with them. "No matter, I shall leave you to –"

Her head whipped back around to him, her curls bouncing on her shoulders. "Of course I shall go," she said. "I could not pass up such an opportunity to further my education. Mother could not but approve. And I am with the vicar, so of course I am... safe."

I hope to God you are. He offered his arm, and she placed her hand in the crook of his elbow. "You can just come inside to select the books you can carry home, and I shall arrange the delivery of the rest later."

They continued through the farming paths, by-passing the village on the way to the vicarage. For the first extended period since they first met, neither spoke. William chanced glances at her from time to time, as often as he dared. She was looking at the sky, the grass, the trees. He longed to ask what fantastical thoughts were skipping through her mind, for he knew the appearance of listlessness or distraction was in reality an artist's brain at work, interpreting the world through a kaleidoscopic lens. As he took a breath to finally give into his curiosity, Cecilia suddenly stopped.

"Oh, look!" she breathed, pointing at the ground.

William glanced at the grass and then back at her. "What is it?" he asked, mystified by what message the blades were speaking to her. He could see why she had gained her reputation for eccentricity, but he wanted to discover what she really was.

"Here." She knelt in the grass, and caressed a small blush of blue.

He checked the fields and yards quickly, to make sure they didn't have an audience. Then he dropped one knee and studied her object. It was a clump of violas, a shade of brilliant indigo.

"It is a miracle these are blooming so late in the season," she said. "Are they not resplendent? If I could but find some paint pigment in such a rich shade, in order to capture their beauty." Her eyes lifted to him and she smiled.

How fragile she was, not unlike the tiny flowers. How complex and beautiful and pure. It would take a unique man to understand the workings of her mind, and he supposed, her heart. He prayed she would find such a man even in her limited environs. He had seen no evidence thus far that Barrington would fulfil the requirements, but he should give the man the benefit of the doubt. After all, William would not be there long enough to see who Cecilia married. He cleared his throat, watching her finger the delicate petals. "Mr Jones does not stock an indigo oil? Or could not order one in?"

She shook her head. "My pin money only allows for watercolours, which Mr Jones does order for me, but I have never had a full complement of oils."

He reached down to the tiny blooms, dangerously close to her hand. "Will you mind if I pick one for you?" he asked gently.

She smiled a little and her blue eyes shone as she gave a slight shake of her head.

He carefully plucked a stem from the outside of the clump, and they both watched as the sunlight pierced the petals and seemed to create an azure aura around the tiny treasure. He smiled and held it out to her.

She took it from him with a sparkling countenance, twirling it between her fingers.

William stood. "Shall we continue?" he asked, offering her a hand up.

Chapter Twelve

Cecilia smiled and put her hand in his, rising back to her full height. Neither was wearing gloves, which was socially beyond the pale, but she didn't care. For those few moments she delighted in the strength and gentleness of his fingers, and the broad palm which nested her own. The touch sent a tingle up her arm, shooting to her heart like fire. Before releasing her hand, he looped it back through his arm, and she revelled in the sense of his possession of even a small part of her.

She felt as if she were floating as they made their way through the glebe, the back garden and into the vicarage.

He stopped on the threshold with a start. "Oh, it is Emma's afternoon off," he said. "We shall be quite alone. Perhaps you should wait outside, and I will fetch some books for you."

Cecilia did not reply at first, overcome by disappointment. She wanted to see all the books, not just the few she could carry. But as the vicar he was sensible of propriety, and she didn't want to appear as though she were not. "Well," she said with drooping eyes, "if that is what you think is best."

She dared to peer up at him, and when she met his eyes she saw the struggle taking place there. "On the other hand, it would be best for your – education... if you select the books which appeal to your artistic sensibility. I can leave you in the library while you peruse them."

She broke into a grin, much relieved. "What a good idea." She placed her hand in the crook of his elbow again, and allowed him to lead her down the hallway and off through a door on the left.

The little library was mostly taken up by a large desk, set up against a window overlooking the front garden, the surface taken up with piles of paper covered in scrawled notes, letters and a bible. The walls at either end were entirely made up of shelves, with those on the left being full with older volumes, and those on the right being only partially filled with recent hard covers.

"Those were left here by Mr Johnson," explained William, indicating the older books. "My selection is somewhat lacking I am afraid, mostly what I acquired during my time at Cambridge." He picked up a volume on biology and flipped through it before returning it back to the shelf. "They are recent publications, though, with the latest knowledge and" – his hand waved over one of the lower shelves – "artists."

Cecilia still hovered in the doorway.

"Come," he said, reaching out to her. "I shall show you the texts."

She started towards him, suddenly aware of how his tall, broad frame almost filled up the entire space between the desk and the shelves. The light from the window shone through his curls, creating a halo effect. She moved towards his eyes, the dark orbs seeming to eagerly draw her in as a moth to flame.

"Here," he said, crouching down to the shelf and pointing. "These are about the Renaissance – mainly architecture, sculpture..." He ran his hand along the spines, and stopped on one. "This one is painting."

He stood and handed it to her, but as she took it her attention was on the way his genuine smile crinkled up the edges of his eyes.

"And these are baroque; I never really did care for those styles – a bit too frilly, do you not think?"

He'd screwed up his nose, and a giggle escaped her mouth. "I will decide for myself," she said.

He nodded, smiling again, and turned back to the shelf. "Now these are more recent – the return to the classical style here, and these ones I bought at the Academy in London. The new landscape painters – Wilson, Gainsborough, Constable."

"Oh yes," Cecilia breathed, almost not believing her luck. "How wonderful. I shall want to look at those directly." She reached out towards the books, but was hindered by the heavy tome she already held.

William turned toward the desk. "I will clear a space for you," he said, stacking his papers up to make an area for her at the front of the desk.

"Oh please, do not go to any trouble."

He pulled out the seat for her. "It is no trouble at all. You look through all the books you like, and how about you choose two to take with you? You can exchange them for more when you have read them."

"I am most grateful, Mr Brook," she said, placing her volume on the desk. Her mind began to swirl with the possibilities of so much learning. "I shall have to find a way to do something nice for you."

William squeezed between the chair and the wall on his way to the door. She caught a whiff of his masculine scent, and it made her head spin in a way that art could not. She turned her head as her eyes followed him involuntarily.

"Please do not feel obliged," he said. "You have already given me more than you could know." His dark eyes seemed to be glowing, and then he blinked and stepped through the door. He called over his shoulder, "I shall leave you to make your choice."

Once he was gone, Cecilia was temporarily overcome by the emotion beating through her heart, consuming her mind. She gazed out the window at the roses and foxgloves, but what she saw was the blooming of something infinitely precious in her own being. He was so kind, so generous, and yet so mysterious. A man of the world, and yet also a man of the cloth. When he looked at her in a certain way, it was as if the rest of the world fell away, and it was just the two of them, needing to share themselves with each other. She felt an emotional and intellectual connection with him she had never experienced with anyone before. And yet, she knew there was more. More in the strong breadth of his shoulders, which she longed to cling to. More in the sharp line of his jaw, which she yearned to caress. And much more in those determined lips, that always spoke the truth, which she ached to kiss.

She gasped at the realisation, and yanked her eyes back to the books. *I want to kiss the vicar.* She'd never wanted to kiss anyone before. Mama would be scandalised, would she not? Not only because she wanted to lavish physical affection on a man to whom she was not betrothed, but because the man in question was a third son who was obligated to earn his money. He was a gentleman, to be sure, but he lacked a title and independent wealth.

She shook her head in an attempt to clear the nonsense. Surely he thought of her only as an under-educated woman – girl – in his parish, and he'd taken pity on her ignorance. He had far more important things to think about than a love-starved country miss. And surely far more important things to feel, to give her more than sympathy.

She took off her bonnet and opened the first book, and was soon poring over the coloured plates of Raphael, daVinci and Titian. The beautiful colours, the delicacy with which the subjects were rendered, the meticulous depiction of tiny landscapes as symbolic backgrounds... all was so inspiring and overwhelming that she never proceeded past this first book by the time William came back to check on her.

✍

Even hunched over his desk, engrossed in absorbing artistic endeavour from centuries before, she was beautiful. She hadn't noticed his appearance in the doorway, and he indulged himself for a few moments, drinking in the sinuous curves of her shoulders, her lustrous blond curls trailing from the crown of her head to the nape of her neck, and one slender, graceful arm extended onto the desk.

During the time he'd been away from the library, he'd meant to see what food Emma had left out for dinner, and then review the notes of the vestry meeting. He'd gotten as far as the kitchen, but then sat at the table for half an hour, remembering. His mind was possessed by the sight of her figure as he'd been able to examine it when he'd stood again after crouching by the bottom shelf. He hoped she hadn't noticed how he could not draw his eyes away from her hips, her torso, and more... and that he hadn't completely given himself away when he'd looked in her eyes. He had taken the full half hour to calm his desires. Whatever he was feeling was not proper for a man of God. He could not fight the longing to take her in his arms as if she were his, yet he also felt a powerful urge to protect her and be gentle, for surely she was fragile; a treasure to be guarded and savoured.

She turned the page and her head with it, and he caught sight of her full cheek, admiring the soft arc of pale skin. When his eyes trailed to her lips, she became conscious of his presence, and he watched them in delight as they formed the shape of his name.

"Why, Mr Brook," she said, rotating in the chair. "I am in some sort of heaven. I have seen some of these works in black and white before, but never so many, and never in vivid colour. I almost dare not take these books from your library – they must be very expensive."

"Nonsense," he said. "They are there to be read, and I do not think it is wise for you to visit with me in order to do so. As to the expense, you need not worry about damaging them. I was afforded an allowance for books when I was at university."

She closed the book and rose from the chair, then leaned back against the top of the desk. "You must have enjoyed your time at Cambridge, Mr Brook? Dedicated time to study any of one's interests must be a luxury indeed."

"I must confess it started out as being a welcome respite from my brothers." He panicked, unsure why those candid words had flown out of his mouth. Her eyebrows had jumped up her forehead, but she said nothing. "However," he rushed on, "once ensconced at college I strived to maximise the opportunity for both learning and developing a sense for what my ministry should be." At once reminded of his true purpose, and how far from Amberley that would be, he reined himself in. "Which books will you take home, then?" he asked, moving past her, toward the shelf and bending to draw out the volumes on modern landscape painters.

She peered at the top one he held, moving closer to lean over the cover. "I shall take that one, Gainsborough," she said, "and the one I was just looking at."

William was temporarily overwhelmed by her sweet scent, of jasmine and roses. He cleared his throat and gave her the book. "Here you are." He bent to put the others away.

Cecilia laid the Gainsborough on top of the Renaissance book, and gave a Rococo one back to him. "I must thank you, Mr Brook," she said, her earnest eyes meeting his. "You cannot know how I shall treasure these. There is so much to be discovered."

"The knowledge that they shall help you is enough thanks," he said gruffly. He tried to tell himself the spark in her eyes was merely gratitude.

She picked up her satchel from the desk. "I hope I have not detained you too long," she said.

"I assure you, your presence is always a welcome distraction." *Distracting is right.* He made himself look away from her pretty face, and moved to show her out. At precisely the same moment, she went to the doorway, and bumped into him.

"Pardon me, Miss –"

"Oh Mr Brook, I –"

Awkward laughter ensued on both sides. Their bodies only an inch apart, William watched as Cecilia slowly brought her eyes up to meet his. The startled blue pools morphed into something like wonder, and... affection? She was so naive and trusting. He could not take advantage of her, he *would* not.

His gaze travelled from her petite nose to her cheeks, which grew rosier by the moment, and finally rested on her mouth. Two full lips were also blushing, a little parted. Overpowered, he dropped his head towards them.

Her eyes fluttered shut, and she lifted her face closer toward him.

He smiled and reached to cradle her cheek, entranced. Her jaw was soft yet firm, and he felt her tremble as he rubbed his thumb over her cheek. When his lips were but an inch away from hers, he was hit with a sudden bolt of logic.

He yanked his hand back and practically fell into the hallway. "No!" he cried.

She opened her eyes and put her hands to her cheeks, her eyes wide with horror.

"I cannot," William muttered, shoving a hand into his hair as he began to pace up and down, and despising himself for how close he'd come to compromising her. "I *will* not!"

"Oh, vicar," Cecilia cried, recoiling and bumping into the desk chair. "What you must think of me!"

He stopped pacing and braced himself in the doorway. "It is what I – feel for you that is the problem," he said.

She appeared not to have heard, absorbed in her own humiliation. "I apologise; I do know that it is improper for a lady to offer to kiss a man when she is not betrothed. I want you to know I have never kissed anyone else... never even considered it. I hope this does not alter your opinion of me... although I feel it must. Will you tell my parents?"

"Miss Grant, listen to me," William said, advancing into the room, and then thinking better of it. "I do not think less of you. In fact if you must know – and although imprudent, I think you must – I was on the verge of accepting your... generous offer."

It was folly to continue to remain in her presence in the ridiculously small library. But he did not want to tell her to leave without explaining why he must not commit to anything, or anyone.

He took the books from her and led her into the parlour, indicating she sit next to him on the couch. As he spoke, he was careful to keep his eyes away from her.

"Miss Grant, you have already deduced my desire to minister abroad."

She nodded. "That was your intention before you were granted this living, was it not?"

"Yes. The thing is, I still hope for such an assignment. I am merely... biding my time in Amberley. The dean wished me to mature as a priest, and it was generous of the Barringtons to proceed with his recommendation of me, given my lack of experience leading a parish."

At her silence, he careened on, unable to stem the tide of words. "I never wanted this post. I am sensible of my good fortune, but I desired, even expected, an assignment to the new world. Working with those in desperate physical and spiritual need is at the heart of who I am. Settling into a country parish for the rest of my days feels like a life sentence. As soon as I can, I'll convince Dean Roberts to send me away. And although I want to serve the people of Amberley as best I can during my time here, it is impossible for me to form ... attachments. To anyone."

He finally allowed himself to look at her, but only for a moment. Her brow creased as understanding dawned. "But you are not going to stay?"

He shook his head. "I will ensure there is a new priest in place before I depart."

"I see." Cecilia looked away, and catching the movement of her head, William observed her reaction to the news. Her eyelashes batted against her plump cheek, and with a pang of guilt he realised she was trying not to cry.

"I wanted you to know because I do not want you to think I am without feelings for you. Indeed, quite the contrary."

At this her head swung back to him, her shining eyes boring into his.

"But you see, I must not make strong ties of any sort. Not with anybody. As much as I may want to. At some point in the future I will take my leave, and the places I need to go to are no place for an English lady."

"So you wish to warn me off," she said with a smile, even as a lone tear betrayed her. She hastily wiped it away. "And what makes you so sure you will not be staying?"

William stood, going to the fire and grasping the mantelpiece. "The call to serve in a foreign land has been on my heart since I first decided to join the clergy. I cannot give it up."

She nodded. "I understand. Does that mean we cannot be friends?"

Something tightened about his chest. He wanted to know her more than anything. "I hope that we can, so long as it does not interfere with your... future."

"Oh you mean..." Cecilia blushed. "Yes."

"And of course, I am always available as your spiritual leader, while I remain here."

He sat down beside her again, and had taken her hand in his before he knew what he was doing. Her skin was so soft. She looked down at his hand, and he remembered himself, pulling away.

"I hope you can see that if circumstances were different..."

"They are not though, are they?"

He observed his hands. "No. The ministry is the most important thing in my life. It has to be."

There was a period of silence, and then Cecilia rose. "I should go," she said, crossing the room and taking the books from the table.

William walked with her to the door. Before opening it, he said, "Miss Grant, I must ask that you keep this knowledge to yourself. Both the fact that I intend to leave, and... the reasons why I needed to tell you about it."

She turned to face him. "If that is your wish."

He nodded. "I know I can trust you. It is imperative you do not even tell your friend Amy. Perhaps *especially* her."

"All right." Her eyes filled with urgency. "Mr Brook, you shan't tell my father how I have behaved, will you? I am in enough trouble as it is."

He chuckled. "Are you?"

She smiled sheepishly. "Constantly."

He shook his head. "You can be assured of my confidence. But I do not think it is *you* your father would have the quarrel with. I am the one who invited you in here."

They said their goodbyes, and William went back into his parlour, sinking back into the couch with a long exhale and staring up at the ceiling for a long while. It had to be done. He could not keep the facade going, as much as he wanted to. The idea of her belonging to him was intoxicating, but he must not be diverted from his true path. His closed his eyes and recalled the enchanting sight of her face, upturned to him with eyes closed and lips parted. At least he had pulled back before it was too late. Now she could move on with her destined fate, and so could he.

He went to get up, intent on finding something to eat before re-organising his study in order to work on Sunday's sermon. But something caught his eye. One of her long blond hairs weaved its way across his couch in sinuous waves.

Temptation.

In his mind's eye the golden strand became the serpent of wicked seduction. Yes, he felt a strong bond with her, but he would not let such a trifle as emotions come between him and his true mission. Perhaps the enemy had sent her as a deviation, to sway him from his path. But how could one so lovely and innocent be a force for anything but good?

He longed to pick up the strand and twirl it around his fingers, but he resisted. He went to the fire and picked up a pair of tongs. Managing to pick up the hair on his third attempt, he opened the window and hurled it outside. The wind caught the golden sliver and whisked it away in a flash of silky light.

He nodded in satisfaction. *It is for the best.*

Chapter Thirteen

Cecilia hugged the books to her chest as she made her way through the village, completely in her own world. She walked straight past the blacksmith hammering a broken down cart in the middle of the road, she didn't notice the dust falling on her from a carpet being beaten above, and she paid no mind to the greetings of Mrs Croxley and Miss Hicks from the latter's cottage porch. Her mind and her heart were still in Mr Brook's little library. She needed time to process the incredible flurry of emotions she'd experienced today.

They'd been a great team at the class, although she hoped Mr Brook didn't mind that she'd almost hijacked his lesson. Later when she'd stopped to admire the viola, he hadn't shaken his head and moved on, or become annoyed with her (the response she was used to). Instead he had humoured her, indulged her even, and she felt, for possibly the first time, as if someone had wanted an insight into her fancies, and an understanding of the wonders she loved so much. And there was the touch of his hand, his first touch, which was the greatest wonder of all...

Then he'd let her have free rein of his library, of books she would never have had an opportunity to enjoy. Even at Aunt Honoria's, the fine arts were not a priority for the library. He seemed to understand how much the books would help her, and perhaps he could tell how many hours of enjoyment they would bring her.

That was when the trouble had started. She closed her eyes and took a deep breath, remembering his musky scent as he leaned over her to get at the books.

"Watch it, miss!"

Her eyes flew open and she leapt out the way of a farmer boy driving a cart full of carrots. "Sorry!" she called, blinking and shaking her head dazedly.

Moving off to the side of the road, she walked past the shops and her eyes wandered over the window displays, while she recalled the sight of William after she'd bumped into him in the doorway. Her nose had hit his chest, a sensation of stiff linen and much firmer muscle. Then her eyes had met his solid neck, the curves of his shoulders knitting together at its base. A strong chin peppered with stubble was followed by his noble nose, and his amazingly deep brown eyes were topped by thick dark brows. His chestnut-coloured crop of curls framed the visage charmingly. The entire effect was devastatingly attractive to her, and when he'd leaned towards her it had been the most natural thing in the world to close her eyes and reach her lips towards him.

So natural in fact, that she hadn't even realised what she was doing until he pulled away.

Then she'd felt confusion and embarrassment, shocked she'd just offered herself up to a vicar, of all people. Her shame of such wanton behaviour was soon overshadowed by the knowledge of his internal struggle. Yes he cared for her, but he had decided not to form any kind of attachment. Deliberately refraining from feeling was an alien notion to Cecilia. She always followed her heart and her sensibilities. To be sure, she was frequently in her parents' bad books for just that crime, but it was the only way she knew.

Would she have to consciously rein in her innate tendencies in order to attract and keep a husband? The thought sent a chill down her spine as she walked up the lane towards Harcourt Lodge.

Oh William, she thought, *I know you must be true to your calling.* She liked him all the more because of his convictions. She only wished she'd met him when they were older, when he was ready for a wife. But perhaps they would not know each other in that alternate reality. Surely their time was now. Nonetheless she must accept his decision. Her feelings for him were inappropriate... but in the library... it hadn't felt wrong.

No, Cecilia. She would allow herself to grieve his affection briefly, and then focus on the tasks that lay beyond. Perhaps Mr Barrington was to be her mate. She must try to please her parents. Surely if she succeeded in marriage, she would finally be doing something that would make them proud of her. The idea provided a beam of sunlight in her stormy heart.

Later that night, Lucy helped Cecilia change into her nightdress and conduct her toilette. Cecilia bid the maid good night and headed toward the bed. Something on the floor caught her attention. Diverting from her path, she knelt down, and her heart jumped into her throat. It was the little viola William had picked for her that afternoon. It must have fallen out of her pocket as she removed her dress. It was the only floral gift she'd ever been given, and it meant so much more to her than anything expensive she might have hoped to receive in town.

She gently fingered the delicate petals, as if they were somehow tied to the magic of the day. Knowing she should not be sentimental given William's unswerving dedication to bachelorhood, she walked to the window with the intention of throwing it out, into the night. As she pushed the window open, cool damp air hit her face, and her hair streamed out over her shoulders. She closed her eyes for a moment and took in a deep breath, and then she held the flower out over the dark abyss. With a pang, her fingers tightened around the blossom, and she yanked her hand back inside. She felt as if she was about to drop her very heart out of the window.

She couldn't let go, not yet. She closed the window and went to the books William had given her. Turning to the middle of the thicker volume, she laid the flower in the centre of the page and carefully closed the book shut. Her heart, so newly awakened, would need to forget him and seek happiness elsewhere. But if he was only going to be in Amberley for a short duration, surely she could let her tender feelings subside slowly. After all, what if she were never to feel such things for anyone else?

❧❦

William left the house of the widow Kendrick the following day. He'd changed her linen, swept the floors, and fed her a bowl of leek and potato soup. Then he'd tucked a blanket about her on the couch and read some psalms to her.

As he left Mrs Kendrick's cottage and started back towards the vicarage, he could no longer keep Cecilia from his mind.

Her words haunted him. *I have never kissed anyone else.* Yet she had offered her lips up to him. Did her words means she felt such for him as she'd never felt for anyone else? Could it be her heart, which seemed untouchable to the general populace, was under his command?

Why would she choose him? He was certainly not within the scope of her mother's search. Even though he was a gentleman, he could not provide the luxurious life Mrs Grant clearly desired for her daughter, and certainly no title. And surely he was too priggish and dull for such a vivacious and bewitching creature.

But perhaps he'd listened to her, and tried to understand her, and perhaps he'd also betrayed his cursed male frailties and attraction to her beauty. When she'd looked up at him in close quarters in his library, and instinctually closed her eyes, was it his own expression that compelled her to do so? Perhaps he'd reeled her in, only to toss her back. He must be more guarded in his behaviour, to all the ladies in Amberley village.

He barged into his house and into the parlour, falling into an arm chair. He propped his elbows on his knees and buried his face in his palms. For a few moments his thoughts were filled again with the loveliness of her face, and the feel of her skin beneath his fingers, and he found himself imagining the feeling of his lips on hers.

He groaned a little and pushed his fingers into his eyelids, ashamed at himself. He was a man of God. He was above such feelings. Perhaps one day he might yearn for a family and so require a wife, but certainly not yet. Any misplaced feelings he might harbour for Miss Grant would fade soon enough, either naturally or by his leaving.

His thoughts were interrupted by the sounds of his maid arriving and then depositing some supplies in the kitchen. A few moments later she appeared in the parlour with a curtsey. She carried the mail salver and a rag.

William eyed Emma as she carefully polished the tray. *Please no more dinner invitations*, he silently pleaded. To his immense relief, the single item of mail she retrieved from her pocket was from Dean Roberts.

My dear Brook,

Thank you for your letter. I am indeed in good health. St Mary's is certainly quieter during these months, but this is not necessarily a negative.

I am pleased to find you are satisfied with your physical surroundings. I have no doubt you are capable of making any alterations to the house or land as you see fit, in consultation with Lord and Lady Ashworth.

As to your concerns, I am very familiar with the sentiments of resistance and unfamiliarity that new vicars experience. You are not the first, and will not be the last, to have these feelings. You must remember that the villagers have been used to the same vicar for nigh on fifty years. There is a natural period of adjustment. Unless I hear reports of your unsuitability from the parishioners themselves, I will be sure they are merely adjusting in their own way. I have every confidence you will find a balance between their old ways and your improvements.

As to your pleas for a mission abroad, while I am sure you would contribute much to such a project, I am loathe to send one of my most intelligent, capable and caring clergymen off to a foreign country. England needs stewardship as well. I do not wish to imply you will need to serve your whole lifetime in Amberley, as it is likely you will rise through the ranks of the church once you have proven yourself, if you so desire. Perhaps one day you will lead an overseas mission yourself. For now, though, it is my wish that you learn how to manage your own flock, and Amberley seems a perfect proving ground for such a purpose. Here is what I ask William: that you see out a year as vicar of this parish. If you still wish to leave come next August, I will personally recommend you for any project you should choose. I am sure you will agree to such a generous compromise.

Yours,

Etc

William read the note hurriedly, and then a second time, more slowly. Each time his eyes came to rest on those words: "a year". He had been in Amberley but seven weeks, and the dean asked that he endure this fate for another eleven months before he would reconsider. He swallowed the resistance that rose up from his belly. There would be no arguing. He would have to make the best of it and bide his time.

He went to his library and wrote a letter in reply promising to serve faithfully for the full year. *Then I will be free.* He sealed the letter and leaned back in his chair, adjusting to the commitment.

If pressed, he would admit he did enjoy serving the village people, but it was certainly not the kind of challenge he craved. The major problem was how to deal with the ladies who would vie for his hand... and the one he wanted. He must only act with the utmost professionalism. He would treat her with the same detached compassion as every other parishioner.

His feelings were dangerous. His every nerve ending burned with a desire to run before he became irrevocably attached. No good could come of love – it never had. Thomas was but one of a long line of people he'd dared care for, who were either gone or had rejected him. He could not bear one more.

⤜⤏

William was distracted as Emma served him his dinner, only becoming aware of the present when his maid laid out the fifth platter of food. The evening meals had grown increasingly elaborate as the farmers' tithes had continued to restock the vicarage's food stores.

"Really, Emma," he said, "you only need dish up one plate for me. Do not go to all this bother."

Her face fell. "But you're a gentleman, sir, and isn't this how gentlemen like their food served?" Her chin started to wobble.

"Now don't get upset, Emma." He hastily took up a dish of chicken. *Women!* "You can show off your fine skills when I host the parishioners."

She nodded, and after a moment, bobbed a curtsey. "I'll leave you to your supper."

William sighed. The idea of a year of meals alone seemed like punishment. "Will you not join me?"

Emma's mouth dropped open, and a serving spoon clattered to the floor. "But, sir! That would not be proper. I would much rather eat in the kitchen. I – I don't mind."

"I would prefer it if you would sit with me, even if I cannot persuade you to eat. Let us get to know each other a little more." If he was going to have to remain here for now, he might as well find out more about her.

She sat at the far end of the table, perching on the very edge of her chair. "What do you want to know, sir?"

William encouraged her to speak about her family and where she grew up. She began tentatively, but was soon speaking with some animation about her brothers and sisters, and all the various animals the family kept.

"And what sort of things do you like to do on your afternoon off?"

Emma seemed affronted. "Why, I assure you my activities are perfectly legitimate."

William laughed, and then regretted offending her further. This was the problem with females. They were far too sensitive. "I am sure they are," he said gently. "I only wondered at what sort of things you find enjoyable. Do you always visit your mother, or is there a particular activity you like to do?"

"Aye, sir, I like to go fishing with my younger brothers."

Emma did not dare to ask after his pursuits, or seek any other personal information. She knew her place.

William was well aware of class divisions. After all, he had been brought up in a house with a reasonable army of servants. But he had never learned to ignore them or belittle them. Indeed he'd spent more time with the servants at home than with his own family, and since beginning ecclesiastical works he'd interacted with people across the social spectrums. Emma's need to keep the social orders distinct was jarring to say the least. When he finally dismissed her and she bolted from the dining room, he was overpowered by a deep and penetrating loneliness. He would *not* admit to himself the person whose presence he wanted the most.

Chapter Fourteen

Cecilia sat at the table in the Ashworth Hall kitchen, resting her chin on the backs of her hands in a melancholy fashion. "So you see my dear Amy, there is no hope."

Amy appeared to be studying a knot in the table as she considered Cecilia's confession of love and the subsequent rebuff. At length, she spoke, tracing a finger over the knot. "You must realise your good fortune, Cici," she said. She finally lifted her green eyes and regarded her friend with quiet resignation.

This was not the sympathetic response Cecilia had expected. "Oh yes? What fortune is that? To have known what it feels like to love someone, only to be denied of the right to love them?" Her thoughts jumped ahead wildly. "And then to be married off only for material gain, to one who might never love me?"

Amy grasped her arm suddenly. "You are lucky, dearest, so *very* lucky, in that you are free to find a husband. There are those of us who are... beyond notice. Beneath the notice of gentlemen... or at least, I cannot be noticed with a view to matrimony."

Cecilia gasped, her worries immediately shifting from herself to her friend. "What are you saying, Amy? Has one of the staff made advances upon you?"

Amy shook her head and laughed a little, but it was a bitter sound. "No, no. It is not that." She sighed and rose abruptly. "It is only that you must realise you will at least be married, and have a home of your own, and children. It is more than those of my kind can aspire to."

"Oh Amy," Cecilia said, coming to embrace her friend. "I am sorry to have pitied myself so. You are right. I am – fortunate."

Amy pulled back and wiped at her eyes. "Come now," she said, "let us not be gloomy. Catherine does not need me until she dresses for dinner. Shall we go into the garden? There is such an abundance of strawberries I am sure no-one would notice if a few went missing."

The ladies linked arms and strolled to the kitchen gardens. There, the bright red and green of the strawberries soothed Cecilia's mind, and she revelled in the juicy sweetness of the fruit on her tongue.

Amy's censure gave her a new perspective. She would not dwell on what she could not have, instead choosing to focus on what might be. With a new determination, she resolved to make herself forget Mr Brook, and to make a real effort with Mr Barrington – or indeed any other eligible man she may meet in the future. Now she knew the type of feelings love could inspire, she wanted to see if she could discover that with a gentleman who was free to love her in return.

❧

William focussed resolutely on conducting the Sunday service. He would not admit any distractions, and to that end he kept his eyes on his bible or on the back wall. Once the parishioners began to leave he rushed to the door to farewell them. Mr Grant was about to exit, and he shook the man's hand. Looking out to the churchyard, he saw only the backs of Mrs and Miss Grant as they walked up the path.

He frowned, almost forgetting to bid farewell to Mrs Fortescue. A pointed throat-clearing alerted him to the task.

He hadn't wanted to *speak* to Cecilia as such, but he thought he would at least have a chance to see that she was well. After all his fierce determination *not* to gaze upon her, not seeing her at all produced an infuriating disappointment. Had she hastened from the church specifically to avoid him? He chastised himself for his weak emotions as he saw the last of the villagers out. Loosening his cleric's tie, he sighed deeply. *It will get easier in time.*

Two days later, it was time for another lesson with the schoolchildren.

He made the fatal error of heading through the village on his way, becoming waylaid by nigh on a dozen impromptu conversations with all manner of locals. They'd been so shy to start off with, but now he could hardly hush them up. He hurried to the schoolroom, sure he would be late. He didn't want to keep the children waiting, that was all.

All was quiet as he approached. As he reached out to open the school door, it swung out toward him and Cecilia stepped out.

"Oh Mr Brook! There you are." She stared at him wide-eyed for a moment, and then dropped into a little curtsey. "Good afternoon."

He found himself automatically dropping into a bow without the power of rational thought. When her eyes had connected with his, even though it was only for a moment, his heart had spasmed, and the sight of her at close range seemed to set his skin on fire.

He attempted to compose himself, concentrating on the cuff of her sleeve. "Good afternoon, Miss –"

"Your timing is impeccable. We shall not have to share the schoolroom."

"I –"

"The children are waiting. Good day." She pulled the hood of her green cloak up over her hair, though a few tendrils peeped out over her forehead. Giving him a slight nod, she walked past him without another word.

He stared after her, his mouth hanging open. *Is this how it will be from now on?* Her open, charming nature was gone, replaced by a detachment and formality which was surely appropriate, but hugely disconcerting. She was still entirely too captivating, but the convivial spark they'd cultivated had disappeared. Would they not be friends?

Her face, her figure, lingered in his mind. Even though her behaviour was cold, she still had the power to throw him off balance just as if she'd been trying to seduce him.

He gulped and returned his attention to the school as the sounds of idle children escaped into the air. Taking a deep breath, he crossed the threshold to begin the lesson.

❧

Cecilia stared out the window of the carriage as it rattled down the lane away from Harcourt Lodge, her eyes unfocussed and her ears deaf to her parents' chatter. Their destination was a party at the Fortescues, but Cecilia's mind was on a journey of its own.

First she was back in her pew on Sunday, trying her best not to admire Mr Brook's charismatic preaching or his other… gifts. She had begun by keeping her eyes in her lap, but as the service had gone on she had become increasingly bold. First just a few glances, but then as she focused on the words leaving his mouth, the shapes of his lips transfixed her.

Before long she found herself gazing helplessly at his face, after which she lost all self-control and admired his neck, shoulders and arms, even the broad chest she knew lurked within his vestments. Horrified, she clasped her hands tight together for the final prayer and squeezed her eyes shut. Then she bolted from the pew, leading her family from the church before there was any chance of him discovering the dark stain of her cheeks.

It was clear he had come late for his lesson at the school, just so that he wouldn't have to see her for any longer than was necessary. He was deliberately working to untangle their hearts, and she must do the same. She'd become worried at his absence, and had gone to look for him when he'd approached. On seeing that he was fine, and with the realisation that he must be avoiding her, she had fled before she betrayed her true feelings… which as yet, refused to die.

If he is there tonight, I will not speak to him. The silent promise filled her with sadness.

"Did you hear that, Cecilia?"

Cecilia shook her head to clear her thoughts, which also served to make her mother repeat herself.

"Lady Catherine assured me that, although her elder brother is otherwise engaged in Milton, Mr Barrington will accompany his sisters to the party."

"Is that so, Mama?" Cecilia forced her lips to stretch into a smile, and then voiced her resolution. "I hope to get to know him a little better, to discover if we may like each other."

"Indeed; time is running out. We do not know when he will seek out other society. Whether you love him or not, my dear, you *will* make him want you."

A knot tightened in Cecilia's stomach. "I will do my best, Mama." Her voice quivered. "But there is no guarantee he will like me."

"At least we can say we tried."

"*We*, Mama? It is I who has to attempt to woo him."

Mr Grant finally spoke up from across the carriage. "It is for your own good that your mother perseveres with making you a favourable match. You know not how she frets for your future."

Cecilia knew her father would not enter such a conversation unless she had spoken out of turn. She dare not defy him. "Yes, Papa." She pressed her gloved hand to Mrs Grant's arm. "Thank you, Mama."

On their arrival, Cecilia could not wait to escape the confines of the carriage. A spirited group was already in the Fortescue's salon, which was decorated with an array of foliage and flowers, and brightly lit with a multitude of candles. Miss Jones was at the piano, playing a country air, and the sounds of animated conversation issued forth from the small groups assembled.

One of the party broke away from her companions and rushed to Cecilia's side.

"Amy!" Cecilia embraced her. "I am so glad you are here."

Her friend seemed to be glowing. "I did not think I would be able to come, but the Barringtons allowed the upper servants to have the night off. Mrs Fortescue was so kind as to send a carriage for us."

"I wonder what kind of mischief will happen below stairs tonight, without the butler and housekeeper to keep order!" Cecilia giggled.

"Yes," murmured Amy, "the mind boggles."

"Are the Barringtons here?" Cecilia asked, forcing a light tone. She didn't want to be caught off guard.

"Yes, I believe John, Louisa and Catherine are in the next room, playing cards."

Amy's countenance was suddenly sombre. Cecilia regretted reminding her friend of her employers on a night off. "Come, dearest," she said, linking her arm through Amy's. "Let us sit by the window and talk, just as we used to do."

Amy smiled. "Oh yes, do let's."

They weren't seated for five minutes before Mr Barrington entered the room and cleared his throat.

All eyes were instantly upon him. Cecilia held her breath. He was certainly the model of a fine Englishman in his blue coat and shining gold waistcoat. She must not be intimidated.

"We require a fourth for whist. Who will join us?"

His smile was engaging, and when his eyes scanned the room they came to rest on her. She stood, and was about to speak when Mrs Grant approached him.

"Cecilia would love to join you," she said loudly.

Cecilia crossed the room in quick strides, aware of the barely-concealed sniggers in her wake. Why must Mama be so obvious and embarrass her in this way? She attempted to cover her blush with a smile, and said, "I will join the group, if you will have me."

Barrington's dark eyes twinkled. "Of course." He offered his arm, and she let him lead her to the card room, where she exchanged curtsies with his sisters. He led her to a card table, and withdrew a chair for her.

"Shall we be partners?" he asked, taking the seat opposite her.

His crooked smile unsettled her. "Er, yes," she squeaked, "if you like."

Lady Catherine sat next to her with her sister opposite, and Barrington shuffled the pack of cards before dealing cards to each player.

"Hearts are trumps," he said, and when Cecilia met his gaze his expression startled her. His eyes bored into hers, and there was the same opaque sparkle she'd seen at the ball. There was warmth, but also some kind of danger. She wasn't sure if her pulse quickened in fear or excitement, but she had a feeling he was not wholly uninterested in her.

The game began, and the Barringtons chatted idly about their visit to Milton earlier that day. Cecilia continued to feel Mr Barrington's eyes on her as she played, and she tried her best not to blush, contributing to the conversation where she could.

A group of older townspeople entered the room for a game of quadrille, and then –

"What is *he* doing here?"

At Barrington's words, the three ladies cast their eyes to the door. It was Mr Brook. He caught sight of Cecilia and winced. She also started involuntarily as affection for him suddenly blazed through her.

"Come to spy on us, no doubt."

Reminded of her companions, Cecilia turned back to study her cards, a blur of black and red swimming in her tortured mind. Why must he continue to have this effect on her?

Lady Louisa's comment rang in her ears, and she wanted to defend him. She felt herself colouring deeper, and her relief was immense when Lady Catherine spoke up.

"He is part of Amberley society now," she said. "He must be in want of friends."

Out of the corner of her eye, Cecilia saw William cross the room to talk with the elderly players.

"In want is right," Barrington muttered. "He needs to learn a thing or two about minding his manners."

Cecilia's breath caught, and she regarded Barrington in confusion. Whatever could he mean?

He smiled at her. "Miss Grant?"

"Yes?"

"It is your turn." He leaned across the table, his face perilously close to hers. He held her spellbound with his all-consuming gaze, and she could feel his breath on her mouth. Suddenly he reached out and tilted her cards down with his finger, glancing at the hand. "You must play the Jack of Spades, Miss Grant," he said softly, and his expression turned playful, as if he was daring her to do something else entirely. The flames of the candlelight danced in his eyes.

A door slammed, and Cecilia turned to discover William had left the room.

Barrington chuckled and lounged back in his chair. "Now ladies, we may continue unfettered. Catherine, remind us of the scores?"

Cecilia found herself short of breath, and it was several moments before she composed herself enough to lay her card down.

The game continued on without incident. Cecilia did not distinguish herself as a conversationalist, but she did not humiliate herself either. She remained agitated by Barrington's puzzling behaviour. At the conclusion of the game, she returned to the salon with the Barringtons, and procured a glass of ratafia. She fell into easy conversation with the three Misses Stockton, relieved to be devoid of male company for a while.

"Good evening, ladies." Mr Brook appeared behind their little group, and was immediately admitted to the circle by the girls.

Cecilia curtsied but did not echo their return greeting. She did not trust herself to look at him, let alone speak. She did not want to disappoint him by betraying her continued regard.

"Are you all enjoying the party?" William asked.

The Stockton girls began to speak all at once, and Cecilia began to back away, hoping no-one would notice if she slipped away to re-order her thoughts. She edged along the refreshment table away from everyone, pausing at the far corner and turning her back on the crowd. She attempted to still her spinning emotions, gripping the table top with both hands.

"I say, Miss Grant."

Cecilia froze. She knew that voice. Her plan to escape had failed. Did he not realise how he was torturing her? How was she supposed to stop thinking about him when he was always there?

She jumped when something touched her arm, and she looked down to see William's hand there. He removed it hastily. Still regarding her forearm, she barely managed to say, "Yes, Mr Brook?"

He cleared his throat. "I – I do hope our little... incident... will not hinder our... friendship. I would still like to be... of service to you."

Service? What did that mean? As much as she would dearly love to be his friend, she needed some distance in order to control her emotions. Still, he must have felt she was being uncivil, which was certainly not her intention.

"I am much obliged, Mr Brook. I apologise if I have been impolite." She raised her eyes to meet his, willing herself not to flinch as his gaze set her heart to pounding.

⟡⟡⟡

Now William had her attention, he hardly knew what to say. His heart overflowed with all the things he longed to express, if only he would allow himself to love her.

His curiosity was brimming over – did Barrington behave as a gentleman during their game, and did she encourage him? Dressed as she was in a striking scarlet dress which seemed to accentuate the curves of her body to an unfair degree, he was certain she could have any man in the world if she only paid him some attention. He must speak.

"How are you liking the books?" Inwardly he cringed at such a trivial remark, however appropriate it may be.

She smiled, in such a way that her whole being seemed to radiate joy. "Very much, I thank you. I treasure them."

"I am very pleased to hear it." He was even more pleased that an action of his, however small, had made her so happy.

"I shall return them to you as soon as I can."

Her manner was more formal again, although she seemed almost agitated as she appeared to study his waistcoat. Was she angry with him? In refusing her affections, had he made her heart turn bitter toward him?

"No," he said, "please keep them as long as you like. Forever if that pleases you."

"You are very good, sir." She curtseyed quickly, and darted into the hallway.

Sir? His betraying feet took off after her. It was exactly what he had intended, was it not? For a measure of coolness between them, to ensure nothing improper could develop. He was safe now; she would not pursue his friendship any more than she would with any other fellow.

As he quickened his pace and leapt in front of her, he questioned his own sanity. Why was he so desperate to make things right between them... why did he feel an overwhelming sadness at the prospect of losing her friendship? It was only because he was lonely and she shared some of his interests, and he had an altruistic need to help her develop her talents, was it not? Surely it was nothing to do with the way her soft blond curls framed her face, her elegant long limbs, or the sweet mix of confusion and warmth in her expression.

"Is this not what you wanted, Mr Brook?" she whispered. "To prevent any possibility of attachment. I – I am doing my best to abide by your wishes."

The earnest, haunted look in her eyes broke his heart. She was indeed acting on his instructions, and it was certainly for the best. But he could not endure the thought of being in Amberley with Cecilia so near, and to have her be a stranger. "It is my wish that we might learn to be friends," he said carefully. "We cannot avoid each other entirely."

She appeared to consider that, for a seemingly interminable length of time. "Well," she said at last, "friends are honest with each other, are they not?"

He regarded her warily.

"Tell me, Mr Brook, what are you hiding? Is there something you are running from? Why are you so desperate to leave England... to leave Amberley?"

The questions shocked him like a blow to the gut, striking the familiar fear of vulnerability in his heart. His strange physical reaction was to laugh in an attempt to make her words absurd, but the sound was bizarre and choked. "Do not be ridiculous," he sputtered. "What could I possibly be running from? I have – nothing."

At his admission, he hung his head, defeated. Surely she would hear no more. But she did not leave him.

"If I may be so bold," she said gently, "you do have an abundance of talents and kindness, and you could have all the delights this world has to offer... if only you would let yourself." She moved a little closer. "It is my opinion you need not go abroad to give of yourself fully."

He studied her and shook his head. How did she manage to speak words right into his heart? How could he avoid telling her everything, or did he want to? He took a breath. "Miss Grant –"

"I apologise, Mr Brook." She covered her face with her hand for a moment. "I have spoken out of turn. You must find me terribly inappropriate." She stepped back again, and a blush crossed her cheeks. "I am sure you are used to ladies with more studied manners, who remain refined and only speak of the weather."

He was not sure if he was relieved or disappointed to have the subject drop. "No indeed, Miss Grant," he said, noticing how she looked even more beautiful when she was embarrassed. "It is refreshing to find a lady who has the courage to be herself."

Cecilia laughed. "Call it not courage, Mr Brook. I assure you I do not act with any sort of intention. If my behaviour is out of the ordinary for gentlewomen, it is not due to any sort of studied rebellion."

He offered her his arm. "And so it is all the more charming."

As she took his elbow, a weight lifted from his shoulders. They began to walk back down the hallway, toward the sounds of dancing. "My mother despairs I will never find a man who will appreciate my foibles," she said. "She is constantly telling me to keep quiet, to stay at home, and to train my thoughts on domestic matters."

"Think of them not as foibles, Miss Grant," he said, close to her ear. "I believe our unique quirks are to be celebrated, not exorcised."

She turned to him just before they re-entered the salon, and the smile she gave him was one of shared appreciation and understanding.

He smiled back.

Chapter Fifteen

Gunshots pierced the air, and there were shouts of victory as two grouse fell from the sky. William congratulated Mr Morton on his shot once the smoke cleared.

He didn't have the slightest intention of killing anything, but he knew he could not refuse Lord Ashworth's invitation to join the shooting party. The opportunity to further engage with the gentlemen of Amberley also could not be passed up. Not that he wanted to form lasting friendships of course... but it would be nice to have some male company.

He observed the progress of the shoot as the beaters drove out the game. After some time, he found himself near Mr Barrington.

The gentleman took his freshly loaded gun from a gamekeeper, and raised it to his shoulder, squinting down the barrel. "Miss Grant looked frightfully fetching last night, did she not?"

His sudden words made William jump. He'd spent most of the morning attempting *not* to remember the party, or to let the image of her linger in his mind. They hadn't danced together, or even spoken again, but he'd been aware of her presence for the whole night. He'd tried to avoid watching her dance with Barrington, and failed miserably.

He couldn't think of a suitable reply, and when Barrington finally lowered the gun and looked in his direction, he just shrugged.

Barrington grasped him by the shoulder as if they were close friends. "Do not try to tell me you did not notice her, my good man. I am sure every man in the room was taken with her delightful form, and those delicate features. She is at the height of her bloom. I was quite entranced."

"You – you are welcome to her," William stammered, staring resolutely at Barrington's chin.

"Why thank you," Barrington said with a slight bow. "I was not aware I needed your permission to carry on with a local wench."

Carry on? Wench? "You would not dare," William said between clenched teeth, glaring into those maddeningly calm eyes. "You are supposed to marry her, you clod."

As soon as the words left his mouth, he regretted them. The denigrating glare directed at him made it clear he'd overstepped the mark.

"Now now, dear vicar," Barrington chided softly. "Mind how you behave toward your benefactors." He stepped away and gazed out over the fields. "It is quite clear that is what the mother has in mind. 'Tis a pity about her lack of dowry, and her family being too low for mine. I will have choices aplenty in London in the coming seasons."

William let out a relieved breath in spite of himself, which Barrington seemed to pick up on.

"Still," he went on, "if I wanted her desperately I could probably bring Lord and Lady A around."

"And do you?"

"Pardon?"

"Do you *want* her?"

Barrington turned to him and smiled. "I have not yet decided," he said, fiddling idly with his cravat. "Are you quite sure *you* don't?"

William coughed. "What an absurd notion! I have no plans to marry."

Barrington laughed. "Well, we will see what my mother has to say about that!"

There was a flurry of activity as a flock of birds swooped overhead. Barrington immediately fired.

"Well done, sir," the gamekeeper shouted, "you've got her!"

"Right you are," Barrington said, with a quick backward glance at William, "I believe I do."

☙❧

William had a restless night's sleep. He relived their conversation with a sour taste in his mouth, and tension tugging at his heart.

How could he in good conscience encourage the match between Barrington and Miss Grant? When she was such an innocent, and William suspected him of some sort of indecent behaviour? The gentleman's language earlier had certainly not been respectful. Surely William should not stand idly by and let her fall into such a hopeless, and undoubtedly loveless, situation.

But it was none of his business. It was the Grants' decision where their daughter should marry, and if Mrs Grant was successful in her suit who was he to deny Cecilia a life of privilege?

Yet she was one of the souls in his temporary care. And – dash it all – he still cared too much. Enough to wish for her future happiness, for an alliance based on love, even only potential love. He allowed himself to think back to the previous night for the first time. Oh how lovely, and lively she looked. It did his hungry spirit good just to look upon her beauty and purity. He had never known a woman like her, such a wonderfully complex mixture of acuity, creativity and guilelessness. And when she had spoken to him, when those lustrous eyes had shined into his... It was all he could do to restrain himself from kissing her or running from the house. His own mind taunted him with the earlier memory of her lips, raised to meet his.

Then he remembered the devilish gleam in Barrington's eyes when he'd talked of her. There was not a man who sought to discover the intricacies of her mind.

He tossed in his bed. Even if he did seek to prevent the match, how on earth would he go about it? Perhaps he should try to engineer the hopes of another man. Stockton's son had seemed keen at the ball. But manipulating his parishioners was surely a sin. And he could never see her parents agreeing to that in any case.

For a brief moment, his betraying thoughts wondered what they would say if he offered his hand, in order to save her. That would be a noble gesture, would it not? It would have nothing to do with his own selfish emotions. A rush of possibilities flowed through his mind's eye. A ring on her finger, a kiss at the altar, and then...

He bolted upright, sweating.

Dropping his feet over the edge of the bed, he reached for the candle and took it over to the embers in the grate, igniting a small flame. He picked up his bible and settled back into bed.

Temptation be damned. He must devote his thoughts to holier matters, and pray for his future... which was hopefully far, far away from here.

౭∾ᐟ

William's brain was busy as the vestry worked through the items of business at the next meeting. It was his intention to make a list of all the reasons why Miss Grant would not be a suitable wife... if he wanted a wife, which of course, he didn't. Despite his best efforts to conjure up a long list, he could only fix on one possible fault. When he finally embarked on his missions abroad, she would not be of any practical use. She was too much a lady; too delicate. She would probably swoon at the sight of uncultured heathens. If he was to take a wife, her tasks would be infinitely more demanding than teaching drawing or embellishing silly novels for old women.

"Now for the most important item in the agenda."

Mrs Fortescue's pompous tones pierced through William's musings and he sat up straighter, nodding at her seriously.

"The annual village fair. At the meeting before last we agreed on the date, and I am pleased to confirm that all of our regular attractions and merchants have promised their attendance."

There were general noises of approbation from the group.

"Now Mr Brook, you will be judging the cakes."

William's mouth dropped open. "The cakes, Mrs Fortescue? Well, that does sound like an agreeable job, but one I am hopelessly under-qualified to perform. I would hate to wrong the good bakers of Amberley with a faulty opinion."

She stared at him. "Very well," she said, pursing her lips. "You can judge the giant pumpkins perhaps, or the cows?"

Mr Stockton cleared his throat. "Not the cows, Mrs Fortescue. Old Mr Rushby has been judging them for fifteen years. He would be horribly put out."

"Yes, I suppose you are right. How about judging –"

"I do not wish to *judge* anything," William said, not meaning to reveal his exasperation so profoundly. "I want to *do* something."

The other members of the vestry exchanged blank looks.

"Do something, Mr Brook?" Mr Grant enquired.

"Why, yes. Is this not the type of fête with rope walkers, conjurers, musicians and other such amusements?"

"Of course."

"Well, I want to do something more than judge the attempts of others. I wish to contribute in some way."

"What is it you want to do?" Mr Lindsay asked.

William broke into a sheepish smile. "I know not as of yet. I will need to consider it. At the very least I will participate in contests during the fair, be they physical or mental."

Mr Fortescue spoke up uncharacteristically. "Mr Johnson was content to watch from the side-lines, and perhaps award a ribbon or two."

"It would behove you to remember, gentlemen, that I am not Mr Johnson."

⤜⊷⤛

A week later, William spent the afternoon delivering parcels of food to the poorest cottagers in the village. On his way back from his last visit at the farthest cottage on Farmer Russell's land, he heard an ear-splitting masculine scream.

He immediately sprinted off the road, over a low hedge and across a paddock towards the sound. After mounting a stile, he saw a figure at the other end of the field near a cart. And fast approaching from the nearby wood was another person, a woman. As they both hurried to the scene, his heart exploded in his chest as he made out the form of Cecilia – Miss Grant. He thought abstractedly she must have been sketching the lilies by the Russell's pond. His labourer had remarked they were in fine form.

They approached the man, the young Mr Russell, at about the same time. Any embarrassment or awkwardness they may have felt upon meeting vanished instantly. Their tenuous friendship would need to be forged in these unfortunate circumstances.

Henry lay on his back next to a dirt track, writhing in pain. A large cart laden with hay was on the track several feet away with long reins dangling, and there was no sign of a horse.

William dropped to his knees beside the man, and noticed his left shoulder was askew. "What happened?" he asked.

Henry's eyes were wild, and his words were a ragged pant. "There was a fox... spooked my horse. He broke free of the cart... I was thrown... my shoulder... and the wheel ran over my leg..."

Cecilia knelt on the other side of Henry and put her hand on his forehead.

Concerned the man could lash out, and sure she would faint over the sight of his shoulder, William said, "Miss Grant, stay back please."

"Nonsense," she said, a ripple of irritation flitting across her brow. "Where is his injury?" She then took in his other shoulder, and her eyes widened in horror. "Oh, I see..." she said. Her colour paled, and she moved back, but she didn't swoon.

Henry cried out in pain. William's heart wrenched, and he despaired as he realised they were probably half an hour's walk from the nearest house.

"I will try to set his shoulder," he said steadily. "We cannot leave him like this while we fetch the physician."

Cecilia nodded, and trust was implicit in her eyes.

"I have seen it done once. I will need your help. Here, help me remove his jacket and shirt."

Together they slowly completed the agonising process of removing Mr Russell's garments. Cecilia peeled back the arm of his jacket on his good side, and then William slipped it underneath him and down his arm. He ripped the arm off the shirt and down the side seams. Their patient yelled and swore and thrashed on the ground.

The appearance of his dislocated limb made even William queasy, and he marvelled at Cecilia's resolve to stay opposite him. Her hair stuck to nervous sweat on her forehead.

William knew Henry was experiencing the worst kind of pain. "Have you any spirits?" he asked the wretched man.

Henry eyed him warily and jerked his head towards the cart. "Brandy. In my bag."

William looked at Cecilia and she nodded, running over to the cart. She returned a few moments later with the bag, retrieving a flask from one of the exterior pockets.

William took it and unscrewed the top, nudging it to farmer's lips. "Take a few nips," he said. "I shan't condemn you for it under the circumstances."

Henry attempted a smile but then grimaced in pain, and he gulped down three mouthfuls of the brandy before his head fell back to the ground.

"Now I need you to hold him down," he said to Cecilia. "He will want to resist when I try to put the shoulder back in."

She nodded again and braced herself against Henry, pushing one arm down on his good shoulder, and the other across his torso. William rolled Henry over a little. Then he grabbed his neck with one hand and the dangling arm in the other, and heaved with all his might, first out and then over into the joint.

Henry screamed and then went limp, unconscious with the pain. William panicked, and for a moment he forgot about the shoulder as he stared at the man's eyes rolling back in his head. Then he looked down and saw that the shoulder was in its rightful place, and the chest still rising and falling, and he let out a huge breath.

"He is not dying, is he?" Cecilia cried.

William had momentarily forgotten she was there. "No, he is not. But I think we should try to wake him. Can you fetch some water from the stream down there? Perhaps there is a bucket in the cart."

He sat back on his heels for a moment after she left, his blood still pumping madly with the effort of putting Henry's shoulder back in place. Then he took the farmer's jacket and laid it across his chest and torso.

Cecilia came back up towards him, heaving a full bucket as she half-ran along. William was suddenly remorseful for having her undertake the physical job. He rushed to take the pail from her, and they came back to kneel beside Henry together. Cecilia moved around to sit behind the man, taking his head carefully in her lap. William soaked Henry's shirtsleeve in the water and handed it to her, and she bathed his face with it.

At first there were no signs of life, but soon Henry's eyes began to flicker, and he began to focus on her face.

"That's better," murmured William. "Now, about this leg."

Henry's left trouser leg was now soaked in blood, and William tore it apart to expose the wound. The flesh was horribly crushed just below the knee and bleeding profusely. He heard Cecilia gasp.

"We need to bind the wound," William said, immediately throwing off his jacket and pulling his shirt from his breeches.

"No," Cecilia said, "use my petticoat. It is much easier to tear several lengths of fabric." Without delay, she gently manoeuvred Henry's head onto the ground, and then hoisted her skirt enough to expose the white undergarment. She began to rip at it feebly with shaking fingers.

"Allow me, please," said William. "If you don't mind, it will be easier if you remove it."

She nodded and stood, and he turned his back. In only a few moments he felt a tap on his shoulder, and he turned to find her handing him the garment.

He ripped the fabric vigorously, tearing four lengths. Before he'd finished, she was already carefully winding the first around the wound. He knelt beside their patient again as he became more cognisant, and gave him some more brandy.

Blood soaked through the bandages but Cecilia kept working, occasionally swiping the hair out of her eyes. She knotted up the fourth layer and sat back on her heels. She looked out over the fields then at Henry. "Where is your horse now?" she asked him.

Henry pointed weakly to his left. "Ran off over that hill."

As William followed the direction indicated, his heart began to pound for a new reason. Since falling off a horse as a boy, he had suffered from a debilitating fear of them. He'd always managed to find some excuse to avoid going on hunts, and he'd limited his travel to where coaches and chaises could take him. The thought of taming a spooked horse sent terror shooting through his veins.

"Do you want me to look for it?" Cecilia's voice broke through his private horror, and he met her earnest eyes. She would willingly do it, and she would probably do a better job. But he could not be responsible for her being kicked, trodden on or worse. And he was sure Henry would prefer to have her nursing him.

"No, I will go," he said, though he remained on the ground for a few moments longer. He forced his legs to straighten. "If we can get the horse tethered again, we can drive him to Mr Lindsay's house."

He set off at a jog across the fields, looking back once to see Cecilia mopping Henry's brow. She'd make a fine nurse. He wouldn't wish such a fate on her though – she was far too gentle and innocent.

Once he'd ascended to the ridge of the hill, he saw a horse some hundred yards away, grazing in a field with its reins trailing in the grass behind it. He slowed to a walk and approached the animal carefully.

The horse looked up and tossed its head with a soft neigh.

"Hello there," William said, ashamed at the tremor in his voice. "Your master needs you – please be co-operative."

He stepped within a foot of the animal, and his tyrannical memories came flooding back. He'd been riding back home just before a storm. A sharp crack of lightning had spooked the horse, and it reared up, violently tossing William to the ground. Then it had stamped about, slamming a hoof into his ribs before galloping off home.

The worst bit was the length of time he waited for someone to come looking for him. He would have thought a groom would raise the alarm on the return of his mount, but William had lain in pain for some time before he mustered the strength to stumble home in the smothering darkness and rain. Each harried step brought home his isolation, despair and loneliness. They didn't even miss him; they didn't care at all.

He found himself fingering the scars along his ribs as he remembered. A quiet whinny from the horse brought him back to the present. *I will not let my family triumph over me*, he told himself. *I can master this fear.*

He extended trembling fingers toward the horse's nose. It didn't look as if it would bite him, but its eyes watched his every movement. At last the tips of his fingers grazed its nose, and the horse shook its head a little. William drew his hand back in a flash. He took a deep breath. *I must do this. Poor Russell might bleed to death.*

He touched the horse's head again, gently stroking him repeatedly. This time the horse didn't move; it only blinked a couple of times.

"There, now," William said in a low voice. He brought his other hand up and placed it on the horse's neck, and when that was successful he moved around to the side of the animal. He stooped for a moment to pick the reins up off the ground, and eyed the horse's bare back. There was no way he was going to get up there without a saddle, so leading the horse back would have to do. He pulled the reins up over the horse's head, and yanked on them tentatively.

The horse whinnied, tossed its head and stamped a foot.

"Now, come on," William coaxed. "I must take you back to your master." He pulled more firmly on the reins, and the horse reared up, kicking out. As the hooves flailed near to his face, he froze in horror as all the fear stored up since his childhood came back to consume him.

Chapter Sixteen

Cecilia scooped some water up from the bucket and let it trickle into Henry's waiting mouth. "There you are."

He swallowed and licked his lips.

"More?"

He shook his head and croaked, "Thank you."

She smiled, covering the queasiness and panic that had held her captive ever since she had come on the scene. Where was Mr Brook? Surely the horse had not gone far? She glanced at the wound on Henry's leg. The blood had now soaked all the way through the top bandages and there was a growing pool of crimson in the grass. The cloth seemed useless, and her patient was surely growing paler by the minute. What could she do to help him? She contemplated leaving him to summon help, but she clung to faith in William's return.

When Henry began to drift in and out of consciousness, she rose, determined to find someone. She turned toward the rippling grasses one more time, and huge relief washed over her as a figure appeared. It was indeed William, leading the wayward horse behind him.

Seeing her, he waved and quickened his pace. When he at last was at her side, she just barely resisted the urge to throw her arms around him and sob.

"You are back," were the foolish words to escape her mouth.

He nodded and smiled weakly, and she noticed he was even more

137

drenched in sweat. He must have had to run after the beast.

"How is he?" he asked quietly.

She shook her head and shrugged helplessly.

"We must make haste."

She helped him re-tether the horse, and he instructed her to take Henry's legs above the knee, while he lifted the man up under his shoulders.

He met her eyes as they crouched. "One... two... three!" The last word was stifled in the effort of lifting Henry. They quickly transported him to the cart, and William hoisted him on in one last burst of strength. The injured man cried out on the impact.

"Sorry old chap," William said, "but we have to get you some proper help."

Cecilia went back for the bucket and Henry's clothes, placing them in the cart.

"Will you ride with us?"

She whirled around to face William, who had one foot up on the cart. The walk was not too long for her to accomplish on her own. She walked several times further on most days. But truth be told, her knees were wobbling and every part of her ached. She doubted she could make it to the edge of the paddock without collapsing. She nodded her exhausted head.

William mounted the cart and reached across to help her up. Even through the despair and worry, the feel of his hands around hers was startling, then comforting. He lifted her onto the seat as if she weighed nothing, catching her upper arms to steady her before they sat down side by side in one motion. There was only an inch between them, and his leg brushed against hers as he leaned forward to take up the reins.

She shivered, praying he didn't notice. Suddenly the trials of the past hour were not the cause of her faint head.

❧❧

William was careful not to drive too fast back to the village. Despite the desperate need to get Henry Russell to the physician, he feared aggravating the man's injuries should they fly over any bumps in the road.

He focussed on the task at hand, and they drove in silence. He glanced over his shoulder, but the hay on the cart obscured his view of Henry. He prayed fervently for the man's survival.

A sound beside him broke into his prayers. Realising Cecilia had sniffed, he turned to her and saw tear-streaked cheeks. He took in her blood-stained dress, clinging to her legs. She was visibly shaking. He paused for a moment, weighing up propriety with the need to comfort her, and then put his arm around her.

"Thank you for your assistance," he said huskily. "I do not know how I would have managed without you."

She managed a shaky smile. "We are a good team, I think," she said.

"Indeed," he said, and he gave her shoulder a gentle squeeze.

"I only hope we are not too late, and that poor Mr Russell will not be permanently disfigured." She sighed heavily, and he was all too aware of her warmth as she leaned into him.

William cleared his throat. "I will set you down at the lane to your house," he said. "No doubt your mother is expecting you."

"No doubt," she replied with a weary nod. "But is there anything else I can do to help?"

"Thank you but no. My main concern is finding Mr Lindsay at home."

"Do not worry – I believe he is attending sessions at home every afternoon this week."

They reached the lane which led to Harcourt Lodge, and William pulled the horse up. He jumped down to offer a hand to Cecilia. To his cursed delight, she offered both, and he slipped his own under her arms to lift her to the ground. When she landed, they were inches apart. It was as if he was locked into her eyes, which appeared fatigued yet resolutely beautiful.

Henry moaned.

"I must hurry," he murmured, stepping back to let her pass and pushing his fingers through his hair.

"Yes," she said, and she hurried down the lane as he mounted the cart.

☙❧

Cecilia closed the main door as quietly as she could, listening for the sounds of her family. She could hear her mother's voice in the drawing room, and she crept quietly past. The door to her father's study was closed, and she hoped he was safely inside.

When she was almost at the stairs, a door behind her opened.

"There you are, Cecilia!" Mrs Grant called. "This is the third time this week you've almost missed dinner. What do you have to say for yourself?"

Cecilia turned slowly around, knowing she must look a fright.

Indeed, Mrs Grant covered a gasp with her hand.

"What is that on your dress? And where is your *petticoat*?"

"Gone," Cecilia said simply. She looked down at her dress and noticed the blood stains for the first time.

"What –"

"Mama, I am too tired to explain everything to you at present. Rest assured my virtue remains intact. Now if you will excuse me, I will bathe."

Cecilia was thoroughly exhausted by the time she was finally cleaned off and in bed, asking Lucy to bring her a simple dinner in her room. But she felt a very gratifying satisfaction in helping Henry Russell, and also in being useful to Mr Brook. She remembered how decisive and brave he was, and she sighed. She touched her shoulder where his hand had been as he'd held her on the cart. She'd felt protected, safe, at home. As long as she was with him, no harm could come to her. Never mind the fact that he had lifted her as if she were as light as a feather.

She could esteem him from afar and he wouldn't know just how much she admired his heroism. She told a wide-eyed Lucy the story, leaving out the part about their cosy cart ride, and the maid promised to make enquiries the following day after Mr Russell's health.

❧

In the morning William knocked at Mr Lindsay's door, intent on the same mission. He'd been in the house for three hours the previous day: helping shift Mr Russell, praying as the physician examined him, and worrying as the man drifted in and out of consciousness. Finally after night had fallen he'd been ushered from the house, assured he could be of no further use.

"Henry survived the night, and he took breakfast this morning," the physician told him as they passed through the vestibule. "I am fairly sure he will pull through. Let us see if he is awake."

He led William into the now familiar bedroom where the patient resided. Henry Russell was indeed awake, his eyes hungrily observing them as they entered the room.

"And how is my patient?" William asked with a chuckle.

To his surprise, Henry reached out his good arm and took William's hand in a firm grip. "I am in your debt, Brook. Lindsay says my leg was only just saved. Without it, God knows I'd be useless as a farmer. You have only to name your price, and I will do anything to pay it."

William waved the suggestion away with a dismissive hand. "Nonsense. Any other man would have performed the same service." There was no way he would have confided how much effort the rescue had in fact cost him – conquering his fear of horses, and causing Miss Grant grief and immodesty.

"You must let me do something as a way of thanks," Henry insisted.

William smiled. "Fine, then. You may buy me a pint at the public house."

"Agreed." Henry grinned. "And if anyone in the village says a bad word against you they will have to answer to me."

Now that William could be sure Henry would survive intact, his mind was free to contemplate other matters. In the ensuing days, he focussed on *not* thinking of how brave and useful Cecilia was, the girl who everyone thought was a peculiar lightweight. He must *not* think about lifting her in his arms – twice – and the feeling of her slight, soft yet firm body under his hands. And he especially wouldn't think about how he could see right through her petticoat-less dress while they drove Henry to the village, and the perfection of her long shapely limbs barely inches from his own.

Dash it all. She'd been calm, practical, caring, and efficient. In short, absolutely terrific. Now what possible excuse could he come up with, in order not to fall desperately in love with her? Her beauty was mesmerising, her intelligence unique and intriguing, her compassion admirable and her wit captivating. It was as if she had been designed deliberately as the perfect trap to ensnare his heart. How was he to resist, and strike off into the world alone as he'd always intended?

As these thoughts tortured him, he tossed an apple back and forth between his hands. Suddenly, he knew what he would do at the fête. Perhaps Henry could assist him after all. But first he would need to pay a visit to Mr Jones' shop.

Chapter Seventeen

True to his word, Henry Russell was a strong ally from that point forward. He seemed to have spread his own version of the gospel – the doctrine of Brook the Brave. William noticed a definite increase in respect from most corners of the village. He began to execute his regular duties with a new enthusiasm, sensing the past feelings of resentment towards him falling away.

On a stormy day a week after the accident, William sprinted home through the rain. He ran up to his bedroom and peeled off his sodden jacket, before stripping off the soggy shirt. He was about to unbutton his breeches when the door burst open.

Emma sailed over the threshold, humming a country air.

"Oh Emma, I say –"

At the sound of his words, her eyes flew to him, then grew as round as saucers, and her mouth fell open. "Oh, Mr Brook!" Collecting herself, she threw her gaze heavenward. "I'm terribly sorry. I thought you were out on your visits."

William laughed softly, even as colour crept up his chest. "It is quite all right, Emma. I was caught in a sudden downpour and had to return home to change. Are those for me?"

Emma glanced down at the pile of freshly starched, ironed and folded shirts she held to her bosom. "Oh yes!" She held them out to him, and when she saw his bare torso again she reached new heights of crimson, her eyes finding the ceiling once more. "Here you are, sir."

William took the shirts and set them on the corner of the bed. "Just when I needed a new shirt. You are a treasure, Emma, always anticipating my needs."

"Th - thank you, sir. I'll be off, sir." She curtsied three times as she backed out of the room.

William shook out one of the shirts and held his breath for a moment, until he was sure the door was firmly closed. Then he let himself laugh for a few moments, before wincing as he put on the shirt. It was starched far too stiffly for his liking, and it felt more like leather than linen on his bare skin. Still, he didn't have the heart to criticise her. He'd certainly injured her maidenly sensibilities. He wondered if she would be able to look him in the eye for the rest of the week.

She seemed to have recovered her dignity two days later, when she encountered her master in the hallway shortly after a knock at the front door. As had become an all too frequent ritual, they bumped into each other as he exited his library.

"Really, Mr Brook, you must let me answer the door," she said with an air of vexation. "A gentleman does not greet his own visitors."

William raised an eyebrow and his mouth quirked. "I apologise, Emma. It shan't happen again." He gestured toward the door. "Do proceed."

The maid turned on her heel with her nose in the air and marched down to open the door. Before opening it, she hissed, "Go and sit in the parlour!"

William started. "Yes, madam," he murmured, before following her instructions.

Shortly thereafter, Emma announced Mr Jones. The gentleman hurried into the room carrying a large parcel, clearly very pleased with himself.

"Do you have them already, Mr Jones?" William asked after shaking his hand. "That was very speedy."

"I managed to source them in Shrewsbury, sir. They came with my weekly supplies today." He passed the package to William. "Thought I'd better deliver them myself, Mr Brook, seeing as you wanted to keep it secret-like."

"Thank you, Mr Jones," William said with an ironic smile, "I appreciate your discretion." He didn't voice his opinion that the spectacle of Mr Jones walking through the village to his door with a large parcel would undoubtedly provoke suspicion.

He fixed the shopkeeper with a firm stare. "Now, I trust I can count on you to keep this to yourself?"

Mr Jones sat up straighter and offered his lopsided smile. "Certainly, certainly."

William waited until the shopkeeper was well gone. Then he tucked the package under his arm and headed out the back door towards the Russell's farm.

Practising his skill for the fête was a welcome change of focus over the next several days. Of course, he was not intending to impress anyone in particular. Not at all. In fact he didn't really understand why he felt so compelled to make an impression at the harvest fair. He only had to endure nine more months in Amberley, and soon they'd have forgotten all about him.

He paused in his practice to consider that thought. How soon it would be before it was as if he never came? An inexplicable sadness washed across his heart. Perhaps they would remember his performance at the fête – and that must be why he wanted to do a good job. He wondered where he would be in a year's time, and the old excitement about adventure abroad bubbled up inside him, chasing away any melancholy.

☙❧

As the rustle of autumn leaves filled the air, so anticipation and excitement about the harvest fair crackled on the wind in Amberley. The day of the fête arrived at last, and the village bustled as the main street crowded with arrivals from near and far.

The village was too small to support a regiment of militia, but some soldiers from Milton came to Amberley for the day, and their redcoats were a sight to behold. Various merchants and performers installed themselves in the traditional fields on the Ashworth estate, and soon the usual quiet country meadows thronged with eager crowds. Excepting weekly church services, the fair was the only time when all social classes were free to mingle, and when all servants were at liberty to join the revelry.

It was a night of freedom for one and all, where, especially once the Barringtons took themselves off home for the evening, everyone could do as they pleased, and associate with whomever they liked.

Cecilia strolled among friends and neighbours in a dress the colour of sunshine, a matching ribbon threaded through her hair. She found Amy, and together they sampled cakes, browsed crafts, laughed at the puppet show and gasped over the high-rope walker. They rounded a corner and there was William, bended on one knee to pin a blue ribbon to the chest of a little boy, who held the prize-winning lamb tethered on a rope. The child beamed proudly, and William ruffled the boy's curly locks as he stood. Amy pulled Cecilia towards the exhibits of giant vegetables before they were noticed.

Much hilarity ensued when the ladies tied their legs together and attempted to run in the three-legged race. All eyes were then on the men of the village as they engaged in a tug-of-war. Cecilia tried not to be obvious as she admired William's strength and tenacity. His face contorted as he pulled on the rope, and the muscles in his neck flexed. Indeed, his thighs bulged in his breeches. She fanned herself with one hand and tore her eyes away.

She sighed. This was how it had been since Henry's accident. They maintained a comfortable distance. While they may observe each other, they had not talked. It was just as well.

As the sun dropped to the horizon, country string music filled the air. Amy and Cecilia purchased pies for supper, and sat on a hay bale together as rows of lanterns were lit around the fields.

"Look," said Cecilia, pointing, "the Barringtons are leaving."

Their departure signalled the start of the real party. Amy said nothing, but they both watched as Lord and Lady Ashworth made their way toward the carriages, with Viscount Marsham and the two misses Barrington in tow.

"Except where is Mr..." Amy began. "Mr B–"

All at once a gentleman appeared before them.

"Mr Barrington!" Amy said in an odd high-pitched voice.

Both ladies rose, and Barrington reached for Cecilia's hand, aiding her to a standing position in a fluid motion. The action accentuated his tall, strong frame, and the fading light cast deep shadows across his sculpted features.

"Miss Grant," he said, his eyes not leaving her face, and his deep tones travelling across the thin night air. "How lovely you look this evening."

"You are on your way home, I presume," Cecilia said evenly. She was determined not to make herself a fool in his company again.

Barrington smiled. "I could not leave without a dance with the most beautiful lady at the fair."

She smiled and blushed as was no doubt expected, but his compliments were so regular as to no longer provoke her to giggles. She thought she heard some sort of squeak from Amy and turned to her friend.

"Will you join the dance, Amy?"

Amy did not speak, giving only the barest shake of her head. "I find myself uncommonly fatigued," she said. "Please go on and I will – I will watch."

Cecilia smiled at her and then at Barrington, indicating he could lead her to the assembling dancers. The dance was an energetic reel and did not leave much leisure for talking. Part way through, she glimpsed her mother, grinning from the side lines. Barrington reached for her hands, and laughed as he twirled her around. She smiled back, glad to be pleasing him.

At the conclusion of the dance, Barrington placed Cecilia's hand in the crook of his elbow and led her away.

As they left the crowd and headed into the descending night, she grew uneasy. "I would rather not go any further, if you do not mind," she said.

If anyone found them alone in the dark, her reputation would be in tatters. But Mr Barrington would surely not compromise himself either, and be forced to enter into marriage against his will.

"I only want to speak with you away from the noise," he said lightly, as if she were a fool to be concerned.

Cecilia glanced at the trees they were moving towards. Their limbs swayed in the evening breeze, and the moonlight cast strange shadows on the ground. The sound of a bizarre laughter reached her ears, as if ghouls were lurking in the shadows.

A peculiar coldness enveloped her, and the hard glare in Barrington's eyes did nothing to soothe her. When they were quite alone, he finally stopped pulling her along and turned to face her. She removed her hand from his arm, but he took it and raised it to his lips.

"You seemed to enjoy yourself at the fair today," he said with a smile.

She nodded, unable to speak, her hand still in his.

"Do you know, Miss Grant, Cecilia, there is quite another sort of fun to be had." He drew her closer, and ran his other hand up the back of her arm. His fingers traced across her shoulder before coming to rest at the base of her neck.

She shivered. "I – I am sure I do not know what you mean."

He stepped closer and locked her gaze in his, and she sucked in a breath as her heart began to pound wildly. "Yes perhaps you do not, but I will show you. You are sure to like it."

He let go of her hand and seized her waist, pulling her to him so that they were pressed together. His body was as hard and unyielding as stone, and panic pulsed through her. He grasped the back of her head and pulled it back, and then his dark eyes descended toward her.

"No Mr Barrington, I will not!" She yanked free of his grip, and jumped back, stumbling in the dewy grass.

Barrington chuckled, a low, chilling sound. "Very well, Miss Grant, I meant no harm. I shall leave you to the fête, and I will return to the hall with my family."

The mildness of his tone made her feel an idiot for protesting so vehemently. Was there any chance he was in love with her, and merely wanted a little affection before declaring himself?

He must have only meant that they should get to know each other a little better, away from the crowds where they might be disturbed. She had been foolish and may have lost her only chance at forming a bond with him. She only wished his embrace had felt more natural, instead of inciting a desperate panic. Perhaps she would learn to like it in time.

"Goodnight, Mr Barrington," she blurted out as he turned to leave.

He stopped, turned back, and touched the brim of his hat in a slow, deliberate motion. The moon illuminated a sheen in his eyes, a raw flash of something primal she had never seen the like of.

Chapter Eighteen

From his position at the hay wain amongst the farmers, William had been all too aware of Cecilia's dance with Barrington, and their subsequent hasty stroll from view. He began to walk in that direction, a sense of foreboding pulsing through his body. At the sound of a raised female voice, he began to run into the darkness. If Barrington hurt her, he would not be responsible for his actions.

He stopped and scanned the pastures, an eerie jumble of light and shadow. How far had the blackguard taken her? He could hear some sort of movement in a nearby tree, and headed in that direction. Frantic with worry, he took a breath to call her name.

He bumped into something, and when it omitted a cry he realised it was some*one*. "Cecilia?"

Her translucent eyes shone into his, filling with tears.

"Oh, it *is* you! Thank the Lord!"

She did not seem to be in a state of disarray, but she clung to his shoulders as if her life depended on it. "Mr Brook, how glad I am to see you," she said, the words flying out of her mouth in a torrent.

Before he knew what he was doing he had an arm about her waist, supporting her. "Miss Grant," he said softly, urgently. "Are you quite all right?" He cupped her cheek with his other hand, and then stroked her hair, desperate to soothe her.

She took a few shuddering breaths. "Yes, I am... f-fine."

He pulled back, searching her face. "Are you quite sure?"

At the sound of galloping hooves, they both looked toward the ridgeline. The silhouette of Barrington riding from the fête was clear against the rising moon.

"Yes, quite sure," Cecilia said. "Thank you, Mr Brook." The tremor in her voice betrayed her, but in her eyes he could not see any sign of harm. She was shaken, but not traumatised. He was only glad he had not waited any longer before coming in search of her.

Suddenly aware that he was also guilty of keeping her alone in the darkness, he took her hand and squeezed it, before looping it around his arm. It was an action that was becoming all too frequent, and all too pleasurable.

"Shall I escort you back to your friends?" he said.

"Yes – that is, I would not dream of detaining you from... wherever it was you were going."

He only shook his head in reply, leading her back to the party, past a growing pile of old timber being prepared for a bonfire. He procured her a mug of cider in order to calm her nerves, taking one for himself as an afterthought.

The band struck up a new tune, and he tried not to notice the way her hips pulsed to the rhythm. It was time to leave her.

"If you are no longer in need of my services..."

She turned to him with a smile. "Do you know this song, Mr Brook?"

The melody emanating from the violin was vaguely familiar. He shrugged.

She reached for his hand. "You look as though you need to dance."

"Pardon?" She was already dragging him towards the crush of revellers. His hand broke free but he stumbled after her anyway. Surely one little dance couldn't hurt.

They fell into step with the other dancers: the ladies in a circle facing out towards the men. Cecilia grinned at him as they started to dance, and her joy was contagious. Any trace of anxiety she may have endured recently had gone. It was as if the sparkle of her spirit lifted his own. He couldn't remember the last time he had done something purely for the pleasure of it.

They linked arms and skipped in a circle, their eyes never leaving each other. He really was quite giddy, and perhaps not only as a result of the cider or the many times he'd spun around. He lost all sensation of his body, not knowing if he danced the correct steps or kept in time with the rhythm. All he knew was her.

When the dance was over, he turned away. His face on fire, he ran a hand through his hair and stalked away. He would leave her to continue in the revelry. He must take some time to regain control of his senses.

He took solace in a tree across the field, with lanterns strung in the boughs. He sat on a low branch and leaned against the trunk, gasping for air. He was crossing some sort of line, he was sure of it. He must stop his feelings from spiralling out of control... mustn't he?

"Mr Brook, are you unwell?"

William removed the hand in which he'd buried his face, and saw the object of his consternation standing in front of him, the lantern-light dancing across her delicate features.

"I am sorry to disturb you," she said timidly. "I only wondered if you need some assistance."

He stifled a bitter laugh, which sounded like a cough. "I am well, I assure you."

He eyed her warily as she perched on the edge of the branch. "You seem troubled. You must miss the guidance of your parents? Your father?"

He should have resented the intrusion, both of her physical presence and the personal nature of her questions. But her expression was so gentle and concerned, and he could not bring himself to send her away. She was the only woman in his life, next to his mother, who had ever tried to get beneath his carefully-maintained façade, and certainly the only one he had ever been tempted to let in.

"I never really knew them, Miss Grant," he began, holding onto the sympathy and strength in her eyes. His heart constricted painfully as he ventured into territory buried deep in his soul. "My mother became sickly after giving birth to me, and died when I was four." His voice broke. "My father followed two years later."

She gasped. "How dreadful," she whispered.

"With twelve years between me and my next brother, I was always treated as a misfit, an outcast. I never felt comfortable at home with my brothers; not one of the family. I took any excuse to get away.

"The church became my home. The rector took me under his wing when I was a boy... he found me hiding in the churchyard. I helped him with jobs around the chapel, and then later I began to accompany him on visits tending to the poor. I never imagined doing anything else with my life."

Cecilia nodded, tears in her eyes.

"So you see, the only constant father I have had in my life is God in heaven. I was even restless in London... I would roam the streets at night, searching for heathens to convert." He studied his hands, now vulnerable and afraid. Perhaps she would quietly leave him alone with his wretchedness.

Her hand covered his own, her fingers curling around his. Her touch warmed him from the inside out. "The fleeting nature of your work seems to lend an odd sort of security," she said. "Being confined in Amberley would make you feel entrapped. Could it be you avoid any lasting connections, because the pain of losing people is too great?"

Her discovery alarmed him, and his eyes flew to hers. In them he found only understanding, not judgement. He swallowed back a tide of emotion, and nodded.

She tightened her grip on his hand and gave him a tender smile. Then she turned to watch the lighting of the bonfire. He followed her gaze, drinking in her company.

The weightiness of the moment passed, and his heart began to beat steadily again.

"Are you always so serious, Mr Brook?" He jumped at her abrupt words, and was surprised to see a smile dancing on her lips. Her tone was not patronising or accusing, merely curious.

He shrugged. "The world is a serious place."

"Why yes," she said, "but there is also so much joy and beauty to be found if you look for it."

He considered that, and frowned. "I suppose I always look for the needy and the darkness of the world."

"In order to bring hope and healing."

He smiled. "Yes... or that is my intention, at least."

"I am sure you do more good than you know."

"Thank you, but I must tell you my help is not always welcome."

She was silent for a moment, then leaned toward him suddenly, her face alight with apparent inspiration. Her heavenly aroma teased his nostrils. "Have you been to the ruined abbey in Hartman's Valley?"

He looked at her askance and shook his head.

"I shall take you there tomorrow."

He attempted to pull away from her, but he was already up against the tree trunk. "Uh..."

"Meet me near the Stocktons' old granary at three o'clock. Will you have the afternoon free?"

He nodded helplessly.

"Then it is settled." She beamed. "You shan't feel trapped there."

"Ah, there you are, Brook."

William started. Henry Russell stood before them. He jerked his hand away from Cecilia's.

"The dancing's over," Henry said. "Are you ready?"

William jumped to his feet. "Certainly. Excuse me, Miss Grant." He dared not look at her again.

A new kind of nerves skipped in his stomach as he made his way back through the crowd. He took his place in front of the assembled masses, who were now highly spirited and eyeing him with a mix of anticipation and suspicion.

He took a deep breath, and turned to Henry. They exchanged a nod, and Henry passed him a red ball, followed by a yellow one. William caught them both in his right hand, and a third green ball in his left. He began to juggle the balls, and the crowded cheered.

Once he was in a regular rhythm, he began to incorporate the variations and tricks he'd learned, to more applause. Miraculously, he did not drop the balls. Henry threw him a fourth ball, then a fifth. William began to sweat with the intense concentration.

When at last he ceased the motion of the balls, the crowd clapped. "Thank you," he said, "but the show is not over!"

Henry had stolen away, and he reappeared with three torches, freshly lit from the bonfire. He threw one toward William, and there was a communal gasp. William caught it carefully, to loud cheers, and then received the other two. The applause continued to grow as he juggled the torches, throwing them alternately high in the air.

For his final trick, he threw two of the torches up, and spun in a circle before catching them. He kneeled before the crowd brandishing all three, triumphant. As a rousing cheer rose up, he surveyed the faces of the villagers, many of whom he now counted as friends. They looked surprised and impressed, just as he'd wanted. And he knew that he cared more than he should about winning their approbation.

An enormous boom sounded, and an explosion of colour illuminated the sky. William threw his torches on the bonfire, and then joined the throng watching the fireworks.

Something compelled him to gaze out across the sea of faces, and his reward was the sight of Cecilia, who met his glance and grinned at him. As the painted lights radiated in her eyes, he felt closer to her than ever. His heart was bursting just like the firecrackers. He couldn't be sure, but a new kind of exhilaration seemed to be winning out over panic.

❦

When Cecilia was finally left alone, she collapsed into bed with the exhaustion of an imprisoned mind. She didn't want to talk any more of Mr Barrington, although her mother had grilled her for word-by-word details of the evening. She didn't want to praise the Barrington girls' gowns, or comment on how well Mary Stockton was turning out. And she especially didn't want to imagine her life away from her friends and family, even if it did mean a house of her own and seasons in London.

All she wanted to think of was William. There was only William, and she was quite sure there only ever would be. She was consumed totally by him in his presence, and now she longed to be consumed once more.

With the realisation that she had her eyes squeezed shut and was gripping her pillow with both hands, she rolled over onto her back and let out a huge sigh. The rushing of the wind through the trees outside echoed her restlessness. She stared up at the ceiling, at the dark beams, and felt as if they were only inches above her head, oppressing her.

Reliving the terror of Barrington's embrace, then the relief of William's, she was torn between an alliance she was obligated to seek, and a true love she could not have. She might be able to have one man, while desperately craving the other.

William thought himself safe from her affections, and it was in that security that he had unburdened himself, shared some of his secrets. She must not scare him away. She could not allow him to suspect that, rather than dissipating, her feelings for him had only blossomed. He trusted that she would not ask for any more of him than he was willing to give, and he'd made it clear he was not able to give his heart.

She *was* falling for him... no, she already had. She ached to be with him, with every fibre of her being. And while she knew she couldn't have him, she would enjoy being with him while she could, even though he would not know of her true desires. For all she knew, it might be her only chance to know such depth of emotion.

She believed he had fostered a romantic attachment for her once – or at least that he'd been tempted to care. His experience had probably taught him to suppress any sort of feeling he didn't want. He was surely biding his time before he could be free of Amberley, and free of them all.

He would go soon, and she would marry Barrington or another such gentleman. It was his destiny to seek other paths, and he'd made it clear she was to play no part in it.

But always she would hold him in her heart, remembering him as the one man above all others in her eyes, the only one who truly understood her heart and mind. She would cherish her love for him as a comfort for the lonely times ahead.

At least she would have loved deeply, absolutely, and she would carry that passion throughout her life to her grave. Her only fear was that she would betray herself before he took his leave from Amberley, and he would feel something like pity for her. No, she must be friendly enough to keep him near, but she must not be tempted into revealing the fond longings of her heart. He must leave with a clear conscience.

She rolled over and hugged her pillow. Her blood pulsed with the excitement of meeting him tomorrow, alone. She would take him to her special place. She hoped he would understand its significance; the hold it had on her heart. And perhaps it would give him mental relief from all the worries he held on his shoulders. She knew he cared so deeply about everyone he met, and she wished she could share the burden. If only he would let her in.

She tossed the other way. It wasn't to be. Maybe he wouldn't even meet her tomorrow. He would probably forget all about her and their outing. He would have more important things to do; more important people to visit. She screwed her eyes shut again, squeezing out tears. After sobbing for half an hour, sheer physical and emotional exhaustion pulled sleep over her like a veil.

Chapter Nineteen

William rose early, and set about polishing the morning's sermon. Attendance of the church service was sparse, as he'd anticipated: many of Amberley's residents had over-indulged at the fête. His eyes were now used to slipping quickly past the Grants' pew, and this morning was no exception. However, as he manned the door to bid the parishioners farewell, he and Cecilia shared a brief smile. As their eyes met he was sure there was a new spark of closeness, understanding, and of anticipation. As quick as the moment began, it was over and she was gone.

Sunday lunch was generally spent with a parish family, and this week he visited with the Mortons. The banker and his wife welcomed him warmly, but he was too agitated to savour the spread they had prepared, and too preoccupied to linger over conversations afterwards.

He found his way to the meeting place fifteen minutes early, trying not to rush but unable to stop his tumbling feet from racing to the spot. He'd been careful to be sure no-one had seen him leave the fringes of the village. As he waited for Cecilia, he picked up one leaf at a time, absent-mindedly tearing them to shreds.

The appointed hour came and went, but the lady did not appear. William's anticipation turned to worry. He was reminded of Cecilia's flighty nature. She was often in a world of her own, paying no heed to the expectations of the world. She may have forgotten all about their appointment. Excitement became annoyance; curiosity dissolved into frustration.

He was aware that patience was not one of his virtues. While he displayed remarkable compassion and tolerance with those in need, when he wanted something to happen for himself, he wanted it *now*. He knew not how to calm himself. It was dashed inconsiderate, that's what it was. Couldn't she respect that he had other things to do with his time? The world didn't revolve around her.

He tried to ignore the hurt simmering beneath his anger. She did not care enough about him to remember her invitation. He was a fool to think she could still have feelings for him. She'd probably long since moved on from her fancy. Why on earth could he not move on?

What was he even doing here, engaging in a clandestine meeting with a young single lady? If anyone saw, would both their reputations not be in tatters? He panicked, and took several steps back in the direction he'd come from. Could the fallout end not only his career, but his chances at any respectable living in the future? He'd do anything to avoid having to depend on his brother for money.

His mind in a whirl, he paced about nervously. He wanted to be free of all this confusion. He must arrange a meeting with Lord Ashworth and tactfully resign his position. He checked his fob watch; twenty past the hour. He told himself she wasn't coming, and while trying to suppress the ridiculous feelings of pain and disappointment, he decided to go directly to Ashworth Hall.

He took one step forward, and then froze. Blond curls rose up over the crest of the hill, and he held his breath as Cecilia's beautiful face appeared. When she saw him her lips stretched into a wide smile, and she waved. He admired the long slim arm extending from her shawl, her hand gloveless. Her lithe figure swayed smoothly in a deep burgundy dress as she rushed towards him. William forced himself to breathe, but the sight of her approaching – glowing, eager, lovely – dissolved all irritation. How lucky he was to be in her presence.

She stopped a few feet in front of him, breathing hard. "I am sorry, Will – Mr Brook. I know I must be late. I do not know the exact time, but I was detained at home. My mother insisted I finish my work before I could leave the house." She reached a tentative hand towards his sleeve, and then withdrew it hastily. "I do hope you are not mad with me."

"Of course not," he said gruffly. "I only hope the abbey is not too far away that we shall have to give it up for today."

Concern flitted across her features. "It is not above a half hour's walk away," she said. "I should still like to go, if you are willing."

He was more than willing. He swallowed his enthusiasm. "Let us go," he said.

Cecilia indicated the direction, and they walked side by side. As usual, she observed the world around her keenly, and for once, he took the time to do the same.

It was a soft day, as the Irish would say. The clouds hung low in the sky, caressing the tops of the surrounding hills, but the first rain had not yet fallen. The misty covering seemed to blanket them, furthering the illusion that they were the only two people in the vicinity, or at least the only two that mattered. They walked along an old farm track, beneath a stand of elms which were turning shades of burnished gold. Climbing a ridgeline, they descended into a valley, following a deserted riverbank along for a mile or so. The wind rustled through sporadic stands of weeping willows, their leafy limbs stroking the rocky riverbed.

William looked about, still paranoid prying eyes would condemn their secret excursion. There were a few small cottages clinging to the sides of the hills, but he couldn't see anyone around. He turned to regard his companion, and any trepidation fled, replaced with joy and excitement. Wasn't she teaching him to make the most of every moment? Well by heaven he would.

At the end of the valley, they rounded the base of a hill, and then cut through a field which rose to a crest. At the top of the small ascent, Cecilia said, "There," then she began to run down the slope.

William gazed out over a plain, surrounded by rolling hills, with a small village nestled at the far end. Off to the east, there lay the ruins of a large abbey. A large central chamber, missing its roof, formed the main building. A cloister sprang out from one side of the nave, and a tower, missing one of its walls, stood at the near end. The structure was positioned on a point formed by a river's bend, with a grove of mature trees standing in a horse-shoe around it. As he watched Cecilia half-run, half-skip towards it, a ray of sunshine pierced the clouds, illuminating her claret-coloured dress, and prompting him to chase after her.

He sprinted down through the dense grass, disturbing butterflies, bees and flies as he went. He caught up with Cecilia just as she was slowing, about a dozen yards from the abbey.

She turned to him at the sound of his approach, and came to a halt. "Is it not magnificent?" she breathed.

As William pulled his eyes from her flushed cheeks and sparkling eyes back to the building, he had to agree. It was enormous, and splendid in its decay. The base of the structure had been seized by tall clumps of grass, and a tangle of ivy wound around the tower. Moss claimed a good deal of the other walls. William began to walk around to the south side of the abbey, stepping tentatively into the cloister. He gazed up at the soaring arches, some crumbling.

Cecilia passed by him. "There is a magical air about this place," she said, "which I can never quite capture with my paint brush or pencil."

For a moment, William was overcome with grief for the way of life that was destroyed here. The sins of two and a half centuries before would have everlasting repercussions. He wondered at what sort of people lived here, how they saw their calling, and how they served the Lord from this place.

When he entered the voluminous nave, Cecilia was already there, staring through the empty shells of a huge stained glass window at the western end. The design was set into an arch shape, with a large circular window in a rose pattern at the top. On either side below were two smaller roses, and elaborate curves formed into seven tall windows at the bottom. The sun broke through the clouds above them, and shafts of light speared through the holes, streaming through the air towards them.

Cecilia closed her eyes and spoke without turning to him. "Imagine the whole space filled with glittering coloured lights," she said. "Can you see it?"

William drew near her and also turned his face into the rays, closing his eyes. At first, just the glow of the sunbeams pierced through his eyelids. But then, something warm touched his hand. He nearly jumped a mile when he realised it was Cecilia. She gently wrapped her fingers around his, and her soft warmth radiated up his arm and into his heart. Suddenly the world inside his mind filled with a dazzling array of colours, as he imagined the light striking through brightly stained glass, with hundreds of hues shimmering through the hall and shooting up into the sky.

"I can see it!" he whispered.

He rubbed his fingers over her hand, and her eyes opened, meeting his. Their bright blue radiance outshone even his vision of the window.

She smiled, and he realised he was already smiling, too. "Thank you," he said.

She squeezed his hand. "I can always find peace here," she said. "More than anywhere else." She turned towards the rear of the building, pulling him with her. "Come, let us ascend the tower."

As they passed through a doorway by the vestibule, their hands naturally broke apart. William followed Cecilia to a flight of stairs inside the tower. They began climbing within walls, but were soon exposed to the outside each time they wound around the north side of the tower.

"Be careful!" he called, as he peered over the perilous precipice. He had not the head for heights.

She laughed without looking back. "Have no fear, Mr Brook, only a gale could knock me off."

They reached the top, and he joined her at the one remaining wall fully intact. His eyes followed the lines of the ivy climbing up the others. The bright verdant leaves and vines seemed to be holding up the piles of stone as they rose toward the sky. Then he took in the lady next to him as she stood gazing out over the view, inhaling deeply as her hair waved freely back from her head in the wind.

"Do you often come up here?" he asked, as he willed himself to look out over the edge.

She nodded. "During the warmer months, I come every few weeks. When I need to clear my head."

His own head grew hazy. "I have to say it worries me, the thought of you scampering about here. You could so easily fall."

Cecilia laid a hand on his forearm. "Your concern is touching but unnecessary, or at least futile." She flashed him a sheepish smile, and then gasped. "Look!" she cried, pointing.

William forced his eyes out over the landscape, and immediately saw her object. A huge rainbow arced across the sky, originating from within the bosom of a curling grey cloud, and stretching across the ether before pouring into a deep green meadow. The sun shone on the other side.

"It connects the light and the dark, do you see?"

"Yes," he said, comprehending more than she knew. He continued to admire the ribbon of luminosity, when out of the corner of his eye he caught a flash of burgundy. He spun around to see her escaping down the stairwell. "Cecilia – Miss Grant!"

Swallowing the fear that she – or he – would topple off the edge, he started after her, keeping his eyes on each successive step. He heard her laughter echoing throughout the nave as he landed in the vestibule. Now on solid ground, his competitive instincts took over and he ran into the building.

In the main chamber, she was nowhere to be found. His eyes darted to the cloisters, and he caught a glimpse of her shawl. "Aha, I've got you!" he called, chasing after it. But when he got there, she was gone again. Another betraying giggle rang out, echoing around the stone at first, and then dying away on the wind. He ran around to the far end of the abbey. He couldn't see her, but at last spied a small empty doorway leading back inside to a tiny chapel. He ducked in and finally had her in his sights.

"Miss Grant, whatever are you playing at?" he panted.

She backed up against the wall, also out of breath, and said nothing, though her wicked grin glowed in the dim light.

William advanced on her slowly, only stopping a few inches away. "Well, I have caught you, fair and square, my little sprite." He laid his hand on the wall just above her head, blocking her escape with his arm and body.

Her grin turned into a quivering smile. "So you have," she said. "Alas, I have no prize to give you."

"You," he breathed, "are the prize." Her delectable scent enveloped him, her eyes drawing him in. Almost without power to control his actions, he moved in closer still and dropped his head towards hers.

"Why Mr Brook," she said softly, "I do believe there is a sentimental spirit in you after all." She held his eyes until they were almost nose to nose, and then she blinked hard for a moment, before suddenly ducking under his arm and fleeing from the building.

William's head crashed against the wall, but he didn't feel pain, only a restless, burning, exciting hunger for her. Recovering, he ran outside and saw her disappearing into the trees. It was a compulsion he could no longer deny, and any sense of propriety flew out of his mind.

He found her leaning back against the trunk of a tree near the bend in the river, gazing out over the tumbling water. When she saw him, her smile was timid, and he was suddenly tentative, his swift pace dropping to hesitant steps. If he dared cross the boundaries of their friendship, what would lie beyond? Would he destroy everything they'd cultivated? Perhaps her running from him was a message that whatever romantic feelings she had felt two months ago had been fleeting, and she had long since began to fall for her intended husband.

He stopped several feet from her, all boldness lost. "I – I am sorry Miss Grant, for being so close to you just now. I must have made you terribly uncomfortable."

She turned clouded eyes upon him. "Not uncomfortable, Mr Brook. I am quite at ease around you. Too much so, I fear." She looked away again, her eyes following the curve of the river.

He took a few steps nearer. Did he dare hope she meant she still cared? "I do not wish to make you afraid," he said.

"Do not misunderstand me – I want to abide by your wishes... to be sensible... which is not my natural inclination, as you must know."

They shared a smile, and he drew nearer still, to within a foot of her. How ironic that he had instructed her to curb her emotions, but he was the one out of control. Her efforts on his behalf made his soul ache.

I can no longer be sensible. The sun was now full upon them, and as the sound of the river flooded his ears, his emotions finally rushed from his heart to the surface.

"Miss Grant, I will be frank." His pulse quickened as the words tumbled forth. "I cannot seem to drive you from my mind. I long to spend time with you. Selfishly, I need you. My world is a brighter place with you in it."

Her eyes misted over, and her silence was enough encouragement for him to go on.

"I know you are intended for someone else, and I would not presume to offer for you against your parents' wishes."

"And what of your own wishes, Mr Brook?" she asked softly. "Your desire to go off and conquer the world, unhindered by a wife?"

William swallowed. How well she knew him. "I cannot deny that I still harbour the ambition to minister abroad. But the urgent fervour I once felt has been… overtaken, by compassion for the people of Amberley… and my love for you."

Immediately Cecilia's dewy eyes overflowed into tears. "How I have longed for you to say those words," she said. "I convinced myself I could keep my heart safe, but I lost it to you long ago."

William choked on his emotion, worried his wildly beating heart might explode. *She loves me!*

His voice broke as he said, "Then I am the most fortunate man in the world." He fought to restrain himself from pulling her into an embrace and smothering her with kisses. As it was he stepped to within a few inches of her, grinning down at her enchanting countenance and wishing he were able to express all of the feelings within him. He reached for her hand, but at the same moment she used it to wipe away her tears.

She took a steadying breath. "Well, you can have me, Mr Brook," she said, and a mischievous sparkle lit her eyes, "if you can catch me."

He laughed as she darted away into the trees. And she said she had not the talent for flirting. He shook his head and started after her, following the burgundy of her dress, the chase only serving to further ignite his passion. Seeing her intended direction, he sprinted around to the other side of an oak tree, just as she was attempting to exit that way. His boot caught the edge of her shoe, and she cried out as she lost her balance, falling.

William broke her fall just inches from the ground, his arm whipping around her waist and the other cradling her head. They crashed into the grass together, the long lush blades cushioning them like a thick green mattress.

In the seconds while they recovered, William was only aware of the feel of her in his hands: the small shapely waist and soft silky curls. Cecilia's eyes flickered open, and they stared at each other for a long moment. Adoration shone from her crystal clear eyes, and he made no attempt to hide his regard for her.

Her lips were parted and she took in short, shallow breaths. As he absorbed every exquisite arc of her face, they curved into a tiny, sweet smile. He let his head fall slowly towards hers, moving his hand from behind her head, to cradle her jaw.

As his lips touched hers, he gave in, body and soul. His world did revolve around her and he couldn't deny it any more. His other hand tightened about her waist as she responded with gentle, delicious pressure, her fingertips weaving through his hair. She was so innocently ardent, and he kissed her with tender passion, savouring her softness and sweet taste. She met a profound and urgent need deep within him, which he hadn't even known existed. His fierce independence had simply been misplaced. He needed her to be whole now, and together they could take on the world.

He lost himself in her, for what length of time he could not say. He only knew he loved her, and she wanted him too. When a cool breeze came to them, her hair tickled his cheek, and some idea of what he was doing entered his mind.

He made himself pull back, still holding her. He felt what he had done was right in his heart, but he knew it was far beyond the bounds of respectability. If anyone saw them, she would be ruined. He should be more responsible. Even though he knew it would go no further, he had already taken advantage of her naivety. "I'm sorry!" he whispered, stroking the side of her cheek.

"I'm not," she breathed, nuzzling into his hand.

He shook his head in wonderment. "I surrender. I cannot resist you any longer. If I need to remain in Amberley in order to be with you, so be it."

Chapter Twenty

Cecilia had spent so long dwelling within her imagination: wanting, dreaming, willing this moment to happen. Now that she was here with him, living it, she wondered if it were really true. It was too fantastic, too wonderful, too perfect. A less optimistic person would already be looking for what could go wrong, but she only wanted to dwell in this moment forever. She smiled up at William as he held her, completely relaxed in the carpet of grass and warmed by the autumn sun. He understood her, and he wanted her just as she was. There would be no gift sweeter for the rest of her life.

William sat up and ran a hand through his hair, his words still hanging on the breeze. *I surrender.*

Cecilia hadn't replied yet, but she hoped her kisses and smiles spoke the volumes she was feeling.

He glanced back down at her, the wrinkle on his brow telling her he was back in realist mode. "I will try not to manhandle you again," he said bashfully, "until everything is official between us."

She laughed. "I am not very good at discouraging you, either."

His eyes darkened with intensity and he pulled her up to sit opposite him. "I would go to the ends of the earth for you, Cecilia, but only if you desire it." He gazed through the trees. "And if your father is willing, and your mother agreeable. And if I can manage the finances so that..."

"Hush." She put a hand over his mouth for a moment, silencing him.

How his cares tore at her heart. He was such a practical, worrisome man, who always needed to have plans in place and all his ducks in a row. He breathed out, and she spoke, needing to soothe his anxieties. "I am willing. I am *wanting*. That is all that matters. Everything will fall into place, sooner or later. You shall see." She gave him an encouraging smile, and soon the creases on his brow relaxed.

He leaned in and took her in his arms, the affection in his eyes sending sparks through her. "See, this is why I need you, my dear. How can I fret and fluster when you are near to bring me back to earth? No, to heaven." He tipped up her jaw, and touched his lips to hers with slow deliberation.

She shivered in ecstasy, and he drew back just as slowly.

He smiled and drew her to her feet. "Now, my love, I think we had best be getting back."

A shadow fell on them, and Cecilia looked up to see grey clouds racing overhead. She was happy to let William take her hand and loop it through his arm. In her heart the small symbol of possession illustrated how she would soon belong wholly to him.

They began the walk across the meadows and up the hill. Cecilia did not feel the ground beneath her feet. She waltzed on a cloud of happiness, only aware of William, nothing but him. Her usual observation of colour, light and movement was dulled to obscurity, as every sense was overtaken by her love for him, her desire to drink in his face, his words, his touch, his smell, his kiss.

She was suddenly shy, feeling too much to look him in the eye. She fingered her lips, remembering his touch, and the strength and tenderness of his arms encircling her. A blush set her cheeks on fire.

He handed her over a stile, and they walked on a narrow path by the river for a while, single file. When they were again side by side, at first he did not give her his arm. Instead their hands hung by their sides inches apart. Cecilia could sense where his hand was without looking, and she fought the temptation to grab it, even though she desperately wanted to. She didn't want him to think she was a wanton hussy.

After a few minutes the backs of their knuckles brushed together, as lightly as the touch of a feather. Her skin tingled all over. On the next gait, his fingers caressed hers, just for an instant. Delight rippled over her body. Then, finally, he intertwined his index and middle finger with hers, before taking her hand in a certain grasp. Heat flooded her senses. She took a gasp of air, realising she'd been holding her breath, and squeezed his hand back. They were connected; whole.

Once their world was united, the world around them came back to her in an explosion of shades and sounds. Light flooded her eyes, and she was drawn to the robin chirping above them with all his might, then the auburn shades of the leaves as they floated to the ground.

She looked over at William to find his eyes already on her.

"You are so beautiful," he said. "I cannot quite believe you want to be mine."

"Believe it," she said, taking in his exquisite chocolate-brown eyes, finely chiselled features and masses of curly hair. "I am quite overpowered by my attraction to you. If you'll recall my scandalous behaviour previously you will surmise I always was."

He chuckled. "Well, I do want you to think seriously about marriage, to be sure I can make you happy. It is for the rest of your life, and I would not want you to enter into it unless you are absolutely sure no other man will do."

She gave an exasperated sigh. "Mr Brook, do stop trying to talk me out of it. I have never felt even a trace of love for any other man."

He did not speak for a moment, and a glance at his features revealed a stain on his cheeks and a sparkle in his eyes. "Well," he said softly, "I dare not issue an official proposal until we have your family's consent."

A slight uneasiness settled over Cecilia's heart. As far as her parents were concerned, she was wooing Mr Barrington in earnest. "I will speak to my mother first," she said, "to soften her to the idea. It may take a little persuasion but I am sure they will come around."

William nodded. "For my part, I will see Mr Morton at the counting house and begin to put my affairs in order. I fear my finances are not such that your parents will approve. I may need to convince my brother Charles to grant me a portion, so that I may evidence I can keep you in the style you deserve."

His brow furrowed again. She ran her hand over it as if to paint over his cares. "Do not fret, my love. I have a feeling everything will be all right in the end."

He smiled. "Yes, as a man of God I should have more faith, should I not?"

"At least, less worry."

William came to a stop. "I think it best we part here," he said, turning to face her. "Dearest, if it were up to me, I would marry you tomorrow. I only need a little time to prove my prospects. I cannot rush the most important undertaking of my life." He raised her hand and examined it, as if it was a priceless treasure. He turned it over, then trailed his own fingers lightly from her wrist, into the soft valley of her palm, and then along her slim fingers.

His touch sent a thousand shivers shooting through her body. She reached up with the other hand and pushed her fingers through the dark curls by his temple. As she stroked his cheekbone he closed his eyes briefly, and sighed as she travelled over his jaw.

He smiled at her and held her eyes as he took her hand to his lips and gently pressed them to it just above her knuckles. "Goodbye, Cecilia," he said.

The sound of her Christian name was another thrill.

"Goodbye, William," she replied. "I pray it will not be long until I share your other name."

꙳❦ᕽ

William made his way to the counting house the following morning. He explained his intentions to Mr Morton, and asked after what funds he had in reserve in the accounts he'd transferred from London. He'd never been one to track every penny, always quick to give anything he had to those less fortunate. But surely there would be something remaining of the allowance previously granted to him by his brother.

Mr Morton's eyeglasses slid down his nose as he inspected the papers in front of him.

William held his breath and leaned forward, trying to read the columns of numbers. He knew his annual stipend would be enough to cover a family's bare essentials, but given what he knew of the Grants, he would need to prove he had an alternate source of income. Carefully managed, a small fund could provide enough interest to allow for the occasional luxury.

Finally, Mr Morton looked up, and pushed his glasses back up. He sighed, and shook his head. "I am afraid, Mr Brook, you arrived in Amberley with savings of only ten pounds."

William started. "Ten pounds?"

Mr Morton nodded. "It seems your travelling expenses consumed a fair amount of your brother's last deposit."

"I see." William swallowed and sat back in his chair. It was worse than he thought. If ever something happened to him which meant he could no longer perform his duties, he would have no funds to fall back on. He could not ask for Cecilia's hand without some sort of security; it was not fair to her. The very idea of asking Charles for money made his skin crawl. But he would do it, if it meant proving his worth to the Grants and securing the hand of his beloved.

"Er, thank you, Mr Morton," he said. He rose from his chair.

The portly gentleman cleared his throat. "Mrs Morton and I are driving to Milton this afternoon, Brook. Might you like to accompany us?"

William smiled, attempting to conceal the extent of his enthusiasm. "Why yes, that would be a welcome change. And do you know, I do have a little money saved at home. I know just what I would like to spend it on."

Chapter Twenty-One

Cecilia kept the happy news to herself for two days, residing in a parallel world of bliss. She hummed to herself as she went about her daily duties, she covered canvasses in bright colours, and her cheekbones began to ache with smiling. Lucy began to look at her strangely, and she knew she could not live in the land of infinite possibilities forever. She must work to bring her plans to fruition.

She chose her moment with care, deciding to broach the subject subtly with her mother, and hoping her father would be steered by her.

Her heart pounded hard against her ribcage as she held a shaking needle against her embroidered handkerchief. For some reason she could not tell Mrs Grant how strong her feelings were. Her instinct told her that her mother may deny her requests only because she had decided on this course of action on her own, rather than being prompted to by her parent. She figured that if Mrs Grant could only come to the conclusion herself, the road would be that much easier. She cleared her throat.

"What do you think of Mr Brook, Mama?"

Mrs Grant paused in her own work for a moment, and glanced up with a quirked eyebrow. "Think of him, Cecilia?"

"Only I wondered if, as the son of a high-born gentleman and as a man with a secure living, he may be considered a fine husband."

Mrs Grant put her work to one side and removed her spectacles, levelling a stare at her daughter. "That is what I had suspected you meant.

And if you will speak so frankly, I will return the favour. He is unsuitable."

Cecilia lost any thought of nonchalance. "But why?" she cried. "Name me one reason why he is not a good choice. It cannot be because he is a younger son."

"He is without any hope of a title, my dear. Even if Mr Barrington is not the heir at present, he may outlive his brother and you would be a countess."

"Can you please forget about Mr Barrington for one minute?"

"Cecilia, lower your tone. The servants will hear."

"I am sorry," she whispered, trying to suppress tears.

"Do I need to remind you of your faithful promise to try with Barrington?"

Cecilia shook her head. "I only thought..." She sighed. "Surely Mama, if I will be settled in a degree of comfort and be happy, that is the most important thing."

Mrs Grant was silent.

"You *do* wish to see me happy?" Cecilia asked incredulously.

"Love is but one ingredient of happiness," her mother said slowly. "I wish to ensure your long-term happiness by focussing on the parts of married life you are overlooking."

"Do you mean wealth and status? Mama, you know very well I have never cared for those things."

"He has no carriages, Cecilia, not even horses. No staff to speak of, only a maid-of-all-work. No opportunity to travel to London or elsewhere. I acknowledge we are not part of the *ton*, but can you not see that this would make you lower?"

Cecilia crossed her arms. "I care not."

Mrs Grant harrumphed, taking only a few moments to regroup. "Do you really think you can carry on as you are? You will have responsibilities as a wife no matter the choice of your partner. But only think of the freedom you would have as an aristocratic wife. Married to Mr Brook, who knows the manner of manual tasks you may have to undertake. You may not even have time for your art. And tell me, who will pay for your paints if you are a vicar's wife?"

"Mama, I believe Mr Brook is not destitute. He will show you how he intends to provide for me and" – she swallowed a lump in her throat – "a family."

Mrs Grant shook her head. "The subject is closed. I will not hear of you marrying anyone else until Mr Barrington is engaged elsewhere."

"No!" Cecilia could not understand her mother's obstinacy. "Mama, why are you so decidedly against my marrying for love? Marrying a perfectly upstanding citizen, a gentleman, who will love me devotedly and provide me a home in Amberley?"

Mrs Grant set her mouth in a straight line. "Cecilia, you have always been too sentimental, and too short-sighted. This is your one chance to try for a life of prestige and ease. You are at present not the best judge of how to secure your future wellbeing."

"I believe my heart is the best judge."

Mrs Grant looked away for a moment, and then renewed fire sparked her eyes when she turned back. "You would not have the funds for a nursemaid. What will you do when you have children? You cannot possibly manage on your own."

"There are many mothers in Amberley who survive perfectly well without *any* maids, Mama."

"But they are not *ladies*, Cecilia. We must keep up particular standards."

"I am sure my friends would help me. I would have hoped *you* would help me."

Mrs Grant also crossed her arms. "Well, what about everything else you would be giving up?"

Cecilia sighed loudly. "Such as?"

"A house in London, fully staffed. A fleet of carriages suitable for any conditions. The opportunity to go to the theatre, the park, to balls, and be assured that you are rubbing shoulders with the best of Society."

"Mama, I have never had these things. I do not think I should miss them."

"But I –" Mrs Grant clamped her hand over her mouth, her eyes wide.

Suddenly realisation dawned. "But *you* miss them, don't you Mama?"

For a moment, Mrs Grant couldn't speak. Then she sputtered, "How dare you?" and turned her back to her daughter.

"You grew up with those things," Cecilia said, as her understanding awakened. "And the title – you are jealous of Aunt Honoria, are you not?"

There were several strained moments of silence, and then Mrs Grant took a deep breath and met her daughter's eyes.

"Do you not see, Cecilia?" she asked softly. "I married your father for love, and look what it got me: a life of seclusion in this backwater. Meanwhile, Honoria married her viscount and is constantly writing to me of all her triumphs and gay pastimes. Even my substantial dowry was not enough to sustain a life of reasonable leisure. Your father and I outstripped our income in our early years, with only a few seasons in London after marriage before we had to scale back. I only wanted the comforts I had enjoyed as a girl. But even those were soon beyond my reach..."

Her words dissolved into the air, and she gazed out the window, lost in her melancholy.

Her revelations caused Cecilia's mind to spin. Mrs Grant had never talked in this way.

For her entire life, she had genuinely believed that her mother had her best interests at heart, motivated by a parent's unselfish love. She had trusted her completely to guide her life decisions and behaviour. While sometimes Cecilia's lackadaisical actions seemed in opposition to Mrs Grant's designs for her, she had never intentionally disobeyed her.

But now she knew she could no longer rely on her mother's plans. She must think, and act, for herself.

Mrs Grant finally broke the silence. "I will say this, Cecilia. I am sure Mr Grant will hear whatever Mr Brook has to say, but the vicar will need to have a very strong suit indeed if we are to even consider it. In the meantime, you will not set foot outside this house without a chaperone."

☙❧

True to her word, Mrs Grant watched her daughter like a hawk, monitoring her every movement. She invented all manner of tasks to keep Cecilia indoors, and her cause was helped by several days of rain. Though the family did venture forth for church, they left swiftly at the end of the service, only exchanging brief greetings in the churchyard with their closest acquaintances before rushing home. A morning visit to the

Fortescues was the only other sanctioned activity.

Cecilia was nearly driven mad in yearning to meet with William. She dreamed of his kiss, and replayed his wondrous declaration of love over in her mind a hundred times. Being able to see him during church, and yet not being able to speak to him, had been the sweetest torture of her life.

All her hopes of being able to converse with him lay on the next lesson at the school, two days later. Mrs Grant had agreed she should go for charity's sake, but Lucy was commanded to never leave her side.

As her mother dithered with a list of items for them to purchase from Jones' on their return, Cecilia paced the room anxiously.

"Please Mama, may I go now? I will be late for the children."

Mrs Grant folded the list in half and creased the fold with deliberation before handing it to Lucy. "Did you finish writing to your aunt?" she asked Cecilia.

"Yes!"

"Very well, off you go. Do not be late home."

"No, Mama." Cecilia grabbed Lucy and flew from the house.

☙❧

William snatched up the paper from his desk and crushed it in his hand, before tossing it in the fire. He buried his face in his hands and moaned. He'd attempted several drafts of a letter to Charles, but he had not found a way to beg for money tactfully. It was a wretched business.

He checked the hour, and jumped up with a start. He must hurry if he was to reach the schoolhouse in time to attend Cecilia's art lesson. He reached for his bible, and then ran to his room to retrieve his coat and a package from his bureau. He only hoped her lesson had not been reassigned to a different day or time.

He trudged through the damp autumn earth. Chances were that Charles might refuse his request, or grant him some minuscule token. His future happiness depended on the result of the exchange.

Perhaps he would wait to see the outcome of Cecilia's talk with her parents. The road ahead may be smoother than he imagined. His mind filled with images of his beloved, and his steps became that much lighter.

When he'd seen Cecilia from the pulpit, his heart had jumped into his mouth, and it had taken all his strength not to run to her. He'd had to avoid gawking at her, afraid he would be tempted to announce his intentions to the entire congregation right there and then.

Though he'd dwelled in the meadows behind the vicarage, and spent an inordinate amount of time strolling by the river, their paths had not crossed. How he longed to gaze into her eyes and take her in his arms, to gain assurance that she still shared his feelings and wishes. By the time he reached the schoolroom, he was almost at a sprint.

He burst through the door, and was instantly drawn to her as she stood next to an easel at the front of the room. She turned to him, and a wave of joy and affection lit her charming features. "Hello, Mr Brook," she breathed.

He hastily composed himself and dropped into a bow. "Miss Grant," he uttered, before diving for the back of the class. He was startled to find Lucy, the Grants' maid, also sitting in the back row. That was odd; she'd never been present on prior occasions. He nodded to her in acknowledgement and returned his attention to Cecilia.

At the end of the art class, Lucy jumped up and made her way to her mistress. William followed, withdrawing his bible. Cecilia packed her things away, and the maid headed toward the door.

Cecilia bounded after her and caught her arm. William could just make out her words above the escalating chatter of the children.

"Lucy, I feel inclined to stay for the lesson."

"Really, Miss? We still need to go to Jones' and Mrs Grant was most insistent that we return home without delay."

"Surely Mama would not object to some extra biblical teaching," Cecilia said, pulling Lucy back past the rows of desks.

William quickly hushed the children and began the lesson. He would later confess in his prayers that he had rushed the story of Moses and the Red Sea. His mind had been on two pools of turquoise perfection at the back of the room.

The schoolmistress arrived just as he was finishing up, and he held the door open for Cecilia and Lucy.

"Miss Grant," he said as formally as he could, "may I escort you back to the village?"

She regarded him through her eyelashes in attempted indifference, but a curve at one corner of her lips betrayed her. "That would be most kind, Mr Brook." She accepted his arm and gave him her satchel, and then they set off at a brisk pace, with Lucy trailing behind. The maid was rotund, and obviously not used to traipsing through fields.

He knew he must speak, but he knew not where to start. How could he begin to communicate all he felt for her? He cleared his throat. "It is so good to see you," he began, almost laughing at the understatement. "Are you well?" He wondered if she would sense he was more curious about her state of mind than her physical wellbeing.

She met his eyes for a moment. "Quite well, thank you," she said with a smile, "though I have been cooped up indoors this past week."

"Yes, I did wonder where you... That is, I hoped you were not ill."

"No, it is only that Mama has been very... attentive."

"Oh? I don't suppose you have had leave to raise a certain subject?"

"That is why she has been attentive." Cecilia glanced behind, and seemingly satisfied with Lucy's distance, told him the gist of her conservation with her mother.

The conclusion was not unexpected, but disturbing nonetheless. Unease fluttered about his heart. "That cannot have been an easy conversation, my dear. I hope it did not cause you pain."

She shrugged. "Certainly not easy, but necessary, I think." She turned hopeful eyes to him. "Did you have good news from Mr Morton, then?"

His heart skipped a beat. "Ah... Sadly, no. I shall have to write to Charles. I confess even though I have attempted a letter, I have not yet found the satisfactory words."

"I understand," she said. "I know you are busy with your duties."

He brought her to an instant halt. "Never too busy for you, my darling Cecilia. Please know you are constantly in my thoughts."

She did not reply, but her blush and the tenderness in her eyes gave him all he needed. He drank in her loveliness for a moment, and placed his free hand over hers, and all was well. Threading his fingers between hers, he hungered to wrap his whole body around her. This would have to do for now.

His eye caught some movement behind them, and he turned to see Lucy gaining on them. "Shall we continue?" he asked, and at her nod he resumed their swift strides. When they were a sufficient distance in front, he reached into his coat pocket and withdrew a package bound in string.

"Here is a small token of my affection," he said, handing it to her surreptitiously.

"Oh, William, I... thank you." Her smile, surprised and delighted, set his senses tingling.

"I went to a shop in Milton," he said. "I described the colour of the violas to them, and well..."

She sucked in a breath, and a spark lit her eyes. "You never did..." she murmured as she pulled at the string. She unwrapped the package, and withdrew a tube of oil paint with an excited squeal. "Oh, I must see the colour!" she cried, biting her lip and regarding the tube with an apparently insatiable curiosity.

William noted that Lucy was temporarily out of sight, behind a grassy knoll. He stopped walking again, and took the wrapping paper from her, holding it flat. She tried to open the tube, but the cap was screwed on too tightly.

"Here," William said, taking it from her and easily removing the cap.

Cecilia gently squeezed a tiny amount of the indigo pigment on to the paper, and gasped. She plucked a blade of grass and used it to swirl the paint around, just as the sun came out and hit the deep, dark colour. "Look," she said, holding it out to him. "It is perfect, exactly what I wanted." She frowned, and turned searching eyes to him. "But William, can you afford this?"

"It is but a small gesture, my love. I shall get you all the colours of the rainbow one day."

She smiled and put the cap back on the paint, before putting it in her reticule. "Thank you," she said.

He offered his arm again, just as Lucy reappeared. Soon afterward, the village was in their sights. William was compelled to mention a subject which had been nagging at his conscience.

"Cecilia," he began, "are you sure you want to be a vicar's wife? You will be left to your own devices for much of the time while I am studying and ministering to people. At other times you shall have to entertain guests."

"Are you worried I shan't show up when our visitors arrive?" she asked with a cheeky grin.

He laughed. "Perhaps I am. No, I am sure you would be the consummate hostess – that is, if you don't mind making the best of slim resources."

"I can learn," she said firmly. "And I can help you with your charity work, and I am quite happy pottering away while you are working on your sermons. I will be a captive audience."

He hadn't thought of that. Perhaps a wife would be useful in ways he had never stopped to consider. He began to slow their pace as they reached the outskirts of Amberley.

"William," Cecilia addressed him suddenly.

"Yes, what is it?"

"You said you would stay in Amberley to be with me."

He nodded.

"You say that now, but I know you will grow restless eventually."

William rubbed his thumb over her hand and sought her eyes. "Wherever you are, that is where I need to be. Amberley has provided me with spiritual opportunities I never knew would be here. It is ministry on a smaller scale, to be sure, but the lives of the people here are just as important as those I might find in another land."

Determination creased her brow. "I could come with you, you know. I am not as ... fragile as I might first appear. I could survive a long sea voyage and help set up a new way of life."

He contemplated this. "Perhaps you could, but let us not speculate about matters beyond our control. At the moment, we need to concentrate on orchestrating our betrothal. Tomorrow may bring us better fortunes."

Chapter Twenty-Two

Cecilia was working in the drawing room with her mother the next morning when there was a brief but urgent rapping on the front door. She heard Lucy's footsteps in the hallway, and after a few moments the maid said, "Of course, I'll be sure that she gets it."

The drawing room door opened, and Lucy practically ran into the room, before abruptly coming to a halt in front of the ladies. She held a note in her hand.

"Yes Lucy, what is it?" Mrs Grant held out her hand to take the missive.

Lucy shook her head. "It's a note for Miss Grant. The footman told me I was to make sure it was delivered into her hands, and her hands only."

"Well, really," said Mrs Grant. "What kind of urgent correspondence could you possibly receive, Cecilia?"

"Thank you, Lucy." Cecilia took the note without a word to her mother. Her brow furrowed as she saw the contents, which were in Amy's style, but only just. The letters were scrawled across the page, and smudged.

> Cecilia, please come quick. I'm in a terrible bother and I don't know what to do. I'll wait for you in the white gazebo.

Mrs Grant watched her daughter's mouth fall open and her eyes widen. "Well, what is it?" she demanded.

Cecilia took a breath and attempted to school her features. She lifted her eyes. "If you will excuse me, Mama, I must go to Amy immediately." She packed up her sewing and handed it to Lucy, who curtsied and left the room. "Do I have leave to take the carriage?"

"Certainly not. What could possibly require it? If you must leave, you can go on foot, and take Lucy with you."

Cecilia stood. "Amy says it is urgent, Mama. I beg you to let me take the carriage. I'll not keep her waiting half an hour. I shall send the carriage back on my arrival, and walk home directly."

Mrs Grant pursed her lips. "Very well. This is a special favour, Cecilia. If you are not home in time for dinner, consider it your *last* favour."

Cecilia didn't wait to respond to her mother's biting words. She fled from the room and called for Joseph to order the carriage. Shortly thereafter she made the anxious journey along the lanes to the lands of Ashworth Hall, and she asked the driver to set her down before they were in view of the hall itself.

"Are you sure, Miss?" the driver called as she jumped out.

"Quite sure, thank you. You may drive home." Cecilia ran into the trees beside the road, over a small mound and through a fernery. There on the other side of an ornamental pond, was the white gazebo, closed in on three sides. It was the farthest structure from the house, hidden from view. She found Amy inside, sitting with one hand to her face. The girl rose to embrace her, exposing tear stains on deathly pale cheeks.

"Amy!" Cecilia wrapped her arms around her friend, before pulling back to search her face. "What on earth is the matter?"

Amy began to pace about in the small structure. "I am so relieved you could come, for I cannot conceal the truth any longer. Oh Cecilia, it is too awful!"

"Come, sit down." Cecilia steered her back to the seat. "It cannot be as bad as you imagine, whatever it is. Did someone accuse you of taking something from the family?" Cecilia knew the other servants, particularly the lower servants, were jealous of Amy's position, hoping they would have risen to her rank. The most efficient way to get someone fired was to frame them for stealing.

Amy shook her head, and then her hand flew to her mouth. "Oh God, it's happening again!" she cried. She ran to the entrance of the gazebo, and doubled over, vomiting onto the clipped grass.

Cecilia dashed to her side, taking her arm and rubbing her back. "Amy, you are sick!" She led her back into the privacy of the gazebo. "Did you eat some perished food? Is anyone else ill?"

"Cici, hush." Amy wiped her mouth and stared at Cecilia with glazed eyes. "I am not sick. I am... with child." As soon as the words left her mouth, a sob shook her being, and she wailed as tears streamed down her cheeks.

Cecilia sat dumbstruck for a moment as the meaning of the words hit her consciousness. She could not believe it. She took Amy's hand. "How do you know? How can you be certain?"

Amy took some deep breaths before attempting to speak. "I have missed "– she gasped for air – "two monthly cycles. I have been ill these past weeks. So far I have managed to conceal it, but today Mrs Hurst caught me being sick, and she guessed the truth."

Cecilia felt tears pricking her own eyes, but she swallowed hard to keep them in check. "But dearest, I did not know you had a sweetheart. Was it one of the footmen?"

Amy started crying again. "No... it was John Barrington."

The words sliced Cecilia in the chest like a knife. "Mr Barrington," she whispered.

Amy nodded miserably. "He said he loved me. He said I was his favourite. He'd kissed me from time to time, more so once we returned from London. He made me feel special. I thought it was all harmless; I loved the way he made me feel. But then... the night of the ball, he asked me to walk with him in the garden. He took me behind the stables and kissed me viciously. Then he took up my skirts and..." She couldn't go on, sobbing and collapsing into the shoulder her friend offered.

"The blackguard," Cecilia said through her teeth.

"It was horrible," Amy said with a hiccup. "Such pain, and it just went on and on. He ripped the top of my dress, and when it was over, he said not a word. He just left me out there in the dark, soiled and shocked. He hasn't come near me since. Not a word."

Cecilia smoothed Amy's hair, her mind reeling and hatred stirring in her gut.

Amy sighed. "I know you'll be angry, Cecilia. It is quite obvious he is your intended. I never encouraged him, but I could not help but enjoy his attentions. I've never had someone tell me such lovely things, or kiss and caress me. I never dreamed he would abuse me like this."

"Do not worry about me," Cecilia said. "I have tried to like him, but... well, do not think about my feelings." She turned to look Amy in the face. "Will you tell him? Perhaps he will do the honourable thing and make you his bride."

Amy laughed bitterly. "That is why I am so distraught. I did tell him today. He – laughed at me, and called me a stupid girl. Then he walked away, and went to tell his mother. Lady Ashworth called me into her parlour, and told me she knows I am with child, though it was clear she does not know it is her son's. She said I can stay until I start to show, but then I am dismissed."

Cecilia nodded, without any words.

"I am ruined. I do not have anyone who could take me in, and I'll never find another position."

An idea occurred to Cecilia. "Maybe Mr Brook will be able to help."

Amy looked horrified. "The vicar? Goodness no! My soul is already damned to hell. I would prefer to delay his judgement for as long as I can. Doubtless he will evict me from the parish."

Cecilia shook her head. "I know he has ministered to unwed mothers in London. He may know somewhere you can go. I only wish you could live with me, but I fear my parents will not allow it."

Amy mulled this over. "Very well, I will stay behind to confess to Mr Brook after church. Will you be with me?"

"Of course I shall."

☙❧

Amy sat with her head bowed, and a single tear took flight from her chin, falling to land upon her gloved right hand. Cecilia held her left in a firm grip. "So you see, Mr Brook," Amy said between gulps of air, "There is no hope. I have nowhere to go... there is no-one who can help me." She dissolved into a fresh bout of tears.

William sat opposite her in the vestry, where the trio had taken shelter when Amy had requested a private conversation. Somehow Cecilia had managed to evade her parents after the service, bringing Amy to his side. The lady's confession filled him with despair and agony. He felt somehow responsible. His instincts had told him Barrington was up to no good, but it appeared even his warning to the man had come too late. His eyes wide in dazed horror, he pushed his hand into his hair and attempted to put his thoughts in order.

"Do you have no relations you could write to, who may offer you shelter?" he asked her.

She shook her head. "There is something you do not know about me, Mr Brook. I am not the natural daughter of the Millers. They adopted me as a baby, and they had no other children. I don't know who my real parents are, and I was never accepted by any extended family. I do not even know any names."

William's heart wrung in sympathy, and he regretted asking the question. "Oh Amy, I am sorry."

"Everyone knows of the adoption," Cecilia told him softly, "but it is never spoken of out of respect for the Millers."

"However am I to provide for the baby? To survive?" Amy lifted her red-rimmed eyes to William. "I cannot bear the thought of doing away with my own child. And I'll not... sell myself. I won't."

He knelt down, to become face to face with Amy. "There is no question you have been led astray, being generally of sound character. We will find a way, without your virtue being further impinged upon."

"We will do our utmost to help you, dear," Cecilia assured her. "I am sure Mr Brook will make it his highest priority to sort something out."

"Of course," William said. "I will devote myself to finding you solace, whether in Amberley or elsewhere. It will take precedence over any other matter – liturgical or personal."

At this he met eyes with Cecilia. She nodded, chewing on her lower lip, and then she looked away. She understood. They would need to postpone pursuing their own happiness until Amy's situation was settled. He could not endeavour to get his affairs in order, or present himself to her parents, while also working on behalf of Amy. And it was entirely inappropriate to be proclaiming their joy in the light of the circumstances. No, their engagement would need to wait for the time being. His heart ached as his resolve strengthened.

"Thank you," squeaked Amy through her tears. "I really do not know what can be done. You know the villagers will see me as a villain who must be banished."

Fury burned through William's veins. "Not if I have anything to say about it," he growled.

Chapter Twenty-Three

Whispers floated on the air of Amberley, and scandal blew on the breeze. At first there were malicious hints from the lower servants of Ashworth Hall, then rumblings among the farming folk and tradesmen, before the full-blown gossip of the spinsters burst the flood banks of delicate morality. Only the gentrified female ears were so far excepted from the secret, but it was surely only a matter of time before the whole village was acquainted with the fall of Miss Amy Miller.

Before long, talk turned to various theories of the child's paternity. The names of every single male of age in Amberley were tossed about like the autumn leaves, and some of the married ones, too. No-one dared to mention the names of the town's patrons outright, but eyebrows were raised and elbows nudged as silent accusations passed between co-conspirators.

William was not blind to the building furore, though the townspeople were quick to close their mouths in his presence. Women would flinch upon seeing him, and hurriedly relocate so they could continue to spin their poison.

He began to dread that week's service, knowing he would not be expected to speak of the matter, but feeling in his heart that he must. His soul was in torment, wanting to hate Barrington but knowing he must only hate the sin. He must set a good example, but it would take all his resolve. Even as he considered what Barrington had done, and how he was intended for Cecilia, his fists clenched and his blood ran hotter. He must repress his toxic feelings if he was to continue in service to the people of Amberley with any kind of composure or conviction.

He ascended the pulpit on Sunday with a heavy heart and was not surprised to note that Miss Miller was absent. His gaze flickered over the front pews, and his stomach turned as he took in the sight of Barrington, sitting in supercilious oblivion as if nothing had happened. He was sure no-one had dared mention anything about Amy to the family. How sad that the people with the most influence on her life were ignorant of the whole affair.

In the one painful moment he allowed himself to look at his beloved Cecilia, the grief in her eyes told him all he needed to know about her friend's condition.

He took a deep breath and began the service. He read from John chapter eight, telling the story of an adulteress. "...and Jesus said unto her, 'Neither do I condemn thee: go, and sin no more.'" He closed his bible slowly and raised his eyes to the congregation.

"A sin has surely been committed here in Amberley" – at this his eyes darted to Barrington involuntarily for the merest of moments – "and we must now demonstrate love and – and... tolerance... for those concerned."

Whispers began to circulate among the pews, the faces of the parishioners a mix of shock and mystification. He went on.

"What would it say about our village if someone is too scared to come to church, for fear of judgement from their fellow residents?"

The murmurings grew louder, and William held up a hand, knowing he'd gone far enough.

Barrington stood immediately after William concluded the service, and led his family from the building. Before she turned to go, Lady Ashworth glanced at William, a searching expression on her face.

As William bade the villagers goodbye, he was not met with the usual chatter or appraisals, and he was not issued an invitation for lunch. Instead, an unexpected visitor appeared at his doorstep that afternoon.

Emma tapped on his library door. "If you please, Mr Brook, Lady Ashworth is in the parlour to see you."

William started. "Lady Ashworth?"

Emma nodded vigorously, and dove out of the way when William dashed from the room, throwing on his jacket.

His patroness was perched on his sofa, quite alone, and she greeted him with a tilt of her head.

"Lady Ashworth, what a pleasant surprise. What can I do for you?"

She indicated he should sit, and met his gaze. Her pale blue eyes were steady and penetrating. "What is it you suspect him of?"

William's pulse began to race. He tugged at the top of his cravat. "I regret to say I do not know your meaning, my lady."

She blew out an impatient breath. "Oh, I think you do. You talked of sin in our midst, and you looked at John."

"I am sure I did not –"

"Oh, but you did. Those seated farther back may have missed it – indeed, I am sure it even escaped Lord Ashworth's notice – but I am certain you suspect him of a misdeed."

William shifted in his seat, beginning to sweat. What had he done? It was not his place to be accusing people of crimes, regardless of whether they deserved it.

"Well?"

The determined set to Lady Ashworth's jaw told William he was cornered. "I think you should ask him yourself, my lady. No doubt he will assure you he is innocent."

"No doubt; that is why I came to you."

William eyed her warily. "I cannot divulge personal information which has been told to me in confidence."

She pursed her lips and appeared to consider this, before meeting his eyes again. "He is my son, Mr Brook. As his mother, and as your patroness, I demand that you tell me the truth." Her gaze softened. "Perhaps I may be able to help in some way?"

William was torn between his need to guard Amy's privacy, and the possibility that Lady Ashworth would indeed ease her burden. He withdrew his handkerchief and mopped his forehead, and made up his mind. "Lady Ashworth, I urge you to consider recent events in your household. That is all I can say."

She regarded him askance, clearly unsatisfied. "Well, I am sure I do not know..." After a minute of contemplation, she gasped, her hand flying to her chest. "Do you mean Miss Miller? She is... and do you think that John..."

William looked away.

"But what proof have you?"

"I cannot possibly say."

She again fixed him with her steely stare. "But you are quite sure."

William's heart thudded in his chest. He gave the barest of nods.

"I see." Lady Ashworth rose from her seat, and straightened her gloves. "Well, I have had enough of his wild ways. This is the final straw."

Whatever could she mean? What action would she take, all because he had implicated Barrington? William leapt up and bounded across to her. "My lady, I beg of you –"

She held up a restraining hand. "Thank you, Mr Brook. Good day."

৵৵

William kept to himself for the days following, in an attempt to let Sunday's dust settle.

He could not keep himself from his work for long though, and the act of delivering food to needy rural families raised his spirits. On returning to the village late one afternoon, he passed close to an alley next to Jones' shop and a sound arrested his attention.

"I hope you're pleased with yourself, young vicar."

William's heart skipped a beat, and sweat pricked his brow. "Why good day, Mr Barrington," he said, pausing before he turned to face the man.

Barrington gave a shout of laughter. "I imagine you think it is a good day, as your little witch hunt has proven quite successful. Thanks to your rather pointed sermonising, not only the whole village knows of my little tête-à-tête, but Lord and Lady A are very much aware. And they seem to think I need to be taught a lesson. No more wild oats for me, so they say. They have insisted I go down to Mulberry Manor within the month, to begin managing the property. My allowance is cut off, and I shan't get a penny more until I get down to that wretched cottage and start collecting rents. Apparently there is a curmudgeonly manager there who will keep me prisoner and send reports to my father. If I escape for even a week

189

during my first year, even to visit friends or go to London for the season, I will be disinherited."

William held back a smile, keeping his expression neutral. He said nothing, despite the temptation to tell Barrington that was hardly a punishment as far as he was concerned.

The gentleman's cold tirade continued. "And it is all down to you, my dear chap. I will be far from any civilised company, forced to do *work*, and without the pleasure of any... well..." – he grinned wickedly – "pleasures. But I am sure I will still find something to amuse me."

William's skin crawled. "Have you not learned your lesson?" he asked, then he regretted speaking a moment later, biting his lip.

In one sudden motion, Barrington dragged him into the alley and pinned him to the wall, his hands firmly around the vicar's cravat. "I'll teach *you* a lesson, you scoundrel. Mark my words; you'll not leave Amberley before I take my revenge."

William stared him straight in the eye. "Do as you will, Barrington. You cannot hurt me."

Barrington laughed, and abruptly released William. "We shall see, dear vicar. Do you know, Mama has insisted I swiftly marry a girl within the vicinity of Mulberry, to engender goodwill in the community. But I rather think I should like to take a bride with me to, er, comfort me."

He looked back at William, but though his gaze hardened, he said nothing.

"Surely you must know I have been nursing passionate feelings for the delectable Miss Grant."

William could not hide a slight flinch at the sound of her name, but he was determined not to strike out in wrath.

Barrington laughed again. "Don't you see, you could never give her everything she needs. I will give her all she could desire – and more."

He sauntered around William in a circle and began to speak with affected indifference.

"She's pretty enough, and although her dowry will be miniscule I will be able to leave her at the country house while I go to town to seek out... other diversions."

When there was still no response, Barrington again closed the gap between them with one long stride.

"She's ripe for the picking, don't you think? Do you know, I seem to recall you once telling me I was *welcome* to her."

William's fists clenched at his sides, and it took him a few breaths to steady his voice. "I will be on my way," he said evenly, and then he attempted to step past Barrington, who caught him by the arm.

"It may seem a little presumptuous, my *dear* fellow, but allow me to express my delight in the fact that you will preside over the marriage ceremony. It all seems rather fitting, don't you think?"

William yanked his arm out of Barrington's grasp, and could not hold back a murderous stare. "Good *day*, sir," he said, and he ran from the alley, slowing to a brisk walk once he reached the street. Barrington's low snigger seeped after him.

Let him go and propose to Cecilia, William thought angrily. Just let him try. Even if her parents insisted on the match, surely once they were sensible of his nefarious character they would not wish such a man on their daughter. Would Cecilia have the courage to tell them all she knew? Would she see it as a betrayal of Amy's trust? Surely it was only a matter of time before the gossip reached their ears in any case.

He could not intervene. He must let things take their course. Only when he had secured his situation – whether in Amberley or elsewhere – and could prove he could give Cecilia the life she deserved, could he seek to ask for her hand. Indeed, perhaps seeing the result of Barrington's suit could aid his own.

He shivered. The thought of the match made his blood run cold. Could he really lose her forever? Once home, he dropped to his knees and prayed for Cecilia with all his might.

Chapter Twenty-Four

Cecilia stared out the window with a half-trimmed bonnet in her lap, her thoughts plagued by Amy and William. Poor Amy, who could now not venture out in public without fear of judgement. And William, the one man who might bring comfort, was so frustratingly near yet out of reach.

A figure appeared, dismounting from a horse, and she gasped.

Barrington saw her and tipped his hat with a crooked smile.

Seething with hatred and revulsion, she dropped her eyes and remained rigid throughout the sounds of his arrival and admission into the drawing room. She rose as he entered and affected a curtsey, but did not speak or look at him.

"Mr Barrington, you are most welcome," Mrs Grant said. "Do sit down. We'll have tea, thank you Lucy."

"Pray, do not order tea purely for my sake," Barrington said. "Indeed, I wondered as, since it is so fine, I might prevail upon Miss Grant to join me for a walk."

Cecilia held her breath and her pulse quickened.

She directed a frown at her mother, just as Mrs Grant flushed with obvious satisfaction. "Of course, I am sure I may spare her for a little while."

"Mama," Cecilia blurted, and both stared at her. "I need to continue with my work."

"Nonsense child, when you have been so conscientious? I insist you go with Mr Barrington."

"But..."

"Go on. *Now*."

Barrington held out his hand, but she dodged him, edging around the room and out the door.

As Cecilia walked along beside Barrington, her usual sensations of colour and sound were mute. Instead she was intensely and insipidly conscious of her companion. She could smell cigar smoke, a musky scent and some sort of liquor. She kept her eyes averted, but she was all too aware of his bulk looming next to her, his dark blue coat, elaborate cravat and shiny gold waistcoat.

She was certainly not going to talk to him. She yearned to push him into the ditch.

Unfortunately, he chose that moment to break the silence.

"My dear Miss Grant," he began, and she could feel his breath on her cheek. "You can be in no illusion as to the purpose of my visit."

Cecilia still would not look at him. "No indeed, Mr Barrington," she said evenly, "I am at a loss."

Barrington chuckled. "I think you are more skilled in the art of flirtation than you know. You must know I have long admired your beauty and spirit."

She gave no answer.

He took hold of her elbow to pull her to a stop, and she winced, yanking her arm away. "Come now, Miss Grant," he said. "Your modesty is charming, but you need not worry. My intentions are honourable."

She gave an incredulous grunt, but still remained mute. She stood still, but she did not look him in the face.

"I am shortly to take up my inheritance in Hampshire. A delightful country residence in what I am told are very picturesque grounds. Eminently suitable for an artist such as yourself."

Cecilia studied a leaf on the ground. It was dark brown and crushed on one side, a far cry from the lush green it had once been. She was suddenly aware of something on her chin, and she jumped when she realised it was her suitor, tilting her face up towards him. She looked up at him in spite of herself, taking in those hard dark brown eyes – nearly black – which she had once thought handsome, and his self-satisfied smile. How his arrogance and presumption were such a contrast to William. Though her love didn't lack for confidence, his first concern was for the welfare and feelings of others. This man only wanted to ensure his own comfort. She focussed on Barrington's angular chin, and lifted her own out of his grasp.

"I will be taking a wife with me," Barrington went on, much like someone would discuss their horse or a valet. But then his voice did soften slightly as he said, "And I assure you it would give me great satisfaction if you agree to marry me."

Cecilia nearly screamed, but she bit her tongue to hold back her rage. "No," she said curtly, turning away and striding off down the lane.

"Pardon me?" Barrington chased after her, matching her pace with furious footsteps.

"I said no. There is nothing in the world that would convince me to marry you. You are not worthy to be called a gentleman."

His right eyebrow raised, but he did not show any other signs of emotion. They walked in silence for several moments. Then his colour rose, and he addressed her again. "I cannot believe you are actually refusing me. Are you mad? You'd be mistress of a country estate, have use of a house in town, and a far higher income than you deserve."

"And I cannot believe you would assume I don't know about your... dalliance with Amy. Her life is ruined because of you."

"Come now Miss Grant, a little 'dalliance' as you put it, is not uncommon. Any man cannot expect to be held to the same standards as women."

"The man I marry will hold to those standards, and many others which you have failed to grasp."

Barrington's chin rose. "Expecting an offer, are we?"

"No," Cecilia growled, not wanting him to think she was refusing him on any grounds other than his own deficiencies. "But I care not if I am never married."

He gave her a pitying look. "My dear, your mother will never accept that." He brightened. "In fact, I believe I shall take you back home right now and tell her we are engaged. You will be powerless to refuse."

She narrowed her eyes. "Not when I tell her what you have done."

"You would not dare. You mother's been angling for you to marry me for months."

"That may be so, but now there is no possible way I could go through with it."

They were inches apart now, shouting in each other's faces.

Barrington stepped back, and turned away for a moment. Facing her again, he took a deep breath in and out. "Fine, then. I won't take a harpy for a wife, even if I could leave you in the country for most of the year. I do not want *you* either."

Cecilia nodded in satisfaction. "I am glad you agree, sir. I will not be needing an escort home."

"Well, *I* have to go that way as well," he said through gritted teeth.

"Then *wait*, while I get a head start." She spun on her heel and stalked off, incensed.

She could never forget what he had done to Amy, and now she had also seen him for the pig he really was. She forced herself to focus on the road ahead until she was nearly around the first bend, then she peeked back over her shoulder to ensure he wasn't following her. She exhaled in relief when she saw him leaning up against a tree, kicking at the dirt. What a narrow escape.

Mrs Grant, however, did not see it that way. "Have you taken leave of your senses?" she shrieked. "I cannot believe you would dare to refuse him."

Cecilia held her chin high. "I have."

Mrs Grant stared at her daughter for a few moments. "I do not know how you could be so wilfully disobedient."

Cecilia took a breath. "When I tell you what sort of man Mr Barrington is, you may be glad of my decision."

"I doubt it. What do you mean?"

"I would rather not tell you, to protect Amy. But you will find out soon enough. Mr Barrington forced himself on Amy and has impregnated her."

Mrs Grant gasped. "How can you say such a thing?"

"It is true. In fact, I confronted him just now and he did not attempt to deny it. He even defended his behaviour as normal among worldly men."

Mrs Grant sank onto a chair. "How is Amy? Has she been dismissed?"

"Her condition is known and it is only a matter of months before she will have to leave. She knows not how she will support the babe."

"Surely Mr Barrington will offer some help, if only monetary?"

Cecilia shrugged helplessly. "I hope he will be made to see sense."

"Well!" Mrs Grant was silent for several minutes.

Cecilia knew not what to do, so unaccustomed was she to the lack of speech.

"I know what we shall do," her mother said finally.

Cecilia sat up straighter. "Yes?" Perhaps her mother knew of a family who would be sympathetic and agree to house Amy and her baby.

"I have failed to secure you a worthy husband, but I will not have you languish in Amberley for the rest of your days."

"Mama, really..." Disappointment and ire sank in Cecilia's stomach. Did her mother have no empathy? Were her matrimonial prospects really the most important thing right now?

"And while we cannot afford to all go to London," Mrs Grant said, with growing enthusiasm, "we can send you to my sister. I am sure she will be all too pleased to take up the task, seeing as she's always seen fit to instruct me. I will set my pride aside for your good."

It was obvious Cecilia was supposed to be monumentally grateful for the sacrifice her mother was making. "If you are to set aside pride," she said evenly, "will you not allow me to remain by Amy's side, to assist her wherever I can?"

"I understand you want to help your friend, dear." Mrs Grant gave Cecilia a longsuffering look. "But there's really very little you can do. If you choose to give her charity once you are comfortably settled, that is your decision – or your husband's, rather."

"Could – could we not house Amy here? In one of my brother's rooms?"

Indignant sparks flew from Mrs Grant's eyes. "Certainly not. I'll not have our good name sullied by endorsing an illegitimate child."

Cecilia was on her feet in an instant. "Mama!"

Mrs Grant didn't blink. "Calm yourself, Cecilia. You shan't get a husband if you are forever flying into hysterics."

Cecilia glared at her mother and spoke through gritted teeth. "I don't *want* to live with Aunt Honoria and ingratiate myself to hapless peers."

"You will do as you are told."

"But I am needed here."

"Needed? Do not flatter yourself. No-one will miss your little art classes or story-book readings."

Tears threatened to spill over, but Cecilia blinked them back. "You don't understand," she said, all too aware she was verging on a wail. "My heart is here."

"Let me guess," Mrs Grant said coldly. "With the vicar."

Cecilia's eyes flashed, but she did not reply.

"We have been over this, Cecilia. The match is not suitable. Fortunately, your aunt is very clever and is happily situated among peer aplenty. She shall succeed where I have failed. She will purchase you all the new dresses you need to impress the gentlemen. You can become her ward."

"You cannot make me go," Cecilia said, looking down at her mother with her chin held high.

"Indeed I can. I will write..."

Cecilia ran from the room, up to her own, whereupon she threw herself on the bed and wept. Her one solace was that her aunt would not be in London until after Christmas. Surely she'd be engaged to William by then?

῾❦

When William arrived at the vestry meeting, it was clear that Amy's misfortunes were now common knowledge. While no names were mentioned, the gentlemen were subdued, and no one seemed quite able to look him in the eye.

"Well, Mr Brook," Mr Morton said, "what a week we've had."

"Terrible business," said Mr Stockton.

Mr Lindsay cleared his throat. "I assure you, vicar, Amberley is usually free of scandals such as this."

"At least, you have never known about them before," mumbled William into his meeting minutes.

"Pardon me, vicar?"

William smiled politely. "Nothing. While this is undoubtedly a terrible occurrence, it takes quite something to shock me. You recall, I have come from London."

"Indeed, Mr Brook," said Lindsay. "We look to you for guidance as how to put this right and move on with our lives."

William raised an eyebrow. "*Our* lives?"

"To be sure. This has caused upset in the village. We need to restore order and morality as soon as possible."

William eyeballed the man. "I do not worry for the general morality of Amberley; in fact I am sure once the instigator of the troubles leaves, most of the population will go on as before. My main concern is for the victim of this horrible episode."

He met the eyes of Mr Fortescue, and the gentleman looked away.

When he received no response, William continued on. "She was an innocent, and we must help her."

Mr Grant broke the stunned silence. "But surely you are not suggesting she be allowed to remain in Amberley. We cannot have a bastard child growing up within our society."

Mrs Fortescue fanned herself with the minutes and stared intently at the wall.

William spread his hands on the table. "The facts are these. Miss Miller is without family to help her. She is estranged from relatives, none of whom could afford to keep her. If we do not take mercy on her, she will only be fit for the workhouse. Would you wish that on a simple girl who enjoyed the attentions of a man who told her he loved her, and then forced himself on her?"

Mrs Fortescue closed her eyes and put her fingertips to her temples as if in pain.

William sighed. "I do not think we will resolve this now, but we need to investigate all the options within and without the village. Let us continue with the meeting."

⥤⥢

William was nearly driven mad in his longing to see Cecilia; to look into her eyes, to hold her again. She haunted his dreams and invaded his thoughts. He was dying to know if Barrington had proposed, and if so, if she had managed to escape. Now that her season of art classes had

198

concluded, he had no hope of meeting with her.

He found himself at the end of the lane which lead to Harcourt Lodge. He could call on the family in his usual capacity – a friendly clerical call. He started down the lane.

But Mrs Grant knew of his suit, and without anything to recommend himself, he may only make things worse. And it was highly unlikely he could converse privately with Cecilia. He turned back towards the main road.

Still, even just the sight of her would lift his spirits… although her mother may hide her from sight.

He stared down at the house wistfully. What a fool love had made him. He didn't even know his own mind anymore. It was such sweet agony.

At that moment, a splash of blue caught his eye. He nearly fell over.

"Cecilia!" he whispered. She ran swiftly from the house, having exited via the garden at the back. He could just make out her painting satchel slung over her shoulder. *Well done, my cunning little convict!*

He began to feel dizzy, and realised he'd been holding his breath. Sucking in some air, he began to move along the road in parallel to her steps. This was the chance he'd been desperate for, if only he could make it past the village without being seen. He cut behind a cottage and began to follow the path through the meadows, just as Cecilia disappeared in a clump of trees. He quickened his pace. Surely she was heading for the river.

He successfully passed behind the centre of the town without being detected, and when he reached the fork in the road which led up to Ashworth Hall, he sighted Cecilia again.

The sound of pounding horse hooves distracted him. Who should come thundering up the lane, but Barrington himself.

He took a couple of strides back in the direction of his beloved, but in an instant his nemesis was upon him, pulling his horse up directly in William's path.

Barrington looked over his shoulder, catching a last glance of Cecilia before she disappeared from view. He laughed. "Chasing after her, are you?"

William set his mouth in a hard line. "Kindly let me pass."

Barrington dismounted. "And deny me your company? I will have a word with you, if you please." He tied his horse to a nearby tree and beckoned for William to join him in the copse.

William blew out a hard breath. It seemed he would find out the truth, one way or the other. His heart beat in painful yearning to catch up with Cecilia. But if he needed to face Barrington down in order to be rid of him, so be it. He affected a slight bow and walked into the trees. "I am at your service."

"Ha! Apparently, but all evidence to the contrary. Perhaps I should be of service to you, and let it slip that you are embarking on private rendezvous with Miss Grant. That would ruin both of you, would it not?"

William's blood boiled. The gentlemen were slowly making their way deeper into the woods. "You have no proof we have ever met in private, Barrington. Even today, I was only intending to ensure she was not shaken by any encounter with *you*."

Barrington raised an eyebrow. "Ah, what noble intentions you have. Perhaps a little shaking would be good for her. But I think I have you to blame for her stubborn rebuttal of my proposals. She would not have refused me before you wormed your way into our lives."

His abhorrence was tempered with relief. Thank the Lord Cecilia was not betrothed to him. "Certainly," he replied sardonically, "I am sure it has nothing to do with you. Is that all you wish to tell me?"

Barrington stopped walking and turned to face William. "Only that you deserve her, the wilful bacon-brained fool."

Rage pumped through William's veins. "Don't tempt me, Barrington," he growled.

Barrington laughed. "Tempt you to do what, Brook? Commit some sort of sin, I imagine?"

William took an enormous breath in an effort to calm himself. He would not be provoked. He would not let this animal win over his self-control. "Good day, Barrington. Why don't you get yourself to London and hook yourself a bride. The sooner you fly off to Hampshire the better." He began to walk away. He heard Barrington's footsteps stalking up behind him, and his shoulder was grasped in a vice-like grip.

He could feel Barrington's breath in his ear. "I would have had her, you know," he said softly. "If it weren't for that tart Amy, the delicious

Miss Grant would have belonged to me."

"Barrington..." William clenched his fists, and then ignored the dragons raging in his belly, struggling free.

Barrington leapt around in front of him, nose to nose. "I am sure she was already dreaming of our wedding night. I know I was."

"That's enough!" William roared. In a split second his fist had shot into Barrington's stomach. The scoundrel doubled up over his arm, winded. William stared at him for a moment, his fury blinding his shame at having intentionally wounded another human being. He drew his arm back, and began to back away. "Do not speak of her like that – do not even dare to think –"

Barrington coughed and stood nearly upright. His hazy eyes washed over William and he laughed. "Nice, Brook," he panted. "Didn't think you had it in you." He bowed his head again, and then took two huge paces towards William, smashing his right fist across the vicar's face.

William cried out in shock, but he didn't feel any pain at that moment. After a few seconds he turned his head back to Barrington, looking him right in the eye. "Go, Barrington. Leave Amberley this instant and never come back."

Barrington came closer, his face twisted with malice. "Or what, church boy? What can you possibly do to me?" He landed a punch into William's ribs.

He stumbled backward and gasped for air. "The Almighty will judge," he croaked. "I know not whether your punishment will be in this life or the next."

"A cowardly rebuttal if ever I've heard one." He kicked William hard, just below the knee. "You know," he said lightly, walking around William in a circle, "I think Miss Grant spends many an afternoon by the river, painting. She has a talent, does she not?" He took hold of William's head and forced eye contact. "I think I might find her there before I head back to the Hall, and see what other talents she has. A little parting gift for poor Mr Barrington." He let go of William's head and slapped him hard across the face. "Or a gift for Mr Brook? You won't have to break her in."

A primal scream ripped forth from William's soul, and at the same time his right arm drew back like a bowstring before slamming hard into Barrington's nose with the whole force of his body, and the violence of righteous anger.

There was a huge cracking sound. Barrington tottered backwards, and blood began to stream from his nose. At first his wide eyes held William's, and then they rolled around in their sockets before shooting up into his head, as Barrington fell over backwards with a thud.

William stared at his lifeless form, comprehending what he'd done. He tried to suppress the triumphant sensation that threatened to consume his being, but it was no good. He went over to Barrington and leant over his bloodied face. "God help the female who finds herself shackled to you. I only hope the poor woman does not fancy herself in love. Good riddance, sir."

William stumbled over to a tree and grasped at the trunk to support his weight. As shock subsided, the pain in his ribs, legs and face began to throb. Tears mingled with the blood on his cheeks, as shame overwhelmed his triumph. "Forgive me, Lord," he sobbed, over and over.

Ten minutes later, William was no longer hysterical and Barrington was beginning to stir. He made his way to a stream and washed himself as best he could, the wounds stinging. There was no possible way he could approach Cecilia in this state. Instead, he crept in the back entrance to the vicarage.

There was no concealing his wounds from Emma, and it was some time before her exclamations ceased. William would not satisfy her curiosity as to the source of his injuries, but he could see assumption in her eyes. He refused her pleas to summon Mr Lindsay, but he did pen a note for immediate delivery to the Dean in Milton, begging for a replacement to take the Sunday service.

Emma bandaged his face and torso and then assisted him into bed. As he stared up at the ceiling for hours on end, he was crushed by the weight of his failures. How could he have dared aspire to convert pagans abroad, when it seemed he was unfit to shepherd even the good people of Amberley? His reckless errors of judgement had divided the community, and his efforts to help Amy with her practical needs had so far come to nothing. And a pure and lasting love, so tantalisingly close, could be out of his reach forever.

Chapter Twenty-Five

William remained at home for nearly a week, waiting for his swelling to go down and his bruises to fade. He detested his own reflection, the sight of his disfigured face in the mirror an unwelcome reminder of his weaknesses.

His absence was well-noted, and he was touched by the notes of sympathy he received. He sensed Cecilia's concern even from his distance, though he knew it was not in her power to write to him before they were officially engaged. He only hoped he was not causing her grief.

Emma reported that Barrington had left Amberley under the cover of darkness, though most of his possessions remained at Ashworth Hall. Gossip among the servants identified his destination was most likely London, in order to gather supplies for his relocation to Hampshire. William hoped he would not have to encounter the man again, but there was a deep-seated foreboding nagging at him, warning that all was not resolved.

He used the time at home to send off desperate queries to the last of his contacts on Amy's behalf, and he finally authored a letter to his brother which he could endure sending. When he was well enough to kneel, he stayed at his bedside for hours, seeking God's counsel on how he could move on from his mistakes.

He was satisfied that his features were sufficiently recovered to perform the service that week. As he stood in the entryway to greet the arrivals, their genuine enquiries as to his health raised his spirits. When Cecilia entered with her parents, she gave him her hand.

"I – we were so worried about you," she said. "What was the matter? Are you now well?"

He smiled, deep into her eyes. "It was nothing but a trifle, I assure you. I only wanted a little rest."

"Come, Cecilia," said Mrs Grant, pulling her away.

Her hand was yanked from his grasp. She looked back at him and gave him a small, secret smile.

His heart soared, and he had tears in his eyes when he turned to greet the widow Kendrick. *She still loves me.*

His peace of mind was short-lived. William visited Jones' shop the following morning, and as he stood outside afterwards talking to Mr Stockton, Barrington rode into the village from the east.

He tipped his hat jovially to all passers-by, and when he saw William and Stockton, he pulled up alongside.

"Good day, gentlemen. Fine weather, is it not?"

"Aye, sir," Mr Stockton said, with a little bow.

William said nothing.

"I have called a special meeting of the vestry tomorrow," Barrington said. "I thought I must have the chance to say goodbye, properly."

William caught his eyes for only a moment, but in them he saw such a deathly dark glare that his blood immediately ran cold.

"I look forward to seeing you there," Barrington said, directing an empty smile at both gentlemen. Then he kicked his mount back to a walk, and slowly made his way towards Ashworth Hall.

❧

William's frustration was palpable. He had written to every parish within a hundred miles, and begged for mercy from the Reverend Mother at the convent in Shrewsbury. He'd sent word to all of his friends in London and Cambridge.

But nothing. Not even the smallest hope of finding a place for Amy.

He sat with his forehead resting on his fists at the vestry meeting table as he surveyed a letter from a rector in Ludlow. Even a reply had been something of a miracle, and he'd seized on the note in such excitement he'd nearly torn it apart. But the few scant lines contained only sympathy; no substance. "I regret I know not of any appropriate shelter for the young woman of whom you speak..." was all he needed to know.

The obvious solution was to shelter Amy in his own home - but even he knew cohabiting with an unmarried mother was a step too far over moral boundaries.

As he racked his brain for where to turn next, he didn't notice that the rest of the vestry members had entered, and were now huddled in the opposite corner. Their whisperings grew increasingly loud, but still William did not look up.

He must visit every resident of Amberley and appeal to their Christian nature, he decided. The knowledge that half the families could only just afford to feed themselves, let alone a mother and babe, deflated his resolve somewhat, but he must make the richer families, who were probably more proud and reluctant to invite scandal, realise that every good turn would go rewarded in the next life.

"You must be mistaken!"

"How dare you!"

The loud shouts finally drew William from his thoughts. He raised his eyes in time to see Mr Lindsay charging at him, with the rest of the group on his heels. He stood abruptly, scraping his chair on the floor.

"Mr Brook," Lindsay said, "what is the meaning of this?"

William knew not what they were speaking of, and he regarded them with a mix of confusion and calm. "Do tell me, sir, and then we will both know."

Mr Grant cleared his throat. "This is a rumour, that is to say, Mr Barrington has recently returned from London and while in attendance at St Mary's he discovered something..."

"Yes?"

William eyed each of the vestry members in turn, eager to unveil the mystery. Mrs Fortescue had turned an odd shade of crimson, and she would not look him in the eye.

"Barrington?" He tried to keep his expression neutral while addressing the man, who lurked at the back of the group, and was not entirely sure of his success.

"It is not my place to accuse you of anything," he said sweetly.

"Accuse? What accusations? You obviously know something which you have relayed to these good people. I demand someone tell me at once what is going on!"

Mr Stockton broke free of the group and blurted out, "Did you frequent the House of Lillian in London?"

William nearly fell over his chair. In that moment it was as if his world stopped turning. *Where did this come from? And how on earth can I explain it?* "No, frequent is the wrong word," he said in a measured tone.

"But you did, er, visit there, regularly?"

"Yes," William said without shrinking, "but I only –"

"Mr Brook," Mr Jones spoke up, "even one visit is damning."

"Completely inappropriate for a vicar," said Lindsay. "Our vicar."

"But you don't understand," William said, desperation creeping up his spine. "My reason was to see one lady in particular."

"Oh!" Mrs Fortescue clung to her husband in a near swoon.

"That is, I had a perfectly valid task to undertake." Beads of sweat moistened William's top lip.

"Can you not tell us the reason?" Mr Morton asked, his eyes pleading.

"I am afraid I cannot." He blew out a breath and hung his head as his thoughts whirled, and then he raised his eyes. "Confidences and the sanctity of my vows prevent me from disclosing exactly what my business was."

"I think we can guess!" snorted Mr Jones.

"You shall just have to trust me, to take my word when I say I have done nothing wrong."

"Even if we did believe you," Mr Grant said, "the townspeople will only think the worst. And once their trust is broken, there is little point in your continued service."

"But surely after these months I have spent here, dutifully serving the congregation..."

"A drop in the bucket, I'm afraid," Lindsay said. "An indiscretion such as this will blot out all good works. We will soon have someone else in your post, and you shall be forgotten."

His words hung heavy on the air, and wrapped around William's heart like a vice.

But not forgiven.

The vestry meeting was called to a hasty close. It was clear they all expected William to leave first, and he held the eyes of each member as he passed them, trying to assure them of his innocence. Coming to Barrington last, he met with a satisfied smirk. It was quite obvious Barrington's "goodbye" was this poisoned chalice.

He did not feel the earth beneath his feet as he found his way back to the vicarage with unseeing eyes. The shock of this exposure numbed his senses for a good hour before he was able to put his thoughts into any kind of order. He sat like a statue in his study, only his thumb moving over the spine of his bible. How he wished Thomas was there to share his burdens with. His friend must be near his destination by now.

He could guess at Barrington's methods of extracting the incriminating information. Mayhap his conversations with Thomas had been overheard by another deacon or churchwarden, jealous of William's favour with Dean Roberts. With enough bribery, even clerical lips could be made to loosen.

He glanced at the letter on his desk, which he had sealed only that morning. There was little pointing in sending it now – even the granting of some charitable funds couldn't see him out of this mess.

This scandal could threaten not just his position in Amberley, but his whole future. He could see his missions abroad slipping out of his grasp, and his very livelihood in England disappearing. What would he do if he couldn't work in the church? His own personal ambition to serve God and help his fellow man aside, where would he seek income? Even the army or navy seemed out of reach, given the cost of a commission and the stain of this disgrace, not to mention his own conscience loathing the notion of wounding other innocent men. But if he could not find a way in... he would have to return to the family estate and depend on the generosity of his brothers for the rest of his life. And to William, that was a fate worse than death.

As he began to hyperventilate, his thoughts and feelings were consumed by the worry which plagued him above all others. Would Cecilia believe him? And could they ever be together?

Cecilia met Amy in the village on the following afternoon, with the intention of spending her afternoon off together shopping and strolling as they used to do. Cecilia hoped that a pleasant few hours might give Amy a little relief from her troubles. She was already browsing the new ribbons at Jones' when Amy burst through the door, the little bell jangling furiously.

"Cici?" she cried.

Cecilia emerged from one of the aisles a few moments later. "Here I am, dearest," she said, closing the gap between them and dropping a kiss onto each of her friend's cheeks before grasping her hands. "How are you?" She searched Amy's eyes, dismayed to see anguish clearly drawn on her features.

"I need to consult with you in private," Amy whispered.

Cecilia nodded. "Perhaps we can take tea, and return to shopping later?"

Amy's brow furrowed. "Perhaps. Let us go, dear." She took Cecilia's elbow and steered her out of the shop.

"Good day, ladies!" called Mr Jones from the back of the shop. They were gone before the last syllable reached their ears.

"What is it?" Cecilia hissed when they were in the street. "Are you unwell?"

"No," Amy said quietly. "Well, a little, but that is not what I need to discuss with you. We must speak alone."

The ladies passed down the alleyway which led to a meadow dissected by a stream. They settled on a bench beneath an oak tree, and Amy glanced about furtively.

"I believe it is safe," she said, her eyes still a little wild.

"Dearest, what is it?" Cecilia pressed her arm urgently. "Keep me in suspense no longer."

Amy turned to look her friend in the eye. "Cecilia, are you engaged to Mr Brook?"

Cecilia frowned. "It is not yet official. But I am sure it will come to pass." A smile enveloped her lips. "We love each other dearly."

Amy looked at her hands. "I have some news; that is, there is a rumour."

"Yes?"

Amy took a deep breath and met Cecilia's eyes. "There is word among the servants, though I believe it was not started there... it is a story about Mr Brook, and something he did in London."

Cecilia's heart began throbbing painfully. "Is he already engaged to another? It cannot be!"

"No, it is not that," Amy said steadily, "and dear, do try to keep your voice down."

"I am sorry," Cecilia said, on the verge of tears. "But you must tell me what it is."

Amy took up both of Cecilia's hands. "The rumour is that Mr Brook availed the services of a – a lady of the night. On many occasions."

A mix of shock and anger hit Cecilia with such force, she felt as though she'd been slapped in the face. "It cannot be true!" she whispered. "I know him – he has been earnestly pursuing his calling his whole life. It is against his very nature."

"I know it is unlikely," said Amy, "but you must see the implications of even the suggestion of it. He is sure to be dismissed, and likely struck off, and I do not know how you shall obtain consent to marry him."

Cecilia stood and began pacing about in agitation. "But I am sure, once he knows of this gossip, he will prove it is false. He will deny it. He must deny it to *me*." She began choking on tears, and Amy came up beside her, taking her in her arms.

"Now, my dear, do not get into such a state in an exposed place such as this. Would you like to go to him?"

Cecilia nodded.

"Then we must go through the village, and you must not betray your knowledge of the rumour, or your emotions."

Cecilia cried against Amy's shoulder for another few minutes and then began to breathe in jagged breaths, trying to control herself. Amy withdrew a handkerchief and dabbed at her face.

"There now, that's better," she said, inspecting Cecilia's visage. "I will visit him with you so as not to arouse suspicion – you must think of your reputation too, my dear."

Cecilia nodded, nearly collapsing against her friend as she was shepherded down the alley. She righted herself and held her head high when they walked through the main street. She was not blind to the pitying stares directed her way, or the whispered conversations in her wake.

When they reached the vicarage, Amy put a supporting arm around Cecilia's waist and rapped on the door. Emma admitted them to the parlour, and in only a few moments William rushed into the room.

"Cecilia! My love," he said, hastily buttoning up the top of his shirt before crossing to her in two long strides and taking her hands.

He looked as though he hadn't slept in days. Deep, dark shadows lay beneath his eyes, the lines on his forehead seemed deeper, and his shoulders slumped. But his face still radiated adoration for her, even as his eyes were filled with concern.

"Hello, William," she said softly, aching to pull him into her arms.

Amy cleared her throat, and William whipped around to find her standing behind him.

"Miss Miller," he said, affecting a hasty bow. "How... good of you to come."

"Good day, Mr Brook," she said, and she looked from one to the other. "I will leave you to talk for a while, which I would say is against my better judgement, but we all know I have none."

"Thank you," William said, with an acknowledging nod.

"I shall be just across the hall, Cecilia," she said as she walked past them. She pulled the door to behind her, without closing it.

William led her to the couch, and they both sat down. Cecilia tried to look at him without betraying her anxiety, but she must have failed, for immediately he asked, "What have you heard?"

"Nothing but some vicious gossip," she said, trying to sound dismissive but coming off a little angry.

William blew out a breath. "I will spare you the indecency of having to mention it," he said. "Someone – I know not who, but I have my suspicions – has spread a rumour to do with my association with a certain woman in London... of ill repute."

His eyes didn't leave her face as he spoke, which gave her some confidence. Surely if he had something to hide, he would be ashamed. She nodded, annoyed with herself for blushing.

Still holding her hands, he gently rubbed her fingers with his thumbs. "I want you to know I am innocent," he said, staring straight into her eyes. "I am unable to share with you the details of my activities – I am promised by the strict confidences of my profession not to reveal any information. Do you understand?"

A confusing rush of emotions pulled at Cecilia's heart. His profession of innocence was relieving, but the secretive nature of the circumstances in question must surely render him guilty by the general populace. "I understand you cannot betray those who seek your counsel," she said. Her mind was racing too much to say more. Could that really be the extent of his explanation?

William sighed, and he withdrew one hand in order to put his fist to his chin as he looked away, thinking. "Cecilia, I have dwelled in worlds I hope you will never have the misfortune to know. I have seen both men and women in their lowliest states. In all cases I have been moved to help in any way I can. This – person – that I have helped is just one of many types of people, and she meant no more or less to me than anyone else. I wish I could tell you who she was, and what happened, but the story may damage more than just my reputation."

Cecilia leaned forward and pressed a hand to his knee. "But William, you must clear your name. You will be struck off... I cannot think what will happen to you. And I cannot abide thinking about you being sent away, without me."

He turned back to her. "Nor can I, my precious angel. But tell me, can you believe me?"

How could he doubt her, even for an instant? "Of course I do." In that moment, having heard him speak of so much history before they met, she realised how little she did know of him. Even though she trusted him implicitly, she worried about what other shadows might cross their future paths.

"I trust you," she said. "But William, can you promise me you did not... you have not..."

He smiled at her earnestly. "I promise Cecilia, with all my heart." His voice broke on the words. "My body is as chaste as yours, and I hope, one day..."

Cecilia's cheeks burned so red she thought they might catch on fire. She giggled when she saw that William was suffering from the same affliction. "Me too," she whispered.

As she studied his face, she noticed a small bright scar on his cheekbone. She reached out to touch it, and his eyes closed briefly. "William, however did you get this?"

He frowned, and a sigh escaped his lips. "It was... an accident. An error of judgement that I will do my utmost not to repeat."

A pointed throat-clearing emerged from the hallway.

"If we have more time in the future," William said, "I will tell you all about it."

At his words, Cecilia was reminded she had not shared something with him. Her mother had already written to Aunt Honoria regarding her relocation to London.

"Is there something you wish to tell me, dearest?" William searched her face and then cupped her chin in one hand.

As the tips of his fingers grazed her neck she shivered. She smiled at him as her cares seemed to melt into his touch. Now was not the time to burden him further, when still so much was unknown. "Only that I am yours forever," she whispered.

Chapter Twenty-Six

William remained in the parlour for a long time after he bade the ladies goodbye, his mind possessed by his beloved. His heart had broken at the sight of her face: eyes which had been troubled over Amy's misfortunes were now desolate and doubting. He hated that she was hurting, and worst of all, he and he alone was the cause. He longed to erase her worries, but given the chance he would not change the past actions which had led to this scandal. It was part of who he was.

Despite having no evidence with which to prove his innocence, she trusted him wholeheartedly. If ever there was an angel sent from heaven, his Cecilia was one. He knew not what he had done to deserve her heart, but now that it was his he would treasure it above all else. Her sweet declaration would stay with him always. But how could they be together with his future so uncertain?

He only wished he could spare her his shared humiliation. He wanted to take her to London right now to show her the truth. If only such a thing were possible.

At the sound of a carriage he looked outside to see the Ashworth crest. He was momentarily struck dumb with horror. Perhaps his judgement was to come this very moment, and he would never see Cecilia again.

Steeling himself, he watched as the carriage door opened. A lone footman exited the vehicle, and marched towards the house.

William gathered his coat and hat. "Emma," he called, "I am going out." He opened the front door just as the footman raised his arm to knock.

"Mr Brook!" The man took a second to recover his composure, before straightening again. "Lord Ashworth requests your presence at the Hall."

"Yes, yes, let us go," William said, anxious to learn his fate.

Quarter of an hour later in Lord Ashworth's study, William's patron had given him a chance to defend himself, and stared at him incredulously when he did not attempt to explain his actions.

"Will you not just deny that you ever laid eyes on the woman?" Ashworth sputtered.

William shook his head. "I cannot," he said. "It would be a lie."

Ashworth sighed. "If it was anyone else, of course we could simply sweep it under the rug. But as our vicar... well, it is just not the done thing. The village people must see strong leadership. If they don't obey their priest, I could have insubordination on my hands."

William held his breath. Ashworth leaned forward in his chair and laced his fingers together.

"I do not want to dismiss you outright," he said, "despite strong persuasion from certain quarters. I think you are doing good things in Amberley. Therefore I have appealed to Dean Roberts for his guidance in this matter. He is a trusted friend, and the villagers will not argue with his decision."

"I understand," said William, beginning to breathe again. "I thank you for not acting rashly. I wish to remain in your service."

Ashworth nodded. "It is a great pity, my boy," he said, coming around to rest a hand on William's shoulder in a startling display of affection. "I was sure you would see out your days here in the village."

William gulped. "I too," he said, though the words passing his lips stunned him.

⁂

As William walked through the village the next morning, he felt all eyes on him, much like the very first time he had walked the main street. This time, the whispers were not as quiet, and when he caught the eyes of some villagers they were indignant and incredulous in turn. William schooled his features, and did not rush his gait. He went about his business as he usually would, and carried out his duties over the next few days as if nothing had happened.

There was a church pew conspicuously empty at the Sunday service, and Amy's reappearance confirmed she knew Barrington was gone. There were other parishioners missing as well however, and William sensed there was a kind of boycott. He'd lost the faith of his flock.

A few days later, Emma presented him with some mail as he worked in his library. He'd received no invitations of late. Even the Stocktons had given up on marrying him to one of their daughters. There was only one letter today in a strange hand, and it was uncommonly battered. William felt a little deflated not to have received a missive from the dean himself, to reassure him all was not lost. Still, this could be news for Amy.

He studied the sender's address, and the mystery only deepened. "Africa?" he murmured. "Whatever could that be..."

He broke what was left of the seal, and took in the scrawled missive.

"No!" William sprang to his feet, and then gripped the edge of the desk, gasping for air. He bowed his head and a cry of anguish tore from his spirit.

Thomas was dead. He'd succumbed to a fever on the sea journey. On his sickbed, Thomas had included William in his next of kin to be notified. His acknowledgement of their strong friendship – nay, brotherhood – even to the last, shattered William's heart.

He stumbled over to the wall as sobs wracked his body. Slowly sinking to the floor, his vision blurred, and all he could see was Thomas on the day they'd said their farewells.

He had lost the dearest person to him in the world, the only one he had trusted with all his dreams and nightmares. Now he hoped Cecilia would be there to share himself with, but there could never be a replacement for the steadfast friendship and understanding he'd known with Thomas. They'd been cut from the same cloth, with the same goals and hopes.

"It should have been me," William whispered. He had surely been the stronger force in driving the two men towards an adventure in far off lands. It was his fault Thomas was gone. He should have been on that ship instead.

His fear of forming attachments was well-founded. The weight of guilt, grief and his own selfish ambitions threatened to consume him.

❧❦

Cecilia ran down the lane to Harcourt Lodge, with poor Lucy trailing behind. *If I hear one more person gossiping about William, I'll wring their neck.*

From a distance she saw the front door open, and her father helped Mrs Croxley into her gig. Cecilia slowed her pace, her eyes narrowed. As the gig drew past, the old woman greeted her with a smile, the kind of triumphant smile she wore after imparting some particularly juicy gossip.

Cecilia entered the house quietly, hoping she could make it to her bedroom undetected.

"Is that you, Cecilia?" Her father's voice preceded his presence in the hallway.

She sighed as she hung her bonnet on a hook, before turning to face him. "Hello, Papa."

"Your mother and I need to speak with you," he said. His serious tone set her nerves on edge.

She followed him into the drawing room and kissed her mother's proffered cheek before sitting on a chair opposite. Mr Grant took up a newspaper across the room.

"Cecilia," said Mrs Grant with an arched brow, "you will never guess what I just heard about Mr Brook."

"I know," Cecilia said wearily.

"You know?" She regarded her daughter with interest. "And what of your admiration for him now?"

"It is not true, Mama. I know it is not true."

"Oh, you *know*, do you? Has love blinded you thus? Well, I will tell you one thing. Any hope you may have had of marrying him is over. I will not have you aligned with someone tarnished by scandal."

"Marrying?" Mr Grant said from his seat near the window. "What's this?"

Mrs Grant waved a trivialising hand. "It does not signify." She brandished a letter in Cecilia's face. "Look what I have here."

Cecilia leaned over and reached for the paper, but Mrs Grant snatched it back, and held her spectacles up to her eyes as she read. "It is from Honoria," she said.

Cecilia's heart began to race. "Yes?"

"She is delighted with the prospect of hosting you in London for the season. In fact, she will meet you in town early, so that you may procure new gowns in time for the opening of Parliament. The Viscount will join you in January."

Cecilia's throat constricted. "How early?" she croaked.

Mrs Grant met her eyes. "You will leave in a week."

"What?" She gripped the arms of her chair and her knuckles turned white. She turned wide eyes to her father. "Papa, do you really want to send me away?"

Mr Grant set his newspaper aside and sighed. "I believe a change of scene would do you good."

Tears pricked Cecilia's eyes and she looked away. "I see." If her father agreed with the plan as well, there would be no arguing. Her heart throbbed in agony, as thoughts of William raced through her mind.

"It is really the only thing I can think to do, Cecilia," Mrs Grant said, with a hint of sympathy. "I had hoped for something else by now, but... you know."

Cecilia blinked and tears escaped down her cheeks. "And you will not come with me?"

Mrs Grant shook her head. "We cannot justify the expense. It is sensible to save the funds for your dowry. Honoria has agreed to fund your journey and living costs, and I cannot ask for more than that. Besides, I think it will be perhaps better to leave her to her own devices with regards to the management of your prospects. We never were able to agree on how to go about things."

"And so you may not meet the man Aunt Honoria pairs me with?"

"That may be so, but we trust her judgement. We can arrange to meet the gentleman once a betrothal is in place."

Cecilia could not believe she was even pretending to go along with the farcical idea that she could be engaged to a stranger in mere months. Her heart was with William and she could not even consider giving it to someone else.

She must find a way to let him know, and reassure him of her enduring affection. She hoped that he would wait for her, even through his trials. Would they ever find a way to be together?

❧

Grief kept William a prisoner in the vicarage for three days. Emma was his only company, and he kept his distance from her as well, preferring to dwell in his bedroom with the curtains closed. When would he learn what was to become of him? What further tragedies could possibly befall him?

He finally took tea in the parlour on Saturday, and he contemplated dressing properly so as to venture into the outside world. Perhaps Cecilia could be in the village. It would be a sweet balm for his soul to see her.

At the sound of furious rapping on the vicarage door, both William and Emma came running, and collided in the entry way.

"Sorry, sorry," William said, steadying her. He sent her back to the kitchen and threw open the door, wondering which of his accusers had arrived. Instead, Dean Roberts himself stood on the doorstep.

"Mr Dean, what a pleasant surprise." William reached out his hand.

Roberts ignored it and pushed his way inside. "We will see about that, young man," he said.

He entered the parlour and sat down on a chair without invitation, and William joined him hastily. "Mr Dean, you must be tired. Are you arrived direct from London? I will get you some tea."

"No." Roberts shook his head and sighed. "Brook, I have received word of scandal... sins of the flesh, disrespect of your benefactors ... and that you are upsetting the townspeople instead of appeasing them. Care to explain what on earth is going on?"

William's heart began to pound a panicked beat. He'd never seen the Dean so incensed. He took a fortifying breath. "Very well." He began to tell Roberts all of the pertinent details, right from his noting Barrington's improper behaviour at the ball, to Amy's disgrace and his staunch defence of her, Barrington's exposure and finally his revenge.

Roberts shook his head. "You were never one for the quiet life, were you, Brook? And what of these allegations?"

William squared his shoulders. "I know the lady in question, but the contentions are false."

Roberts closed his eyes and covered his face with one hand, as if at a loss of what to say. A few agonising moments later, he regarded William again. "Even if it is not true, it looks very bad. Could you not have been more selective in those you chose to help? Could you not have restricted your movements to our parish members, rather than roaming about the city like a vagrant?"

"Mr Dean, I –"

"Do you not see, Brook, what light this paints me in? I stuck my neck out for you. I went out of my way to assure the Barringtons you were more mature than your years. I convinced them a young priest with energy and vitality was just what the parish needed. I could not predict that your very spirit would be the cause of your downfall."

The man appeared to run out of steam. His face had turned bright red, and he ran a finger alongside the inside of his collar, from which his fleshy chin protruded.

A horrible defeat settled on William as he felt the weight of disappointing this father figure in his life. "I have done my best, sir," he said.

"Well, Brook," Roberts continued, "I think it is time to grant your wish. Perhaps you do need to be shipped off to a foreign country, if you will only serve to divide townspeople against each other. But there will be no church planting or bible translating or ministering to the heathens just yet... I shall assign you somewhere remote, where your physical strength will be utilised in basic practical deeds."

William gaped at him, unable to comprehend this proposition. The old part of himself begged him to jump at the chance to escape. It would be a fresh start, a way out. But he knew he was changed now. He knew what it was to be part of somewhere, to belong, and he knew what it was to love.

"With all due respect," he said slowly, "I would rather stay in Amberley, if you see me fit to continue here. Sir, I now see how right you were. I have so much to learn. I regret the position I now find myself in, with my very rectitude being questioned. I know not how I will regain the trust of the people, but I would like to try."

Roberts stared at him open-mouthed. "My, what a change of heart.

And there you were, only three months ago, writing to beg your hasty removal."

"I, uh, find I have gained affection for the townspeople." He blushed maddeningly.

"Ah, I see," the Dean said with a knowing nod. "Well, it is unlikely her family will allow the match now."

William bowed his head. "I am aware of that."

Roberts shook his head again. "You are a young man of such compassion, such potential. How great a pity it would be if you were not able to realise it. However, this is a matter of some delicacy."

He stood and walked about the room, with one arm behind his back and the other covering his mouth.

"Here is what will happen," he said, turning to face William. "Your presence in the village is currently a disturbance. You will leave Amberley for a month – go to your family. I will calm down the parishioners and seek their views on your character and the value of your service.

"There will be a town meeting at Christmas whereupon it will be decided if you will remain. Before that I will give my advice to Ashworth, but I leave your final fate in the hands of the congregation."

William swallowed. "That sounds fair. I would not want to stay against their wishes."

Roberts came to stand directly in front of William. "Make no mistake, Brook. If I decide to remove you from this post, it is unlikely you will find work as even a curate. You must prepare yourself for uncertain prospects."

"I understand, sir."

"You will give your last service tomorrow, and then on Monday be gone."

Chapter Twenty-Seven

There was something different about William's manner as he led the service. Even through these last trying weeks, his confidence in interpreting the gospel had not faltered. But today, Cecilia noticed a slight hesitation in his words, and a sort of sad resignation in his eyes. The church was only half-full today, with even more villagers choosing to abstain from his teachings. As she'd entered the church, William had not been there to greet her family. Instead, she was alarmed to find another cleric manning the door. Had they found a replacement so soon? She began to breathe again when she saw William standing alone by the lectern, his focus seemingly on the crucifix at the head of the chapel.

Cecilia tried to listen to William's words as he preached, but she spent much of the service trying to decide what she would tell him, and all she needed to ask, in the few moments he would be with her family after the service. The message, "I am to be sent to live with my Aunt in London" was obviously crucial, but she wanted desperately to then clarify how they might ever see each other again, what was going to happen to him, and if he knew more about Amy.

At the conclusion of the benediction she remained where she was as usual, waiting for those in the first rows of pews to leave. She was determined to remain for as long as possible, to allow William the time to reach the back of the church. But Mrs Grant swept her up and steered her out into the aisle.

Cecilia turned back toward William when they reached the end of the aisle and began to walk the short distance to the exit. She stared at him desperately, but he was entangled with Mrs Fortescue, and only noticed her accelerated departure a moment before she disappeared out the door. She saw the shock register on his face. She was ushered straight into the carriage, and from the window she saw him run out of the church. That was the last she saw of him that day.

At home, she went directly to her room and cried a little in frustration, waiting for Lucy to help her out of her Sunday clothes. At length the maid appeared, hastily slamming the door behind her and approaching her mistress with a decidedly conspiratorial countenance.

"Lucy? What is it?"

Lucy did not reply immediately, instead fishing around in her right pocket. She produced a folded piece of paper, which she handed to Cecilia. "It's from him, miss. The vicar."

Cecilia ran forward and snatched it up. "Thank you, Lucy! But how…"

"He was awful crafty-like, miss. He shook my hand and slipped it into my fingers. He ain't never shaken my hand before. He told me very quietly I must give it to you and nobody else."

"And no-one saw?"

Lucy shook her head. "And I didn't tell anyone, neither."

"You are a true friend, Lucy," Cecilia said, at which her maid beamed. "Please return to me in ten minutes."

Lucy nodded and left the room.

Cecilia settled on the edge of the bed and rapidly unfolded the note. Inscribed in William's hand were these words:

> My dearest Cecilia,
> I must see you, before we are parted.

Parted? Did he know about her forthcoming journey?

> Meet me tomorrow morning at half-past seven, in White's grove.
> If you cannot, I will understand, but if possible do send me a

return missive today so I may rest assured you received mine.

In the case that we cannot talk before we are separated, please know that I love you with all my heart, and I will do my utmost to be with you again and to make you my bride. However, I shall not ask that you wait for me, but make yourself or your family content with an alliance that may present itself in the meanwhile.

Until tomorrow I hope, I remain your devoted,

William

Cecilia gasped for air as a tear slid down her cheek. His declarations of love thrilled her, yet his reference to impending doom and the idea of her marrying someone else devastated her. What separation did he speak of? If he was to leave permanently, surely he would have said something this morning?

She read the beginning of the note again. He had chosen that hour because she should be able to escape the house undetected by her family. Some servants would be up, but her father never left his room for breakfast until nine, and her mother scarcely before ten. She should be able to be away for at least an hour before she was missed.

Lucy returned and helped her change her dress. Cecilia then ordered a bath, and proceeded to invent other excuses to avoid her family and remain in her room for the rest of the day. She did come down for dinner, but ate silently and quickly, returning to her room without spending time with her mother.

She rang for Lucy and performed her evening toilette two hours earlier than usual. The maid promised to wake her mistress up covertly at seven the following morning. Her parents might think she was sulking, but in truth she wanted to be well-rested for William, and she hoped the hours would fly by more quickly if she was in slumber.

It wasn't to be. She lay awake for almost the whole night.

When Lucy crept into her room and gently shook her shoulder, she had only drifted into a deep sleep a short time before. They got her ready silently in the frigid air, and Cecilia tiptoed out of the conservatory French doors, gasping at the chill of the late November morning.

Her shoes crunched over the frost as she swiftly turned behind the house and out to the boundary of their lands. She was sure the whole village could hear her progress, but nothing stirred, save some blackbirds beginning their chorus. The sun was just turning the rim of the hills an apricot orange, and a mist rose up from the river.

She made her way up over a bluff and down along the track into a copse by a stone wall. As soon as she was hidden from view she saw William standing among the tree trunks. Immediately he ran towards her, and after a slight pause to smile at her and look into her eyes, he drew her into his arms.

"Cecilia," he murmured as he nuzzled into her hair and neck, his words almost a sigh.

"Good morning, my darling," she said, pressing her cheek against his and revelling in his strength enveloping her. She relaxed against him, and was suddenly aware that every part of her was touching him. She had hugged male relatives on occasion, so she must have been this close to a man before, albeit briefly. But as she ran her hands up his back and felt him drag his lips tenderly over her neck, a delicious warmth flooded her body, the like of which she'd never known.

He pulled back, taking her hands and beholding her properly. "How I have missed you," he said, his velvety brown eyes liquid pools of adoration.

"And I you," she said, squeezing his hands. "I was in agony when Mama tore me away after the service."

"If you could have heard my heart beat once I realised," he said. "When I missed the chance to give you the note myself I guarded the door, intent on cornering your maid."

She smiled at him fondly. "Oh William, I know we must not have much time. How are we to say all the things that need to be said?"

He sighed. "I suppose we must begin with the most important. I have some news which you will not much care for."

Her hand flew to her mouth. "What is it?"

"Dean Roberts is arrived from London. The rumours about me outraged him so much he flew here with righteous vengeance."

"Oh dear. I know how you respect him. Are you badly shaken? What did he say?"

"I managed to calm him, somewhat, but he told me to leave the village at once and go to my family estate. He will investigate matters and determine what my future will be."

She nodded, the blood draining from her face. They had even less time than she thought. "And thus you are banished," she said. "And I shall have to leave before you find out your fate."

His face darkened and he took in a sharp breath. "Leave?"

Cecilia nodded sadly. "I am to be sent to my aunt in London, in order to be matched with a suitable husband. Mama was vexed when I refused Mr Barrington, and now she has washed her hands of me."

William stepped back a little, his eyes wide. "London! But surely, you will not leave before the season."

Her heart ached and she shook her head. "I am to leave on Thursday. There is much to be done to prepare before Parliament brings the best families to London in January."

He blew out a slow breath. "I see. There will be Christmas parties and entertainments to attend, no doubt. And then you shall be as good as betrothed."

She stepped towards him. "But I did not get engaged in my last season."

"Now your beauty is blooming so brightly, I have no doubt you will need to beat them off with a stick. And if I am ruined –"

"William, it matters not…"

He held up a hand. "If I am ruined, and I cannot provide the life you are worthy of, I will not expect you to carry through with your promises. I shall release you from any obligations."

Her breath caught in her throat. "No, my love, I shall stand by you."

"We cannot marry if I have not the means to support us."

Desperate to change the subject, she said, "Is there any progress on what will happen to Amy?"

He shook his head. "I have tried to convince all the families who could shelter her that it is doing the Lord's work, but they all cry off. So far my search for a respectable charity house nearby has failed, but I will continue to make enquiries from afar."

Cecilia gazed through the trees. "Whatever will she do?"

"If it comes down to it, her best option would be to get to Shrewsbury and beg for shelter at the Cathedral. I fear she will long be a target for devious men."

She felt sick inside, and William took her hand, pressing it gently. With his other hand, he reached into his jacket and withdrew a card.

"This is my family's address, if you need to get word to me." He handed it to her. "It is not so far from London. Perhaps I can visit you."

Hope sprang up within Cecilia, but was almost immediately crushed by despair. "It is no good, Aunt Honoria will never agree to our match. You will not be admitted to the house." Reckless inspiration struck her. "We could run away. Over the border to Gretna Green."

He touched his fingers to her lips. "Hush, I will not consider it. You deserve a dignified marriage, not a guilty one." He tipped her chin up toward him and she found reassurance in his eyes. "Do not give up hope yet. I may yet arrange things to make myself appear more eligible."

"But how?" She could not stop the rising panic. "What shall we do if you are sent abroad?"

"I will do anything in my power to have you with me, whether in England or not."

"And we cannot write to each other without a betrothal. Even if I tried I know the mail would not leave the house."

"If I need to get word to you, I will," he said simply. "You know how determined I am."

She smiled. "Yes, I do."

He took her face in both his hands, and drew it towards his, taking her lips in a soft, lingering kiss.

☙❧

Her eyes remained closed for a few moments after he drew back, but when she opened them her shining topaz irises spoke of love and soothed his soul.

Still holding her jaw, he said, "I only wish that you will find a way to contact me, if you are to marry another."

Cecilia gasped, and a sudden tear rolled down one cheek. "It is unthinkable," she whispered.

He let go, and took her hands again. "Even so, you must prepare yourself. We cannot know the plans the Almighty has for us, and if there is one thing I have learned it is that you cannot force them. No matter how much you think your desires are in tune with his plans, sometimes he has something else, something ultimately more fulfilling, in mind."

She frowned. "Do you feel you have served your purpose in Amberley, William?"

"I cannot help feeling there is more to be done, but I hope I have been of use during these... trials." He attempted a smile. "Perhaps the purpose was for me to meet you. Perhaps our – friendship – will bring about other good. We shall know in time."

Her chin quivered. "But what will I do without you?"

He took a deep breath, and gently stroked her cheek. "Let us not think about that now," he said, thinking of how much she had changed him for the better, even as he spoke the words. "All we have is today, and we shall endure it as best we can."

She nodded and smiled a little. "You are right. Our last moments together – for now – should not be tainted with sadness and worry for a future we know not of."

He sat on the stonewall and patted the spot next to him, which she instantly availed herself of, nuzzling into his chest as he wrapped his arm about her. His mind strayed to Thomas, as it often did.

She chose that moment to raise her head, and her eyes widened when they met his.

"William?" She sat up straighter and stroked his cheek with the back of her hand. "There is something else. What is it?"

He hesitated, his old instincts reluctant to let the hurt come to the surface. But as he took in the pure compassion of her expression, he succumbed to the relief of sharing the burden.

He let out a shuddering breath. "It is Thomas," he said, his voice breaking. "He died on the way to India."

She gasped. "Oh, my dear..." She put both of her arms around him, and he collapsed onto her shoulder, breathing in her quiet strength. His façade of calm assurance broke, and he let himself receive her comfort as she whispered consoling words. He was so used to being the one to provide sympathy and support to others, needing to have all the answers. It was a revelation to give up control and be vulnerable, in complete trust and security.

There they remained in silence for several minutes, William drinking in her closeness. When he'd composed himself, he sat up and smiled at her, trying to memorise every curve of her face. "I feel as though I should give you a gift," he said. "Some token of my affection."

"I still have your books –"

"Which you may keep."

"And the exquisite oil paint, and your note... and the viola."

He looked down at her suddenly. "The viola? You kept it?"

She nodded. "So you see it is I that has not given *you* anything."

No, you have given me everything. "The memory of your beauty – and your beautiful spirit – is enough," he said.

"William!" She blushed. "Who knew a vicar could say such sentimental things."

As he took in every inch of her features, his eyes rested on a curl which wafted about her cheek. "But… would you mind ever so if I took a small lock of your hair?"

She shook her head, and the objects in question bobbed about charmingly, as if in competition to be picked as his prize. "But you had better take one from the back."

She swivelled around, and for a moment he was overcome by the loveliness of her long graceful neck and her smooth shoulders. Unable to tear his eyes away, he fished in his pocket for his pen knife, at last withdrawing it and selecting the longest tendril. He sliced up through the hair and, on seeing the golden strands now orphaned in his hand, was engulfed momentarily by despair.

Cecilia turned back around, saying, "Did you get it?"

He met her eyes and nodded. He withdrew his handkerchief and placed the lock in the centre, folding it up carefully. "It is nothing really, compared to its owner," he said, "but it will remind me of the golden-haired angel who brought light into my life."

A shiver shook her. "William, do not talk as if I am gone, or dead."

He put the handkerchief back in his pocket and took her hands. "No, you are right, we must hope for the best."

"When do you leave Amberley?"

"I must leave for Cambridgeshire today, almost this minute."

She gasped.

"I shall return here to await the Dean's conclusions," he continued, "and to face the judgement of the people at a special meeting. I may not end up in Amberley, but I must return in an attempt to clear my name."

She put her hand over his. "I will try to convince Roberts you have behaved in a godly manner, if I am able to talk to him."

"He will think you are biased," he said with a rueful smile. "Everyone seems to know about us."

"As well they should," she said, "for we shall be together, no matter what they all think."

He laughed softly and stood, also bringing her to her feet. "Ah, my defiant little miss. You did always have a shocking lack of respect for society's mores."

"And you, my dear vicar, would never be content with a staid woman who always did as she is told."

He grinned at her, and gave her an affectionate tap on the nose before sliding his arms around her waist. "How well you know me. I love you, Cecilia."

She melted against him. "And I you, William."

He sealed their declarations with a kiss, more passionate than they had ever shared. When he at last broke off from her eager response, his head spinning, he wondered if it could really be a sin to kiss a maiden, when he had committed his whole heart to her, when she was so lovely and pure, and when it provoked the most heavenly feelings ever stirred within him.

Chapter Twenty-Eight

William had written to Charles to warn of his impending arrival. He knew not whether to expect his elder brother to be home, as they had not been in contact since William's visit to the London townhouse. Charles could be away at a house party or hunting stags in Scotland for all he knew. At any other time, William would have almost wished him away, but on this occasion he needed to speak with his brother. He doubted his second brother George would be there as he was stationed in France.

He did not take all of his belongings with him. Even if he was to be extradited from the village for good, at least having some possessions within the vicarage would allow him an excuse to return. As he gathered up the necessary personal items, he stopped by the library for his bible and some lessons he was working on. His attention was drawn to the gap on the shelf, where the fine arts books had been. They were with Cecilia and oh, how he longed to be in their place. What was she doing now? Having breakfast with her parents as though nothing had happened?

In truth he was sorely tempted to storm over there, pick her up, and whisk her off to Gretna Green. Then he could take her to his family estate and present her as his very own, and spare her the trouble of having to be put on show by Aunt Honoria. They could face his trial in Amberley together.

But it wasn't to be. She deserved to have a respectable marriage, endorsed by her parents and with the blessing of the whole community. Perhaps, he thought with a glance skyward, their union was not God's will. His heart protested vehemently. He must do whatever he could to win her, before accepting an alternative fate.

At the sound of the hackney coach pulling up, William left the house and carried his bag down the garden path. Emma tried valiantly to suppress her emotions, but when he reached out to her, she collapsed into his bosom and sobbed.

"I shall be back, Emma," he said, "mark my words. We will be bumping into each other in the hallway again before you know it."

Her cries gave way to laughter, and she swiped her tears away as she stepped back. "I'll hold you to that, sir."

William stepped up into the coach, and took a final look at the vicarage before the vehicle moved away. He didn't want to be at his childhood home, where he was resented. But he knew not where else he could go.

You can go away, and never come back. The treacherous voice from deep inside his old wounds whispered to his conscience. It would be easier, less painful, to abandon all hope and run away, perhaps to the continent at first. He was banished; this was his perfect opportunity to escape. He'd do what Thomas never should have done.

But for some reason, he had an inexplicable conviction that his work in Amberley was not finished, that somehow the residents needed him... that there were storms yet to be weathered, and he wouldn't weather them alone.

As they drove through the village, his conviction became stronger and stronger. His sense of belonging was palpable as the faces of each villager came to mind, along with their stories. Perhaps it would be the last time he saw the main street as a resident himself. That saddened him beyond measure. It had been the very first place in the world where he had had a purpose all of his own, an existence and destiny he could shape, and a role only he could fill in the lives of these people. While the pull to adventure abroad tempted him, perhaps it was all a horrible gamble that would pale in comparison to what he had here.

Cecilia could feel Amy's protruding stomach as she embraced her friend in the kitchen at Ashworth Hall. Knowing eyes would recognise the slightly altered draping of Amy's dress.

"They will let me stay until Christmas," Amy told her when they were seated alone at the large table, "and then I am on my own."

Cecilia battled to restrain her emotions. "Will you go to the convent in Shrewsbury?"

Amy nodded.

"They – they will certainly force you to leave the child?"

"I believe so." Amy sighed and threw up her hands in a helpless gesture. "I intend to beg for some sort of employment there, but I do not fancy my chances." She took hold of her belly. "I must leave him to be brought up in an orphanage, if he is to survive at all." She looked at Cecilia through her lashes. "I've taken to calling him Ben, you know. I think I" – she choked back a cry – "I already love him. He is a part of me, even though he represents such filth and sorrow."

Cecilia pulled her chair closer and put her arm around Amy, knowing it was cold comfort. "I only wish someone could go with you," she said, her mind racing. "I could run away..."

Amy put a restraining hand on Cecilia's arm. "No. This is my burden. I would not have your reputation, your future, sullied by leaving your family's protection. This is something I must do on my own. I have just enough funds for the journey."

Her resigned determination wrenched Cecilia's heart. "And what then of your fate? If the convent will not employ you?"

"I will visit every shop in the town, every seamstress, every milliner... I must find employment. And if I cannot..."

Their eyes met, sharing knowledge of the worst.

Cecilia shook her head. "You must not give up – there will be a position for you somewhere. You have ladylike manners, and would be perfectly suited to work in a shop."

"If I am able to procure a reference." Amy looked away. "I even pleaded with John – Mr Barrington – to take me as his mistress... to do with me what he will, if he would only provide a situation for me somewhere." Her eyes darkened. "But he said a woman's body after childbirth was forever altered, and of no use to him."

Cecilia fought the urge to retch. Recovering, she was anxious to break the silence. "If you are settled at an address, send word to my aunts'. Even before then, I will anxiously await any news."

Amy smiled. "Nonsense, you'll be too busy catching a husband." At Cecilia's protest, she laid a finger to her friend's lips. "It will cause me further distress if you worry for me, dearest. It will cheer me to know you are settled well."

The very idea of settling with anyone except William made Cecilia descend even further into melancholy, and her expression must have revealed her emotions.

"You will miss Mr Brook," Amy said softly.

Cecilia nodded. "All of this is unjust in the extreme. How can everyone believe this story without attempting to prove it? Will no one seek out the truth?"

A spark flew from Amy's eyes. "My dear," she said slowly, "you will be in London. If no-one else will look for the facts…"

The suggestion hit Cecilia like a lightning bolt. "Of course! If ever I can escape from Aunt Honoria's watch, I can attempt to discover what really happened."

Amy nodded. "But how will you progress? I'm lead to believe the clergy who betrayed William have been well bribed to stay silent."

"I must do something. As you rightly point out, in London I will be closer than anyone to the truth. I only need a starting point from which to make enquiries." Another idea crashed into her brain. "And I know exactly who to ask."

❧

As William approached the house, the evening sun at its rear cast long shadows over the entrance, so that before the coach pulled up, it was enveloped in the darkness.

Similarly, a shadow fell across his heart. He emerged from the carriage and gazed up at the red brick manor, in the Brook family for several generations. To him it felt less like a home, and more like a prison. He'd barely been back since he left for Cambridge eight years ago.

Charles did not appear from the huge main doors, but a few of the staff filed outside. In his eyes they looked upon him with disapproval.

The accidental, unwanted youngest son. The one who killed their mistress.

He'd forgotten how cold the manor could be. Though the fire lit in his room soon took the chill off, moving around the halls and corridors required a swift foot to avoid shivering. Most of the rooms in the house had walls covered with dark wood panelling, so even those with south-facing windows seemed darker than they ought. As he walked back down the main staircase, memories of his childhood flooded his mind. Of creeping around the hallways so as not to disturb the family, used as he was to their belittling insults. Of hiding in the library under a table or in a dark nook, and finally, of timing his escape through the servants' quarters to avoid being seen. He would then find the rector and shadow him, absorbing his teachings and helping him see to the needs of the parish.

As he searched in vain for Charles, he became that little boy again. With each step, all his old insecurities and inadequacies threatened to devour him. He stopped and clutched at a side table in the vestibule, trying to calm his rapid breathing.

His own reflection confronted him in a grand mirror above the table. The man staring back at him was a surprise. In his eyes he saw a new confidence, a new hope, born of unconditional love. Despite his recent troubles, he no longer yearned for escape. He had a new purpose, in life and in love.

He was not that little boy any more. As a man he had responsibilities to fulfil, and a new life to lead. He would not leave this house until he had what he needed to make his dreams come true.

"Well, if it isn't the vagabond vicar, returned home at last."

The voice sent a chill down William's spine. He turned around slowly, and squared his shoulders.

"Hello, Charles."

He wasn't hiding anymore.

Chapter Twenty-Nine

Cecilia guessed Mrs Croxley would be in her usual spot bordering the village green. It was a prime opportunity for townspeople observation. Indeed she wondered what Mrs Croxley had learned about *her* as she'd wandered past this place... perhaps with William?

She carried her basket along the street on the pretence of a shopping errand. She'd stuffed a large chequered cloth into the basket, to disguise its betraying emptiness. She even swung the basket back and forth as she strolled toward the green, congratulating herself on the appearance of carefree nonchalance. Inwardly the shivered as she crossed the shadows cast by the clock tower, and then she caught sight of her quarry. Mrs Croxley sat on the stone bench in the sunniest spot next to the green, her hands busy with lace-making.

She held her breath, hoping the woman hadn't seen her start. She kept up a studied casual pace, swinging the basket as she walked towards Jones'.

"Cooo-eee! Miss Gra-ant!"

Cecilia stopped in her tracks at the sound of the shrill cry. She couldn't hide her smile. The woman was so predictable, thank goodness. She'd fallen right into the trap. Turning, she changed her wry expression to studied friendliness, and strode towards the woman. "Why Mrs Croxley, how lovely to see you. I take it you are enjoying the sun?"

"Indeed, my dear, indeed. No doubt your mother has sent you on an important mission. Or are you in search of trinkets or art materials?"

Cecilia's pulse quickened. Lying was not her forte. "More of an important mission," she said, then giggled a little too loudly. That was not a lie. It was important in the extreme. And fortunately, she did not have to expend any effort in leading the conversation.

"The village does seem to be quiet without Mr Brook, does it not?"

Cecilia endeavoured to disguise the small gasp which escaped on the mention of William's name. How she ached for him.

Mrs Croxley's hands paused for a moment and she leaned forward with hungry eyes, her mouth open.

Cecilia lowered her gaze for a moment in an effort to compose herself. "His absence will surely be felt by many," she replied slowly.

"To be sure, it will. In particular I believe some young females may see their hopes dashed if he is to never return."

At the very idea Cecilia swayed a little, her head swimming in anguish.

Mrs Croxley smiled, a horrid knowing smile, and Cecilia knew she'd let down her guard. The old woman's self-satisfied expression revealed she'd obtained her goal; the reason she'd called Cecilia over in the first place.

"You are a particular friend of the vicar's, are you not?"

Cecilia's heart hammered in her chest. How she longed to shout of her love, but William had made her promise not to, to guard against further hurt should the worst happen. "Mr Brook is certainly a good friend to me," she said, "as he was – *is* to a good many people."

Mrs Croxley's eyes flashed. "Ah, it seems he has been a little *too* friendly in the past."

Anger boiled in Cecilia's stomach. "We cannot be quick to judge," she said in a rush, and then she quickly drew breath, remembering to measure her words. "Mr Brook is a good man. Can anyone believe these allegations?"

"I have it on good authority that there are eye witnesses," Mrs Croxley said in a patronising sing-song tone.

Pain and panic pressed on Cecilia's heart. The shock and sadness of the accusation hit her afresh once again. It only served to strengthen her resolve. It was time to finish this conversation, before she fell into a swoon. "Does the vestry even know of the name of the, er, establishment?"

"Indeed they do, Miss Grant. Mrs Fortescue told me. It is the House of Lillian." She settled into a cloud of smugness.

House of Lillian. House of Lillian. Cecilia repeated the name like a mantra in an effort to burn it on her brain. "I see," she murmured. "What a fine memory you have, Mrs Croxley."

"I pride myself on it, Miss Grant." She looked about furtively and then leaned forward again. "I hear the dean from London will confer with Lord Ashworth, and there will be a town meeting at which Mr Brook's fate will be decided."

Cecilia knew the most effective way to make her forthcoming absence known. Indeed, this would almost be like a reward to Mrs Croxley for her unknowing co-operation. "I shall not be present," she said, smoothing her skirt with care. She jumped when her hand was taken up and squeezed.

"Too painful, dear?"

Cecilia forced herself to look into the woman's eyes, and tried to discern whether the compassion she saw there was true or a selfish pretence. Even if she had remained, it probably would have been distressing to see William on a trial of sorts, but she would have at least been there to stand up for him, stand by him.

"No indeed," she said with a tilt of her chin. "I will be away, visiting my aunt."

Mrs Croxley let go of Cecilia's hand and sat back, resuming her spinning. "Lady Holcombe, I take it?"

"Yes, Mrs Croxley. I am to reside at her house in London for a time."

"How nice for you to get away, dear," Mrs Croxley said. "Although I must confess, there was talk you would disappear in another direction."

Cecilia raised her brows. "Oh yes?"

Mrs Croxley smiled indulgently. "Indeed. There was a whisper that naughty Mr Barrington would take a wife before he fled to Hampshire."

How dare she even mention his name? It sounded as a curse to Cecilia's ears. "I pity the young woman who bears his name," she spat out. She instantly regretted voicing the bitter words before this audience.

Mrs Croxley chuckled. "There were those of us who wondered if your family might succeed in forging an alliance."

Cecilia could tolerate no more, and fearing her tongue would betray her further, decided to take her leave. "I must bid you a good day, Mrs Croxley," she said between her teeth, though she tried to keep her voice light. "I dare not keep my mother waiting." She spun on her heel and took a deep breath before starting off.

"You'll be missed, my dear," Mrs Croxley called after her.

"I think it highly unlikely," Cecilia muttered under her breath as she stalked towards Jones'. "You will miss only the gossip I may have provided."

She threw open the door to the shop and once inside, collapsed against it. Staring at the ceiling with unseeing eyes, she recited the name of the brothel to herself one more time.

"May I help you, Miss Grant?"

Cecilia gasped, her hand flying to her mouth.

Mr Jones stood in front of her, his smile disappearing. "Are you quite all right?"

"Oh yes, of course," Cecilia said with a laugh. "I was only lost in my thoughts."

They stared at each other for a moment. "How may I be of assistance?" Mr Jones prompted.

"Ah. Yes." Cecilia scanned the shop. "I am in need of..." – she walked around a rack of coats towards the bonnets – "...some ribbons please, Mr Jones. I see you have some lovely new colours."

Mr Jones followed her and ran his hands over his stock, beaming. "As a matter of fact Miss Grant, they arrived only yesterday."

Cecilia smiled at him. "I shall take half a yard of each, please," she said.

"Certainly!" Mr Jones ran away to fetch his scissors.

Mama will scold me for spending so much. No matter: if she had to go away she might as well have something nice to dress her bonnets with.

❧

Joseph helped Cecilia into the coach. He was to be her escort for the trip to London.

Tears flooded down her cheeks as she settled onto the seat, and she barely noticed the manservant as he sat opposite.

"There now, miss, don't be sad."

Cecilia choked on a breath. "Have you ever truly loved someone, Joseph?"

Joseph's eyes widened, then he looked down at his hands and sniffed. "Perhaps I have, miss."

"Then you know the sorrow of parting," she said. "It feels as if your heart will never mend."

Joseph met her eyes again, his own filled with emotion. "I do know, miss," he said, with a crack in his voice. "But we have a long journey ahead of us. Try to occupy your mind with other things, else I may need to carry you from the carriage at the coaching inn."

Cecilia smiled a little. "I will try Joseph, for your sake. I would not want to cause you injury."

∎

William endured an uneasy armistice with Charles for several days, as he gathered his thoughts and judged the man's moods, seeking the best time to make his case. He stood his ground in moments when it was clear Charles wished him absent, but when he was at last overpowered by the need to get some space himself, his footsteps automatically directed him to the church.

He paused as he entered the churchyard, surprised by conflicting emotions. The graveyard and the church itself were so familiar, and yet something was different. The building seemed smaller than he remembered somehow, and the trees which overhung the yard appeared more gnarled as their limbs stretched over the gravestones. Still, it was more of a home to him than the manor had ever been. He couldn't wait to find the rector.

He stepped into the church, and instantly felt at ease, taking in the many pews and the stained-glass window. "Hello?"

A stranger dressed in cleric's robes emerged from one of the chapels at the rear of the building. "Yes, may I help you, my son?"

"Good day to you. I am seeking the rector, Mr Phillips? He is an old friend."

The man shook his head. "The rector is away visiting his daughter in

Suffolk. I am performing his duties as curate for two months."

Disappointment crashed over William like a tidal wave. There was no-one in the village who understood him like Mr Phillips. "I see," he murmured. "Well, if you do not mind, I will spend some quiet time in contemplation."

"Very good, sir. Do let me know if you need anything."

William sat in the family pew automatically, attempting to sort through his feelings. Without the man, the building seemed to lose the homely quality it possessed in William's youth. He chastised himself. This was a house of worship, not merely his escape for surrogate parental affection.

In the stillness, he was alone with his God, and unable to hide from his emotions.

He had to finally admit it to himself: his desire to leave England really was running away: the ultimate escape for hurt – both in the past and the future. As a missionary he had thought he would move with the need, and would not allow himself to commit his heart. Even without the pull of Amberley, he could see his motivations had been wrong. There was no escaping deep human connections, nor should he try.

He couldn't run from himself... he would carry the hurt with him wherever he went. Opening up to Cecilia's love had shown him a life he'd been missing out on. He had more to give than just a vicar's love. He could be a husband, a father, a friend... roles he'd scarce allowed himself to hope for. There were so many rich experiences he had been denying himself out of fear. Now, without any distractions or justifications, it was all too clear.

He gazed up at the vaulted ceiling. It would be some years yet before the rector would leave this mortal coil, but even then William doubted he would aspire to take up this particular living. This town was not his home; he would always feel an imposter here.

He got up and left the empty church. The silence was overbearing.

Cecilia barely had time to settle into London before the whirlwind of activity began. Aunt Honoria kept her busy at all hours of the day, leaving her no time to pursue any enquiries on William's behalf. In all the flurry of dress fittings, calling on acquaintances, and even dance lessons, she had not had any time to herself.

It seemed many fashionable families had come to London early and would spend Christmas in the shops and tea houses. Invitations to dinner, parties and balls began to circulate.

With the numerous morning visits, and sojourns in the park during the fashionable hour, the names and faces became a blur. Cecilia was sensible of the assessing looks cast in her direction by members of both sexes, but she kept her eyes to herself. Before she knew it, days had turned into weeks. Her wardrobe began to swell with new dresses, and she began to dread her first formal engagements.

When at last she had a few hours of leisure one morning, she allowed herself to dream of her life as she wished it to be. She touched her lips, remembering the taste of William in their last all-consuming kiss. She brought her paints to the drawing room, and drew a picture which flowed from her hands in a direct stream from her heart.

So consumed was she in her art, she didn't notice her aunt entering the room, and fairly hit the ceiling at the words spoken over her shoulder.

"What a pretty cottage."

"Aunt Honoria!" Her heart hammered wildly. "I did not know you were there." She blinked and regarded her work, and she was only then sensible of what she'd illustrated. It was the vicarage of Amberley, the place her emotions now called home. Along with the house itself, she'd painted the vegetable garden William had planted to the side, and the church in the background. In front of the garden gate, there was a dash of purple, which only she knew were violas.

"I am sure I have seen that before," Aunt Honoria said, coming around to sit opposite her niece at the little table.

Cecilia took a breath, unwilling to reveal what it meant to her. "It is – it is in Amberley," she said finally.

Aunt Honoria nodded. "That explains it. A very pleasant scene."

"You have no idea," she mumbled.

"I beg your pardon, Cecilia?"

She shook her head to quash the conversation, and returned her attention to the page. She dipped her brush in the black pigment, and began to paint a figure working in the garden. She remembered that day just three short months ago, when her heart first began to stir for him, when she'd seen him as more than a vicar... as a man. He'd been in her heart ever since, and would ever be.

"Aunt Honoria," she said, her voice wavering. "Am I to have any influence in who will ask for my hand?"

Honoria put a hand to her niece's chin. "Child, are you on the verge of tears?" Her eyes narrowed as she searched Cecilia's face. "I declare, I begin to wonder if you are more afraid if we do find you a husband, than if we do not. Is there something you are not telling me?"

Cecilia contemplated confiding in her aunt. She hated deception, and perhaps if Honoria knew she'd already given her love to another, she might be able to help. But looking into the older woman's eyes, she did not read compassion there. Suddenly she knew that if Honoria was aware of her intention to avoid being matched with a man during this season, it would only make her aunt even more determined to see her committed to a "suitable" match, and make for more awkward interactions between them.

She decided on a response. "Only that I would like my feelings to be taken into account when you consider who should offer for me."

"Why of course, my dear," Aunt Honoria said, sitting back in her chair with a smile. "But first I will advise you on precisely whom it is appropriate for you to develop feelings for."

Cecilia sighed and return to her artwork. Her heart had already decided on that score, and it did not care to play by anyone's rules, whether appropriate or not.

Chapter Thirty

The following day was dedicated to preparing Cecilia for her first ball. She was puffed, primped and pinched until she could bear it no more. Upon arrival, her senses were so overwhelmed by the colours, scents and sounds, that it was all she could do to follow Aunt Honoria through the crush.

She curtsied when introduced, and put a smile on her face when addressed. Aunt Honoria supervised the entries in her dance card as they encountered various gentlemen. Cecilia did not look any of them in the eye.

As the evening progressed, she fell deeper and deeper into melancholy. She willed her feet to move about the floor, but each step she danced towards these gentlemen was another step away from William, and another crack in her bleeding heart.

Her disposition was not lost on her aunt, and she was confronted immediately on re-entering the carriage for the homeward journey.

"Now Cecilia, if that is how you conduct yourself at social gatherings it is no wonder you haven't any proposals. I have never seen a young lady with such a stubbornly sullen countenance. I do not recall you being thus during your first season, only that you seemed shy or nervous. What is the matter with you?"

Cecilia winced, but not at the rubbing in of her apparent lack of suitors. She yearned to tell the world she *had* had a proposal: two in fact.

One from a lying rake who would have made her rich, and one from a wonderful man who would make her richer still.

"I am sorry to disappoint you, Aunt," was the extent of her reply. She dared not promise any improvement in her behaviour. Her mind was wandering toward how she may get out of the townhouse in the coming days in order to clear William's name.

A dreadful storm precluded her from venturing out for three days, and her hours were filled with thoughts of her beloved and composing letters to Amy. The following day her plans were stymied by morning callers. She was summoned to the drawing room, and glanced at the visiting family briefing as she made her curtsey. Her attention was caught by a young man, who stared earnestly back at her. He appeared to be accompanied by his mother and a sister, introduced as the Roxboroughs.

Her eyes flew to Aunt Honoria, whose expression made it clear she did not intend to waste this opportunity. Cecilia's breath left her body. This was different to her mother's futile attempts to introduce her to country suitors. This was serious. Her aunt was well within her powers to encourage a courtship and even a proposal, and she had limited power to delay the process. Her time may be running out. Oh, when would William come for her?

The only available chair in the room was conspicuous in its proximity to the gentleman in question. She perched on it cautiously, and was surprised to see a familiarity in the man's eyes, which she couldn't help noticing were animated and kindly.

"Do you not remember, Miss Grant?" he whispered. "We danced together on Wednesday evening."

Cecilia barely refrained from saying, "oh, did we?" She caught herself just in time – she didn't need to offend the gentleman. He was being very good about it, regarding her with a mix of disbelief and amusement.

"Of course," she said. "How nice to see you again." She dropped her eyes to her lap, where they remained through the small talk which followed, and into the tea service.

"Lady Holcombe."

Cecilia jumped at the sound of the deep baritone voice from beside her.

"May I obtain your consent to take Miss Grant for a stroll? The pavements are quite dried out."

Cecilia tried to hide her involuntary cringe.

"Certainly, Lord Roxborough," Aunt Honoria cooed. "I shall ring for Mary to accompany you."

Cecilia's palms began to sweat. "Aunt Honoria –"

Her aunt directed her a pointed smile and turned to ring the bell. "Some air will do you good, my dear," she said.

Before she knew it, Cecilia had been bustled out the door with the baron, and while she accepted his arm, as they began to walk she kept her body as far from his as possible. The maid Mary followed a few steps behind. They began a slow circuit of Golden Square. The sun was high but it gave little warmth. Cecilia observed the bare branches of the trees and shivered, pulling her cloak tighter about her.

Lord Roxborough cleared his throat. "I did not see you in town this past season, Miss Grant."

"No," she said, her voice quivering. "I remained in the country and have only been in London these past weeks."

"I see. Well, I am very glad you are arrived."

The feeling in his voice drew her to look at him, and his expression was open and eager. He did seem like an amiable gentleman, and was certainly not displeasing to the eye, but her heart drummed in her chest in vehement protest. Without thinking, she yanked her hand from his arm.

His brows shot up, his mouth dropping open. They walked along in awkward silence.

"Miss Grant," he began anew, "I had thought you were merely shy the other night, but now I suspect there are other forces at work."

He stepped in front of her, and she stumbled to avoid bumping into him. She heard Mary exclaim behind her, and looked back to see the maid on her heels, before making a tactful retreat of several paces.

"I am not one for dancing around the heart of the matter," Lord Roxborough said. "I will tell you that you have bewitched me, and I should like very much to court you."

Cecilia gasped. How could she have bewitched him, when they had hardly spoken more than a dozen words to each other?

"But I suspect that beneath your veil of politeness, you would much rather be somewhere else." He dipped his head, attempting to meet her gaze. "*With* someone else."

Her eyes finally flashed to his. His were not angry, merely understanding.

"Am I right?"

Cecilia's breathing accelerated as she shrank under his penetrating stare. This man was dangerous. He was someone she could not dislike, and he already knew too much. He would likely provide the material comfort her family desired for her. If she had met him earlier in the year, she may have accepted him as a suitor. She may not have found love with William. She shuddered. Not then, not now. William had offered to give her up, but she would not give up on him.

She didn't want to lie to Lord Roxborough, or give him false hope. She wished he were disagreeable, so she had an excuse to spurn him. There was something about him which convinced her he deserved the truth.

She sighed. "I am sorry, Lord Roxborough. You are quite correct. I have promised myself to another, but our circumstances are not such at present..." She clamped a hand over her mouth. "Oh dear, you shan't tell anyone, shall you?"

His mouth curved into a gentle smile. "You have nothing to fear. And you do not need to explain further. I only hope he is worthy of you. Do let me know if I can be of any assistance."

Cecilia returned his smile. "Thank you." She could use a friend and ally in this hazardous city. He offered his arm again, and she put her hand back in the crook as they continued on.

Suddenly struck by an idea, she took a breath and her eyes darted to the side. Dare she ask him? He would think her mad, peculiar, or immoral. But she was familiar with people misunderstanding her, and this was certainly the time to lay concern for her reputation aside, if only it could help William.

"As a matter of fact," she said, "I believe there is something you could do to help."

He quirked an eyebrow. "Oh?"

A blush immediately poured over her chest and neck. "I hope not to offend you..."

"I very much doubt you could," he said.

She laughed awkwardly. *We shall see about that.* "I cannot tell you why I need to know this information, only that it will be of great assistance to a friend of mine. I wondered if I could trouble you to find an address for me."

His furrowed brow ironed out. "Of course, Miss Grant."

She barrelled on, afraid she would lose her nerve. "Only, it is for a... business. You will think it inappropriate." She pulled him to a stop and looked him squarely in the eye. "You would be doing me a great service if you could get word to me of the whereabouts of the House of Lillian."

"The House of..." Lord Roxborough's eyes threatened to grow into saucers. "You cannot mean..."

Cecilia nodded. "The very one. I cannot explain my business, but it is very important."

He swallowed, his Adam's apple travelling down and up his neck rapidly. "I would not be a gentleman if my service caused you to come to harm," he said.

She could not seem to find enough air, or any words to persuade him. "Please," she whispered.

He stared at her for a long moment. "Very well, I will get you the address." He walked on. "I will ask my sister to write to you, enclosing my directions. I will not tell her what it, er... is."

She squeezed his arm in gratitude. "I would be eternally in your debt."

"No indeed. But tell me, Miss Grant. Are you in some sort of trouble?"

"No, my lord, you must believe my enquiries are in aid of an honourable cause. I may prevent the ruin of a virtuous man."

He nodded. "I understand you are resolute. But you must see to it that no-one else sees my note. Your aunt would have me roasted on a spit if she knew I'd given you directions to a brothel."

She caught his wary smile. "Let us not contemplate what she might do if she were to learn I visited one."

⤳⋘

William gathered his courage and sought out his brother. He found him in their father's study. The door was partially open, and he saw Charles within. He reclined in the huge leather seat, with his feet resting on the corner of the desk, crossed at the ankles. He smoked a pipe, and stared out the window.

Hard at work as ever, I see. William knocked on the door and entered.

Charles' gaze flicked to him. "What is it, brother mine?" He drew on the pipe. "Can you not see I am busy?"

William raised an eyebrow, and took the chair opposite his brother without an invitation. "Charles, I have something in particular I need to discuss with you."

"Well, I did assume something was afoot, given the sudden nature of your visit." Charles condescended to take his feet off the desk, and he turned to face his brother. "Do tell."

William sighed, deciding honesty was the best course of action. "Here are the circumstances."

He explained the current state of affairs in relation to his post, including his inadvertent implicating of his patron's son in a rape, and the unearthing of his visits to the House of Lillian.

Charles didn't attempt to interrupt him, his only response a slight lift of his eyebrows at the conclusion of the story. He took a long breath on his pipe. "Hardly a crime."

"That is not true," William said through clenched teeth. "I have not succumbed to that particular temptation."

Charles whistled softly. "Still white as a lamb, eh? A little boy, who has not yet become a man." He leaned forward onto his elbows and sucked on the pipe. "Have you never wondered what it feels like to possess a woman?"

His words were lighter than the clouds of smoke which puffed from his lips, but William shot daggers through them with his eyes.

He took a breath. "I assure you I have seen more sex and depravity than most my age, but the Lord has helped me to rise above it."

Charles laughed softly. "What a shame."

William's skin crawled. He could barely stand to be in the same room as his own flesh and blood. How could it be that they were made of the same substance? It was clear he was not going to arouse any sympathy in Charles. He racked his brain for a new plan of attack, but his brother spoke again.

"It is just as well our father did not live to see the spineless milksop you have become."

"That is enough," William spat out, and he pushed the chair back, turning on his heel. As he headed for the door, all the emotions of his childhood years engulfed him. He was overpowered by the urge to escape, and it took all his self-control not to physically run. He wanted to be far from this room, this house, this county, this country.

"Go ahead," Charles said as William grabbed the handle and threw open the door. "Run away, just as you always do. Run off on one of your mercy missions, or go and hide in the church. You are not wanted here, anyway."

The words, "Fine then, I will," teetered on William's tongue. But another, stronger impulse overtook him. The instinct of an obstinate younger sibling to always do the opposite of his superior's bidding rose up to dominate his stubborn streak. Charles wanted him to go, and suddenly his conscience begged him to consider the alternatives.

As he struggled with his emotions, his one solace, Cecilia, came fresh to his mind. What was it she said about how he always looked for the darkness, how he focussed on the problems of life? He closed his eyes and began to imagine how she might look for the good.

First he felt the worn metal under his fingers. He remembered as a boy how he would yank open this door to his father's study without knocking, and run over to the desk where the older man would sit hunched over business papers.

At first Sir Gregory Brook's countenance was one of irritation. His eyebrows protruding over stormy eyes, he might utter, "What is the meaning of this?"

But upon seeing the small intruder, the lines on his forehead would soften, his eyes would lighten, and often the stern mouth would curve into a smile. "My boy," he would sometimes say, "eluded your poor nurse maid again?"

As he fingered the handle, William mouthed the words, "my boy," and smiled, remembering how his father would let him sit on the desk and babble nonsense for as long as he liked. Only now he realised how busy his father must have been, and although it was never voiced, he now knew the gift of his time was a sign of love.

Opening his eyes, he gazed down the hallway. Instead of the dark passage, he saw a long racetrack, where a young William sprinted down, with the butler in pursuit. He could hear his own laughter echoing off the walls, and then the deeper rumble of the butler's own merriment after it.

His imagination followed his juvenile self through to the grand hall, up the staircase and along to his mother's room. There, instead of just bursting in, he would carefully turn the door handle so as not to make a sound, and then creep into the room and to Lady Brook's bedside. If she was asleep, sometimes he would stand just inside the threshold and watch her, captivated. However if she had noticed his entrance, she would always beckon him closer, and smile as he climbed up onto her bed.

He snuggled right up close to her, and she pulled him in with a weak but fond arm.

"My little William," she would say, "what a comfort you are to me."

Long hidden feelings arose in William; love and security and comfort. Those sensations had long been quashed by his brothers and by his own aloofness. They had taken his sense of belonging and the surety of his parents' love, eroded from the time he was six years old. Well, not now. Not anymore.

He'd become so fixated on escape as a solution, he'd never tried to face down his demons. The pain was too raw; the emptiness too overwhelming. But now, as he confronted the past and found comfort instead of despair, he knew what he must do. He knew who he was, and he had finally realised there was no need to escape at all.

"Well?" Charles' patronising and lazy, yet somehow demanding tone broke through his reverie.

William brushed the back of his hand across his eyes to clear his emotion and then turned to face his brother, his head held high. "This house is just as much mine as it is yours," he began, then seeing Charles' mouth open in protest, he held up his hand. "I will not be treated as an unwelcome stranger any longer. And when I leave, it will not be to run away, but to begin a wonderful new life."

He again saw his mother in his mind's eye. He wished he could have known her longer, that she could have seen him grow up, been proud of him, and that she could have met Cecilia. He would not deny his own children the right to know their history, and to have family.

"When I return, I shall bring a wife and she will be treated with respect. If we are so fortunate as to have offspring, they will be welcomed to the manor."

He paused. Clearly Charles needed a moment to recover from this sudden display of assertiveness. "Certainly brother," he said, "I cannot deny admittance to blood relatives."

William nodded. "And if you *ever* tell my wife or my children that they are not wanted, you shall face my sword at dawn."

Charles' eyebrows shot up, and he looked away for a moment. "Understood," he mumbled. Fencing was the one sport in which he had always been bested by his brothers.

Chapter Thirty-One

Lord Roxborough did not let on to Aunt Honoria that Cecilia had discouraged him, and apparent cooperation seemed to be sufficient to allow her a little freedom in the days that followed. She was given consent to venture out on her own, with Mary to attend her.

They left the townhouse, and headed east towards Covent Garden through the damp morning. Cecilia clutched the paper in her pocket, though she knew she would not need to consult it. She'd memorised Lord Roxborough's directions meticulously.

Her main concern was her escort. There was no way she was going to have Mary accompanying her on this quest. Even if she would prefer the company in the part of town she must visit, she could not risk even the slightest chance of her mission becoming gossip fodder in the servants' hall, and then in the wider public.

She scanned the buildings they passed desperately, wondering how she could possibly venture on alone. After two blocks, she pulled the maid to a halt. They were at the lending library, the only safe place Cecilia could think of to leave Mary while she hurried off to her strange destination.

"Mary, I would like to go on a private errand, if you please. Please choose any books you like and I shall pay the lending fees. I will return as soon as I can."

Mary's mouth formed into a hard straight line. "Miss, I'm obliged to stay with you. You cannot go alone."

"Oh but I must, Mary." Cecilia's chest tightened. "I have a secret, er, task to undertake for a friend."

"Oh, a present?" Suddenly Mary was downcast. "You do not trust my judgement. I assure you, I am an excellent helper when it comes to gifts."

Cecilia sighed, taking in her maid's upturned chin and beseeching look. "If you will stay here for just a short while, I will give you as many ribbons as you like."

Mary's eyes sparked. The bribe, such as it was, had worked.

Once the maid was safely ensconced in the library, Cecilia hurried off. In just under an hour, she returned and found the maid poring over novels deep within the rows of books.

"Here I am, Mary." She helped the maid to withdraw the books, and they were soon back on their way to Aunt Honoria.

"Did you find what you was looking for, Miss?" Mary inquired.

Cecilia took pause. "Not quite," she said slowly. "I rather think I will buy my friend a bonnet instead. What do you think?"

Mary clapped her hands together, eyes shining. "Oh yes, Miss. I'm sure a bonnet will be just the thing. Will we look for one tomorrow?"

Cecilia grinned. "Indeed we shall." She knew how fond her maid was of headgear, and she kept her exact intentions a secret. Indeed, Mary talked of nothing else for the entire journey home. Cecilia hoped the distraction was enough to help her forget the day's oddities, and the pretence of the gift would sufficiently disguise her activities on the morrow. William's future could very well depend on it.

☙❧

After their showdown in the study, a different sort of dynamic existed between the Brook brothers. There was a begrudging respect from Charles and a new ambiance pervaded the atmosphere.

William was content to enjoy the peace for a few days, but he knew he must get to the heart of the matter. It was almost time to return to Amberley for his day of reckoning.

The brothers took dinner together, until now a rare occasion indeed, and then William waited until Charles was comfortably settled back in his chair with a glass of port in his hand.

He took a bolstering sip from his own glass, and turned to face his brother. "Charles, I need to ask one favour of you, and if you grant it you may rest assured I will never ask again."

A flicker of irritation crossed over Charles' features. "If it pains you so much to ask, and if it will pain me, as you infer, then perhaps it is wiser not to proceed with your request."

William took a slow breath in and out. "As I have already implied, I have found the woman I want for my wife. She is the dearest creature in the world, of landed gentry, and her parents wished more for her than to marry into the church."

"Quite. Is it the girl who is up the creek?"

William lurched towards him, but then held himself back. "No, it is not."

Charles raised an eyebrow. "Calm down, old boy. You always were wanting to play the martyr, saving other people. It was a natural assumption."

William adjusted his cravat. "My preference for Miss Grant is based entirely on love, respect and friendship. I cannot really expect you to understand so pure a notion."

"Is she a looker?"

William sighed. "Yes. She is the most beautiful creature I have ever beheld."

"Well that –"

"If we can come to the point, brother –"

"Come now, William," Charles said with a condescending smile, "I am only showing an interest."

He leaned forward in earnest. "I believe you must know what I am asking of you. My income is such that I can support myself, but a wife and family must do without the little luxuries which make life comfortable. I have only one maid, no carriage, and no means for employing a curate or the funds to take my wife on a honeymoon. If you cannot, er, spare any capital, I shall quite understand. You are well within your birthright to refuse. However, what I ask is for one lump sum that I can keep in the four percents, which will help convince her parents that she will not be marrying into poverty."

Charles nodded slowly, running his index finger up and down his nose. "I see." He appeared to ruminate for a few moments. "Let me consider it, brother dear. I shall give you my answer before you depart."

William had seen a glimmer in Charles' eyes which seemed to betray his intention to assist. In a return to his old habits, he would enjoy torturing William by delaying the communication of his decision. "Thank you, Charles," he said. "I must move with reasonable haste... Miss Grant is now in London and may end committed to another fellow before long."

"And *you* may be transported somewhere, I believe."

William shook his head. "I would not be so sure of that. I intend to stand my ground."

"This is a turn up for the books, old chap. Not six months ago you would have taken anything, even transportation to the Americas, if it meant you could convert heathens. And now... well, love has conquered you."

William allowed a smile. "True, but I have also discovered the impact one can have on a small community. I have learned I can be of service no matter where I am. As long as I have the woman I love at my side, all will be well."

❧

Snow swirled around the main street of Amberley as William's hired coach manoeuvred through the carts and milling villagers. Glancing out of the window, he was sensible of the curious stares, and perhaps one or two antagonistic glares.

He jumped out of the vehicle as soon as it pulled to a stop, and looked up the vicarage hungrily. A lump immediately settled in his throat as he surveyed the shuttered windows and familiar stone walls. *Home.*

Movement caught his eye. Emma had parted the parlour curtains, and on seeing him she waved frantically, sporting the grin of a Cheshire cat. She met him in the hallway and crushed him in a fierce hug, before stepping back shyly, a shade of crimson enveloping her.

"Er, welcome home, sir," she said, dipping into an embarrassed curtsey.

William swallowed back tears. "Thank you, Emma," he managed. He let her fuss about him, helping him out of his coat and assisting him to his room. He accepted her offer of fried eggs, sitting at the little kitchen table as she prepared them.

"Is there any news, Emma? Of Miss Miller or… about me?"

Emma swivelled around from her position at the fry pan, the sizzle and smell of butter permeating the small room. "No, sir. That is, Amy will have to leave the big house next week, and that man Roberts from London has been asking everyone about you. But he hasn't asked me to pack up the rest of your things."

William nodded. He would have to seek his own satisfaction on both counts. To that end, he made short work of his eggs, and hurried over to Ashworth Hall. He was admitted to the drawing room, where the Earl and Countess were taking tea with Dean Roberts.

Lord Ashworth rose and crossed the room to shake William's hand, a smile crinkling his eyes. "Good to see you, Brook. Do sit down."

William also shook Roberts' hand before taking a chair near the tea table, and accepting a cup from Lady Ashworth. A quarter hour of chit-chat followed, with enquiries on both sides regarding the health of each family, talk about the war and even the weather. William was fairly bursting to steer the conversation toward his position as the vicar of Amberley.

It was the dean who finally addressed the matter. "Now Brook, about this wretched affair. I find you have already accomplished a great many things in your short time here, as I believed you would. Many of the people are eager to sing your praises."

Lord Ashworth raised his tea cup to William in a sort of congratulatory salute.

"But, there is a great deal of confusion and a feeling of betrayal concerning your alleged behaviour in London from some quarters. I am still of the opinion that the parishioners must have faith in their spiritual leader, and to that end there will be a town meeting two days hence, at which we will determine if the majority are in favour of your return."

William nodded, though his heart galloped in his chest. "That is fair. I appreciate your vote of confidence, sir." He took a deep breath. "Your lordship, I wondered if I might visit with some of your servants while I am here."

Lord Ashworth's expression took on a bemused surprise which spoke of puzzlement as to why anyone would want to do that. He shrugged. "Certainly, certainly."

His queries established that Amy was busy assisting her mistress, and would not be available to speak with him. He remained below stairs for a good hour, catching up with the various staff members, but also in the hope Amy might appear. She did not. He trudged back along the muddy roads to the vicarage, intent on preparing his emotions and mind for his day of reckoning.

Chapter Thirty-Two

Christmas loomed on the calendar. Cecilia remained silent as Mary removed her ball gown and jewellery. Memories of the evening churned through her mind: superficial smiles on the ladies, roaming eyes on the gentlemen, and a cacophony of music and dance. It was all a beautiful, shining trap, and her heart stung dreadfully. As Mary brushed out her hair, a single tear fell down her cheek. She swiped it away before the maid noticed, shaking her head when asked if she needed anything else.

Left alone, her feelings overflowed. With each passing day, she was plagued by deeper doubt and confusion. If William was struck off, it might be kinder to him if she did accept another husband. She didn't want to be a burden on him. Perhaps he would find a good life in the new world. Would she be doing him a favour if she freed him from the encumbrance of creating a life for them, of worrying for her comfort?

She was sure he would be content no matter where he ended up, whether that was in the Americas or the swamps of the Far East. Even only as a soldier in France, surely it would be less painful to sever ties here in England.

She must find out his fate. Amy was the only person she could possibly write to who would give her the unbiased facts. She sat down to pen a letter, but then wondered how could she possibly ask her to write about William's troubles when she had so many of her own?

She choked on her tears and pressed her fingers to her lips. How would she ever know what was happening to him? Perhaps she could enquire if his brothers were in town, and get to him that way? Could she feign illness and beg to recover back in Amberley? She took several deep breaths, trying to calm herself. William had said he would come to her in London, did he not? She would persevere, and save herself for him, and trust that he would somehow reach her to let her know what lay ahead.

She had never shared herself with another human being so fully. She was quite sure she would never find that experience with anyone else ever again. And she certainly could not give even an ounce of her heart to another.

She opened the bureau drawer and withdrew the Gainsborough book from William's library. She carefully flicked through the pages, stopping about half way through. She reached for the little dried viola, taking it up and gingerly fingering it. She would go to the ends of the earth to make him happy. And regardless of whether he was to be her life partner or not, she knew without a shadow of a doubt she would belong to him, forever and always.

⁂

"Mr Brook saved my life." Henry Russell's hazel eyes shone. "He is a decent man and I'm proud to call him a friend. I want him to stay."

William was overcome by Henry's brief yet humbling declaration. Their eyes connected, and he gave him a nod which he hoped expressed his thanks. Henry was the tenth villager to stand up at the town meeting and give his argument. So far, the sentiments were largely positive. William still sweated profusely as he sat at the front of the hall with Lord and Lady Ashworth and Dean Roberts.

The widow Kendrick struggled to her feet. "He has a kind soul," she said. "I believe his place is here."

Mr Morton cleared his throat. "He is a rational thinker, and a hard worker," the man said, flashing a brief smile at William before returning to his seat.

The schoolmistress raised her hand. "The children have never shown quite so much interest in learning the Scriptures."

Murmurs of approval echoed around the hall. "Capital," Lord

Ashworth said. "Would anyone else care to speak?"

"Yes." Mr Lindsay bolted upright. "This is all well and good, but our vicar must be an upstanding citizen of high moral standards. *Not* a hypocrite."

Mrs Stockton waved her hand. "How can he lecture us up there, week after week, when he's going around doing who knows what behind our backs? It just isn't right."

The noises in the hall turned into angry rumblings. William wondered if Mrs Stockton's bad will was more about his reluctance to marry any of her daughters.

"And he defended that hussy Amy!" someone shouted from the back of the room.

Indignant cries rose to fever pitch. Lord Ashworth raised his palms and attempted to quiet the crowd. "Silence, silence. We ought to hear from Mr Brook." He turned to William. "What have you to say for yourself?"

William had considered what he might say, drafting a rebuttal for any and all allegations he might face. But now, none of the details seemed to matter. He only wanted them to know who he was, and to decide based on his character alone.

He stood before a sea of faces, many hostile. "I have always endeavoured to give my all in the service of others," he began. "It has been my privilege and honour to live and work among you –"

The town hall doors burst open. A couple entered, strangers to the townspeople, but William's mouth dropped open in shock.

Lord Ashworth shielded his eyes against the light streaming through the open door. "I say, what is the meaning of this?"

The woman strode up the central aisle, and addressed his lordship. "I am Mrs Stanley, but I was Shirley Allsopp... and I went by the name of Becky when I worked at the House of Lillian in London."

There was a collective gasp from the assembly. Lord Ashworth opened his mouth and closed it again, looking to the dean.

"I beg of you to let me tell my story, especially where it concerns Mr Brook." She looked towards William and smiled, giving him a little wave. He felt his insides lightening as he returned the gesture, though he observed the incredulity of the parishioners. He would not deny their connection, not even now. *Especially* now.

Dean Roberts spoke up. "Have you come from London in order to give your testimony?"

Mrs Stanley nodded. "We can't really afford such a journey, but I convinced Mr Stanley of its import." Her husband, standing at her side, reached out to grasp her hand.

"Indeed." Roberts addressed the crowd. "I believe we should hear what this lady has to say."

"Lady?!" someone shouted in derision.

Lord Ashworth gestured for Mrs Stanley to join him at the front of the hall. "Please tell us the truth," he said.

She nodded seriously, and then turned to face the audience, taking a deep breath. "I was brought up by good God-fearing people. My parents were milliners and I used to help in the shop. But I was seduced by the vices of London. I befriended gentlemen who seemed amusing, but were drinking and gambling away their fortunes.

"I became addicted to opium, and my father threw me out. I could not find anyone to – support me, so I turned to... other work." She coloured, and cleared her throat. "The opium took over my life... I would do almost anything to get it. I was so sick...

"The night William found me, I was in the shallows of the Thames, having been beaten by some gentleman or other, intending to drown myself. He took me back to his quarters, and he and his friend nursed me back to health. They tried to stop me from going back to my – profession, but I was too ashamed to go back to my family.

"So, William would visit me at the House of Lillian during the day, bringing me good food and reading the Scriptures to me. He never laid a hand on me, though I admit I did try to tempt him. And I have it on good authority that he never got up to hijinks with the other girls either. We all used to gossip about how handsome he was; how we wouldn't make him pay."

There were outraged calls from the villagers. "Look what filth this man has brought to Amberley!" "That's quite enough, thank you miss!"

"Go on," Lady Ashworth said to Mrs Stanley.

"After some months, he convinced me to seek penance. I went back to my parents and they allowed me to work in their shop. I'm now married to a good man, and I will bring my children up to be good Christians." She faced William. "I know that Mr Brook saved me. You should all be grateful to have him."

She shared a smile with William and he mouthed 'thank you'. He knew how much this confession had cost her, how painful the journey to the past must be. He never would have exposed her secret, to allow her to continue in her new life without any discrimination. But she had somehow found him, and found it in her heart to risk her reputation to help him.

She spoke again, as if she had heard his thoughts. "I know William endeavoured to keep my past a secret from everyone, and I know he would not have asked me to reveal my story. But I was paid a visit in London by a charming young lady, a Miss Grant, I believe?"

A general murmur rippled through the crowd.

My darling Cecilia, thought William, suddenly distraught, *visited a brothel?* His shock was mirrored in the faces of her parents. For a panicked instant he worried that Cecilia's efforts to clear his name would stymie their chance at matrimonial happiness.

"She had gone so far as to make enquiries at my former, er, place of employment," Mrs Stanley went on, "and tracked me down to the shop. She told me what a right pickle dear Mr Brook was in, and I agreed I would try to come to Amberley."

"Er, thank you, Mrs Stanley," Lord Ashworth said.

She dipped her head at him respectfully.

There came a shout from within the room. "But how do we know this woman is who she says she is? Brook might have called on a friend to play the part."

All heads swivelled back to Mrs Stanley. She showed no signs of discomfort. "You can ask me anything about that place," she said confidently. "I can tell you names, dates, the decor of the, uh, rooms..."

Dean Roberts held up a hand. "I do not think that will be necessary, thank you." He addressed the room. "It is my opinion we can have faith that the lady's story is true."

"And what say you," Lord Ashworth said to him, "now we have heard this tale?"

Roberts stroked his chin. "I always knew young Brook practised somewhat unconventional methods in his attempts to save the world, travelling to who knows where to preach and tend to the needs of the poor. I did not realise the extent of his missions, but now I must say his intentions do seem to have been honourable. I can see no reason why he should not remain in his post, unless his conduct has otherwise been wanting. From what the good people of this town have told me, he is an asset to you. I leave it to your elders to determine his fate."

Lord Ashworth nodded. "The vestry will vote on behalf of the village," he said.

William regarded the vestry members and their wives, all sitting in the front row. It was clear to him which way each would vote – those who would not look him in the eye were undoubtedly against him. His suspicions were correct: when Lord Ashworth asked them to raise their hands if they were in favour of his retention, only Mr Morton and Mr Grant raised their hands at first.

He shifted in his seat uncomfortably. Lord Ashworth also raised his hand, but there was still one more vote needed. As the seconds passed, William began to fear the worst.

Mr and Mrs Fortescue sat whispering fervently. Only Mr Fortescue would have a vote, and his wife spoke into his ear with a great deal of passion.

"Well?" Lord Ashworth said, eyeballing the two of them.

Their discussion ceased, and they both looked at him. Then, Mr Fortescue cleared his throat, and slowly raised his hand.

It was done. He was saved. The hall erupted into applause, and all became a blur as William's hand was repeatedly wrung by his supporters.

"We will have order, please!" entreated Lord Ashworth. Some minutes later, most had returned to their seats, although William noticed the absence of some disgruntled villagers. He would make it his personal mission to win them over. "Do we have any other business?" Ashworth called.

There was silence.

"Well, then, I shall declare this meeting –"

Suddenly Mrs Fortescue shot out of her chair and cried, "We will take Miss Miller in!"

There were gasps from the crowd.

Ashworth took a moment to absorb this. "Indeed?"

Mrs Fortescue appeared to gather her thoughts. "I must agree that Miss Miller has been insensible, naive, foolhardy, and she will now pay the price for the rest of her life. As good Christian people, and as Mr Brook reminds us, we must take pity on her, having mercy on her sins, and show her the love our Lord would."

A few incredulous whispers floated through the air.

"To that end," she continued, "we are willing to do our part. I hereby announce that we will take the girl in, and provide shelter to her and the babe. We have more than we can ever consume, and I will do my best to ensure the child is raised to be a respectable, genteel citizen."

Dizziness washed over William temporarily. One more surprise today might finish him off. Of all the people to become Amy's saviour, he had not counted on Mrs Fortescue. It seemed that underneath that domineering exterior, there was a heart after all. And in the space of minutes, she'd saved two lives. A miracle indeed.

Chapter Thirty-Three

A veil of chatter washed over the room after the meeting was finally adjourned, and everyone began to take their leave. William stayed where he was for a moment, his heart overflowing with gratitude and relief. Never would he have thought that he would fight so hard to remain in such a place as this. But he now knew that it was exactly what he needed – much more than the village people needed him. He fought a lump rising in his throat as his eyes roamed over the souls he had known nothing of just six months ago.

Then he noticed the Grants heading for the door, and he dashed into the aisle after them. His way was blocked by well-wishers, wanting to shake his hand or slap him on the back. He smiled, thanked, and pushed through.

He caught up with the couple just as they started down the lane.

"Oh Mr Grant!" he called. "Mrs Grant. If I might have a word?"

Mr Grant glanced behind and slowed his wife by taking her elbow. "Certainly, Mr Brook."

William approached and took Mr Grant's outstretched hand.

"Congratulations are in order, I believe," the gentleman said. "Amberley seems to have taken you to heart."

"The feeling is mutual," William replied with a smile, "though I hardly know what I have gotten myself into."

Thankfully the Grants shared his chuckle, though Mrs Grant's eyes darted about.

"I wondered," William said quickly, "if I may have an audience with both of you... today, perhaps?"

Mr Grant deferred diplomatically to his wife.

"We have no prior engagements," she said, rather stiffly. "You may come this afternoon for tea."

As William held a teacup to his lips four hours later, he held Mrs Grant's suspicious gaze. The woman was shrewd; she knew he was here on more than church business.

They seemed to be silently negotiating while Mr Grant talked on about how the village had not known this much excitement since the plague of 1786. He praised William's noble, if risky, loyalty to Mrs Stanley.

Mrs Grant put her teacup back on the low table. "You are a determined young man, are you not, Mr Brook?"

"I possess a certain stubborn streak, to be sure, Mrs Grant." He smiled.

"And there is something else you are seeking, above your position as vicar in this village."

"Indeed there is."

Mr Grant looked from one to the other as if they were speaking a foreign language.

"Well?" Mrs Grant raised her eyebrows at William.

She's not going to let me off easily, then, if at all.

"Mr and Mrs Grant, I believe you know I love your daughter, and she has given me hope of a return affection. I have come in order to beg for her hand. I... cannot pretend to be indifferent to your objection to the match."

"Objection?" Mr Grant interjected.

"Yes," said his wife shortly.

"You desire Miss Grant to be matched with a peer of the realm," William said, "or at least a gentleman with his own house in town and a large country estate. Though I am a gentleman, my occupation and dedication to my post here in Amberley renders me bound to execute my duties, and my wife will need to accept compromises on fine living."

"Exactly so, Mr Brook," Mrs Grant said.

"Your dedication is an inspiration," said her husband indignantly. "Any young lady should be pleased to accept your hand, and – and if she is too grand to be glad of it, then you should be better off without her."

Mrs Grant glared at him, and he glared back.

"In fact," he went on, "I believe our young Mr Brook could take his pick of the marriageable girls in a five-mile radius. I'll confess to hearing Stockton and Jones discussing his merits as a son-in-law."

William was without words momentarily, and could only look at the older gentleman with grateful wonder. He never dreamed his case could be pleaded so well on another man's tongue.

Mrs Grant took a breath. "Now –"

Her husband addressed her directly. "I was very much in favour of the plan to hitch her to young Barrington. It would have set her up comfortably and certainly improved our social standing. But look at what a villain Barrington turned out to be. Regardless of our Cecilia's faults, she deserves to be loved, or at least well-treated. I shall not have her miserable and ignored. Even a rich beau from London will need to answer to me, to ensure his good intentions."

The strength and passion of his words seemed to have moved Mrs Grant near tears. She nodded meekly.

Mr Grant finally turned back to William. "Now, young Brook, tell me of *your* intentions."

William had prepared for this exact moment. For the entire journey back from Cambridgeshire – even before he knew his place in Amberley was assured – he thought of all the reasons why he should marry Cecilia. From his gentle upbringing, to his education, to the security of his prospects, to his agreement with his brother, he'd practised his arguments over and over, until he knew word for word what he would say to convince them. His reasoning was sound, logical even. Surely with such reason before them they could not deny him.

Now, with the eyes of those who held his future in their hands upon him, all his prepared speeches took leave of his brain. He racked his mind for the words, but instead they came bubbling up from his heart.

"I love Cecilia with all my heart – all I am," he said, his voice breaking. "She has... turned my world upside down. When I look in her eyes, I can see a beautiful soul. She is the most precious thing to me here on this earth. As for my intentions? I intend to cherish your daughter with my mind, body and soul. If there is anything I can do to secure her happiness, you can be sure I will go to the ends of the earth to achieve it.

"As to material comfort, my brother, the heir, has granted me five thousand pounds to invest in the four percents, which will supplement the living enough to allow us to spend the occasional season in town or travel abroad. I want to see Cecilia's face when she sees the treasures of Florence, Rome and Paris. I will make our honeymoon a feast for her senses, as well as a spiritual pilgrimage for me. If only you will allow me to take her hand... I promise you to treasure it always."

Coming back to reality, William realised he was standing in the centre of the room, just a few feet from Mr and Mrs Grant. They stared at him without speaking for several moments. Collecting himself, he retreated back to his chair and waited. Each second of silence plunged him deeper into suspenseful misery.

Finally, there was movement. Without looking at her, Mr Grant reached out for his wife's hand. She clasped his firmly, and then their heads turned toward each other. Mr Grant raised his eyebrows ever so slightly, and his wife gave a slight bob of the head, a tear escaping from one eye.

Mr Grant stood and strode over to William. "I should have known a man who can preach so well would express his feelings eloquently. Although," he smiled, "we have never heard you speak quite like *that* from the pulpit."

"Indeed not, sir," William said shakily. "Matters of romantic love are quite a different article to scripture." He almost whispered, *Well?*

Mr Grant reached for William's hand, dragging him to his feet and pumping his arm up and down. "It would be an honour to have you in the family, my boy. I knew it would take a special man to truly understand an extraordinary girl like my Cecilia, but I think she has found her match. We can have confidence she will be comfortable, but more importantly, happy."

William took an unsteady breath, and a grin spread across his face. "Thank you, sir," he said, and then looking over Mr Grant's shoulder at his wife, "and you too, Mrs Grant."

She rose from her chair to join the gentlemen. "Do not thank us yet," she replied, looking grave. "I believe Cecilia has already attended several society events in London. I shall write and ask Honoria to send her home. I do hope it is not too late."

William nodded. "Please do write." He stopped for a moment to consider, his thoughts tumbling over themselves with possibilities. "Actually," he said, "if you are agreeable, I will go to her in London. I will give her aunt a note containing your blessing, and I will court Cecilia and ask her formally for her hand."

"Very well," Mrs Grant said, as her husband nodded. "I suppose," she said slowly, "you might take the opportunity to show her off at a few balls as well. After all, she will have so many lovely new gowns... it would be a shame not to put them to good use. Perhaps an excuse for you to consider a new evening jacket as well."

It was really quite a performance, the way she still managed to get her way but disguised it as a favour to her future son-in-law. William almost laughed in spite of himself. "If you do not mind, I shall certainly show her off," he said, becoming more carefree by the second. "We may also take in art exhibitions and a theatre production or two."

Mrs Grant didn't mind at all. "We will allow it," she said, "but only once you are formally betrothed."

William couldn't have struck a better bargain if he'd tried.

※

William tossed articles of clothing into his valise, far too exhilarated to bother folding anything. He'd ordered a hackney coach for the morning. In two days hence he would be in London. It would be the start of a new life.

A knock at the front door barely intruded into his thoughts. For once, he was glad to leave Emma to it. Soon, however, there was a tapping at his bedroom door.

His maid bobbed quickly. "It's Mrs Fortescue, sir."

William stopped in his tracks. "Oh?"

He tidied himself up and met the lady in the parlour. She was alone.

"My dear Mrs Fortescue," he said once they were seated, "allow me to express my gratitude and indeed – my wonder..."

She shook her head. "Mr Brook, I know what you are going to say and

I assure you, it is quite unnecessary." She met his eyes, and for the first time since he'd met her, she had an air of vulnerability. "Given all we have learned today," she said slowly, "I know anything I say to you will be kept in strict confidence."

He smiled and nodded. "Of course."

"Then I must tell you a story of my past." She shifted on the couch, and sighed. "I am the daughter of a wealthy tradesman in Milton. I was indulged; spoiled. I took my family's protection for granted, and at fifteen, I allowed myself to be tricked into... that is, I found myself with child."

William could not hide his shock, but he quickly recovered, motioning for her to continue.

"I was sent to a farm near here for my confinement, and my daughter was immediately placed in the care of the Millers, a barren couple and friends of my guardians."

The puzzle pieces slammed together in William's brain. *Mrs Fortescue is Amy's mother!*

"My family asked me to return once I was well, but I could not bear to live without knowing how my child grew up. So I stayed at the farm, helping with mending and the like, and eventually I managed to catch Mr Fortescue's eye at the fair. No-one else in Amberley knows why I came to be there.

"I watched out for Amelia. I funded her clothing and education. It was my careful influence on Lady Ashworth which secured her the position at the Hall. I rather hoped that she would meet a nice man during their travels to London... I had no idea that young rake was imposing himself on her." Her face contorted as if the words were bitter on her tongue. "In a way, I blame myself. She had no-one to warn her; no-one to tell her about the wicked ways of the male sex." She paused. "No offence meant, Mr Brook."

"None taken, I assure you."

"Offering her a sanctuary is the least I can do. I know it must look strange to the world, but I cannot bear the thought of her in a workhouse."

William took a slow breath, his mind catching up. At length, he looked up. "Will you tell her the truth?"

"Perhaps one day. The most important thing is having her settled and making a home for the child." Her chin wobbled. "My grandchild."

William closed the distance between them and sat next to her on the couch, placing a hand on her shoulder. "God bless you both."

Chapter Thirty-Four

Never had a journey been so lengthy and tedious. William's flight to London was not only plagued by muddy roads and a crowding in the stagecoach; his own mind seemed to oppress him. He began to convince himself that Cecilia had fallen prey to a dashing peer selected by her aunt. Had the charms of London turned her head away from Amberley... from him?

Returning to the city for the first time in six months, he marvelled at his change in perspective since his last departure. London no longer pulled his heart in every which direction with the call to serve anyone and everyone. Now he had a focus in which to concentrate his energies, and most importantly, a home for his affections. As he grew closer and closer to Cecilia, his very blood seemed to flow faster, every nerve coming alive.

On arrival at the Brook townhouse, he only paused to deposit his luggage in the foyer and adjust his cravat in a mirror. He stared back at himself, feeling he was only now becoming the man his father would have been proud of.

Time to convince the aunt to give up the search. He ran a hand through his hair and left the building, setting off on foot.

Once admitted to the Holcombe apartments, he presented his card and removed his great coat, straightening his jacket. He watched as the footman walked away, then was suddenly unable to wait, running after the man.

The footman pushed a door open, and began, "A gentleman caller, Lady Holcombe. A Mr –"

William pushed past him into the room. There, Cecilia and her aunt sat with needlework in their laps. "Brook," he panted, first giving a clumsy bow to Lady Holcombe, then advancing on Cecilia before he knew what his feet were doing. She was a vision, an angel. Her deep blue eyes pierced his soul, and a torrent of emotions flooded his heart.

"William!" cried Cecilia, on her feet in an instant, and then she clamped a hand to her mouth. "I mean, Mr Brook!" she said through her fingers.

The aunt's gaze travelled from the eager young man regarding her niece with unbridled adulation, to Cecilia's glowing cheeks and tear-brimmed eyes. She knew at once her position as London matchmaker was redundant. There was nothing to be done.

❦

William escorted his new bride the short distance from the church to the vicarage, their new home together. The cheers from the townspeople were thunderous, but he did not hear them. He was only sensible of the treasure on his arm. He caught her eye, and she gave him a bashful smile.

"Now, you know we probably will not be here forever," he said. "I could be assigned to London or another town, or even go to the mission field."

"I know," she said merrily, "but I care not as long as I am with you."

As they saw the cottage, adorned with bright decorations by the villagers, and gazed out to the hills beyond, his words evaporated. Perhaps they would stay, after all.

Author's Note: Thank You

Thank you for reading *The Vagabond Vicar*. I very much hope you enjoyed it.

I would greatly appreciate it if you would leave a review for this book at Goodreads or your online retailer.

You don't have to leave Amberley just yet! In the next book, *Gloved Heart*, you'll find out what happens to Amy. Turn the page to read the first chapter.

Visit my website www.charlottebrentwood.com to sign up for my email newsletter to find out about my next releases and other news about my books.

Ways to connect with Charlotte:

Email:	charlotte.brentwood@gmail.com
Facebook:	www.facebook.com/charbrentwood
Twitter:	www.twitter.com/charbrentwood
Pinterest:	www.pinterest.com/charbrentwood
BookBub:	www.bookbub.com/authors/charlotte-brentwood

HEARTS OF AMBERLEY
BOOK TWO

Gloved Heart

A tender, moving story of hope and healing, unbreakable bonds and steadfast love, *Gloved Heart* is a bestselling proper regency romance.

"A different take on historical romance, both fresh and full of heart, this one is a true reading treasure chest gem!"
"*Gloved Heart* had me hooked by the first few pages. This lovely romance set in regency times is perfect for fans of this genre. I adored this story."
"This is a beautiful, romantic & charming novel. 5 stars"
"A gorgeous, sweet Regency Romance I absolutely adored!"
"This is an adorable, heartwarming regency romance that will truly make you smile. I absolutely loved this book."

Can she ever trust again?

Amy Miller is struggling to come to terms with her new life as a mother, while being a reluctant guest in a rigid gentry household. A victim of abuse, she is determined to never trust a man again.

Henry Russell has loved Amy for as long as he can remember, but his family want nothing to do with her. A chance encounter with Amy rekindles a friendship which might save both of them.

The discovery of a secret which holds the key to Amy's past will change them forever, and jeopardise any chance they have for happiness. Can Henry show Amy that true love will give her everything she could ever need?

Gloved Heart - Excerpt

Chapter One

Amberley, Shropshire
June 1806

Screams echoed in every corner of the room, and in her mind.
There was agony, humiliation and confusion… Her dress torn, her skin ripped, and a man intent on possessing her, no matter the cost. She had never felt more helpless, worthless, or alone.

Amy woke with tears pouring down her cheeks, but the incessant cries she could hear were not her own.

It was the consequence of that hideous night: a baby born of sin. Motherhood had been thrust upon her, her life irrevocably altered.

The baby's cries escalated, and she forced herself from the bed. Her nightdress was saturated from the neck to the waist. Her milk flowed freely whenever he cried, or at the mere thought of feeding him. She couldn't even control her own body these days, let alone the course of her life.

She hurried down the hall to the nursery, but the crying stopped before she opened the door.

Good heavens! Is he alive?

She threw the door open. In the moonlight sat the wet nurse, already feeding her child. Amy's heart nearly burst out of her chest with relief when she saw her son, healthy.

The woman looked up and saw her, then focussed her attention on the child again.

Amy stepped forward.

"I'll take him, please."

The nurse didn't move. "He needs feeding, miss."

"I can do that. I want to."

"Nonsense, miss. You're to leave that to me."

"But–"

"Mrs Fortescue wouldn't hear of you feeding him. Go back to bed. You need your rest."

Amy nodded wearily. She did not want to disturb her son by fighting over him. She rubbed her pounding temples, on the edge of giving up. Benjamin was only a few weeks old, but he was already fodder for battle. Despite her guardian's orders, Amy had often managed to feed Benjamin herself, at all hours of the day and night. She was so tired she didn't know who she was anymore. It would be easier to go back to bed.

But her breasts ached, and there was a longing somewhere deeper inside her, too. For what purpose did she need rest? Lord knew Mrs Fortescue wouldn't let her lift a finger with any household duties. She felt impotent and purposeless. Tending to her son was the one thing she *could* do.

She unbuttoned the top of her night-rail and reached for him, saying with as much authority as she could muster, "Give him to me."

The baby started at the sound of her voice, detaching from the nurse's breast. Amy scooped him up and he began whimpering. She rushed to the chair on the other side of the cradle and settled into it, cuddling him and nudging him to her throbbing breast. He opened his mouth wide, latched on, and began to suck vigorously.

She sighed and began to relax as sweet release came. Little Benjamin wriggled closer to her, and her heart skipped a beat. She had been so afraid she would resent or despise this little wonder of a creature, but a seed of love had been planted in the first moment she held him in her arms. It had only grown since.

The nurse also sighed and trudged from the room.

Amy barely noticed. She gently caressed Benjamin's cheek with her fingertip, stroked his wisp of hair, and tapped the tip of his tiny nose.

"Hello, little one," she whispered. "You take as much as you need. I'll look after you."

When he was satiated, Benjamin opened his eyes. A connection sparked between them, visceral and sweet. A few moments later, he fell asleep, and Amy pulled him in close to her. She rested her head back and closed her eyes as fulfilment, love and contentment flowed through her. She had never known something this powerful could exist.

Now, he was the only reason she had to live.

౭ఞ

Later that morning, Amy ran a finger down her gleaming silver hairbrush as she sat in front of her dresser. She had never possessed anything so beautiful before coming to live in this house. There was a comb of tortoiseshell, hair pins of ivory and silk ribbons so smooth they slipped through her fingers in glossy waves.

Her dresses consisted of cast-offs from the Barringtons, which fit well enough, and some gowns from Mrs Fortescue herself, many of which Amy still needed to take in to fit her leaner frame. The fabrics were all so much finer than she was used to, some with delicate lace or intricate embroidery. Far *too* fine for someone like her.

They were all lovely things a lady should have – not an imposter who didn't belong.

A large mirror was affixed to the back of the dresser, and Amy's deep green eyes stared back at her, clear as day. Previously she'd had only a small, rusted pane and an approximation of her likeness.

She reached for the hairbrush again, her fingers curling around the shiny silver handle.

"I'll take that!"

The hairbrush was whisked from her hand. She gasped, whirling around on her seat. "Jenny!"

"Good morning, miss," the maid said crisply. She began to remove the curling papers from Amy's hair. Her auburn curls were ill-formed, at best. The maid tut-tutted, as if Amy had purposely underachieved, and then started to brush her hair with strokes that were not altogether gentle.

Amy reached above her head. "Give me that, please. I can do it myself."

"Poppycock." Jenny sniffed. "You're a *lady* now." Her tone indicated she believed the opposite was true.

And well Amy knew it. Though she had been given her own room on the first floor, though she had freedom from earning wages, she was still the adopted daughter of a tenant farmer, her true lineage a mystery. She had lately been a lady's maid herself and had never dreamed she would ever have someone else brush her hair or help her dress. Jenny was a parlour maid who had been tasked with attending to Amy, and it was clear she resented the extra work. Or perhaps she felt that Amy did not deserve to be attended upon. Amy wished the Fortescues had not thought to give her the help. It only served to remind her that she did not fit in.

She remained silent while she was helped into stays, a petticoat and a morning gown. Jenny then arranged her hair in a simple chignon, leaving her crinkled hair carefully exposed.

The maid reached beneath the bed to retrieve her chamber pot. Glancing at the contents she asked, "Will that be all, miss?"

"Yes, Jenny," Amy croaked. "Thank you."

Once alone again, she took a few deep breaths in order to recover her composure before leaving the room. She went directly to the nursery to check on Benjamin, who was slumbering sweetly under the watch of a nurse. Her heart warmed, she was now able to face the breakfast table with a degree of equanimity.

Amy had come to live at Briarwood, the Fortescues' home, when her swelling figure had made her position at the big house untenable – and she had been desperate. If not for their charity, she would be in a workhouse, and she dreaded to think what would have become of her baby.

Surely the Fortescues had only taken her in to make a show of their benevolence. How long before their goodwill turned sour? She had told herself time and again she should be grateful and bend to their ways, but her natural temper was quick, her hackles easily raised. It was sometimes very difficult to hold her tongue.

She had not been seated with her toast and ham for more than ten seconds when the lady of the house, the only other person in the room, addressed her from directly across the table.

"I hear you are in the habit of dismissing the night nurse and attending to the babe yourself."

Amy looked her straight in the eye. "Yes, I have done so."

Mrs Fortescue heaved a sigh. "I have given you nurses so you may rest. Why would you choose not to take advantage of that?"

Indignation rose up within Amy, and she spoke with measured words so as not to lose her temper. "Is it fair to stop me from feeding my very own child?"

"The nurse will not be able to continue nursing if you do not allow her to do it with regularity," Mrs Fortescue shot back. "Is *that* fair?"

"I cannot sleep while he cries," Amy protested. "I need to be with him. He needs *me*."

Something flashed in Mrs Fortescue's eyes. Amy braced herself for the next reproach, but it never came. The older woman swallowed and returned her attention to her breakfast.

She will never understand. How could she? She never had a child of her own. An awkward silence followed, punctuated only by the clinking of knives and forks against plates and cups on saucers.

Amy gobbled up her food, then shoved her chair back and stood. "I will go and see if Benjamin needs anything."

Mrs Fortescue also sprang up. "Nurse Agnes will notify us in that case." She came around to stand in front of her charge, blocking the way.

Amy sucked in a breath. She was not going to give in today. Every fibre in her body yearned for her son. "I have every right to see him whenever I like," she said, then she dodged around Mrs Fortescue and dashed from the room.

"Don't coddle him!" the woman roared after her.

"I'll do whatever I damn well please," Amy muttered, as she ran across the hall and up the stairs. As she reached the landing, she looked towards the nursery and saw Agnes walking into the hallway clutching a chamber pot. The nurse ducked into a neighbouring empty bedroom to relieve herself.

Amy sprinted down to the nursery and within a few seconds had picked up Benjamin and cradled him in her arms. He had been asleep but he stirred, made a little gurgling sound, and his eyes fluttered open.

Entranced by those deep, dark pools, her heart flooded with love anew. She was suddenly overwhelmed with the desire to be alone with him for as long as she wanted. After putting him back in his cradle, she darted about the room, packing necessities in a large cloth. She slung this around her shoulders, picked Benjamin up again, and darted to the door.

There was no sign of the nurse in the hallway. Seizing her chance, Amy walked as fast as she dared down the passage and to the servants' stairs. By some miracle, she made it to the back entrance undetected, and after flinging the door open, she dashed towards a hedge that ran down one side of the house.

Tears filled her eyes, blurring her vision. She hardly knew where she was going, half running across the back garden, through a gate and out into the fields beyond. As she drew in more fresh air, her anger began to dissipate and instead a heady optimism filled her. *Freedom!*

❧

Henry Russell drove his mallet down hard upon the fencepost, crying out with the effort. His anger drove him to execute his task with rather more strength and fervour than was required. He'd volunteered to repair the fence just to get away from his father.

If he contradicts me one more time...

The post was soon in place, and he worked on securing the horizontal railings to it.

He was no longer a child but a man of six-and-twenty. He knew his own mind. But if he dared to express his opinions, they were crushed every time. Was his father really so threatened by him? He slung the mallet over his shoulder and began to trudge back to the farm house.

They were two roosters, cooped up together for far too long. How much longer would he have to put up with this? He longed for his own space, to be able to make his own decisions and control his own fate, as much as a tenant farmer could.

Still incensed, Henry changed course, deciding to go home around the perimeter of the lands his family had leased from the Barringtons for several generations. Surely he should check the health of other fences as well.

Sheep scattered as he traversed a paddock. He then headed up a hill and came to a crest whereupon he could look back across Amberley village. The little huddle of buildings nestled along the valley floor, with the church at one end. In the opposite direction, the main street petered out into houses and the small estates of the landed gentry. The view hadn't changed in his whole life; he doubted it ever would.

He jumped over a gate and started down across the next field, scanning the fences in the meadows. The sight of someone under a tree in the distance made him stop short. Who could that be? It looked like a woman with some sort of bundle. Perhaps she needed assistance. He set down his mallet and began to jog down the hill towards her. It looked as though she was sleeping.

After only a few steps he stopped short and swore softly. It was Amy Miller, as he lived and breathed. He hadn't seen her since she'd had her baby, and hadn't talked to her for many months before that.

His heart pounded, and he began to sweat. He had half a mind to turn around and run in the other direction. Their last proper conversation had been years ago, and they hadn't really been alone since she'd matured into a woman.

What would he say to her? What did she think of him, if anything? He had so much he could tell her, but he knew not how... and this was not the time. She must still be going through so much. His heart ached, throbbed for her.

His feet began to move again, almost of their own volition. He wanted to see her. He needed to. Being in her presence had given him the most happiness he had experienced in his life.

She was not asleep; she merely had her head bowed over her infant. Nearly upon her, he slowed his steps as she hadn't noticed him yet. He was suddenly apprehensive, feeling as if he were intruding even though it was she who was on his land. He drank in the scene. The little child was snuggled into her, its hand grasping her dress. Amy gazed down at him with an expression of wonder and peace.

A twig snapped under his foot and her head whipped up towards him. "Oh! I–" Her arm flew over the child in a protective gesture, and she reached for her bag with the other hand. "Oh, it's only you, Henry," she said with a huge sigh of relief.

Henry's heart sank. He took some tentative steps forward. "Yes, it's only me. Good day, Miss Miller."

She glanced down at the baby and then back up at him. Even at this distance, her green eyes seemed to see right through him. He saw those eyes in his dreams.

"Can I... help you?" He hovered in front of her, desperately awkward.

She broke the eye contact. "No... that is, I am probably... beyond helping."

His breath quickened. What kind of trouble was she in? How could things be worse? Had someone hurt her? His fists clenched, and before he knew what he was doing he was kneeling before her in the grass. "What is it? Are you hurt?"

She raised her face to him once again, tears in her eyes.

"No, I am feeling better than I have since little Benjamin arrived," she said, her voice breaking. "I have... run away." She said this with a shrug and then a little laugh, but she looked as if she might cry. He longed to reach out to her.

"Run away?" he repeated. "What do you mean?"

"I am not supposed to be mothering him, if I am to be a lady. That is what she says. But I cannot stay away from him. He is... a part of me."

Henry tried to absorb all this. "So, you stole him?" He smiled a little.

"Yes, I suppose I did." Her mouth quirked.

"Does anyone know?"

"They likely will by now. I expect I will be in trouble." Her steady stare spoke of defiance, as if she did not care if she was in trouble. Her spirit made him ache all the more. She'd always had that spirit.

A comfortable moment of silence passed, and a breeze swirled around them. It caused the sleeping baby to stir, and he made a few burbling noises before settling down again. Amy caressed his cheek and bent down to kiss his head.

The tender moment took Henry's breath away. How incredible, that this woman had been through such horror and yet was so loving and gentle towards this child.

"How have you been, Miss Amy?" he asked gently. "Are you all right?"

She did not speak immediately, her head still bowed. He wondered if she had heard him. But after a few seconds she raised glistening eyes to him. "It has been the very worst and the very best times of my life."

He nodded, holding her eyes. "I have..." *Hurt for you, worried for you, despaired for you, longed for you.* "I have been thinking of you," he said, finally. "I hope you know I am here, if you should ever need anything. I always have been."

She smiled. "Thank you, Henry. You are a good friend to me."

The sweet moment lingered, while he thought of all he wanted to tell her. Instead, he said nothing, and just enjoyed her company. Then she looked away and her gaze swept over the landscape. "Forgive me, Henry,

I hope all is well with you? Your parents?"

Formalities and politeness. It swept away the notion that his heart had been open to hers just moments earlier. "Ma and Pa are in good health, thank you. The farm is soon to be in the full swing of summer, and most of the animals have produced their offspring. In fact, just last night I helped a sow deliver her piglets."

At this Amy regarded him eagerly. "Ooh, did you? Was there a reason you needed to intervene?"

"Only that it was a long labour and she tired quickly. There were eight piglets in all, and quite a small runt."

Her brow furrowed and she instinctively drew her little one closer. "Will it survive, do you think?"

Henry threw up his hands in a helpless gesture. "I'll do my best to save it."

He was suddenly struck with an idea – a way to stay in her presence a little longer. "Would you like to see the piglets?" he asked. "There are many other young families in the barn too." He wondered if he might have put his foot in it, mentioning families in the light of her situation, but she didn't seem to take offence.

"To be sure, I think that would be just the thing to lift my spirits," she said, gathering up her shawl and the baby's things. "That is, if you have the time to show me."

Henry could hear his father's voice ringing in his ears with a long list of jobs around the farm that needed to be done before sundown. He pushed it to one side. "Of course I have time, Miss Amy, for you."

She smiled at him and his heart broke into a gallop. How could he ever consider being with somebody else? He stood and offered her his hand. "Let me help you up."

She turned towards him and began to reach out, but then she looked upon his hand with something like revulsion and snatched back her own. "No!" She shook her head. "I can manage by myself."

He put his hand in his pocket. "Sorry, miss," he mumbled. He turned around so she could get up without any worry of immodesty.

She thinks me so beneath her, she can't even stand to touch me. He felt lower than the earth beneath his feet. And now, he would have to accompany her across the farm knowing that she thought so little of him.

"Would you rather I just leave you to go?"

She was at his side, saying, "Shall we go?" and then, "Pardon?"

Her eyes drew him in again, bright with anticipation. He shook his head. "Yes, let's go."

Do you want to read more of *Gloved Heart*?

Go to www.charlottebrentwood.com
for ordering information.

About the Author

A bookworm and scribbler for as long as she can remember, Charlotte always dreamed of sharing her stories with the world.

She lives in Auckland, New Zealand and loves exploring her beautiful surroundings. Her "day job" was in digital marketing, but she is currently a stay-at-home mother to two tiny tyrants and married to her real-life hero.